DAMNATION ALLEY

They were all of them bikes.

They swung onto the road behind him.

He could have opened fire. He could have braked and laid down a cloud of flame. It was obvious that they didn't know what they were chasing. He could have launched grenades. He refrained, however.

It could have been him on the lead bike, he decided, all hot on hijack. He felt a certain sad kinship as his hand hovered above the fire-control . . .

When they began to fire, he knew that he'd have to retaliate. He couldn't risk their hitting a gas tank or blowing out his tires.

Their first shots had been in the nature of a warning. He couldn't risk another barrage. If only they knew . . .

The speaker!

He cut in and mashed the button and spoke.

"Listen cats," he said. " All I got's medicine for the sick citizens in Boston. Let me through or you'll hear noise."

A shot followed immediately, so he opened fire with the fifty calibers to the rear.

He saw them fall, but they kept firing. So he launched grenades.

The firing lessened, but didn't cease. So he hit the brakes, then the flame-throwers . .

EDITED BY JOE HALDEMAN
WITH CHARLES G. WAUGH
AND MARTIN HARRY GREENBERG

SUPER-TANKS

ACE SCIENCE FICTION BOOKS
NEW YORK

SUPERTANKS

An Ace Science Fiction Book / published by arrangement with
the editors

PRINTING HISTORY
Ace Science Fiction edition/April 1987

For information address: The Berkley Publishing Group,
200 Madison Avenue, New York, New York 10016.

ISBN: 0-441-79106-9

Ace Science Fiction Books are published
by The Berkley Publishing Group,
200 Madison Avenue, New York, New York 10016.

PRINTED IN THE UNITED STATES OF AMERICA

TABLE OF CONTENTS

INTRODUCTION

by Joe Haldeman

In Vietnam my outfit didn't see tanks often, working as we did in the Central Highlands, where most of the terrain was too vertical for a tank to do anything but drop and break. We sometimes traveled with them in the valleys, though. And had mixed feelings.

The tank guys were more dashing than us grubby grunts. Some of them were allowed to carry macho weapons like Thompson submachine guns and grease guns, rather than the wimpy and temperamental M-16. They always had beer and dope and plenty of ammunition and real food from the PX. Sometimes even clean fatigues and haircuts. Not to mention several inches of steel between them and the bullets. So of course we cordially hated them, in a friendly sort of way, but we didn't really envy them. Nobody could envy them who ever peeked inside the reeking loud hell of a furnace that was the actual reality of a tank in the jungle. And when something big enough to affect a tank did hit one, nobody was likely to walk away from it.

We were combat engineers, so our special relationship with tanks was the rather scary duty of walking along in front of them with mine sweepers: metal detectors that would screech *bleep!* in your earphones if you walked over a mine. Or, more often, a buried spent cartridge case or an old Coke bottle cap. Whatever, you had to stop everything and probe for it, the tank rumbling in idle behind you. If it was actually a mine, of course, it would probably blow up in your face. Other people tended to stand behind the tank while you probed the dirt with your bayonet blade.

We always did this duty ten minutes on, ten minutes off; one engineer swinging the metal detector while the other sat up on the tank, in relative safety.

The following exemplar of life and death with tanks didn't happen to me, for which I'm glad. A friend of mine was riding the tank, waiting for his turn on the road, when there was a sudden sound like a huge cathedral bell ringing once, and he found himself flying through the air. He landed more or less unhurt, with a one-sided firefight going on, all of our guys laying down blistering fields of fire to the left and right of the road, but no enemy answering back. They had done their damage.

The tank had evidently run over a "command-detonated nonmetallic mine." A mine sweeper was useless against them. The only piece of metal in such a weapon might be the small tube that holds the fulminate or the picric acid that sets off the shaped charge of plastic explosive when a safely distant observer sees that the tank is in the right place, and pushes the button. The shaped charge explodes into a torus of plasma, hotter than the surface of the sun, punching upward with hypersonic velocity into and through the steel belly of the tank. The people inside don't live long enough to scream.

The gunfire died down and they opened the hatch of the tank. There wasn't anything inside that vaguely resembled a human being, or even meat. Just a thin layer of red jelly.

This is not to say that tanks were simply dangerous traps. Modern tanks turned the tide of many important battles in Vietnam, such as Hue. They presented an awesome amount of firepower to an enemy generally without comparable weapons; I suspect their psychological impact was often as important as the ordnance they carried.

That ordnance was usually employed against more or less unprotected people, rather than fellow machines—contrary to the way most of us think about tank warfare, thanks to movies and TV and the dashing legends of Rommel *et al.* The ninety-millimeter cannon that was the main weapon of our standard M-48 tank could be loaded with antipersonnel "fléchette" rounds, turning it into a rapid-fire shotgun with a barrel almost four inches in diameter. Other armor carried "quad fifties," four fifty-caliber machine guns firing in unison to create a solid wall of lead, or the onomatopoetic and dreadful pom-pom guns, or terrifying flamethrowers.

It doesn't seem fair to pit a twenty-ton juggernaut so ferociously armed against a little guy in black pajamas. Maybe that's why tanks are such natural material for fiction. In their implacable, impersonal potency they symbolize the fearsome inhumanity of modern warfare. They also give us half of the archetypal David and Goliath story, since one brave man with a hand grenade can disable a tank—or at least die trying.

So what of the future of tanks? I suspect that the tank as we know it is destined for the fate of the cavalry steed. Horses couldn't survive the ubiquity of fully automatic weapons, and I don't think tanks will long hold out against cheap "smart" weapons. When you can put a TV camera into the nose of an armor-piercing bazooka round (all right, "recoilless rifle"), and fiddle a joystick to get one tank with each round—with the tank costing at least a thousand times as much as the round that kills it—then you have grievously reduced the desirability of tanks.

There is a larger, more ghastly, scale to tanks' obsolescence. Military planners with fertile imaginations, maps of Western Europe unfolded on their laps, have pointed out that you could disable thousands of enemy tanks in a single stroke, using one measly neutron bomb. Then you could even take the dead enemies out of the tanks, and use the unharmed machines yourself. But you'd better work fast, since the war will probably be over, one way or another, in forty-five minutes or so.

Enough of the real world, though, with its mundane familiar terrors. Even if tanks are rendered obsolete, relegated to slugging it out in wars between Third-World countries without rich uncles' smart bombs, we'll still write stories about them, as we still write stories about medieval armor, doughty samurai, and steely-eyed cowpokes with Colts riding low on their lean hips. A symbol is a symbol.

Most of the authors of the stories that follow logically make their tanks bigger, faster, and more powerful than the ones that exist now (which makes me want to write a story about a small, slow, defenseless one), and they often give the machine some artificial-intelligence capability, even to the point of having a personality.

Makes for good stories. I still wouldn't get into one if it was made out of kryptonite.

THE HORARS
OF WAR

by Gene Wolfe

The three friends in the trench looked very much alike as they labored in the rain. Their hairless skulls were slickly naked to it, their torsos hairless too, and supple with smooth muscles that ran like oil under the wet gleam.

The two, who really were 2909 and 2911, did not mind the jungle around them although they detested the rain that rusted their weapons, and the snakes and insects, and hated the Enemy. But the one called 2910, the real as well as the official leader of the three, did; and that was because 2909 and 2911 had stainless steel bones; but there was no 2910 and there had never been.

The camp they held was a triangle. In the center, the CP-Aid Station where Lieutenant Kyle and Mr. Brenner slept: a hut of ammo cases packed with dirt whose lower half was dug into the soggy earth. Around it were the mortar pit (NE), the recoilless rifle pit (NW), and Pinocchio's pit (S); and beyond these were the straight lines of the trenches: First Platoon, Second Platoon, Third Platoon (the platoon of the three). Outside of which were the primary wire and an antipersonnel mine field.

And outside that was the jungle. But not completely outside. The jungle set up outposts of its own of swift-sprouting

5

bamboo and elephant grass, and its crawling creatures carried
out untiring patrols of the trenches. The jungle sheltered the
Enemy, taking him to its great fetid breast to be fed while it
sopped up the rain and of it bred its stinging gnats and cen-
tipedes.

An ogre beside him, 2911 drove his shovel into the ooze filling
the trench, lifted it to shoulder height, dumped it; 2910 did the
same thing in his turn, then watched the rain work on the
scoop of mud until it was slowly running back into the trench
again. Following his eyes 2911 looked at him and grinned. The
HORAR's face was broad, hairless, flat-nosed, and high-
cheeked; his teeth were pointed and white like a big dog's.
And he, 2910, knew that that face was his own. Exactly his
own. He told himself it was a dream, but he was very tired and
could not get out.

Somewhere down the trench the bull voice of 2900 announced the evening meal and the others threw down their
tools and jostled past toward the bowls of steaming mash, but
the thought of food nauseated 2910 in his fatigue, and he
stumbled into the bunker he shared with 2909 and 2911. Flat
on his air mattress he could leave the nightmare for a time;
return to the sane world of houses and sidewalks, or merely
sink into the blessed nothingness that was far better . . .

Suddenly he was bolt upright on the cot, blackness still in
his eyes even while his fingers groped with their own thought
for his helmet and weapon. Bugles were blowing from the edge
of the jungle, but he had time to run his hand under the in-
flated pad of the mattress and reassure himself that his hidden
notes were safe before 2900 in the trench outside yelled, "Attack! Fall out! Man your firing points!"

It was one of the stock jokes, one of the jokes so stock, in
fact, that it had ceased to be anything anyone laughed at, to
say "Horar" your firing point (or whatever it was that according to the book should be "manned"). The HORARS in the
squad he led used the expression to 2910 just as he used it with
them, and when 2900 never employed it the omission had at
first unsettled him. But 2900 did not really suspect. 2900 just
took his rank seriously.

He got into position just as the mortars put up a parachute
flare that hung over the camp like a white rose of fire.
Whether because of his brief sleep or the excitement of the

impending fight his fatigue had evaporated, leaving him nervously alert but unsteady. From the jungle a bugle sang, "Ta-taa . . . taa-taa . . ." and off to the platoon's left rear the First opened up with their heavy weapons on a suicide squad they apparently thought they saw on the path leading to the northeast gate. He watched, and after half a minute something stood up on the path and grabbed for its midsection before it fell, so there *was* a suicide squad.

Some one, he told himself. *Someone*. Not *something*. Someone grabbed for *his* midsection. They were all human out there.

The First began letting go with personal weapons as well, each deep cough representing a half dozen dartlike fléchettes flying in an inescapable pattern three feet broad. "Eyes front, 2910!" barked 2900.

There was nothing to be seen out there but a few clumps of elephant grass. Then the white flare burned out. "They ought to put up another one," 2911 on his right said worriedly.

"A star in the east for men not born of women," said 2910 half to himself, and regretted the blasphemy immediately.

"That's where they need it," 2911 agreed. "The first is having it pretty hot over there. But we could use some light here too."

He was not listening. At home in Chicago, during that inexpressibly remote time which ran from a dim memory of playing on a lawn under the supervision of a smiling giantess to that moment two years ago when he had submitted to surgery to lose every body and facial hair he possessed and undergo certain other minor alterations, he had been unconsciously preparing himself for this. Lifting weights and playing football to develop his body while he whetted his mind on a thousand books; all so that he might tell, making others feel at a remove . . .

Another flare went up and there were three dark silhouettes sliding from the next-nearest clump of elephant grass to the nearest. He fired his M-19 at them, then heard the HORARS on either side of him fire too. From the sharp corner where their own platoon met the Second a machine gun opened up with tracer. The nearest grass clump sprang into the air and somersaulted amid spurts of earth.

There was a moment of quiet, then five rounds of high explosive came in right behind them as though aimed for Pinocchio's pit. *Crump. Crump. Crump . . . Crump. Crump.* (2900 would be running to ask Pinocchio if he were hurt.)

Someone else had been moving down the trench toward them, and he could hear the mumble of the new voice become a gasp when the H.E. rounds came in. Then it resumed, a little louder and consequently a bit more easily understood. "How are you? You feel all right? Hit?"

And most of the HORARS answered, "I'm fine, sir," or "We're okay, sir," but because HORARS did have a sense of humor some of them said things like, "How do we transfer to the Marines, sir?" or "My pulse just registered nine thou', sir. 3000 took it with the mortar sight."

We often think of strength as associated with humorlessness, he had written in the news magazine which had, with the Army's cooperation, planted him by subterfuge of surgery among these *H*omolog *OR*ganisms (*A*rmy *R*eplacement *S*imulations). *But*, he had continued, *this is not actually the case. Humor is a prime defense of the mind, and knowing that to strip the mind of it is to leave it shieldless, the Army and the Synthetic Biology Service have wisely included a charming dash in the makeup of these synthesized replacements for human infantry.*

That had been before he discovered that the Army and the SBS had tried mightily to weed that sense of the ridiculous out, but found that if the HORARS were to maintain the desired intelligence level they could not.

Brenner was behind him now, touching his shoulder. "How are you? Feel all right?"

He wanted to say, "I'm half as scared as you are, you dumb Dutchman," but he knew that if he did the fear would sound in his voice; besides, the disrespect would be unthinkable to a HORAR.

He also wanted to say simply "A-okay, sir," because if he did Brenner would pass on to 2911 and he would be safe. But he had a reputation for originality to keep up, and he needed that reputation to cover him when he slipped, as he often did, sidewise of HORAR standards. He answered: "You ought to look in on Pinocchio, sir. I think he's cracking up." From the other end of the squad, 2909's quiet chuckle rewarded him, and Brenner, the man most dangerous to his disguise, continued down the trench. . . .

Fear was necessary because the will to survive was *very*

necessary. And a humanoid form was needed if the HORARS were to utilize the mass of human equipment already on hand. Besides, a human-shaped (*homolog?* no, that merely meant *similar*, *homological*) HORAR had outscored all the fantastic forms SBS had been able to dream up in a super-realistic (public opinion would never have permitted it with human soldiers) test carried out in the Everglades.

(Were they merely duplicating? Had all this been worked out before with some greater war in mind? And had He Himself, the Scientist Himself, come to take the form of His creations to show that He too could bear the unendurable?)

2909 was at his elbow, whispering. "Do you see something, Squad Leader? Over there?" Dawn had come without his noticing.

With fingers clumsy from fatigue he switched the control of his M-19 to the lower, 40mm grenade-launching barrel. The grenade made a brief flash at the spot 2909 had indicated. "No," he said, "I don't see anything now." The fine, soft rain which had been falling all night was getting stronger. The dark clouds seemed to roof the world. (Was he fated to reenact what had been done for mankind? It could happen. The Enemy took humans captive, but there was nothing they would not do to HORAR prisoners. Occasionally patrols found the bodies spread-eagled, with bamboo stakes driven through their limbs; and he could only be taken for a HORAR. He thought of a watercolor of the crucifixion he had seen once. Would the color of his own blood be crimson lake?)

From the CP the observation ornithocopter rose on flapping wings.

"I haven't heard one of the mines go for quite a while," 2909 said. Then there came the phony-sounding bang that so often during the past few weeks had closed similar probing attacks. Squares of paper were suddenly fluttering all over the camp.

"Propaganda shell," 2909 said unnecessarily, and 2911 climbed casually out of the trench to get a leaflet, then jumped back to his position. "Same as last week," he said, smoothing out the damp rice paper.

Looking over his shoulder, 2910 saw that he was correct. For some reason the Enemy never directed his propaganda at the HORARS, although it was no secret that reading skills were implanted in HORAR minds with the rest of their instinctive training. Instead it was always aimed at the humans in the camp, and played heavily on the distaste they were supposed to feel at being "confined with half-living flesh still stinking of chemicals." Privately, 2910 thought they might have done better, at least with Lieutenant Kyle, to have dropped that approach and played up sex. He also got the impression from the propaganda that the Enemy thought there were far more humans in the camp than there actually were.

Well, the Army—with far better opportunities to know—was wrong as well. With a few key generals excepted, the Army thought there were only two . . .

He had made the All-American. How long ago it seemed. No coach, no sportswriter had ever compared his stocky, muscular physique with a HORAR's. And he had majored in journalism, had been ambitious. How many men, with a little surgical help, could have passed here?

"Think it sees anything?" he heard 2911 ask 2909. They were looking upward at the "bird" sailing overhead.

The ornithocopter could do everything a real bird could except lay eggs. It could literally land on a strand of wire. It could ride thermals like a vulture, and dive like a hawk. And the bird motion of its wings was wonderfully efficient, saving power-plant weight that could be used for zoom lenses and telecameras. He wished he were in the CP watching the monitor screen with Lieutenant Kyle instead of standing with his face a scant foot above the mud (they had tried stalked eyes like a crab's in the Everglades, he remembered, but the stalks had become infected by a fungus . . .).

As though in answer to his wish, 2900 called, "Show some snap for once, 2910. He says He wants us in the CP."

When he himself thought *He, He* meant God; but 2900 meant Lieutenant Kyle. That was why 2900 was a platoon leader, no doubt; that and the irrational prestige of a round number. He climbed out of the trench and followed him to the CP. They needed a communicating trench, but that was something there hadn't been time for yet.

Brenner had someone (2788? looked like him, but he couldn't be certain) down on his table. Shrapnel, probably from a grenade. Brenner did not look up as they came in, but 2910 could see his face was still white with fear although the attack had been over for a full quarter of an hour. He and 2900 ignored the SBS man and saluted Lieutenant Kyle.

The company commander smiled. "Stand at ease, HORARS. Have any trouble in your sector?"

2900 said, "No, sir. The light machine gun got one group of three and 2910 here knocked off a group of two. Not much of an attack on our front, sir."

Lieutenant Kyle nodded. "I thought your platoon had the easiest time of it, 2900, and that's why I've picked you to run a patrol for me this morning."

"That's fine with us, sir."

"You'll have Pinocchio, and I thought you'd want to go yourself and take 2910's gang."

He glanced at 2910. "Your squad still at full strength?"

2910 said, "Yes, sir," making an effort to keep this face impassive. He wanted to say: I shouldn't have to go on patrol. I'm human as you are, Kyle, and patrolling is for things grown in tubes, things fleshed out around metal skeletons, things with no family and no childhood behind them.

Things like my friends.

He added, "We've been the luckiest squad in the company, sir."

"Fine. Let's hope your luck holds, 2910." Kyle's attention switched back to 2900. "I've gotten under the leaf canopy with the ornithocopter and done everything except make it walk around like a chicken. I can't find a thing and it's drawn no fire, so you ought to be okay. You'll make a complete circuit of the camp without getting out of range of mortar support. Understand?"

2900 and 2910 saluted, about-faced, and marched out. 2910 could feel the pulse in his neck; he flexed and unflexed his hands unobtrusively as he walked. 2900 asked, "Think we'll catch any of them?" It was an unbending for him—the easy camaraderie of anticipated action.

"I'd say so. I don't think the CO's had long enough with the bird to make certain of anything except that their main force has pulled out of range. I hope so."

And that's the truth, he thought. Because a good hot fire fight would probably do it—round the whole thing out so I can get out of here.

Every two weeks a helicopter brought supplies and, when they were needed, replacements. Each trip it also carried a correspondent whose supposed duty was to interview the commanders of the camps the copter visited. The reporter's name was Keith Thomas, and for the past two months he had been the only human being with whom 2910 could take off his mask.

Thomas carried scribbled pages from the notebook under 2910's air mattress when he left, and each time he came managed to find some corner in which they could speak in private for a few seconds. 2910 read his mail then and gave it back. It embarrassed him to realize that the older reporter viewed him with something not far removed from hero worship.

I can get out of here, he repeated to himself. Write it up and tell Keith we're ready to use the letter.

2900 ordered crisply, "Fall in your squad. I'll get Pinocchio and meet you at the south gate."

"Right." He was suddenly seized with a desire to tell someone, even 2900, about the letter. Keith Thomas had it, and it was really only an undated note, but it was signed by a famous general at Corps Headquarters. Without explanation it directed that number 2910 be detached from his present assignment and placed under the temporary orders of Mr. K. Thomas, Accredited Correspondent. And Keith would use it any time he asked him to. In fact, he had wanted to on his last trip.

He could not remember giving the order, but the squad was falling in, lining up in the rain for his inspection almost as smartly as they had on the drill field back at the crèche. He gave "At ease" and looked them over while he outlined the objectives of the patrol. As always, their weapons were immaculate despite the dampness, their massive bodies ramrod-straight, their uniforms as clean as conditions permitted.

The L.A. Rams with guns, he thought proudly. Barking "On phones," he flipped the switch on his helmet that would permit 2900 to knit him and the squad together with Pinocchio in a unified tactical unit. Another order and the HORARS deployed around Pinocchio with the smoothness of repeated drill, the wire closing the south gate was drawn back, and the patrol moved out.

With his turret retracted, Pinocchio the robot tank stood just three feet high, and was no wider than an automobile; but he was as long as three, so that from a distance he had something of the look of a railroad flatcar. In the jungle his narrow front enabled him to slip between the trunks of the unconquerable giant hardwoods, and the power in his treads could flatten saplings and bamboo. Yet resilient organics and sintered metals had turned the rumble of the old, manned tanks to a soft hiss for Pinnochio. Where the jungle was free of undergrowth he moved as silently as a hospital cart.

His immediate precursor had been named "Punch," apparently in the sort of simpering depreciation which found "Shillelagh" acceptable for a war rocket. "Punch"—a bust in the mouth.

But Punch, which like Pinocchio had possessed a computer brain and no need of a crew (or for that matter room for one except for an exposed vestigial seat on his deck), had required wires to communicate with the infantry around him. Radio had been tried, but the problems posed by static, jamming, and outright enemy forgery of instructions had been too much for Punch.

Then an improved model had done away with those wires and some imaginative officer had remembered that "Mr. Punch" had been a knockabout marionette—and the wireless improvement was suddenly very easy to name. But, like Punch and its fairy-tale namesake, it was vulnerable if it went out into the world alone.

A brave man (and the Enemy had many) could hide himself until Pinocchio was within touching distance. And a well-instructed one could then place a hand grenade or a bottle of gasoline where it would destroy him. Pinocchio's three-inch-thick armor needed the protection of flesh, and since he cost as much as a small city and could (if properly protected) fight a regiment to a stand, he got it.

Two scouts from 2910's squad preceded him through the jungle, forming the point of the diamond. Flankers moved on either side of him "beating the bush" and, when it seemed advisable, firing a pattern of fléchettes into any suspicious-looking piece of undergrowth. Cheerful, reliable 2909, the assistant squad leader, with one other HORAR formed the rear guard. As patrol leader 2900's position was behind Pinocchio, and as squad leader 2910's was in front.

The jungle was quiet with an eerie stillness, and it was dark under the big trees. "Though I walk in the valley of the shadow . . ."

Made tiny by the phones, 2900 squeaked in his ear, "Keep the left flankers farther out!" 2910 acknowledged and trotted over to put his own stamp on the correction, although the flankers, 2913, 2914, and 2915, had already heard it and were moving to obey. There was almost no chance of trouble this soon, but that was no excuse for a slovenly formation. As he squeezed between two trees something caught his eye and he halted for a moment to examine it. It was a skull; a skull of bone rather than a smooth HORAR skull of steel, and so probably an Enemy's.

A big "E" Enemy's, he thought to himself. A man to whom the normal HORAR conditioning of exaggerated respect bordering on worship did not apply.

Tiny and tinny. "Something holding you up, 2910?"

"Be right there." He tossed the skull aside. A man whom even a HORAR could disobey; a man even a HORAR could kill. The skull had looked old, but it could not have been old. The ants would have picked it clean in a few days, and in a few weeks it would rot. But it was probably at least seventeen or eighteen years old.

The ornithocopter passed them on flapping wings, flying its own search pattern. The patrol went on.

Casually 2910 asked his helmet mike, "How far are we going? Far as the creek?"

2900's voice squeaked, "We'll work our way down the bank a quarter mile, then cut west," then with noticeable sarcasm added, "if that's okay with you?"

Unexpectedly Lieutenant Kyle's voice came over the phones. "2910's your second in command, 2900. He has a duty to keep himself informed of your plans."

But 2910, realizing that a real HORAR would not have asked the question, suddenly also realized that he knew more about HORARS than the company commander did. It was not surprising, he ate and slept with them in a way Kyle could not, but it was disquieting. He probably knew more than Brenner, strict biological mechanics excepted, as well.

The scouts had reported that they could see the sluggish jungle stream they called the creek when Lieutenant Kyle's voice came over the phones again. As routinely as he had delivered his mild rebuke to 2900 he announced, "Situation Red here. An apparent battalion-level attack hitting the North Point. Let's suck it back in, patrol."

Pinocchio swiveled 180 degrees by locking his right tread, and the squad turned in a clockwise circle around him. Kyle said distantly, "The recoilesses don't seem to have found the range yet, so I'm going out to give them a hand. Mr. Brenner will be holding down the radio for the next few minutes."

2900 transmitted, "We're on our way, sir."

Then 2910 saw a burst of automatic weapon's fire cut his scouts down. In an instant the jungle was a pandemonium of sound.

Pinocchio's radar had traced the bullets back to their source and his main armament slammed a 155mm shell at it, but crossfire was suddenly slicing in from all around them. The bullets striking Pinocchio's turret screamed away like damned souls. 2910 saw grenades arc out of nowhere and something struck his thigh with terrible force. He made himself say, "I'm hit, 2909; take the squad," before he looked at it. Mortar shells were dropping in now and if his assistant acknowledged, he did not hear.

A bit of jagged metal from a grenade or a mortar round had laid the thigh open, but apparently missed the big artery supplying the lower leg. There was no spurt, only a rapid welling of blood, and shock still held the injury numb. Forcing himself, he pulled apart the lips of the wound to make sure it was clear of foreign matter. It was very deep but the bone was not broken; at least so it seemed.

Keeping as low as he could, he used his trench knife to cut away the cloth of his trousers leg, then rigged a tourniquet with his belt. His aid packet contained a pad of gauze, and tape to hold it in place. When he had finished he lay still, holding his M-19 and looking for a spot where its fire might do some good. Pinocchio was firing his turret machine gun in routine bursts, sanitizing likely-looking patches of jungle; otherwise the fight seemed to have quieted down.

2900's voice in his ear called, "Wounded? We got any wounded?"

He managed to say, "Me. 2910." A HORAR would feel some pain, but not nearly as much as a man. He would have to fake the insensitivity as best he could. Suddenly it occurred to him that he would be invalided out, would not have to use the letter, and he was glad.

"We thought you bought it, 2910. Glad you're still around."

Then Brenner's voice cutting through the transmission jumpy with panic: "We're being overrun here! Get the Pinocchio back at once."

In spite of his pain 2910 felt contempt. Only Brenner would
say "*the* Pinocchio." 2900 sent, "Coming, sir," and unexpectedly was standing over him, lifting him up.

He tried to look around for the squad. "We lose many?"

"Four dead and you." Perhaps no other human would have
detected the pain in 2900's harsh voice. "You can't walk with
that, can you?"

"I couldn't keep up."

"You ride Pinocchio then." With surprising gentleness the
platoon leader lifted him into the little seat the robot tank's
director used when road speeds made running impractical.
What was left of the squad formed a skirmish line ahead. As
they began to trot forward he could hear 2900 calling, "Base
camp! Base camp! What's your situation there, sir?"

"Lieutenant Kyle's dead," Brenner's voice came back.
"3003 just came in and told me Kyle's dead!"

"Are you holding?"

"I don't know." More faintly 2910 could hear him asking,
"Are they holding, 3003?"

"Use the periscope, sir. Or if it still works, the bird."

Brenner chattered, "I don't know if we're holding or not.
3003 was hit and now he's dead. I don't think he knew anyway. You've got to hurry."

It was contrary to regulations, but 2910 flipped off his
helmet phone to avoid hearing 2900's patient reply. With
Brenner no longer gibbering in his ears he could hear not too
distantly the sound of explosions which must be coming from
the camp. Small-arms' fire made an almost incessant buzz as a
background for the whizz—bang! of incoming shells and the
coughing of the camp's own mortars.

Then the jungle was past and the camp lay in front of
them. Geysers of mud seemed to be erupting from it every-
where. The squad broke into a full run, and even while
he rolled, Pinocchio was firing his 155 in support of the camp.

They faked us out, 2910 reflected. His leg throbbed pain-
fully but distantly and he felt light-headed and dizzy—as
though he were an ornithocopter hovering in the misty rain
over his own body. With the light-headedness came a strange
clarity of mind.

They faked us out. They got us used to little probes that
pulled off at sunrise, and then when we sent Pinocchio out
they were going to ambush us and take the camp. It suddenly

occurred to him and he might find himself still on this exposed seat in the middle of the battle; they were already approaching the edge of the mine field, and the HORARS ahead were moving into squad column so as not to overlap the edges of the cleared lane. "Where are we going, Pinocchio?" he asked, then realized his phone was still off. He reactivated it and repeated the question.

Pinocchio droned, "Injured HORAR personnel will be delivered to the Command Post for Synthetic Biololgy Service attention," but 2910 was no longer listening. In front of them he could hear what sounded like fifty bugles signaling for another Enemy attack.

The south side of the triangular camp was deserted, as though the remainder of their platoon had been called away to reinforce the First and Second; but with the sweeping illogic of war there was no Enemy where they might have entered unresisted.

"Request assistance from Synthetic Biology Service for injured HORAR personnel," Pinocchio was saying. Talking did not interfere with his firing the 155, but when Brenner did not come out after a minute or more, 2910 managed to swing himself down, catching his weight on his good leg. Pinocchio rolled away at once.

The CP bunker was twisted out of shape, and he could see where several near-misses had come close to knocking it out completely. Brenner's white face appeared in the doorway as he was about to go in. "Who's that?"

"2910. I've been hit—let me come in and lie down."

"They won't send us an air strike. I radioed for one and they say this whole part of the country's socked in; they say they wouldn't be able to find us."

"Get out of the door. I'm hit and I want to come in and lie down." At the last moment he remembered to add, "Sir."

Brenner moved reluctantly aside. It was dim in the bunker but not dark.

"You want me to look at that leg?"

2910 had found an empty stretcher, and he laid himself on it, moving awkwardly to keep from flexing his wound. "You don't have to," he said. "Look after some of the others." It wouldn't do for Brenner to begin poking around. Even rattled as he was he might notice something.

The SBS man went back to his radio instead. His frantic

voice sounded remote and faint. It was ecstasy to lie down.

At some vast distance, voices were succeeding voices, argument meeting argument, far off. He wondered where he was.

Then he heard the guns and knew. He tried to roll onto his side and at the second attempt managed to do it, although the light-headedness was worse than ever. 2893 was lying on the stretcher next to him, and 2893 was dead.

At the other end of the room, the end that was technically the CP, he could hear Brenner talking to 2900. "If there were a chance," Brenner was saying, "you know I'd do it, Platoon Leader."

"What's happening?" he asked. "What's the matter?" He was too dazed to keep up the HORAR role well, but neither of them noticed.

"It's a division," Brenner said. "A whole Enemy division. We can't hold off that kind of force."

He raised himself on his elbow. "What do you mean?"

"I talked to them . . . I raised them on the radio, and it's a whole division. They got one of their officers who could speak English to talk to me. They want us to surrender."

"*They* say it's a division, sir," 2900 put in evenly.

2910 shook his head, trying to clear it. "Even if it were, with Pinocchio—"

"The Pinocchio's gone."

2900 said soberly, "We tried to counterattack, 2910, and they knocked Pinocchio out and threw us back. How are you feeling?"

"They've got at least a division," Brenner repeated stubbornly.

2910's mind was racing now, but it was as though it were running endless wind sprints on a treadmill. If Brenner were going to give up, 2900 would never even consider disobeying, no matter how much he might disagree. There were various ways, though, in which he could convince Brenner he was a human being—given time. And Brenner could, Brenner would, tell the Enemy, so that he too would be saved. Eventually the war would be over and he could go home. No one would blame him. If Brenner were going—

Brenner was asking, "How many effectives left?"

"Less than forty, sir." There was nothing in 2900's tone to indicate that a surrender meant certain death to him, but it was true. The Enemy took only human prisoners. (Could 2900 be convinced? Could he make any of the HORARS under-stand, when they had eaten and joked with him, knew no physiology, and thought all men not Enemy demigods? Would you believe him if he were to try to take command?)

He could see Brenner gnawing at his lower lip. "I'm going to surrender," the SBS man said at last. A big one, mortar or bombardment rocket, exploded near the CP, but he appeared not to notice it. There was a wondering, hesitant note in his voice—as though he were still trying to accustom himself to the idea.

"Sir—" 2900 began.

"I forbid you to question my orders." The SBS man sounded firmer now. "But I'll ask them to make an exception this time, Platoon Leader. Not to do"—his voice faltered slightly—"what they usually do to nonhumans."

"It's not that," 2900 said stolidly. "It's the folding up. We don't mind dying, sir, but we want to die fighting."

One of the wounded moaned, and 2910 wondered for a moment if he, like himself, had been listening.

Brenner's self-control snapped. "You'll die any damn way I tell you!"

"Wait." It was suddenly difficult for 2910 to talk, but he managed to get their attention. "2900, Mr. Brenner hasn't ac-tually ordered you to surrender yet, and you're needed on the line. Go now and let me talk to him." He saw the HORAR leader hesitate and added, "He can reach you on your helmet phone if he wants to; but go now and fight."

With a jerky motion 2900 turned and ducked out the nar-row bunker door. Brenner, taken by surprise, said, "What is it, 2910? What's gotten into you?"

He tried to rise, but he was too weak. "Come here, Mr. Brenner," he said. When the SBS man did not move he added, "I know a way out."

"Through the jungle?" Brenner scoffed in his shaken voice. "That's absurd." But he came. He leaned over the stretcher, and before he could catch his balance 2910 had pulled him down.

"What are you doing?"

"Can't you tell? That's the point of my trench knife you feel on your neck."

Brenner tried to struggle, then subsided when the pressure

of the knife became too great. "You—can't—do this."

"I can. Because I'm not a HORAR. I'm a man, Brenner, and it's very important for you to understand that." He felt rather than saw the look of incredulity on Brenner's face. "I'm a reporter, and two years ago when the Simulations in this group were ready for activation I was planted among them. I trained with them and now I've fought with them, and if you've been reading the right magazine you must have seen some of the stories I've filed. And since you're a civilian too, with no more right to command than I have, I'm taking charge." He could sense Brenner's swallow.

"Those stories were frauds—it's a trick to gain public acceptance of the HORARS. Even back in Washington everybody in SBS knows about them."

The chuckle hurt, but 2910 chuckled. "Then why've I got this knife at your neck, Mr. Brenner?"

The SBS man was shaking. "Don't you see how it was, 2910? No human could live as a HORAR does, running miles without tiring and only sleeping a couple of hours a night, so we did the next best thing. Believe me, I was briefed on it all when I was assigned to this camp; I know all about you, 2910."

"What do you mean?"

"Damn it, let me go. You're a HORAR, and you can't treat a human like this." He winced as the knife pressed cruelly against his throat, then blurted, "They couldn't make a reporter a HORAR, so they *took* a HORAR. They took you, 2910, and made you a reporter. They implanted all the memories of an actual man in your mind at the same time they ran the regular instinct tapes. They gave you a soul, if you like, but you are a HORAR."

"They must have thought that up as a cover for me, Brenner. That's what they told you so you wouldn't report it or try to deactivate me when I acted unlike the others. I'm a man."

"You couldn't be."

"People are tougher than you think, Brenner; you've never tried."

"I'm telling you—"

"Take the bandage off my leg."

"What?"

He pressed again with the point of the knife. "The bandage. Take it off."

When it was off he directed, "Now spread the lips of the wound." With shaking fingers Brenner did so. "You see the bone? Go deeper if you have to. What is it?"

Brenner twisted his neck to look at him directly, his eyes rolling. "It's stainless steel."

2910 looked then and saw the bright metal at the bottom of the cleft of bleeding flesh; the knife slid into Brenner's throat without resistance, almost as though it moved itself. He wiped the blade on Brenner's dead arm before he sheathed it.

Ten minutes later when 2900 returned to the CP he said nothing; but 2910 saw his eyes and knew that 2900 knew. From his stretcher he said, "You're in full command now."

2900 glanced again at Brenner's body. A second later he said slowly, "He was a sort of Enemy, wasn't he? Because he wanted to surrender, and Lieutenant Kyle would never have done that."

"Yes, he was."

"But I couldn't think of it that way while he was alive." 2900 looked at him thoughtfully. "You know, you have something, 2910. A spark. Something the rest of us lack." For a moment he fingered his chin with one huge hand. "That's why I made you a squad leader; that and to get you out of some work, because sometimes you couldn't seem to keep up. But you've that spark, somehow."

2910 said, "I know. How is it out there?"

"We're still holding. How do you feel?"

"Dizzy. There's a sort of black stuff all around the sides when I see. Listen, will you tell me something, if you can, before you go?"

"Of course."

"If a human's leg is broken very badly, what I believe they call a compound spiral fracture, is it possible for the human doctors to take out a section of the bone and replace it with a metal substitute?"

"I don't know," 2900 answered. "What does it matter?"

Vaguely 2910 said, "I think I knew of a football player once they did that to. At least, I seem now to remember it . . . I had forgotten for a moment."

Outside the bugles were blowing again.

Near him the dying HORAR moaned.

An American news magazine sometimes carries, just inside its front cover among the advertisements, a column devoted to news of its own people. Two weeks after a correspondent named Thomas filed the last article of a series which had attracted national and even international attention, the following item appeared there:

The death of a staffer in war is no unique occurrence in the history of this publication, but there is a particular poignancy about that of the young man whose stories, paradoxically, to conceal his number have been signed only with his name (*see* PRESS). The airborne relief force, which arrived too late to save the camp at which he had resigned his humanity to work and fight, reports that he apparently died assisting the assigned SBS specialist in caring for the creatures whose lot he had, as nearly as a human can, made his own. Both he and the specialist were bayonetted when the camp was overrun.

I MADE YOU

by Walter M. Miller, Jr.

It had disposed of the enemy, and it was weary. It sat on the
crag by night. Gaunt, frigid, wounded, it sat under the black
sky and listened to the land with its feet, while only its dishlike
ear moved in slow patterns that searched the surface of the land
and the sky. The land was silent, airless. Nothing moved,
except the feeble thing that scratched in the cave. It was good
that nothing moved. It hated sound and motion. It was in its
nature to hate them. About the thing in the cave, it could do
nothing until dawn. The thing muttered in the rocks—

*"Help me! Are you all dead? Can't you hear me? This is
Sawyer. Sawyer calling anybody, Sawyer calling anybody—"*

The mutterings were irregular, without pattern. It filtered
them out, refusing to listen. All was seeping cold. The sun was
gone, and there had been near-blackness for two hundred and
fifty hours, except for the dim light of the sky-orb which gave
no food, and the stars by which it told the time.

It sat wounded on the crag and expected the enemy. The
enemy had come charging into the world out of the unworld
during the late afternoon. The enemy had come brazenly, with
neither defensive maneuvering nor offensive fire. It had destroyed them easily—first the big lumbering enemy that rumbled along on wheels, and then the small enemies that scurried

23

away from the gutted hulk. It had picked them off one at a time, except for the one that crept into the cave and hid itself beyond a break in the tunnel.

It waited for the thing to emerge. From its vantage point atop the crag, it could scan broken terrain for miles around, the craters and crags and fissures, the barren expanse of dust flat that stretched to the west, and the squarish outlines of the holy place near the tower that was the center of the world. The cave lay at the foot of a cliff to the southeast, only a thousand yards from the crag. It could guard the entrance to the cave with its small spitters, and there was no escape for the lingering trace of enemy.

It bore the mutterings of the hated thing even as it bore the pain of its wounds, patiently, waiting for a time of respite. For many sunrises there had been pain, and still the wounds were unrepaired. The wounds dulled some of its senses and crippled some of its activators. It could no longer follow the flickering beam of energy that would lead it safely into the unworld and across it to the place of creation. It could no longer blink out the pulses that reflected the difference between healer and foe. Now there was only foe.

"Colonel Aubrey, this is Sawyer. Answer me! I'm trapped in a supply cache! I think the others are dead. It blasted us as soon as we came near. Aubrey from Sawyer, Aubrey from Sawyer. Listen! I've got only one cylinder of oxygen left, you hear? Colonel, answer me!"

Vibrations in the rock, nothing more—only a minor irritant to disturb the blessed stasis of the world it guarded. The enemy was destroyed, except for the lingering trace in the cave. The lingering trace was neutralized however, and did not move.

Because of its wounds, it nursed a brooding anger. It could not stop the damage signals that kept firing from its wounded members, but neither could it accomplish the actions that the agonizing signals urged it to accomplish. It sat and suffered and hated on the crag.

It hated the night, for by night there was no food. Each day it devoured sun, strengthened itself for the long, long watch of darkness, but when dawn came, it was feeble again, and hunger was a fierce passion within. It was well, therefore, that there was peace in the night, that it might conserve itself and shield its bowels from the cold. If the cold penetrated the in-

sulating layers, thermal receptors would begin firing warning
signals, and agony would increase. There was much agony.
And, except in time of battle, there was no pleasure except in
devouring sun.

To protect the holy place, to restore stasis to the world, to
kill enemy—these were the pleasures of battle. It knew them.

And it knew the nature of the world. It had learned every
inch of land out to the pain perimeter, beyond which it could
not move. And it had learned the surface features of the
demiworld beyond, learned them by scanning with its long-
range senses. The world, the demiworld, the unworld—these
were Outside, constituting the universe.

*"Help me, help me, help me! This is Captain John Harbin
Sawyer, Autocyber Corps, Instruction and Programming Section, currently of Salvage Expedition Lunar-Sixteen. Isn't
anybody alive on the Moon? Listen! Listen to me! I'm sick.
I've been here God knows how many days . . . in a suit. It
stinks. Did you ever live in a suit for days? I'm sick. Get me
out of here!"*

The enemy's place was unworld. If the enemy approached
closer than the outer range, it must kill; this was a basic truth
that it had known since the day of creation. Only the healers
might move with impunity over all the land, but now the
healers never came. It could no longer call them or recognize
them—because of the wound.

It knew the nature of itself. It learned of itself by introspect-
ing damage, and by internal scanning. It alone was "being."
All else was of the Outside. It knew its functions, its skills, its
limitations. It listened to the land with its feet. It scanned the
surface with many eyes. It tested the skies with a flickering
probe. In the ground, it felt the faint seisms and random
noise. On the surface, it saw the faint glint of starlight, the
heat loss from the cold terrain, and the reflected pulses from
the tower. In the sky, it saw only stars, and heard only the
pulse-echo from the faint orb of Earth overhead. It suffered
the gnawings of ancient pain, and waited for the dawn.

After an hour, the thing began crawling in the cave. It listened
to the faint scraping sounds that came through the rocks. It
lowered a more sensitive pickup and tracked the sounds. The
remnant of enemy was crawling softly toward the mouth of
the cave. It turned a small spitter toward the black scar at the

foot of the Earthlit cliff. It fired a bright burst of tracers toward the cave, and saw them ricochet about the entrance in bright but noiseless streaks over the airless land.

"You dirty greasy deadly monstrosity, let me alone! You ugly juggernaut, I'm Sawyer. Don't you remember? I helped to train you ten years ago. You were a rookie under me . . . heh heh! Just a dumb autocyber rookie . . . with the firepower of a regiment. Let me go. Let me go!"

The enemy-trace crawled toward the entrance again. And again a noiseless burst of machine-gun fire spewed about the cave, driving the enemy fragment back. More vibrations in the rock—

"I'm your friend. The war's over. It's been over for months . . . Earthmonths. Don't you get it, Grumbler? 'Grumbler'— we used to call you that back in your rookie days—before we taught you how to kill. Grumbler. Mobile autocyber fir con-trol. Don't you know your pappy, son?"

The vibrations were an irritant. Suddenly angry, it wheeled around on the crag, gracefully maneuvering its massive bulk. Motors growling, it moved from the crag onto the hillside, turned again, and lumbered down the slope. It charged across the flatlands and braked to a halt fifty yards from the entrance to the cave. Dust geysers sprayed up about its caterpillars and fell like jets of water in the airless night. It listened again. All was silent in the cave.

"Go 'way, sonny," quavered the vibrations after a time. *"Let pappy starve in peace."*

It aimed the small spitter at the center of the black opening and hosed two hundred rounds of tracers into the cave. It waited. Nothing moved inside. It debated the use of a radia-tion grenade, but its arsenal was fast depleting. It listened for a time, watching the cave, looming five times taller than the tiny flesh-thing that cowered inside. Then it turned and lumbered back across the flat to resume its watch from the crag. Distant motion, out beyond the limits of the demiworld, scratched feebly at the threshold of its awareness—but the mo-tion was too remote to disturb.

The thing was scratching in the cave again.

"I'm punctured, do you hear? I'm punctured. A shard of broken rock. Just a small leak, but a slap-patch won't hold. My suit! Aubrey from Sawyer, Aubrey from Sawyer. Base Control from Moonwagon Sixteen, message for you, over. He

he. Gotta observe procedure. I got shot! I'm punctured. Help!"

The thing made whining sounds for a time, then: *"All right, it's only my leg. I'll pump the boot full of water and freeze it. So I lose a leg. Whatthehell, take your time."* The vibrations subsided into whining sounds again.

It settled again on the crag, its activators relaxing into a lethargy that was full of gnawing pain. Patiently it awaited the dawn.

The movement toward the south was increasing. The movement nagged at the outer fringes of the demiworld, until at last the movement became an irritant. Silently, a drill slipped down from its belly. The drill gnawed deep into the rock, then retracted. It slipped a sensitive pickup into the drill hole and listened carefully to the ground.

A faint purring in the rocks—mingled with the whining from the cave.

It compared the purring with recorded memories. It remembered similar purrings. The sound came from a rolling object far to the south. It tried to send the pulses that asked "Are you friend or foe," but the sending organ was inoperative. The movement, therefore, was enemy—but still beyond range of its present weapons.

Lurking anger, and expectation of battle. It stirred restlessly on the crag, but kept its surveillance of the cave. Suddenly there was disturbance on a new sensory channel, vibrations similar to those that came from the cave; but this time the vibrations came across the surface, through the emptiness, transmitted in the long-wave spectra.

"Moonwagon Sixteen from Command Runabout, give us a call. Over."

Then silence. It expected a response from the cave, at first—since it knew that one unit of enemy often exchanged vibratory patterns with another unit of enemy. But no answer came. Perhaps the long-wave energy could not penetrate the cave to reach the thing that cringed inside.

"Salvage Sixteen, this is Aubrey's runabout. What the devil happened to you? Can you read me? Over!"

Tensely it listened on the ground. The purring stopped for a time as the enemy paused. Minutes later, the motion resumed. It awoke an emissary ear twenty kilometers to the south-

west, and commanded the ear to listen, and to transmit the
patterns of the purring noise. Two soundings were taken, and
from them, it derived the enemy's precise position and velocity. The enemy was proceeding to the north, into the edge
of the demiworld. Lurking anger flared into active fury. It
gunned its engines on the crag. It girded itself for battle.

*"Salvage Sixteen, this is Aubrey's runabout. I assume your
radio rig is inoperative. If you can hear us, get this: we're proceeding north to five miles short of magnapult range. We'll
stop there and fire an autocyb rocket into zone Red-Red. The
warhead's a radio-to-sonar transceiver. If you've got a seismitter that's working, the transceiver will act as a relay stage.
Over."*

It ignored the vibratory pattern and rechecked its battle
gear. It introspected its energy storage, and tested its weapon
activators. It summoned an emissary eye and waited a dozen
minutes while the eye crawled crablike from the holy place to
take up a watch post near the entrance of the cave. If the
enemy remnant tried to emerge, the emissary eye would see,
and report, and it could destroy the enemy remnant with a remote grenade catapult.

The purring in the ground was louder. Having prepared
itself for the fray, it came down from the crag and grumbled
southward at cruising speed. It passed the gutted hulk of the
Moonwagon, with its team of overturned tractors. The detonation of the magnapult canister had broken the freight car
sized vehicle in half. The remains of several two-legged enemy
appurtenances were scattered about the area, tiny broken
things in the pale Earthlight. Grumbler ignored them and
charged relentlessly southward.

A sudden wink of light on the southern horizon! Then a tiny
dot of flame arced upward, traversing the heavens. Grumbler
skidded to a halt and tracked its path. A rocket missile. It
would fall somewhere in the east half of zone Red-Red. There
as no time to prepare to shoot it down. Grumbler waited—and
saw that the missile would explode harmlessly in a nonvital
area.

Seconds later, the missile paused in flight, reversing direction and sitting on its jets. It dropped out of sight behind an
outcropping. There was no explosion. Nor was there any activity in the area where the missile had fallen. Grumbler called

an emissary ear, sent it migrating toward the impact point to listen, then continued south toward the pain perimeter.

"Salvage Sixteen, this is Aubrey's runabout," came the long-wave vibrations. *"We just shot the radio-seismitter relay into Red-Red. If you're within five miles of it, you should be able to hear."*

Almost immediately, a response from the cave, heard by the emissary ear that listened to the land near the tower: *"Thank God! He he he he—Oh, thank God!"*

And simultaneously, the same vibratory pattern came in long-wave patterns from the direction of the missile-impact point. Grumbler stopped again, momentarily confused, angrily tempted to lob a magnapult canister across the broken terrain toward the impact point. But the emissary ear reported no physical movement from the area. The enemy to the south was the origin of the disturbances. If it removed the major enemy first, it could remove the minor disturbances later. It moved on to the pain perimeter, occasionally listening to the meaningless vibrations caused by the enemy.

"Salvage Sixteen from Aubrey. I hear you faintly. Who is this, Carhill?"

"Aubrey! A voice—a real voice—or am I going nuts?"

"Sixteen from Aubrey, Sixteen from Aubrey. Stop babbling and tell me who's talking. What's happening in there? Have you got Grumbler immobilized?"

Spasmodic choking was the only response.

"Sixteen from Aubrey. Snap out of it! Listen, Sawyer, I know it's you. Now get hold of yourself, man! What's happened?"

"Dead . . . they're all dead but me."

"STOP THAT IDIOTIC LAUGHING!"

A long silence, then, scarcely audible: *"O.K., I'll hold onto myself. Is it really you, Aubrey?"*

"You're not having hallucinations, Sawyer. We're crossing zone Red in a runabout. Now tell me the situation. We've been trying to call you for days."

"Grumbler let us get ten miles into zone Red-Red, and then he clobbered us with a magnapult canister."

"Wasn't your I.F.F. working?"

"Yes, but Grumbler's isn't. After he blasted the wagon, he

*picked off the other four that got out alive—He he he he . . .
Did you ever see a Sherman tank chase a mouse, Colonel?"*

"Cut it out, Sawyer! Another giggle out of you, and I'll flay
you alive."

"Get me out! My leg! Get me out!"

"If we can. Tell me your present situation."

"My suit . . . I got a small puncture—Had to pump the leg
full of water and freeze it. Now my leg's dead. I can't last
much longer."

"The situation, Sawyer, the situation! Not your aches and
pains."

The vibrations continued, but Grumbler screened them out
for a time. There was rumbling fury on an Earthlit hill.

It sat with its engines idling, listening to the distant movements of the enemy to the south. At the foot of the hill lay the
pain perimeter; even upon the hilltop, it felt the faint twinges
of warning that issued from the tower, thirty kilometers to the
rear at the center of the world. It was in communion with the
tower. If it ventured beyond the perimeter, the communion
would slip out of phase, and there would be blinding pain and
detonation.

The enemy was moving more slowly now, creeping north
across the demiworld. It would be easy to destroy the enemy at
once, if only the supply of rocket missiles were not depleted.
The range of the magnapult hurler was only twenty-five kilometers. The small spitters would reach, but their accuracy was
close to zero at such range. It would have to wait for the
enemy to come closer. It nursed a brooding fury on the hill.

"Listen, Sawyer, if Grumbler's I.F.F. isn't working, why
hasn't he already fired on this runabout?"

"That's what sucked us in too, Colonel. We came into zone
Red and nothing happened. Either he's out of long-range
ammo, or he's getting cagey, or both. Probably both."

"Mmmp! Then we'd better park here and figure something
out."

"Listen . . . there's only one thing you can do. Call for a
telecontrolled missile from the Base."

"To destroy Grumbler? You're out of your head, Sawyer.
If Grumbler's knocked out, the whole area around the excavations gets blown sky high . . . to keep them out of enemy
hands. You know that."

"You expect me to care?"

"Stop screaming, Sawyer. Those excavations are the most valuable property on the Moon. We can't afford to lose them. That's why Grumbler was staked out. If they got blown to rubble, I'd be court-martialed before the debris quit falling."

The response was snarling and sobbing. *"Eight hours oxygen. Eight hours, you hear? You stupid, merciless—"*

The enemy to the south stopped moving at a distance of twenty-eight kilometers from Grumbler's hill—only three thousand meters beyond magnapult range.

A moment of berserk hatred. It lumbered to and fro in a frustrated pattern that was like a monstrous dance, crushing small rocks beneath its treads, showering dust into the valley. Once it charged down toward the pain perimeter, and turned back only after the agony became unbearable. It stopped again on the hill, feeling the weariness of lowered energy supplies in the storage units.

It paused to analyze. It derived a plan.

Gunning its engines, it wheeled slowly around on the hilltop, and glided down the northern slope at a stately pace. It sped northward for half a mile across the flatland, then slowed to a crawl and maneuvered its massive bulk into a fissure, where it had cached an emergency store of energy. The battery-trailer had been freshly charged before the previous sundown. It backed into feeding position and attached the supply cables without hitching itself to the trailer.

It listened occasionally to the enemy while it drank hungrily from the energy store, but the enemy remained motionless. It would need every erg of available energy in order to accomplish its plan. It drained the cache. Tomorrow, when the enemy was gone, it would drag the trailer back to the main feeders for recharging, when the sun rose to drive the generators once again. It kept several caches of energy at strategic positions throughout its domain, that it might never be driven into starved inability to act during the long lunar night. It kept its own house in order, dragging the trailers back to be recharged at regular intervals.

"I don't know what I can do for you, Sawyer," came the noise of the enemy. *"We don't dare destroy Grumbler, and there's not another autocyber crew on the Moon. I'll have to call Terra for replacements. I can't send men into zone Red-Red if Grumbler's running berserk. It'd be murder."*

"For the love of God, Colonel—!"

"Listen, Sawyer, you're the autocyber man. You helped train Grumbler. Can't you think of some way to stop him without detonating the mined area?"

A protracted silence. Grumbler finished feeding and came out of the fissure. It moved westward a few yards, so that a clear stretch of flat land lay between itself and the hill at the edge of the pain perimeter, half a mile away. There it paused and awoke several emissary ears, so that it might derive the most accurate possible fix of the enemy's position. One by one, the emissary ears reported.

"Well, Sawyer?"

"My leg's killing me."

"Can't you think of anything?"

"Yeah—but it won't do me any good. I won't live that long."

"Well, let's hear it."

"Knock out his remote energy storage units, and then run him ragged at night."

"How long would it take?"

"Hours—after you found all his remote supply units and blasted them."

It analyzed the reports of emissary ears, and calculated a precise position. The enemy runabout was 2.7 kilometers beyond the maximum range of the magnapult—as creation had envisioned the maximum. But creation was imperfect, even inside.

It loaded a canister onto the magnapult's spindle. Contrary to the intentions of creation, it left the canister *locked to the loader.* This would cause pain. But it would prevent the canister from moving during the first few microseconds after the switch was closed, while the magnetic field was still building toward full strength. It would not release the canister until the field clutched it fiercely and with full effect, thus imparting slightly greater energy to the canister. This procedure it had invented for itself, thus transcending creation.

"Well, Sawyer, if you can't think of anything else—"

"I DID THINK OF SOMETHING ELSE!" the answering vibrations screamed. *"Call for a telecontrolled missile! Can't you understand, Aubrey? Grumbler murdered eight men from your command."*

"You taught him how, Sawyer."

There was a long and ominous silence. On the flat land to the north of the hill, Grumbler adjusted the elevation of the magnapult slightly, keyed the firing switch to a gyroscope, and prepared to charge. Creation had calculated the maximum range when the weapon was at a standstill.

"He he he he he—" came the patterns from the thing in the cave.

It gunned its engines and clutched the drive shafts. It rolled toward the hill, gathering speed, and its mouth was full of death. Motors strained and howled. Like a thundering bull, it rumbled toward the south. It hit maximum velocity at the foot of the slope. It lurched sharply upward. As the magnapult swept up to correct elevation, the gyroscope closed the circuit.

A surge of energy. The clenching fist of the field gripped the canister, tore it free of the loader, hurled it high over the broken terrain toward the enemy. Grumbler skidded to a halt on the hilltop.

"Listen, Sawyer, I'm sorry, but there's nothing—"

The enemy's voice ended with a dull snap. A flare of light came briefly from the southern horizon, and died.

"He he he he he—" said the thing in the cave.

Grumbler paused.

THRRRUMMMP! came the shock wave through the rocks.

Five emissary ears relayed their recordings of the detonation from various locations. It studied them, it analyzed. The detonation had occured less than fifty meters from the enemy runabout. Satiated, it wheeled around lazily on the hilltop and rolled northward toward the center of the world. All was well.

"Aubrey, you got cut off," grunted the thing in the cave. *"Call me, you coward . . . call me. I want to make certain you hear."*

Grumbler, as a random action, recorded the meaningless noise of the thing in the cave, studied the noise, rebroadcast it on the long-wave frequency: "Aubrey, you got cut off. Call me, you coward . . . call me. I want to make certain you hear."

The seismitter caught the long-wave noise and reintroduced it as vibration in the rocks.

The thing screamed in the cave. Grumbler recorded the screaming noise, and rebroadcast it several times.

"Aubrey . . . Aubrey, where are you . . . AUBREY! Don't desert me, don't leave me here—"

The thing in the cave became silent.

It was a peaceful night. The stars glared unceasingly from the blackness, and the pale terrain was haunted by Earthlight from the dim crescent in the sky. Nothing moved. It was good that nothing moved. The holy place was at peace in the airless world. There was blessed stasis.

Only once did the thing stir again in the cave. So slowly that Grumbler scarcely heard the sound, it crawled to the entrance and lay peering up at the steel behemoth on the crag.

It whispered faintly in the rocks. *"I made you, don't you understand? I'm human. I made you—"*

Then with one leg dragging behind, it pulled itself out into the Earthglow and turned as if to look up at the dim crescent in the sky. Gathering fury, Grumbler stirred on the crag, and lowered the black maw of a grenade launcher.

"I made you," came the meaningless noise.

It hated noise and motion. It was in its nature to hate them. Angrily, the grenade launcher spoke. And then there was blessed stasis for the rest of the night.

ENCOUNTER

by Stephen Leigh

Voll felt so damned useless, and he simply wanted out. A simple enough desire.

The land, his land, spread about him in lonely splendor, the hills choked with brush and the trees turning brown and bare. The painted days of the short autumn weren't long past. Somewhere, near him but unseen, a brook thrashed its way between and round the rocks of its bed. Occasionally, he would stoop and pick up a stone, eventually casting it westward away from the boundaries of his land.

There didn't seem to be much else to do.

The memories kept coming back. Irresistible, they shivered through him like ebony lances, the weapons of dreams. He would try to stop them, thinking of anything else, knowing how he would feel afterward—yet Voll always lost that battle, finally surrendering himself to the past, the surcease from pain always brief and ineffectual.

Night battle. The entire landscape is bathed in red, drenched with the bloody light of the infrared projectors. Mist (or is it steam?) writhes about the silhouetted hulks of two carriers not far from him. He gives the code challenge, waiting to see if they would answer, but they remain silent. They turn to face him, bristling with armor and weapons. Voll smiles as he rises to a crouch. The lust of battle upon him, a berserker, he goes to destroy the vehicles.

By himself. Alone.

No, he thought, leave me alone. Damn!

The terrible confusion of hand-to-hand combat swirls about him. Noise, always noise, that's what he is most aware of: sound so loud that the mind ceases to register all of it and the battle seems to take place in awesome silence. And only the humans scream. The gholas, the resurrected dead of both sides, fight in characteristic, tight-lipped silence. He'd often wondered if that reflected on their previous deaths. Do they no longer fear the spectre, having faced it once? Certainly, the gholas are fearless. They attack, always attack, hacking and clawing at their enemies if they can do nothing else. He'd seen one that might once have been a woman rise as if from her second death and fasten her teeth on her attackers, with her stomach torn open and the entrails dragging on the ground. It/she ignored the soldier's slashing knife, ignored the blood that poured from its side, ignored the fatal wound that would have driven a living being into peaceful shock: it was intent only on taking a life. And then he'd entered the battle, and the ghola and human both fell before him as he swept through untouched.

And he recalled the time he'd descended in wrath upon an animatank, rising from his hiding place on a hillside as it passed below him. He ripped away the plasteel armor, plunged his naked hands into the unprotected vitals, and tore out wiring and circuitry in a bloodless disembowelment. He remembered that the 'tank had screamed, an animal sound that had nothing of metal and grease to it—the death cry of a life. Voll had felt kinship—for an instant—but kin fought against kin in this insane war, so what did it matter?

There were men running from him in terror, knowing who he was, screaming in a litany of agony the word he'd come to hate. "Voll!" Voll: his name—it had come to mean power, it had come to mean hatred. And Voll, without hatred but with power, smashed them as he'd smashed many things: always with remorse, always without rancor, but always . . . Fire arced from his brow, poisons dripped from the steel of his nails, cannons barked from his waist. A man, but something far more. A man to destroy men and the things of men.

A man with no purpose now. Useless, unwanted, but still dangerous.

So he cast his stones, letting them fall where he couldn't go, dropping beyond the barrier that fenced his land, keeping everyone out and keeping him inside. Voll wondered how many stones now lay on the other side. How long, at the rate of, say, seven stones a day before all his land was Outside?

Cleaning the rust-red stains from his hands afterward, watching the clotted blood swirl away in the clean water . . .

"No," he said softly. Voll bent down and picked up another stone, keeping his attention focused on the way the specks of mica caught the sun and the subtle colors tinting the crevices: a pale blue, a smeared mustard yellow. A bird shrieked above him. He watched it wheel and sway, the outstretched pinions catching the updraft from the nearby hills. Voll watched it circle and then quickly stoop, vanishing in a flurry of wings beyond the tangle of leafless trees.

As vivid as any of the memories, he recalled the reaction of those he fought with, those that had made him into the half-machine he was and who wished him well in battle but avoided him in the times between. They chased him away with feigned goodwill and distilled indifference until he sought the battlefields and war because at least there he could do something with his feelings. There he was fit, there he was home, there he was useful.

Voll dropped the stone with a disgusted sound. It fell into the brittle leaves that cloaked the path and was gone. He scuffed at the spot where it had fallen and fragments of leaves scattered in the wind, drifting slowly back to earth. It was going to be a bad day. They came at times, those days when he couldn't control his thoughts, when the ache to be out of here was almost unbearable. The past would unreel without volition, bringing back all the gall and bitterness it contained.

Afterward, they had deemed Voll a mistake, a technological dead end that had been an interesting experiment in time of need. But he was human, or at least once had been, and they simply couldn't junk him as they did other weaponry. No, they were too humane for that, too human.

Voll walked to the accompaniment of crumbling leaves, a rhythmic, dry crackling like explosions of arid fire. He came to a turn in his path where a large hoversign proclaimed warning. The barrier. If he looked closely, he could see the faintest of shimmerings there, in a patch of clear earth that paralleled his path and then turned at right angles to it, barring his way. He walked as near to it as he dared, as he always did, until he could feel the subsonic vibrations of the second warning shield, a basso rumbling. A ground squirrel lay a few meters ahead of him, paws up and unmoving, a casual victim of his imprisonment, though most animals found the subsonics irritating enough and never went into the barrier itself. Voll stepped from the path and snapped a dry length of branch from a nearby dead tree. Then, carefully, he slid the wood underneath the dead animal and flipped it past the barrier. Outside, to where he could never be.

Satisfied, he turned and continued walking, pausing once to pick up another stone.

It was late afternoon when he returned to the house and studio set in a clearing near where the brook emptied into a small lake. Voll checked the transportal they'd set up outside. Nothing much in it today: another supply of meats, a few cans of nondescript vegetables, another bundle of newsfax, and some cloth. Voll carried the meat and cans into the house and left the rest. He carefully packed away the provisions, taking the excessive care of those with much time to waste. Finished with the task, he went to his studio.

The studio was cluttered with his wooden carvings, each piece finely detailed and varnished to a high gloss. The room itself was dominated by a huge log, nearly fifteen meters in height, set on end in the open space in the middle of the studio. Unworked, bark still clung stubbornly to the wood. As Voll surveyed the room, he knew it was time to pack away some of the clutter and send it through the transportal. Occasionally, he would stumble across his name in the newsfax they sent him, imprisoned in the esoteric verbosity of an art critic's column—the news services, with the exception of a few "do you remember" pieces, had forgotten about him. Cerainly not a polished artist, and crude work, read one review, but with the true vigor of a primitif. The work has a brutal, angry strength, and we hope to see more of Voll's work as he hones his craft. So it seemed he had a very minor reputation in the arts, and somewhere a bank account in his name grew slowly. Voll walked around the studio, studying each piece. The

Wounded Deer, writhing in suspended agony; it could go. The same for the *Bust of Ghola*, the *Crippled Bird*. They'd all been around for some time: he knew them, knew each line, and it was to the point where he no longer *saw* them, but simply acknowledged their presence. He wouldn't miss them—pack them up tonight. Not the *Fallen Man With Ghola* though. No, that was his favorite, and he found himself reticent to send it out; afraid, perhaps, that it would be rejected and viewed with distaste. Anyway, he thought, I'll keep it here for a time.

The decisions made, Voll stared across the lake. The westering sun glazed the tip of each ripple, and the east wall of the studio wavered with the twisting of light. There were only a few hours left in which to work—Voll disliked using artificial lighting in the studio. The ceiling was a framework of steel and glass, and the only portions blocked from the outside were the east and south walls.

With a sound halfway between grunt and sigh, Voll moved to the log. He'd pulled it from the forest two days earlier on a whim, feeling that it was time he attempted something on a larger scale. He walked around it, musing. Then, with a motion a shade too fast for a normal man, he stepped to the log and began working. He dug at it with his hands, and shavings began to curl from under his fingernails.

He sang as he worked, off-key and discordant.

He was singing when he returned from his morning walk, a German lieder he halfremembered from early days. The ground was wet and cold water hung in quivering droplets from the bare trees. The clouds, low and thick, were raked by the highest branches of the forest. Voll turned at the door of his cabin and flung the stone in his hand far out into the lake. He heard rather than saw the splash.

Inside, he shook dampness from his arms and brushed at his sodden clothing. It was then that he saw the woman, sitting cross-legged in a chair across the room and staring at him, a tube of some silver metal in her hand. The open end of the tube pointed directly at his chest, and he had no doubts as to its meaning.

For an imperceptible moment, he paused—*a feint to the right, then a quick frontal assault and she'd never know what happened, would never use that strange weapon she holds*—then continued walking to the kitchen.

"You hungry?" The sound of his own voice startled him as much as finding the woman. He didn't think he'd spoken in weeks, but he hid shock and surprise in the habitual rite of fixing a meal. He could see her across the half-wall that separated the kitchen from the living room. Only her head had moved. The cylindrical object still pointed to the door. She looked at Voll: walnut eyes.

Her face was multiswirled with skin dyes around the foci of those dark eyes. Red, violet, lime green: it was a disconcerting effect, giving her face motion even in repose. Voll forced himself to look away.

"You"—she hesitated, then continued—"don't look at all different." Her voice was as quiet and deep as the eyes.

"Umm, thanks," Voll replied, not knowing what she meant. He could not find that face in his memories. "You want soup? It's meat stock." *Control,* he thought. *Pretend you have visitors every day.*

"You don't seem surprised to find me here." The woman rose and came toward the kitchen area, walking slowly and stopping where he could see her clearly. Voll noted that the cylinder was gone, vanished somewhere in the folds of loose clothing she wore.

"I'm sufficiently startled," he said slowly, nodding his head. *Damn right. How did you get past the barrier?* "If the governments can erect a barrier, then I suppose someone else can get by it." A pause. "Not that I thought it would happen so quickly." *Or that anyone would want to enter my little domain.* "Milk, or spring water?"

"You're not curious about me?"

Voll put down the pot in which he was stirring the soup. He looked at her, wiped his hands on his pants. "Hey, you made it in, and I figure that you'll tell me everything when you're ready to do so. And I *am* hungry. Time is one thing of which I have sufficient quantities. Nothing presses me here. And one of the requirements I insisted upon when I agreed to this confinement was that there would be no surveillance devices of any kind on this side of the barrier—so no one can monitor your presence, and you can stay as long as you wish and do what you care to do. We have time."

She seemed to relax suddenly, as Voll turned back to the cooking. She sloughed off an insubstantial tension that had held her body and wrapped her features in ice. She didn't smile, but she found a chair and sat, watching him make his familiar motions.

They ate in silence. Voll kept his attention on the food and hardly looked at her. He wondered if his reticence to talk came from the years of being alone here. He had little desire to start a conversation; had, in fact, nothing to say. He almost resented the intrusion which forced him to pay attention to another person's presence. For her part, the woman made no attempt to disturb him, but he could feel her eyes constantly on him. She watched him warily—and why not? he thought. Was he not Voll, the great killer?

Afterward, he pushed the grease-smeared plate away from him, sitting up in his chair. He put his hands on the table, ready to lever himself up. "I'm going to my studio. Would you like to see it?"

The woman nodded and shrugged simultaneously, rising from her chair. Voll led her to the studio, opened the door, and stepped back. He waited for her reaction, but she said nothing and her face was set in blank stoicism. He walked in behind her—feeling vague disappointment—and closed the door behind them.

The log still dominated the room. Roughly carved now, it was beginning to take on a suggestion of its final shape. Three figures, somewhat elongated, clasped each other and looked into the distance with faces transfixed by obvious, almost melodramatic, horror. At their feet were shapes that resembled discarded weapons, and with them a twisted and distorted dwarf squatted and looked upward at the trio, laughing. Voll caressed the surface of the wood with a hand.

"You don't like it?" His voice had the faintest tremor, and he regretted asking the question, hating the feeling of vulnerability it gave him.

"I'm not sure," she replied. She turned and looked at him, her eyes challenging, and then squinted toward the piece. "I think I may hate it."

Leaning against the eastern wall, affecting a nonchalance he did not feel: "It doesn't matter. They sell Outside, though." His voice added the capitalization.

"I've seen a few. You actually do them with nothing but your hands?"

"For the most part." He walked toward her, his voice easier now that he was on a familiar subject. "Why not, since it's convenient. The nails are beryl-steel, sharpened and retract-able." He held his hands out. Afternoon sun made golden the hairs on the back of his hands. "The nerve endings have been deadened, and they work well as tools. I feel a lot closer to the sculpture."

Her eyes, encased in color, held him. "Did you feel a lot closer to the killing?"

Voll inhaled deeply. He closed his eyes, opened them.

"No," he said softly. A roaring filled his ears and slowly subsided.

She had moved away from him, standing at the window that was the western wall. The sun and light glancing from the water made her outline dance. Voll felt anger rising in him and tried to quell it.

"Look," he said, finally. "I think I may have this figured out. You're a reporter for one of the networks, yah? That doesn't give you leave to come here and goad me, like some caged animal." Even as he said the words, he knew they were false. No, that didn't explain the metal cylinder that had been pointed at him with decided menace, didn't explain how and why she'd slipped past the barrier, didn't explain any of the enigmas that hung about her. But he continued speaking because it was easier than stopping and admitting she'd hurt him.

"You've forgotten that I'm a danger to a peaceable society, something you need to pen up so you normals can pursue your idyllic lives." He spoke the last few words with measured sar-casm, venting some of the bitterness inside. When she said nothing, but continued staring out toward the water, he went on.

"I'm a beast, something subhuman, a deformed and un-wanted child sent away so it won't embarrass the family. Pariah. I could kill you and feel nothing. Isn't that what you believe?" Voll grimaced and raised his hands in sudden aimless disgust. "Ahh, hell."

Strange calm held the woman's features. "I think you know how wrong your guess is, Voll. I told you. We've met before, thought I doubt you bothered to jot down the occasion at the time." She laughed, but the laugh held no humor. "I'm Myrna Dassent. I'm sure the name itself means nothing to you."

She moved away from the window and came halfway across

the room toward him. Her eyes were shadowed: in the shadows, moist highlights glittered and moved. "Do you *want* to hear my story, Voll? I hope not, because you'll listen in any case. I—" Her voice broke and she stopped in mid-sentence, then lifted her chin in a defiance of emotion. "I was an animatank during the war, fighting in a squad with my husband, father, and brother—we believed in keeping the family together—our brains wired to the machinery while our bodies slumbered at home."

"Myrna," began Voll. The name moved oddly on his tongue. He shook his head and gestured to the studio around him. "I don't know you. This is all I do now. I wish it were all I'd ever done. I don't want to hear about you or the war."

She continued as if she hadn't heard him. "One day, we received information that the enemy had some new weapon, some new twist that would strike from hiding and destroy anything within its grasp. That weapon was, according to the reports, loose in our sector. A man, they said, it looks like a man. We laughed, my family and I, feeling secure in the metal bodies of the 'tanks, behind the bulwark of their firepower. It was one of the rare warm and sunny days. Any threat seemed distant, and a *man* could do nothing to us. We continued on our patrol. It was a grand day, the mists just rolling in from the river."

"Myrna," Voll said again.

She glared at him, silencing him with a look. "The mists swept past us as we moved, and from out of that mist, a figure emerged—we hadn't detected him on any of our sensors, hadn't had any indication that we were not alone in this meadow by the river. You, Voll. You were too close to use the lasers—we might hit one another—and you moved quickly, ignoring the sonics we aimed at you. Your hands ripped the power pack from my brother and left him helpless. You tore the shielding from Raoul's—my husband's—side and placed explosives beside the brain compartment, and I heard his screams as they detonated. You crippled my father and me. I don't remember much, then. All I heard were sounds of pain over the communications frequencies. And then you left, fading back into the mists and the slow falling sun, while my father died slowly around me. They were all dead when our people finally came. They managed to save me, get my mind out of the wreckage intact and place it back in my body."

She paused and brushed her dark hair back from her forehead. Voll winced, half-expecting to see gruesome scars there,
though he knew that it was foolish.

"You can't see the marks," she said, guessing his thoughts,
"but they're present, all the same. All I had left were
brainless, warm bodies that would never speak or love. We
were losing battles constantly, then, so I let them be taken to
become gholas. It wasn't patriotism or altruism—I didn't
want to see them. The gholas never returned, and I didn't
care. I . . ." She altered and looked away. Voll started to reach
out to touch her, but drew his hand back. She saw the gesture
and looked at him with eyes full of shocked distaste. He
couldn't look away.

"I had to see you," she said finally. "I had to see what you
were like and what they'd done with you. I'd heard about the
after-war hearings concerning you, of course. Everyone was
interested in Voll's fate. I even thought that I'd kill you, if I
could." She half-turned from him and faced the sculpture,
arms akimbo. "I don't know." A whisper. The sun limned her
with ruddiness.

Voll started to speak, but stopped, not knowing what words
to use. He scratched his left forearm and shifted his weight.
"Look, it's all done with. I don't know what it cost you to
find your way in here, but I'm afraid—well, I don't know
what you've gained by it. You can stay, if you like. I'll show
you a room you can use."

He moved toward the door, opened it, and looked back.
She stood, as motionless as a statue, then slowly followed
him.

Myrna went with him on his daily walk the next day. She
walked alongside him but kept an appreciable distance between them, as if loath to accidentally brush against him.
Whenever the path narrowed, she let him go ahead until it
widened once more.

"I'm not going to hurt you, you know," he said. They had
reached a point where the path wound among tall conifers.
The air smelled of pine, and Voll breathed the fragrant air
deeply.

Myrna shrugged. "So you say."

"My skin isn't rough or cold like a machine's."

"How poetic." She didn't smile.

Voll shook his head. They walked on past the stand of conifers and along the brook. A thin veneer of ice was just beginning to form along the edge of the stream. Voll reached down
and plucked a stone from the cold, racing water. He looked at
the stone and turned it over in his hand. Schist. "Hey, if
you're planning to do something, I wish you'd go ahead.
You're making me damned nervous."

For a moment, then, she *did* smile, a fleeting movement of
the mouth that was almost gone before it could be seen. "I
told you I could kill you. I almost did, when you walked in
yesterday."

"Really?" *A feint to the right . . .*

"Yah."

Voll tossed the stone up, caught it, then heaved it westward.
They heard it crash through branches and land with a distant
thud. Voll glanced at Myrna.

"You always do that?" She walked away from him and
picked at the scaling bark of a tree.

"What?"

"Throw stones."

"It passes the time."

"Until . . . ?"

"Until I get out."

"You're going to get out?" Myrna turned from the tree to
stare at him.

"Yes." No hesitation.

"How?"

"You've managed it, or found someone that could, and I
have a lot more incentive and time, if not the resources. I'll
find a way over, under, or through the barrier when I decide
it's time. I'll get out."

Myrna had a hand inside the pocket of her loose blouse.
Voll wondered if her fingers were touching the cool metal of
the cylinder.

"You agreed to all this," she said, waving her other hand at
the woods about them.

Voll, watching the hidden hand more than her face,
shrugged. "I did." His voice was more bitter than he'd intended. "What choice did I have? They were all afraid of me,
afraid of what they'd made me into. I was given little alternative. They wanted me to undergo a reversal operation, but the
original surgery to alter my body had been both extensive and

dangerous, and I'd almost died then. I don't think it would have been attempted if it had not been wartime and, well, I suppose they thought it might be one way to end the lingering fighting—create a cadre of enhanced fighters. We didn't know then that your people were so close to surrendering. I didn't think I'd survive that second operation. It would have been too easy, too tempting to let something go wrong and then release mournful statements about Voll's expiration during surgery. So I said no, and they said no to letting me go my way unhampered. Here''—he echoed her gesture of a minute before—"is the compromise."

He shrugged again. "I don't know yet that I'd leave if the possibility were open to me. I like it here. All I ask is the freedom to make my own choices; to leave, or to let people come here if I care to see them. They won't agree to that, so I'll force them to deal with me. Yah, I'll break the barrier, in time."

They hiked a while longer, to one corner of the barrier and down another side. Wildlife skittered away from them. Rabbits thrashed through underbrush, unseen animals bounded away, birds scolded them from trees. Once they saw a deer in a nearby clearing. It raised large, sorrowful brown eyes, looked at the intruders, then left the clearing in a flash of white tail.

"If you're going to kill me, why haven't you? You've certainly had chances." The deer vanished in the green light of the forest, and Voll turned to Myrna.

"I don't know. I was more concerned with simply getting in here, scared that the device wasn't going to work and that I'd die at the barrier—I was caught up in a distant hatred for Voll the killer. I never thought of what would happen when I actually saw you. I had you in my mind as some gigantic, deformed parody of a man, something easy to rationalize slaying, and I found that remembered image to be in error. I still hate what you've done, but . . ."

"I hate it, also. I tried to find ways out. Look." Voll held out his hands, palms up, and pulled back the sleeves of his shirt from his wrists. In the morning light, she saw the whitened tracks of deep scars. Voll let her look only a moment before he covered himself again.

"They watched me constantly, then," he said in answer to her unasked question. "It was during the latter months of the war, and they didn't want their shiny, effective, expensive weapon getting hurt through his own self. After the last attempt, they put me through a psych wash-out. I suppose I couldn't commit suicide now even if I still had the desire. I'm surprised you haven't tried a wash-out. Clean out that dingy soul, scrub your ego, id, and superego so they sparkle white in the clean air of rationality. Scour away all those annoying little ridges that gig you every time you stumble across them in your mind. Wonderful."

"It's no solution, just as shutting yourself away wasn't a solution. I thought that your death—"

"You have a weapon? I don't think you could do it yourself."

She glanced at him sidewise. "Yah. It's a variant on the barrier field. It let me in, and it could be easily adjusted to kill—and I wouldn't have to be particularly accurate. I know your quickness. It's developed by the same person that broke your barrier. I paid quite a bit for it."

"Hmmm."

The shadows of branches lined her face, much as the skin dye had done the night before. Today, only her forehead bore the hue of cosmetics, shining a glossy orange. "I'm not planning to give it up, either. Touch me, move toward me, and I may well use it."

Voll looked at her hand, once again inside the blouse pocket, then at her face. He shook his head. "What you don't seem to realize is that you don't have much chance of stopping me." The last words were slow and distinct.

"I doubt that."

"Really?" He looked at the path ahead of them, squinting into the rising sun. He sighed. Voll moved closer to her, slowly and deliberately, his hands at his side, fisted. Myrna backed away, and her right hand flashed silver as she pulled the cylinder from her pocket. Voll had a chance to see it clearly. It was a small, fragile thing. Even in her hand, it was almost lost, innocuous. Yet she *had* passed the barrier with it. She flourished it menacingly as he came toward her. *What are you doing this for? What does it prove?* His thoughts hammered at him.

"It's not a toy, Voll. It functions."

"I know. You're here, after all." He continued moving.

"Dammit! Don't—" Myrna's fingers suddenly convulsed around the triggering mechanism and a low hum became audi-

ble. Voll felt an abrupt tightening in his stomach and a
twisting in his bowels as if some unseen hand were grasping
and turning. He grimaced in pain, but his reflexes had already
moved him. He leaped to the side of the path as Myrna
tracked him, but she followed a touch too slowly as Voll's
long-unused muscles worked. He felt exultation as adrenaline
flooded his system. In one movement, he grasped a protruding
branch from a tree and pulled. The branch, still green, cracked
and split as he tore the limb from the tree—a lengthy, stout
club. He swung it, grunting, as a flare of pain suddenly struck
him. He shouted.

Myrna was still turning as the branch struck her hand. Voll
forced himself to hold back his full strength, so that he would
dislodge the weapon yet not break her hand. The branch hit
her and the small cylinder flew from her hand. Myrna cried
out in pain and held her wrist, falling to her knees as Voll
walked deliberately past her to recover the weapon. He looked
at it, curiously, then aimed it at the kneeling woman.

Myrna's right hand hung limply at her side, cradled in her
other hand. She looked at Voll's face, not at the cylinder he
held.

Voll suddenly remembered that he was still holding the club,
and threw it into the trees. It crashed noisily through underbrush. "You've a lot to learn about handling power,
m'dame." His voice was icily calm. He moved a step closer to
her, so that he could have reached out and touched her face.
She stared defiantly at him.

Voll looked down at her. "There's a first lesson," he said.
"You have to know when and how to use your power." And
he reversed the weapon, holding it out to her.

Startled, it was a moment before she moved to take it with
her good hand. She held it, and then placed it back in her
pocket.

He knelt beside her. "How's your hand?" he asked.

They ate an early supper in the studio, and she watched him
work on the large sculpture. His hands moved slowly, barely
taking any wood with his strokes. His attention was complete.
He smoothed the planes, softened a harsh ridge, and defined
the small details. He took sandpaper and began lightly sanding
the carving. The dust clouded him, hazed with sun, and he
sneezed—quickly, like a cat.

"Yah, I know I could use a field plane, but I like the feel of the sandpaper." Voll looked up to see if he had correctly anticipated her question. Arm in a makeshift sling, she was looking out toward the lake, and she nodded abstractedly at his words, without hearing them. He turned back to the work, squatting on his heels to polish the dwarfish figure at the base.

Myrna glaced from Voll to the late sun over the lake, then back again. She started pacing the room, examining the other, smaller carvings.

"This is all you do?"

Voll looked up from his work and glanced around until he found her. "No. I told you I've been working on ways to bypass the barrier. All that's in a shed out back. And the money I've made from these pieces is going to pay a researcher to work on the field."

"What'd you do after the war, before they put you here?"

Voll stopped sanding and stared out to the lake where the sun was laced by high branches. Then he began working again, punctuating his words with the sibilant rasp of the sandpaper. "Nothing," he said. "I was functionless, an anachronism with no purpose, something that technology had created and now didn't want or need. I hated myself, and I couldn't cope with people well. I was always introspective, and the operations hadn't changed that. I was as frightened of the others as they were of me. I think they were all fearful that I'd turn on them and they'd be unable to stop me before I did a tremendous amount of damage—I knew how to hide, how to conceal myself and then emerge to strike and kill. They'd taught me well."

He blew packed dust from the surface of the sandpaper. "I ended up here, and for a while I was satisfied with the arrangements. But not for long. I began wanting out. I was only a man altered to do a task, and I'd done it. Why should I be punished for that?"

"You do a fair job of defending yourself, for a machine."

Voll laughed, and wondered at the sound of his laughter. Had it been that long? "Yah, so maybe the machine has a little human left in him, neh?"

She didn't reply. Myrna picked up a carving small enough to hold in one hand, held it to the dying light. It was a representation of a man, done in some ebony wood, lying on a litter-strewn battlefield. A ghola stood over him, its knife ready to strike down, while the man lifted an imploring hand. "This one's interesting. Why do you keep it?"

Voll resumed standing. "*Fallen Man With Ghola*? It's my favorite. I don't know why I leave it here. I don't want to get rid of it and never see it again. It means a lot to me."

Myrna placed the carving back on its shelf, but continued to survey it. "It's good, certainly the best of yours I've seen. You saw this?"

"Yah. I saw it." His voice was suddenly pained.

"You know, other people can fight and not become upset at the memories. They even seem to enjoy talking about it, recalling the times."

"They could take off their weapons afterward." He exhaled, loudly and sharply. "And they have something else they're fit to do."

"You can carve."

"You said yourself that they're little better than amateur playthings. I don't delude myself about that. They're curiosities, made by the man-weapon. Otherwise, they wouldn't sell."

Myrna came toward him and for the first time touched him with something other than distaste. She let her uninjured hand rest on his shoulder for a moment before it slid off. Voll glanced at her and saw a half-smile twist her mouth. He couldn't read her eyes.

"I'm tired," she said. "See you in the morning?"

Voll smiled back at her, tentatively, and nodded. "Yah."

The sun touched the edge of the lake with red fire. An oblate, it began to sink. He turned back to his work.

He followed the spoor of the animatank. Where the treads had passed, the earth of the river meadow was gouged and torn. It wasn't too far ahead, for he could hear the rumbling as it smashed and bullied its way through the high grass and he could feel the trembling of the ground beneath him. He knew their sensors might find him shortly, knew that they'd been warned of his presence and were searching for him. That was a bad omen, for his strength lay in surprise and stealth, in striking from an unforeseen angle. The double moons cast twin shadows ahead of him, the right one violet, the left red. He ducked into a small stand of trees to his right. Yes, they'd

found him now, for the rumbling had changed to a soft whin-
ing like a pack of dogs. That meant he had to find cover, for
he couldn't hope to dodge the computer-aimed laser fire. The
'tanks were standing, waiting for him to emerge, and he
twisted desperately looking for an avenue of escape. He could
hear them growling like wolves, now, howling, and with the
howls came a high, keening wail he couldn't identify. The
wolf-growl was loud, as if in triumph, and very close.

Wolves. Voll sat up in bed, trying to shake the dream stupor
from him. Sweat beaded his forehead, but already the dream
was slipping from his memory. Moonlight silvered the floor of
his room and, nearby, he could still hear the noise, softer now
than it had seemed in the dream, but audible. The forest had
its wolves, but they rarely came this close to his house. And he
could hear, intermittently, that strange high cry, a voice of
pure animal terror. He threw the covers from him and went
out, turning on the lights.

Myrna was outside her room, her tunic on and belted. "You
heard it too?"

"Woke me up. Wolves. I'm going out to see, anyway. They
usually don't come this near."

"I'll go with you."

Voll put on his coat and tethered a hoverlamp to a control
belt. Its yellowish glow preceded them. The air was crisp and
cold; frost whitened the ground in irregular patches, the first
vestige of the coming winter. The trees stood out blackly
against the lighter, star-filled sky. Off to their right, wolves
sighed and muttered.

"Sounds like a pair, probably mates. I doubt that they'll
stay when they hear us coming."

Voll stamped into the woods, making no attempt at stealth.
They hadn't gone more than a hundred meters before they
found the animals, standing over a downed body of a large
deer, a doe with blood streaming from a deep wound in its
throat. The two animals faced them, still growling deep in
their throats, blood matting the fur around their jaws. They
backed away slowly, snarling at the intruders. Behind him,
Voll heard Myrna curse as she saw the wounded deer, and then
there came a familiar low humming that swiftly died—even at
the edges of the field, he could feel it, a slight fluttering inside
him. He turned to see the cylinder in her hand, pointed at the

nearest of the wolves. The animal yelped—a sound more like a dog—and it collapsed, whining. Its mate, with a final snarl, fled.

"Why did you do that?" Voll, incredulous, stared at the wolf, which now lay still.

"What?" Myrna's voice was loud with wondering, nervous laughter.

"They were leaving. They weren't any threat to us. They're simply doing what they're supposed to do. There wasn't any reason to kill them." He gestured at the slain wolf.

"I don't understand you."

"Obviously."

Voll shook his head and went to the deer. It feebly attempted to rise, its large eyes rolling in fright and pain. Voll stroked its flank and brought the lamp down to him. He whistled and cursed.

"Anything you can do for it?" asked Myrna.

Voll shrugged. "No. It should've been left for the wolves. It's almost dead."

"Should I kill it?" She held out the cylinder in offering.

"You've done enough with that." Voll took the doe's head between his hands, whispering to the animal in an effort to calm it, and then twisted savagely. A sharp crack split the night air. The deer's body convulsed once, then lay still. Blood steamed in the night air.

Voll stood and wiped his hands on his tunic. Looking at the doe, he spoke to Myrna. "I'm sorry I was upset. There's nothing we can do. I don't need the venison, and the predators do. We'll leave the carcasses to them. I'll move what's left in the morning."

He turned to find her staring at him, at his hands. He looked down at the blood-stained fingers, then at her.

"I can't help their strength," he said. "It's part of me."

"You just twisted his neck . . ." Her voice trailed off into silence.

"Let's go back, heh? There's still hours before daybreak." He moved toward her and started to put an arm around her shoulders. She pulled away, silently, and began walking toward the house. Voll watched her go, wiping his hands against the tunic's coarse fabric. After a time, he bent down and picked up a stone.

•   •   •

In the morning she was gone. It didn't surprise him greatly.
He went into the studio and watched the dawn touch the trees
on the opposite side of the lake. The house cast a wavering
shadow far out over the water and a few feeding fish rippled
the still surface. A shallow mist haunted the shoreline. He
stood watching for some time, as the house's shadow moved
slowly toward the near shore and the light began to scintillate
on the water's surface.

He looked at the studio. There was a carving missing. He
knew without checking which one it would be. *Fallen Man
With Ghola.* He could see the empty space on the shelf where
the piece had sat. A scrap of paper, folded once, sat there
now. He picked it up.

Finally, he unfolded it and read what she'd written.

*Voll: As you said, one should know how to use power. And
I know you could take this weapon from me. I still don't know
why I didn't use it when I had the opportunity, and I don't
want to stay to find that answer.*

*I'll throw the cylinder back over the barrier once I'm out.
You'll find it on or near the path, where it bends to head
toward the hills. Consider it payment for the carving. And
should you want to see* Fallen Man *again, you'll know where
to look. I hope you find your freedom of choice enjoyable—
though remember you don't have to use the device. The barrier also keeps others out, and you might find that to be its
most important function. In any event, I wish you luck.*

The note wasn't signed. Voll placed it back on the mantel.

After a while, for the last time, he went out and threw
stones.

THE COMPUTER CRIED CHARGE!

by George R.R. Martin

The autotanks drove across the hellplain in a double column of fifty, toward the distant mountains where the enemy lay in wait.

Ugly was the word for autotanks. Low, hunched shapes of battledark duralloy, they crawled on woven metal treads over ground that would have melted anything else. Screechgun mounts and the snouts of lasercannon broke their unpleasant symmetry.

Even the dull sheen of their armor was gone, hidden by the thick black heatgrease that oozed from within, shielding them until it cooked and cracked and was covered by a fresh layer.

Beneath the hardened grease: a foot of metal, then a tangled web of weaponry and circuits and motors and computers. Beneath that: the deep-buried synthabrain, fist-sized mind of the autotank. Within that: the programmed mentality of a bloodthirsty moron.

Ugly was the word for autotanks. On most worlds they were an obscene intrusion, a blot, hideous things that crushed out life beneath them with only a rumbling purr, nightmare shapes that touched beauty and left ruin.

Here they belonged.

They moved across a flat, fissured plain of yawning desolation and unending heat. They moved in a world where water was a legend and the rivers ran with white-hot metals, over rocks that hissed at the touch of their treads, around lakes of molten magma. They moved in an awful stillness, save for when the winds came. And that was no relief, for those screaming sulfuric blasts would cook the heatgrease and rip it off and sear and pit the duralloy beneath.

Across the face of the inferno, the autotanks crawled like a line of fat black slugs, ignoring the bluewhite burning blindness that filled up half the sky. Behind them they left a trail of hardened grease cooking on the rocks.

Above: it was not hot in the command center of the dropship *Balaclava,* and the hundred-plus men working there knew it. They knew the ship was high in orbit, safe in the cold womb of space. They could see the readings on their temperature gauges. They could hear the faint whine of the pumps and cooling systems that kept the air circulating in the huge, bustling room.

Yet, in spite of all this, they squirmed and sweated and loosened the collars of their uniforms. They knew it was not hot, but knowledge was no defense. For the main viewscreen filled the entire forward wall with a scene from hell, and they could *see* the lava and the great blue sun that was larger than the mountains and the rocks that baked and cracked and hissed. And the bluewhite brilliance flooded the command center and beat at their eyes, and they could *see* and *feel* the heat that did not exist.

The worst off were the men along the port wall. When they ignored the main viewscreen and tended to their instruments, the same sun pounded at them from a thousand smaller screens. And they had to watch; each screen was the eye of an autotank, down on the face of hell, reporting what it saw.

The telecom men along the starboard wall were much better off, for they watched only blinking lights and wavering lines and dancing needles. But they'd forget at times, and look up at the main screen, and then the heat would wash over them in a torrid rush.

The computer techs were the best off. The dropship's Battlemaster 7000 Tactical Computing System took up the wall directly opposite the main viewscreen; tending it, they had their backs to the sun at all times.

General Russ Triegloff, drop commandant, wasn't so lucky. Moving around the mountainous holocube that filled the center of the room, Triegloff faced the screen as often as not. He was a huge, hairy man, and his brown uniform was already soaked with sweat.

He'd asked Captain Lyford to cut the main viewscreen at least twice. But Lyford, a lean hawk-faced Navy type who wouldn't condescend to perspire if you paid him for it, had politely declined. He was very cool. He'd gotten the dropship into orbit without incident, and now he just wanted to sit back and watch Triegloff worry—and sweat. Every time the general mentioned the heat, Lyford would point to a thermometer and cluck and tell Triegloff that he was working too hard.

So Triegloff had given up on that particular crusade; he had bigger things to worry about. Flanked by a couple of under-commanders and a host of orderlies, he stomped about the room restlessly, watching the holocube from a dozen different angles, studying photos of the enemy positions in the mountains, and thinking furiously.

He calmed a little when Lee Williston, the portly blond civilian who headed the TCS experts, fought his way through the underlings and slapped a stack of computer printouts into Triegloff's hand. "There's seven assault plans there," Williston said. "Projected likelihood of success ranges from thirty-seven to seventy-two percent."

Triegloff moved to a desk beside the holocube, and spread the seven printouts alongside each other. "That's not bad," he said, studying the plans with the quick familiarity of a man who has done this a thousand times before. "The seventy-two percenter has the highest casualty rates, of course."

Williston nodded, and his double chins bounced. "Of course. And that casualty figure includes men and material."

Triegloff looked up, and brought his grizzled eyebrows together. "Men?"

"Yes. Plan four—that's your seventy-two percenter—calls for landing a couple of battalions of assault squads to supplement the armor. That means human casualties, naturally, and pretty high ones."

Triegloff picked up plan four and looked at it carefully. "Yes, I see," he said, flipping through the pages. "I'm tempted, too. Don't like having nothing but autotanks and juggernauts down there. They're tough enough, but not too smart. Can't think on their feet, like a man could, y'know?"

Williston returned a fussy frown. "The war machines will do the job for you, General, if you just program them correctly. I wouldn't recommend choosing plan four, really I wouldn't. The casualties are quite high. Battlemaster has given that plan a 'least recommended' rating, despite the high succuess figure." He pointed.

"Still," said Triegloff. "Men would give us so much more battlefield flexibility . . ." He dropped the printout back to the desk reluctantly. "Well, what else is there?"

"Six other plans," said Williston. "Two have success indices below fifty, however, and I'm sure you wouldn't want them. That leaves four reasonably sound tactical approaches to those emplacements. All of them are roughly equal, except for a few variables."

"Such as?" Triegloff said.

Williston shrugged. "Holes in our data, General. We don't know everything about the enemy position we'd like to know, and Battlemaster's projections can't be fully reliable without full information." He paused and looked around. "Anyone have those photos?" he asked.

An orderly shoved a stack of blown-up aerial photos at the computer man. Williston took them and turned back to Triegloff. "Here," he said, jabbing at a photograph. "These black holes in the cliffside are the biggest problems. Until we know for certain what they are, we won't know which plan to push."

Triegloff, still studying the printouts, barely glanced at the photo. "I can guess what those holes are," he said gruffly. "We picked up energy readings from that area. And not from the big laser turrets, either—those are clearly visible. I figure we got hellglobe tubes down there, built right into the damn mountains."

"Yes, that *is* a possibility," Williston said. "In which case, that whole valley would get a fortification index of four-oh-seven-six. Your autotanks would be decimated attacking something like that; you just don't mess around with those sort of figures. If those *are* hellglobe tubes, plan two is optimal."

Triegloff glanced at plan two. "Right," he said. "A joint autotank-juggernaut assault. Should do it. The juggernauts could use their shields to cover the 'tanks."

"Exactly," Williston said. "However, it's also possible that those holes are caves, or some other natural formation. Or perhaps the only thing inside is more lasercannon. In *that* case, the fortification index drops to two-two-oh-nine. And plan seven becomes optimal."

"No," Triegloff said firmly. "I don't care what Battlemaster projects; those *are* hellglobe tubes. I know it. A hunch, but it makes sense. That valley is the main approach of their whole sector HQ. It'd be held with everything they got, and they got hellglobes."

Williston was about to say something, but a hand on his shoulder shut him up. Captain Lyford, smiling and immaculate in fleet-black, stepped around him and clucked at Triegloff. "I still say we should just lob them to slag from orbit," Lyford said smoothly. "It would save you ever so much trouble, General."

Triegloff grimaced. "Crap," he said. "We want them alive. That's the job. They pulled a fast one, sticking their sector base on a freakish hellhole like this without even a fleet to guard it. And they cost us plenty when we hit that fake that was *supposed* to be their HQ. Now they pay, though; we can grab all their top brass."

Lyford dismissed that. "Whatever you like, General," he said. "I got you here for the drop, so I'll leave the rest up to you. I really should butt out, eh?"

"Your advice is always well taken, Captain," Triegloff said with a wooden voice. "I would appreciate it if you would shut off that damned viewscreen, however. I really don't need it."

Lyford smiled. "Why? It gives a good idea of the terrain down there. But if you insist . . . I mean, I wouldn't want it to bother you, or impair your judgment."

Triegloff frowned, annoyed. "My judgment is not in the least impaired by your viewscreen, Captain," he said. "It's only that it bothers my men. I've made decisions under conditions much worse than this."

He looked down at the seven plans, very decisively, and moved his finger from one to another. There was a brief pause when he touched plan four. But he moved on, and picked up plan two.

"Here," he said, giving the printout to an aide. "Have them program this one."

●   ●   ●

Forward, ever forward, moved the autotanks. The mountains, once a smudge on the distant eastern horizon, now loomed larger and larger ahead of them. And still the double column drove forward, hissing and rumbling, fighting the sulfurwind and the blinding light and the inexorable heat. Only ninety-nine of the column had made it this far; one 'tank was miles behind, alone on the plain where its cooling systems and motors had failed almost simultaneously. There it would remain until its heatgrease finally ran out, and the wind and the sun got at its duralloy flanks to burn and tear.

The others drove on without it. Now, programmed from above, they had a purpose. Now they had a battleplan.

North of them, other long rows of shapes moved in the distance, gradually growing larger. No alarms rang in the autotanks. Dimly, they knew what the others were; a second column, angling southeast to join them. The rendezvous had already been programmed into their consciousness.

The two formations paralleled each other for a long time, driving east on opposite sides of a great crevasse that divided the plain. Once, briefly, they lost sight of each other, when a second, smaller fissure branched off from the main one, and forced the southern formation to make a wide detour.

The other columns waited, however; slowing where the crevasse ran into a lake of redblack magma, and swinging around it. On the shores of that lake, they were augmented by yet another formation of autotanks that had come boiling from the northernmost dropoint at breakneck speed. Beyond the lake, on its eastern banks, the original group finally met and melded with the others.

Now six columns of autotanks resumed their drive toward the enemy, through terrain that grew steadily rougher and more difficult. The mountains ahead had become a row of blackened teeth that bit the bluewhite sun.

Triegloff leaned forward over the corporal, his palms sweaty where they gripped the leather of the man's seatback, his eyes fixed on the readings and the small viewscreen. There was nothing much to see on the screen: a sea of slow-moving black, crossed by very thin, very faint lines.

The other instruments were more informative, and their readings spelled trouble. Triegloff watched in silence, until he suddenly grew aware that Williston was standing beside him.

"The fucking crust broke," Triegloff said, loudly, without looking at the TCS man. "I've got three jugggernauts covered by magma."

Williston said nothing. Battlemaster had chosen the drop-oints for each component of the attack force. If the jugger-nauts had been traveling over ground too weak to support their immense weight, the computer was to blame—at least in Triegloff's eyes.

"We're still functional, General," the corporal said, his attention on the instruments that were monitoring the fate of one of the buried juggernauts. "The duralloy is holding, and I've thrown the cooling systems onto emergency maximum. But the treads can't get any traction, sir. And the readings are edging up toward critical. We've got to get out soon, or we'll have a failure."

Triegloff nodded. "How much time?"

"A half hour, sir," the corporal said. "Maybe a little more."

"Leave them," Williston suggested.

"I intend to," Triegloff said. "A rescue is out of the question—another section of ground might break through, and God knows how many more juggernauts I'd lose *then*."

He turned away from the monitors and faced Williston. "But I've ordered the whole column full-stop. That's not solid rock at all; we were moving over a goddam sea of magma, covered by a crust of hardened rock. Can't go forward."

Williston looked slightly embarrassed. "I'm sorry, General, but Battlemaster can only work with the data it's given. Our sensor readings indicated that route was solid all the way. We'll have to recompute."

"Damn straight," said Triegloff, his tone very disgruntled. "I'm ordering the whole juggernaut squad to edge back, real slow and careful. Take some new readings, and find a branching where they can cut off to a new route."

Williston nodded and moved off quickly, and Triegloff headed back to the big holocube. The holo was a constantly changing computer simulation, assembled by Battlemaster from the data flooding the monitors. It looked almost like an aerial view. Triegloff watched intently. The pattern that had been forming, the attack pattern, was now broken.

"Sir?"

He turned to face an under-commander, wincing as he

looked toward the main viewscreen. "Yes?"

"Should we reprogram the autotanks, General?"

Triegloff hesitated. The sudden snafu had ruined the timing of the assault; the juggernauts would never make the planned rendezvous in time. And without the huge juggernauts and their cumbersome shield machinery, the enemy hellglobes would tear up the smaller autotanks in an attack.

"Waiting won't do any good," Triegloff said. "It'll be hours before we get the juggs around the magma. Have your autotanks proceed as planned, Colonel."

"To the attack point, sir?"

"Yes," said Triegloff. He waved for the colonel to follow him and strode off down the length of the holocube, toward the big viewscreen. Twenty paces brought them to the section of the cube that showed the enemy fortifications. Triegloff braked to a halt, and pointed.

"I'm sticking with the plan we've picked," he said. "We'll run it through Battlemaster once more to be sure, but I don't think there'll be any problems. Instead of attacking at once, though, we'll use the autotanks to soften 'em up a little until the juggernauts get there."

His hand went into the holocube, and stroked a series of low ridges that bracketed the entrance to the most heavily fortified valley. "We've picked up minor energy readings from these ridges—probably low-grade stuff like disruptors and small lasers. Not too important, but they might be bothersome when we charge up the valley—and we're going to have to do that sooner or later. So we might as well knock out the ridges now. Have the autotanks swing by and plaster them. Then move out of range, quick; I doubt they'll waste hellglobes at that distance, but there's no sense taking any chances. Raid 'em like that a couple times. And then when the juggs get there, we can reform and carry out the attack plan."

The colonel nodded. "Sounds good, sir." He noted the coordinates and turned back to his sector. Triegloff, already engrossed in larger considerations, hardly noticed him go.

The colonel relayed the order to the six captains under him. Each captain commanded an autotank attack group a hundred strong. The captains talked to their lieutenants, who did the actual coding. The lieutenants worked out a joint program, and handed it over to the enlisted men on the monitors, who fed it into the command consoles. The consoles chewed up the program, digested it, and spat it down to the autotanks. Then the 'tank computers took over, deciphering the string of impulses and feeding the orders to the synthabrain.

Somewhere, somebody made a mistake.

The last rendezvous was in sight of the valley, when the two big 'tank formations, each composed of three attack groups, linked up to form a single angry metal horde. With that last linkage, the columns broke, and the autotanks assumed battle formation: they covered the last miles in a sprawling arc.

Onward they drove, across death-still rocky foothills and smoking fissures and burning craters, toward the cliffs and the ridges and the valley ahead.

Onward they drove, toward a row of silent mountains that gleamed bluewhite like sharpened teeth, and half-seen emplacements that dotted the peaks like cavities.

Onward they drove, rolling into darkness for the first time when they entered the long shadow thrown by the mountains, moving toward the dark gash in the mountain wall and the ridges that ran across it.

When the ridges were almost a mile away, battle began.

The enemy opened fire first; tiny lights began to wink and blink on top of the ridges, and laser fire spat from the shadows. The autotanks took the light blows, and drove on. The fire grew heavier. 'Tank instruments recorded disruptor fire, and from somewhere a buried projectile gun opened up, and the ground shook to the explosions.

The autotanks closed, relentless. It takes a lot of force to dent duralloy. It takes a lot of heat to cut duralloy. The ridge guns came up short on both counts. The 'tanks shrugged a path through the explosions with only a few dented plates. They ignored the disruptors, light personnel weapons that were useless against armor. They worried about the lasers, but only a little; their own lasercannon were bigger and more deadly than the guns on the ridges.

Half a mile from the first ridge, the autotanks opened up. Heavy laser fire sliced into the ridges, HE rocked the gun emplacements, and the sulfurwinds shrieked with the sound of screechgun fire.

The lead 'tanks fired first; then the others behind them; then the ones behind *them*. The ridges smoked and shook and the enemy guns died and grew silent. Here and there an autotank died too, but the losses were few. The 'tank fire grew steadily heavier, more deadly. Whole sections of the ridges vanished under the pounding; rock cannot absorb punishment like duralloy.

The lead 'tanks reached the first ridge and rolled over it, still firing. The rest of the formation followed, in wave after smoking wave. They climbed over the second ridge, and third, silencing any enemy guns that still moved. They didn't have to climb over the final ridge; it had ceased to exist before they reached it. But they climbed through the debris.

And onward drove the autotanks. Onward, not back. Onward, past the ridges, past the light guns they were ordered to charge. Onward, toward the shadowed valley that yawned before them like the mouth of death.

It had grown very silent in the command center, but Triegloff hardly noticed it. He was absorbed in the new printouts that Battlemaster had just spewed forth, detailing alternate battleplans that took into account the delay in getting the juggernauts into action.

He snapped into awareness when an aide put an uneasy hand on his shoulder. "Yes?" he said.

"Sir," the aide said. He looked up, at the main viewscreen.

Triegloff followed his gaze with narrowed eyes. He saw what he'd expected to see; a battle scene, confused. The autotanks had been assaulting the ridges, as he'd ordered. He hadn't been following the action closely, although he was vaguely aware that it was in progress. Making sure the preliminary went all right was a job for his subordinates; Triegloff was planning the main event.

He had been looking at the screen for a full minute before it hit him. The autotanks were climbing *over* the ridges. And they were continuing.

"They're charging," someone said, very faintly, across the room. "They're charging the main guns."

Triegloff's fists tightened. His eyes roamed the room, found the colonel who commanded the autotanks. He moved to him in a raging rush. "What the *hell* are you doing?"

The colonel stared. "I—a programming error. It must be a programming error."

Triegloff looked back at the screen. The lead 'tanks had entered the valley. The others were following, in waves.

"Damn you," Triegloff shouted. "Don't just *stand there*! Countermand those orders, quick."

The colonel nodded, but didn't move. Triegloff grabbed him with both hands, and shoved him toward the monitors. "*Move it!* Or you won't have a command left . . ."

Onward drove the autotanks, over the ridges and through the shadows, up the rocky valley of hell toward the pockmarked cliffs ahead. And one by one, they began to die.

The enemy waited until three-quarters of the 'tanks were in the valley, waited while the 'tanks pounded the cliffs with HE and scorched them with lasers, waited long minutes while the charging 'tanks did their worst. And then, all at once, they commenced the slaughter.

It was never battle; never; never for a moment. It was just destruction.

From both sides of the valley, lasercannon opened up simultaneously; big lasercannon, the great-granddaddies of the small ridge guns. The valley floor shattered under the impact of a hundred sudden explosions.

And—from a wide black hole in the cliff at the end of the valley—something shot in a fiery blur. The other holes around it spat other fireblurs. Then the first hole spat again. Then the others.

And when the blurs hit and expanded and roared, shimmering globes would appear around them to hold in the fire and the heat. And the targets.

Hellglobes: nukes were all they were. Nukes set off in close proximity to a big shield generator, a generator that would catch the awful energy and hold it tight at the moment of its release. H-bombs in a force fist.

A disruptor can't touch duralloy. Explosions barely dent it. Lasers take long minutes to burn through. But catch a duralloy autotank in a hellglobe, and it writhes and melts and vaporizes in microseconds.

It takes a mountain to hold a shield generator big enough to make hellglobes; the shields have to be enormously strong. The range isn't very good either; you can't throw a shield much farther than you can see. But it's worth it. The only defense against hellglobes is to make sure they don't reach you. The huge juggernauts could have done that, with the mobile shields they mounted.

But autotanks are too small for shields.

Onward drove the autotanks, onward up the valley, onward toward the lasers and tubes and hellglobes, onward into the teeth of the enemy. And as they drove, the hellglobes ate them. In ones and twos and fours, moving or still, firing or silent; it didn't matter. The hellglobes found them and caught them and wrapped them in arms of fire and ate them. The hellglobes that missed ate rocks and carved craters and bit chunks out of the mountains. But few missed; most of them ate autotanks.

The shadow was gone from the valley. In hundreds of places, globes of fire burned brighter than the sun: searingly, unbearably intense. It rained hellglobes.

Onward drove the autotanks, into that rain. The enemy met them with thousands of megatons of nuclear power, but the 'tanks took it and rolled into it unwavering.

For an eternity they rolled into it, vanishing as they crept closer, swallowed up in the carnage. Then, all at once, the survivors went stiff.

And they began to turn.

Retreat: or attempted retreat. But really, it was rout. Back toward the mouth of the valley they rushed, but the hellglobes followed them and ate them as they ran. And when the 'tanks crept past effective hellglobe range, the lasers took over once again.

Still, a handful made it out of the valley.

Above, on the dropship, they watched it all in living color. No one said anything. Not Triegloff, nor Williston, nor even Lyford. Until it was over.

Lyford had been standing shoulder-to-shoulder with Triegloff. Triegloff wasn't certain when he'd arrived, but he was there now. And he looked at the general and spoke. "My God," he said. "What happened?"

Triegloff was ashen. His mind wasn't working properly. He kicked it and tried to get it to think, but it was still seeing those hellglobes pouring down and down and down, and still hearing the awful whine the monitors sounded whenever one of the hellglobes caught an autotank.

Finally he shook his head. "An error," he said slowly, his voice thick. "An—error. Somebody gave the wrong order. Somebody—they charged the wrong guns." He shook his head again, fighting to clear away shock. The command center was still quiet. Telecom instruments had quit chattering, and all along the port wall the viewscreens were out. A few still showed that burning sun, but row on row were now dark and black.

Williston came between Triegloff and the silent, scared Lyford. He handed the general some printouts. "I've programmed this all into Battlemaster," he said. "I assumed you'd be wanting some new attack plans." He shrugged. "You've got three new approaches there, using mostly the juggernauts and whatever autotanks have survived. However, you're going to have to send down some men, I'm afraid. The casualties will be very high, but there's no alternative."

Triegloff looked at the printouts, dully. Then up. "But—the success indices—"

"Yes," said Williston. "Fourteen percent to twenty-six percent, I know; not very encouraging. Still, it's all that's left. The autotanks were an important part of Battlemaster's earlier computations."

Triegloff let the plans drop to the floor, and looked at Williston very hard. "You son of a bitch," he said, something of his old manner returning to his voice in a rush. "*Now* you tell me to send men down—*now* when the odds are hopelessly against them. *Hell!* If I'd sent down men in the first place, none of this would ever have happened."

Williston was unmoved. "General Triegloff, that's not true. You can't blame this reversal on the machines, I'm afraid. The autotanks simply carried out the orders they were given. They attacked when you programmed them to attack, and retreated when you altered the program. Whoever gave the order was at fault, I'm afraid."

Triegloff snorted. "Crap. *Men* would have had the sense to know I didn't mean to send them up against hellglobes naked. They would have been intelligent enough to beam up and question the order, and the misunderstanding would have gotten cleared up pronto. But your damned stupid machines just went ahead blindly and did it. And got themselves wiped out, and fouled up the whole mission. No human being could possibly be that stupid."

Williston answered with a shrug. "Regardless, that's past. I suggest we tend to the present."

•　　•　　•

Down on the surface of hell, thirty-two autotanks crawled across the plain in an uneven double column. A few, seared and damaged, had already dropped behind to die. And several of the others were struggling.

But they moved on, toward the rendezvous with the juggernauts and a new battle to come. Untired and unthinking they moved on.

HANGMAN

by David Drake

The light in the kitchen alcove glittered on Lt. Schilling's
blond curls; glittered also on the frost-spangled window beside
her and from the armor of the tank parked outside. All the
highlights looked cold to Capt. Danny Pritchard as he stepped
closer to the infantry lieutenant.

"Sal—" Pritchard began. From the orderly room behind
them came the babble of the radios ranked against one wall
and, less muted, the laughter of soldiers waiting for action.
"You can't think like a Dutchman anymore. We're Hammer's
Slammers, all of us. We're mercs. Not Dutch, not Frisians—"

"You're not," Lt. Schilling snapped, looking up from the
cup of bitter chocolate she had just drawn from the urn. She
was a short woman and lightly built, but she had the unerring
instinct of a bully who is willing to make a scene for a victim
who is not willing to be part of one. "You're a farmer from
Dunstan, what d'you care about Dutch miners, whatever these
bleeding French do to them. But a lot of us do care, Danny,
and if you had a little compassion—"

"But Sal—" Pritchard repeated, only his right arm moving
as he touched the blond girl's shoulder.

"Get your hands off me, Captain!" she shouted, "That's

69

over!" She shifted the mug of steaming chocolate in her hand.
The voices in the orderly room stilled. Then, simultaneously,
someone turned up the volume of the radios and at least three
people began to talk loudly on unconnected subjects.

Pritchard studied the back of his hand, turned it over to examine the calloused palm as well. He smiled. "Sorry, I'll
remember that," he said in a normal voice. He turned and
stepped back into the orderly room, a brown-haired man of
thirty-four with a good set of muscles to cover his moderate
frame and nothing at all to cover his heart. Those who knew
Danny Pritchard slightly thought him a relaxed man, and he
looked relaxed even now. But waiting around the electric grate
were three troopers who knew Danny very well indeed: the
crew of the *Plow*, Pritchard's command tank.

Kowie drove the beast, a rabbit-eyed man whose fingers
now flipped cards in another game of privy solitaire. His deck
was so dirty that only familiarity allowed him to read the pips.
Kowie's hands and eyes were just as quick at the controls of
the tank, sliding its bulbous hundred and fifty metric tons
through spaces that were only big enough to pass it. When he
had to, he drove nervelessly through objects instead of going
around. Kowie would never be more than a tank driver; but he
was the best tank driver in the regiment.

Rob Jenne was big and as blond as Lt. Schilling. He grinned
up at Pritchard, his expression changing from embarrassment
to relief as he saw that his captain was able to smile also. Jenne
had transferred from combat cars to tanks three years back,
after the Slammers had pulled out of Squire's World. He was
sharp-eyed and calm in a crisis. Twice after his transfer Jenne
had been offered a blower of his own to command if he would
return to combat cars. He had refused both promotions, saying he would stay with tanks or buy back his contract, that
there was no way he was going back to those open-topped cof-
fins again. When a tank commander's slot came open, Jenne
got it; and Pritchard had made the blond sergeant his own
blower chief when a directional mine had retired the previous
man. Now Jenne straddled a chair backwards, his hands flexing a collapsible torsion device that kept his muscles as dense
and hard as they had been the day he was recruited from a
quarry on Burlage.

Line tanks carry only a driver and the blower chief who

directs the tank and its guns when they are not under the direct
charge of the regiment's computer. In addition to those two
and a captain, command tanks have a communications techni-
cian to handle the multiplex burden of radio traffic focused on
the vehicle. Pritchard's commo tech was Margritte DiManzo,
a slender widow who cropped her lustrous hair short so that it
would not interfere with the radio helmet she wore most of her
waking hours. She was off duty now, but she had not removed
the bulky headgear which linked her to the six radios in the
tank parked outside. Their simultaneous sound would have
been unintelligible babbling to most listeners. The blackhaired
woman's training, both conscious and hypnotic, broke that
babbling into a set of discrete conversations. When Pritchard
reentered the room, Margritte was speaking to Jenne. She did
not look up at her commander until Jenne's brightening expression showed her it was safe to do so.

Two commo people and a sergeant with Intelligence tabs
were at consoles in the orderly room. They were from the regiment's HQ Battalion, assigned to Sector Two here on Kobold
but in no sense a part of the sector's combat companies: Capt.
Riis's S Company—infantry—and Pritchard's own tanks.

Riis was the senior captain and in charge of the sector, a
matter which neither he nor Pritchard ever forgot. Sally Schilling led his first platoon. Her aide, a black-haired corporal, sat
with his huge boots up, humming as he polished the pieces of
his field-stripped powergun. Its barrel gleamed orange in the
light of the electric grate. Electricity was more general on Kobold than on some wealthier worlds, since mining and copper
smelting made fusion units a practical necessity. But though
the copper in the transmission cable might well have been
processed on Kobold, the wire had probably been drawn off-
world and shipped back here. Aurore and Friesland had refused to allow even such simple manufactures here on their
joint colony. They had kept Kobold a market and a supplier of
raw materials, but never a rival.

"Going to snow tonight?" Jenne asked.

"Umm, too cold," Pritchard said, walking over to the
grate. He pretended he did not hear Lt. Schilling stepping out
of the alcove. "I figure—"

"Hold it," said Margritte, her index finger curling out for a
volume control before the duty man had time to react. One of

the wall radios boomed loudly to the whole room. Prodding
another switch, Margritte patched the signal separately
through the link implanted in Pritchard's right mastoid.
"—guns and looks like satchel charges. There's only one man
in each truck, but they've been on the horn too and we can
figure on more Frenchies here any—"

"Red Alert," Pritchard ordered, facing his commo tech so
that she could read his lips. "Where is this?"

The headquarters radiomen stood nervously, afraid to interfere but unwilling to let an outsider run their equipment,
however ably. "Red Alert," Margritte was repeating over all
bands. Then, through Pritchard's implant, she said, "It's Patrol Sigma three-nine, near Haacin. Dutch civilians've stopped
three outbound provisions trucks from Barthe's Company."

"Scramble First Platoon," Pritchard said, "but tell 'em to
hold for us to arrive." As Margritte coolly passed on the
order, Pritchard picked up the commo helmet he had laid on
his chair when he followed Lt. Schilling into the kitchen. The
helmet gave him automatic switching and greater range than
the bioelectric unit behind his ear.

The wall radio was saying, "—need some big friendlies fast
or it'll drop in the pot for sure."

"Sigma three-niner," Pritchard said, "this is Michael
One."

"Go ahead, Michael One," replied the distant squad leader.
Pritchard's commo helmet added an airy boundlessness to his
surroundings without really deadening the ambient noise.

"Hold what you've got, boys," the tank captain said.
"There's help on the way."

The door of the orderly room stood ajar the way Pritchard's
crewmen had left it. The captain slammed it shut as he too ran
for his tank. Behind in the orderly room, Lt. Schilling was
snapping out quick directions to her own platoon and to her
awakened commander.

The *Plow* was already floating when Danny reached it. Ice
crystals, spewed from beneath the skirts by the lift fans, made
a blue-white dazzle in the vehicle's running lights. Frost whitened the ladder up the high side of the tank's plenum chamber
and hull. Pritchard paused to pull on his gloves before mounting. Sgt. Jenne, anchoring himself with his left hand on the
turret's storage rack, reached down and lifted his captain

aboard without noticeable effort. Side by side, the two men slid through the hatches to their battle stations.

"Ready," Pritchard said over the intercom.

"Movin' on," replied Kowie, and with his words the tank slid forward over the frozen ground like grease on a hot griddle.

The command post had been a district road-maintenance center before all semblance of central government on Kobold had collapsed. The orderly room and officers' quarters were in the supervisor's house, a comfortable structure with shutters and mottoes embroidered in French on the walls. Some of the hangings had been defaced by short-range gunfire. The crew barracks across the road now served the troopers on headquarters duty. Many of the Slammers could read the Dutch periodicals abandoned there in the breakup. The equipment shed beside the barracks garaged the infantry skimmers because the battery-powered platforms could not shrug off the weather like the huge panzers of M Company. The shed doors were open, pluming the night with heated air as the duty platoon ran for its mounts. Some of the troopers had not yet donned their helmets and body armor. Jenne waved as the tank swept on by; then the road curved and the infantry was lost in the night.

Kobold was a joint colony of Aurore and Friesland. When eighty years of French oppression had driven the Dutch settlers to rebellion, their first act was to hire Hammer's Slammers. The break between Hammer and Friesland had been sharp, but time has a way of blunting anger and letting old habits resume. The regimental language was Dutch, and many of the Slammers' officers were Frisians seconded from their own service. Friesland gained from the men's experience when they returned home; Hammer gained company officers with excellent training from Gröningen Academy.

To counter the Slammers, the settlers of Auroran descent had hired three Francophone regiments. If either group of colonists could have afforded to pay its mercenaries unaided, the fighting would have been immediate and brief. Kobold had been kept deliberately poor by its homeworlds, however; so in their necessities the settlers turned to those homeworlds for financial help.

And neither Aurore nor Friesland wanted a war on Kobold.

Friesland had let its settlers swing almost from the beginning, sloughing their interests for a half share of the copper
produced and concessions elsewhere in its sphere of influence.
The arrangement was still satisfactory to the Council of State,
if Frisian public opinion could be mollified by apparent activity. Aurore was on the brink of war in the Zemla System. Her
Parlement feared another proxy war which could in a moment
explode full-fledged, even though Friesland had been weak-
ened by a decade of severe internal troubles. So Aurore and
Friesland reached a compromise. Then, under threat of aban-
donment, the warring parties were forced to transfer their
mercenaries' contracts to the homeworlds. Finally, Aurore
and Friesland mutually hired the four regiments: the Slammers; Compagnie de Barthe; the Alaudae; the Phenix Moi-
rots. Mercs from either side were mixed and divided among
eight sectors imposed on a map of inhabited Kobold. There
the contract ordered them to keep peace between the factions;
prevent the importation of modern weapons to either side;
and—wait.

But Col. Barthe and the Auroran leaders had come to a further, secret agreement; and although Hammer had learned of
it, he had informed only two men—Maj. Steuben, his aide and
bodyguard; and Capt. Daniel Pritchard.

Pritchard scowled at the memory. Even without the details a
traitor had sold Hammer, it would have been obvious that
Barthe had his own plans. In the other sectors, Hammer's men
and their French counterparts ran joint patrols. Both sides
scattered their camps throughout the sectors, just as the villages of either nationality were scattered. Barthe had split his
sectors in halves, brusquely ordering the Slammers to keep to
the west of the River Aillet because his own troops were mining the east of the basin heavily. Barthe's Company was noted
for its minefields. That skill was one of the reasons they had
been hired by the French. Since most of Kobold was covered
either by forests or by rugged hills, armor was limited to roads
where well-placed mines could stack tanks like crushed boxes.

Hammer listened to Barth's pronouncement and laughed,
despite the anger of most of his staff officers. Beside him,
Joachim Steuben had grinned and traced the line of his cut-
away holster. When Danny Pritchard was informed, he had
only shivered a little and called a vehicle inspection for the

next morning. That had been three months ago . . .

The night streamed by like smoke around the tank. Pritchard lowered his face shield, but he did not drop his seat into
the belly of the tank. Vision blocks within gave a 360° view of
the tank's surroundings, but the farmer in Danny could not
avoid the feeling of blindness within the impenetrable walls.
Jenne sat beside his captain in a cupola fitted with a three-
barreled automatic weapon. He too rode with his head out of
the hatch, but that was only for comradeship. The sergeant
much preferred to be inside. He would button up at the first
sign of hostile action. Jenne was in no sense a coward; it was
just that he had quirks. Most combat veterans do.

Pritchard liked the whistle of the black wind past his
helmet. Warm air from the tank's resistance heaters jetted up
through the hatch and kept his body quite comfortable. The
vehicle's huge mass required the power of a fusion plant to
drive its lift motors, and the additional burden of climate control was inconsequential.

The tankers' face shields automatically augmented the light
of the moon, dim and red because the sun it reflected was dim
and red as well. The boosted light level displayed the walls of
forest, the boles snaking densely to either side of the road. At
Kobold's perihelion, the thin stems grew in days to their full
six-meter heights and spread a ceiling of red-brown leaves the
size of blankets. Now, at aphelion, the chilled, sapless trees
burned with almost explosive intensity. The wood was too
dangerous to use for heating, even if electricity had not been
common; but it fueled the gasogene engines of most vehicles
on the planet.

Jenne gestured ahead. "Blowers," he muttered on the intercom. His hand rested on the gun switch though he knew the
vehicles must be friendly. The *Plow* slowed.

Pritchard nodded agreement. "Michael First, this is
Michael One," he said. "Flash your running lights so we can
be sure it's you."

"Roger," replied the radio. Blue light flickered from the
shapes hulking at the edge of the forest ahead. Kowie throttled
the fans up to cruise, then chopped them and swung expertly
into the midst of the four tanks of the outlying platoon.

"Michael One, this is Sigma One," Capt. Riis's angry voice
demanded in the helmet.

"Go ahead."

"Barthe's sent a battalion across the river. I'm moving Lt. Schilling into position to block 'em and called Central for artillery support. You hold your first platoon at Haacin for reserve and any partisans up from Portela. I'll take direct command of the rest of—"

"Negative, negative, Sigma One!" Pritchard snapped. The *Plow* was accelerating again, second in the line of five tanks. They were beasts of prey sliding across the landscape of snow and black trees at 80 kph and climbing. "Let the French through, Captain. There won't be fighting, repeat, negative fighting."

"There damned well *will* be fighting, Michael One, if Barthe tries to shove a battalion into my section!" Riis thundered back. "Remember, this isn't your command or a joint command. *I'm* in charge here."

"Margritte, patch me through to Battalion," Pritchard hissed on the intercom. The *Plow's* turret was cocked 30° to the right. It covered the forest sweeping by to that side and anything which might be hiding there. Pritchard's mind was on Sally Schilling, riding a skimmer through forest like that flanking the tanks, hurrying with her fifty men to try to stop a battalion's hasty advance.

The commo helmet popped quietly to itself. Pritchard tensed, groping for the words he would need to convince Lt. Col. Miezierk. Miezierk, under whom command of Sectors One and Two was grouped, had been a Frisian regular until five years ago. He was supposed to think like a merc, now, not like a Frisian; but . . .

The voice that suddenly rasped, "Override, override!" was not Miezierk's. "Sigma One, Michael One, this is Regiment."

"Go ahead," Pritchard blurted. Capt. Riis, equally rattled, said "Yes *sir*!" on the three-way link.

"Sigma, your fire order is canceled. Keep your troops on alert, but keep 'em the hell out of Barthe's way."

"But Col. Hammer—"

"Riis, you're not going to start a war tonight. Michael One, can your panzers handle whatever's going on at Haacin without violating the contract?"

"Yes, sir." Pritchard flashed a map briefly on his face shield to check his position. "We're almost there now."

"If you can't handle it, Captain, you'd better hope you're killed in action," Col. Hammer said bluntly. "I haven't nursed this regiment for twenty-three years to lose it because somebody forgets what his job is." Then, more softly— Pritchard could imagine the colonel flicking his eyes side to side to gauge bystanders' reactions—he added, "There's support if you need it, Captain—if they're the ones who breach the contract."

"Affirmative."

"Keep the lid on, boy. Regiment out."

The trees had drunk the whine of the fans. Now the road curved and the tanks banked greasily to join the main highway from Dimo to Portela. The tailings pile of the Haacin Mine loomed to the right and hurled the drive noise back redoubled at the vehicles. The steel skirts of the lead tank touched the road metal momentarily, showering the night with orange sparks. Beyond the mine were the now-empty wheat fields and then the village itself.

Haacin, the largest Dutch settlement in Section Two, sprawled to either side of the highway. Its houses were two- and three-story lumps of cemented mine tailings. They were roofed with tile or plastic rather than shakes of native timber, because of the wood's lethal flammability. The highway was straight and broad. It gave Pritchard a good view of the three cargo vehicles pulled to one side. Men in local dress swarmed about them. Across the road were ten of Hammer's khaki-clad infantry, patrol S-39, whose ported weapons half-threatened, half-protected the trio of drivers in their midst. Occasionally a civilian turned to hurl a curse at Barthe's men, but mostly the Dutch busied themselves with off-loading cartons from the trucks.

Pritchard gave a brief series of commands. The four line tanks grounded in a hedgerow at the edge of the village. Their main guns and automatics faced outward in all directions. Kowie swung the command vehicle around the tank which had been leading it. He cut the fans' angle of attack, slowing the *Plow* without losing the ability to accelerate quickly. The command vehicle eased past the squad of infantry, then grounded behind the rearmost truck. Pritchard felt the fans' hum through the metal of the hull.

"Who's in charge here?" the captain demanded, his voice

booming through the command vehicle's public address system.

The Dutch unloading the trucks halted silently. A squat man in a parka of feathery native fur stepped forward. Unlike many of the other civilians, he was not armed. He did not flinch when Pritchard pinned him with the spotlight of the tank. "I am Paul van Oosten," the man announced in the heavy Dutch of Kobold. "I am mayor of Haacin. But if you mean who leads us in what we are doing here, well . . . perhaps Justice herself does. Klaus, show them what these trucks were carrying to Portela."

Another civilian stepped forward, ripping the top off the box he carried. Flat plastic wafers spilled from it, glittering in the cold light; powergun ammunition, intended for shoulder weapons like those the infantry carried.

"They were taking powerguns to the beasts of Portela to use against us," van Oosten said. He used the slang term "skepsels" to name the Francophone settlers. The mayor's shaven jaw was jutting out in anger.

"Captain!" called one of Barthe's truck drivers, brushing forward through the ring of Hammer's men. "Let me explain."

One of the civilians growled and lifted his heavy musket. Rob Jenne rang his knuckles twice on the receiver of his tribarrel, calling attention to the muzzles as he swept them down across the crowd. The Dutchman froze. Jenne smiled without speaking.

"We were sent to pick up wheat the regiment had purchased," Barthe's man began. Pritchard was not familiar with Barthe's insignia, but from the merc's age and bearing he was a senior sergeant. An unlikely choice to be driving a provisions truck. "One of the vehicles happened to be partly loaded. We didn't take the time to empty it because we were in a hurry to finish the run and go off duty—there was enough room and lift to handle that little bit of gear and the grain besides.

"In any case"—and here the sergeant began pressing, because the tank captain had not cut him off at the first sentence as expected—"you do not, and these fools *surely* do not, have the right to stop Col. Barthe's transport. If you have questions about the way we pick up wheat, that's between your CO and ours. Sir."

Pritchard ran his gloved index finger back and forth below his right eyesocket. He was ice inside, bubbling ice that tore and chilled him and had nothing to do with the weather. He turned back to Mayor van Oosten. "Reload the trucks," he said, hoping that his voice did not break.

"You can't!" van Oosten cried. "These powerguns are the only chance my village, my *people* have to survive when you leave. You know that'll happen, don't you? Friesland and Aurore, they'll come to an agreement, a *trade-off*, they'll call it, and all the troops will leave. It's our lives they're trading! The beasts in Dimo, in Portela if you let these go through, they'll have powerguns that *their* mercenaries gave them. And we—"

Pritchard whispered a prepared order into his helmet mike. The rearmost of the four tanks at the edge of the village fired a single round from its main gun. The night flared cyan as the 200mm bolt struck the middle of the tailings pile a kilometer away. Stone, decomposed by the enormous energy of the shot, recombined in a huge gout of flame. Vapor, lava, and cinders spewed in every direction. After a moment, bits of high-flung rock began pattering down on the roofs of Haacin.

The bolt caused a double thunder-clap, that of the heated air followed by the explosive release of energy at the point of impact. When the reverberations died away there was utter silence in Haacin. On the distant jumble of rock, a dying red glow marked where the charge had hit. The shot had also ignited some saplings rooted among the stones. They had blazed as white torches for a few moments but they were already collapsing as cinders.

"The Slammers are playing this by rules," Pritchard said. Loudspeakers flung his quiet words about the village like the echoes of the shot; but he was really speaking for the recorder in the belly of the tank, preserving his words for a later Bonding Authority hearing. "There'll be no powerguns in civilian hands. Load every bit of this gear back in the truck. Remember, there's satellites up there"—Pritchard waved generally at the sky—"that see everything that happens on Kobold. If one powergun is fired by a civilian in this sector, I'll come for him. I promise you."

The mayor sagged within his furs. Turning to the crowd behind him, he said, "Put the guns back on the truck. So that the Portelans can kill us more easily."

"Are you mad, van Oosten?" demanded the gunman who had earlier threatened Barthe's sergeant.

"Are *you* mad, Kruse?" the mayor shouted back without trying to hide his fury. "D'ye doubt what those tanks would do to Haacin? And do you doubt this butcher"—his back was to Pritchard but there was no doubt as to whóm the mayor meant—"would use them on us? Perhaps tomorrow we could have . . ."

There was motion at the far edge of the crowd, near the corner of a building. Margritte, watching the vision blocks within, called a warning. Pritchard reached for his panic bar—Rob Jenne was traversing the tribarrel. All three of them were too late. The muzzle flash was red and it expanded in Pritchard's eyes as a hammer blow smashed him in the middle of the forehead.

The bullet's impact heaved the tanker up and backwards. His shattered helmet flew off into the night. The unyielding hatch coaming caught him in the small of the back, arching his torso over it as if he were being broken on the wheel. Pritchard's eyes flared with sheets of light. As reaction flung him forward again, he realized he was hearing the reports of Jenne's powergun and that some of the hellish flashes were real.

If the tribarrel's discharges were less brilliant than that of the main gun, then they were more than a hundred times as close to the civilians. The burst snapped within a meter of one bystander, an old man who stumbled backward into a wall. His mouth and staring eyes were three circles of empty terror. Jenne fired seven rounds. Every charge but one struck the sniper or the building he sheltered against. Powdered concrete sprayed from the wall. The sniper's body spun backwards, chest gobbled away by the bolts. His right arm still gripped the musket he had fired at Pritchard. The arm had been flung alone onto the snowy pavement. The electric bite of ozone hung in the air with the ghostly afterimages of the shots. The dead man's clothes were burning, tiny orange flames that rippled into smoke an inch from their bases.

Jenne's big left hand was wrapped in the fabric of Pritchard's jacket, holding the dazed officer upright. "There's another rule you play by," the sergeant roared to the crowd.

"You shoot at Hammer's Slammers and you get your balls kicked between your ears. Sure as god, boys; sure as death." Jenne's right hand swung the muzzles of his weapon across the faces of the civilians. "Now, load the bleeding trucks like the captain said, heroes."

For a brief moment, nothing moved but the threatening powergun. Then a civilian turned and hefted a heavy crate back aboard the truck from which he had just taken it. Empty-handed, the colonist began to sidle away from the vehicle—and from the deadly tribarrel. One by one the other villagers reloaded the hijacked cargo, the guns and ammunition they had hoped would save them in the cataclysm they awaited. One by one they took the blower chief's unspoken leave to return to their houses. One who did not leave was sobbing out her grief over the mangled body of the sniper. None of her neighbors had gone to her side. They could all appreciate—now—what it would have meant if that first shot had led to a general firefight instead of Jenne's selective response.

"Rob, help me get him inside," Pritchard heard Margritte say.

Pritchard braced himself with both hands and leaned away from his sergeant's supporting arm. "No, I'm all right," he croaked. His vision was clear enough, but the landscape was flashing bright and dim with varicolored light.

The side hatch of the turret clanked. Margritte was beside her captain. She had stripped off her cold-weather gear in the belly of the tank and wore only her khaki uniform. "Get back inside there," Pritchard muttered. "It's not safe." He was afraid of falling if he raised a hand to fend her away. He felt an injector prick the swelling flesh over his cheekbones. The flashing colors died away though Pritchard's ears began to ring.

"They carried some into the nearest building," the noncom from Barthe's Company was saying. He spoke in Dutch, having sleep-trained in the language during the transit to Kobold just as Hammer's men had in French.

"Get it," Jenne ordered the civilians still near the trucks. Three of them were already scurrying toward the house the merc had indicated. They were back in moments, carrying the last of the arms chests.

Pritchard surveyed the scene. The cargo had been reloaded, except for the few spilled rounds winking from the pavement. Van Oosten and the furious Kruse were the only villagers still in sight. "All right," Pritchard said to the truck drivers, "get aboard and get moving. And come back by way of Bitzen, not here. I'll arrange an escort for you."

The French noncom winked, grinned, and shouted a quick order to his men. The infantrymen stepped aside silently to pass the truckers. The French mercenaries mounted their vehicles and kicked them to life. Their fans whined and the trucks lifted, sending snow crystals dancing. With gathering speed, they slid westward along the forest-rimmed highway.

Jenne shook his head at the departing trucks, then stiffened as his helmet spat a message. "Captain," he said, "we got company coming."

Pritchard grunted. His own radio helmet had been smashed by the bullet, and his implant would only relay messages on the band to which it had been verbally keyed most recently. "Margritte, start switching for me," he said. His slender commo tech was already slipping back inside through the side hatch. Pritchard's blood raced with the chemicals Margritte had shot into it. His eyes and mind worked perfectly, though all his thoughts seemed to have razor edges on them.

"Use mine," Jenne said, trying to hand the captain his helmet.

"I've got the implant," Pritchard said. He started to shake his head and regretted the motion instantly. "That and Margritte's worth a helmet any day."

"It's a whole battalion," Jenne explained quietly, his eyes scanning the Bever Road down which Command Central had warned that Barthe's troops were coming. "All but the artillery—that's back in Dimo, but it'll range here easy enough. Brought in antitank battery and a couple calliopes, though."

"Slide us up ahead of Michael First," Pritchard ordered his driver. As the *Plow* shuddered, then spun on its axis, the captain dropped his seat into the turret to use the vision blocks. He heard Jenne's seat whirr down beside him and the cupola hatch snick closed. In front of Pritchard's knees, pale in the instrument lights, Margritte DiManzo sat still and open-eyed at her communications console.

"Little friendlies," Pritchard called through his loud-

speakers to the ten infantrymen, "find yourselves a quiet alley
and hope nothing happens. The Lord help you if you fire a
shot without me ordering it." The Lord help us all, Pritchard
thought to himself.

Ahead of the command vehicle, the beetle shapes of First
Platoon began to shift position. "Michael First," Pritchard
ordered sharply, "get back as you were. We're not going to
engage Barthe, we're going to meet him." Maybe.

Kowie slid them alongside, then a little forward of the point
vehicle of the defensive lozenge. They set down. All of the
tanks were buttoned up, save for the hatch over Pritchard's
head. The central vision block was a meter-by-30-cm panel. It
could be set for anything from a 360° view of the tank's surroundings to a one-to-one image of an object a kilometer
away. Pritchard focused and ran the gain to ten magnifica-
tions, then thirty. At the higher power, motion curling along
the snow-smoothed grainfields between Haacin and its mine
resolved into men. Barthe's troops were clad in sooty-white
coveralls and battle armor. The leading elements were
hunched low on the meager platforms of their skimmers.
Magnification and the augmented light made the skittering
images grainy, but the tanker's practiced eye caught the tubes
of rocket launchers clipped to every one of the skimmers. The
skirmish line swelled at two points where self-propelled guns
were strung like beads on the cord of men: antitank weapons,
50mm powerguns firing high-intensity charges. They were
supposed to be able to burn through the heaviest armor.
Barthe's boys had come loaded for bear; oh yes. They thought
they knew just what they were going up against. Well, the
Slammers weren't going to show them they were wrong. Tonight.

"Running lights, everybody," Pritchard ordered. Then,
taking a deep breath, he touched the lift on his seat and raised
himself head and shoulders back into the chill night air. There
was a hand light clipped to Pritchard's jacket. He snapped it
on, aiming the beam down onto the turret top so that the
burnished metal splashed diffused radiance up over him. It
bathed his torso and face plainly for the oncoming infantry.
Through the open hatch, Pritchard could hear Rob cursing.
Just possibly Margritte was mumbling a prayer.

"Batteries at Dimo and Harfleur in Sector One have re-

ceived fire orders and are waiting for a signal to execute," the
implant grated. "If Barthe opens fire, Command Central will
not, repeat, negative, use Michael First or Michael One to
knock down the shells. Your guns will be clear for action,
Michael One."

Pritchard grinned starkly. His face would not have been
pleasant even if livid bruises were not covering almost all of it.
The Slammers' central fire-direction computer used radar and
satellite reconnaissance to track shells in flight. Then the computer took control of any of the regiment's vehicle-mounted
powerguns and swung them onto the target. Central's message
notified Pritchard that he would have full control of his weapons at all times, while guns tens or hundreds of kilometers
away kept his force clear of artillery fire.

Margritte had blocked most of the commo traffic, Pritchard
realized. She had let through only this message that was cru-
cial to what they were about to do. A good commo tech; a very
good person indeed.

The skirmish line grounded. The nearest infantrymen were
within fifty meters of the tanks and their fellows spread off
into the night like lethal wings. Barthe's men rolled off their
skimmers and lay prone. Pritchard began to relax when he
noticed that their rocket launchers were still aboard the skimmers. The antitank weapons were in instant reach, but at least
they were not being leveled for an immediate salvo. Barthe
didn't want to fight the Slammers. His targets were the Dutch
civilians, just as Mayor van Oosten had suggested.

An air-cushion jeep with a driver and two officers aboard
drew close. It hissed slowly through the line of infantry, then
stopped nearly touching the command vehicle's bow armor.
One of the officers dismounted. He was a tall man who was
probably very thin when he was not wearing insulated coveralls and battle armor. He raised his face to Pritchard atop the
high curve of the blower, sweeping up his reflective face shield
as he did so. He was Lt. Col. Benoit, commander of the
French mercenaries in Section Two; a clean-shaven man with
sharp features and a splash of gray hair displaced across his
forehead by his helmet. Benoit grinned and waved at the muzzle of the 200mm powergun pointed at him. Nobody had ever
said Barthe's chief subordinate was a coward.

Pritchard climbed out of the turret to the deck, then slid
down the bow slope to the ground. Benoit was several inches

taller than the tanker, with a force of personality which was
daunting in a way that height alone could never be. It didn't
matter to Pritchard. He worked with tanks and with Col.
Hammer; nothing else was going to face down a man who was
accustomed to those.

"Sgt. Maj. Oberlie reported how well and . . . firmly you
handled their little affair, Captain," Benoit said, extending his
hand to Pritchard. "I'll admit that I was a little concerned that
I would have to rescue my men myself."

"Hammer's Slammers can be depended on to keep their
contracts," the tanker replied, smiling with false warmth. "I
told these squareheads that any civilian caught with a powergun was going to have to answer to me for it. Then we made
sure nobody thinks we were kidding."

Benoit chuckled. Little puffs of vapor spurted from his
mouth with the sounds. "You've been sent to the Gröningen
Academy, have you not, Capt. Pritchard?" the older man
asked. "You understand that I take an interest in my opposite
numbers in this sector."

Pritchard nodded. "The Old Man picked me for the two-
year crash course on Friesland, yeah. Now and again he sends
noncoms he wants to promote."

"But you're not a Frisian, though you have Frisian military
training," the other mercenary continued, nodding to himself.
"As you know, Captain, promotion in some infantry regiments comes much faster than it does in the . . . Slammers. If
you feel a desire to speak to Col. Barthe some time in the
future, I assure you this evening's business will not be forgotten."

"Just doing my job, Colonel," Pritchard simpered. Did
Benoit think a job offer would make a traitor of him? Perhaps. Hammer had bought Barthe's plans for very little, con-
sidering their military worth. "Enforcing the contract, just
like you'd have done if things were the other way around."

Benoit chuckled again and stepped back aboard his jeep.
"Until we meet again, Capt. Pritchard," he said. "For the
moment, I think we'll just proceed on into Portela. That's per-
missible under the contract, of course."

"Swing wide around Haacin, will you?" Pritchard called
back. "The folks there're pretty worked up. Nobody wants
more trouble, do·we?"

Benoit nodded. As his jeep lifted, he spoke into his helmet

communicator. The skirmish company rose awkwardly and set off in a counterclockwise circuit of Haacin. Behind them, in a column reformed from their support positions at the base of the tailings heap, came the truck-mounted men of the other three companies. Pritchard stood and watched until the last of them whined past.

Air stirred by the tank's idling fans leaked out under the skirts. The jets formed tiny deltas of the snow which winked as Pritchard's feet caused eddy currents. In their cold precision, the tanker recalled Col. Benoit's grin.

"Command Central," Pritchard said as he climbed his blower, "Michael One. Everything's smooth here. Over." Then, "Sigma One, this is Michael One. I'll be back as quick as fans'll move me, so if you have anything to say we can discuss it then." Pritchard knew that Capt. Riis must have been burning the net up, trying to raise him for a report or to make demands. It wasn't fair to make Margritte hold the bag now that Pritchard himself was free to respond to the sector chief; but neither did the Dunstan tanker have the energy to argue with Riis just at the moment. Already this night he'd faced death and Col. Benoit. Riis could wait another ten minutes.

The *Plow*'s armor was a tight fit for its crew, the radios, and the central bulk of the main gun with its feed mechanism. The command vehicle rode glass-smooth over the frozen roadway, with none of the jouncing that a rougher surface might bring even through the air cushion. Margritte faced Pritchard over her console, her seat a meter lower than his so that she appeared a suppliant. Her short hair was the lustrous purple-black of a grackle's throat in sunlight. Hidden illumination from the instruments brought her face to life.

"Gee, Captain," Jenne was saying at Pritchard's side, "I wish you'd a let me pick up that squarehead's rifle. I know those ground-pounders. They're just as apt as not to claim the kill credit themselves, and if I can't prove I stepped on the body they might get away with it. I remember on Paradise, me and Piet de Hagen—he was left wing gunner, I was right— both shot at a partisan. And then damned if Central didn't decide the slope had blown herself up with a hand grenade after we'd wounded her. So *neither* of us got the credit. You'd think—"

"Lord's *blood*, Sergeant," Pritchard snarled, "are you so damned proud of killing one of the poor bastards who hired us to protect them?"

Jenne said nothing. Pritchard shrank up inside, realizing what he had said and unable to take the words back. "Oh, Lord, Rob," he said without looking up, "I'm sorry. It . . . I'm shook, that's all."

After a brief silence, the blond sergeant laughed. "Never been shot in the head myself, Captain, but I can see it might shake a fellow, yeah." Jenne let the whine of the fans stand for a moment as the only further comment while he decided whether he would go on. Then he said, "Captain, for a week after I first saw action I meant to get out of the Slammers, even if I had to sweep floors on Curwin for the rest of my life. Finally I decided I'd stick it. I didn't like the . . . rules of the game, but I could learn to play by them.

"And I did. And one rule is, that you get to be as good as you can at killing the people Col. Hammer wants killed. Yeah, I'm proud about that one just now. It was a tough snap shot and I made it. I don't care why we're on Kobold or who brought us here. But I know I'm supposed to kill anybody who shoots at us, and I will."

"Well, I'm glad you did," Pritchard said evenly as he looked the sergeant in the eyes. "You pretty well saved things from getting out of hand by the way you reacted."

As if he had not heard his captain, Jenne went on, "I was afraid if I stayed in the Slammers I'd turn into an animal, like the dogs we trained back home to kill rats in the quarries. And I was right. But it's the way I am now, so I don't seem to mind."

"You do care about those villagers, don't you?" Margritte asked Pritchard unexpectedly.

The captain looked down and found her eyes on him. They were the rich powder-blue of chicory flowers. "You're probably the only person in the regiment who thinks that," he said bitterly. "Except for me. And maybe Col. Hammer . . ."

Margritte smiled, a quick flash and as quickly gone. "There're rule-book soldiers in the Slammers," she said, "captains who'd never believe Barthe was passing arms to the Auroran settlements since he'd signed a contract that said he wouldn't. You aren't that kind. And the Lord knows Col. Hammer isn't, and he's backing you. I've been around you too long, Danny, to believe you like what you see the French doing.''

Pritchard shrugged. His whole face was stiff with bruises and the drugs Margritte had injected to control them. If he'd locked the helmet's chin strap, the bullet's impact would have broken his neck even though the lead itself did not penetrate. "No, I don't like it," the brown-haired captain said. "It reminds me too much of the way the Combine kept us so poor on Dunstan that a thousand of us signed on for birdseed to fight off-planet. Just because it *was* off-planet. And if Kobold only gets cop from the worlds who settled her, then the French skim the best of that. Sure, I'll tell the Lord I feel sorry for the Dutch here.''

Pritchard held the commo tech's eyes with his own as he continued, "But it's just like Rob said, Margritte: I'll do my job, no matter who gets hurt. We can't do a thing to Barthe or the French until they step over the line in a really obvious way. That'll mean a lot of people get hurt too. But that's what I'm waiting for.''

Margritte reached up and touched Pritchard's hand where it rested on his knee. "You'll do something when you can,'' she said quietly.

He turned his palm up so that he could grasp the woman's fingers. What if she knew he was planning an incident, not just waiting for one? "I'll do something, yeah,'' he said. "But it's going to be too late for an awful lot of people.''

Kowie kept the *Plow* at cruising speed until they were actually in the yard of the command post. Then he cocked the fan shafts forward, lifting the bow and bringing the tank's mass around in a curve that killed its velocity and blasted an arc of snow against the building. Someone inside had started to unlatch the door as they heard the vehicle approach. The air spilling from the tank's skirts flung the panel against the inner wall and skidded the man within on his back.

The man was Capt. Riis, Pritchard noted without surprise. Well, the incident wouldn't make the infantry captain any angrier than the rest of the evening had made him already.

Riis had regained his feet by the time Pritchard could jump from the deck of his blower to the fan-cleared ground in front of the building. The Frisian's normally pale face was livid now with rage. He was of the same somatotype as Lt. Col. Benoit, his French counterpart in the sector: tall, thin, and proudly erect. Despite the fact that Riis was only twenty-seven, he was Pritchard's senior in grade by two years. He had kept the rank he held in Friesland's regular army when Col. Hammer recruited him. Many of the Slammers were like Riis, Frisian soldiers who had transferred for the action and pay of a fighting regiment in which their training would be appreciated.

"You cowardly filth!" the infantryman hissed as Pritchard approached. A squad in battle gear stood within the orderly room beyond Riis. He pursed his fine lips to spit.

"Hey Captain!" Rob Jenne called. Riis looked up. Pritchard turned, surprised that the big tank commander was not right on his heels. Jenne still smiled from the *Plow*'s cupola. He waved at the officers with his left hand. His right was on the butterfly trigger of the tribarrel.

The threat, unspoken as it was, made a professional of Riis again. "Come on into my office," he muttered to the tank captain, turning his back on the armored vehicle as if it were only a part of the landscape.

The infantrymen inside parted to pass the captains. Sally Schilling was there. Her eyes were as hard as her porcelain armor as they raked over Pritchard. That didn't matter, he lied to himself tiredly.

Riis's office was at the top of the stairs, a narrow cubicle which had once been a child's bedroom. The sloping roof pressed in on the occupants, though a dormer window brightened the room during daylight. One wall was decorated with a regimental battle flag—not Hammer's rampant lion but a pattern of seven stars on a white field. It had probably come from the unit in which Riis had served on Friesland. Over the door hung another souvenir, a big-bore musket of local manufacture. Riis threw himself into the padded chair behind his desk. "Those bastards were carrying powerguns to Portela!" he snarled at Pritchard.

The tanker nodded. He was leaning with his right shoulder against the doorjamb. "That's what the folks at Haacin thought," he agreed. "If they'll put in a complaint with the Bonding Authority, I'll testify to what I saw."

"Testify, *testify*!" Riis shouted. "We're not lawyers, we're soldiers! You should've seized the trucks right then and—"

"No I should *not* have, Captain!" Pritchard shouted back, holding up a mirror to Riis's anger. "Because if I had, Barthe would've complained to the Authority himself, and we'd at least've been fined. At least! The contract says the Slammers'll cooperate with the other three units in keeping peace on Kobold. Just because we suspect Barthe is violating the contract doesn't give us a right to violate it ourselves. Especially in a way any *simpleton* can see is a violation."

"If Barthe can get away with it, we can," Riis insisted, but he settled back in his chair. He was physically bigger than Pritchard, but the tanker had spent half his life with the Slammers. Years like those mark men; death is never very far behind their eyes.

"I don't think Barthe can get away with it," Pritchard lied quietly, remembering Hammer's advice on how to handle Riis and calm the Frisian without telling him the truth. Barthe's officers had been in on his plans; and one of them had talked. Any regiment might have one traitor.

The tanker lifted down the musket on the wall behind him and began turning it in his fingers. "If the Dutch settlers can prove to the Authority that Barthe's been passing out power-guns to the French," the tanker mused aloud, "well, they're responsible for half Barthe's pay, remember. It's about as bad a violation as you'll find. The Authority'll forfeit his whole bond and pay it over to whoever they decide the injured parties are. That's about three years' gross earnings for Barthe, I'd judge—he won't be able to replace it. And without a bond posted, well, he may get jobs, but they'll be the kind nobody else'd touch for the risk and the pay. His best troops'll sign on with other people. In a year or so, Barthe won't have a regiment anymore."

"He's willing to take the chance," said Riis.

"Col. Hammer isn't!" Pritchard blazed back.

"You don't know that. It isn't the sort of thing the Colonel could say—"

"Say?" Pritchard shouted. He waved the musket at Riis. Its breech was triple-strapped to take the shock of the industrial explosive it used for propellant. Clumsy and large, it was the best that could be produced on a mining colony whose homeworlds had forbidden local manufacturing. "Say? I bet my life against one of these tonight that the colonel wanted us to obey the contract. Do you have the guts to ask him flat out if he wants us to run guns to the Dutch?''

"I don't think that would be proper, Captain," said Riis coldly as he stood up again.

"Then try not to 'think it proper' to go do some bloody stupid stunt on your own—sir," Pritchard retorted. So much for good intentions. Hammer—and Pritchard—had expected Riis's support of the Dutch civilians. They had even planned on it. But the man seemed to have lost all his common sense. Pritchard laid the musket on the desk because his hands were trembling too badly to hang it back on the hooks.

"If it weren't for you, Captain," Riis said, "there's not a Slammer in this sector who'd object to our helping the only decent people on this planet the way we ought to. You've made your decision, and it sickens me. But I've made decisions too."

Pritchard went out without being dismissed. He blundered into the jamb, but he did not try to slam the door. That would have been petty, and there was nothing petty in the tanker's rage.

Blank-faced, he clumped down the stairs. His bunk was in a parlor which had its own door to the outside. Pritchard's crew was still in the *Plow*. There they had listened intently to his half of the argument with Riis, transmitted by the implant. If Pritchard had called for help, Kowie would have sent the command vehicle through the front wall buttoned up, with Jenne ready to shoot if he had to, to rescue his CO. A tank looks huge when seen close up. It is all howling steel and iridium, with black muzzles ready to spew death across a planet. On a battlefield, when the sky is a thousand shrieking colors no god ever made and the earth beneath trembles and gouts in sudden mountains, a tank is a small world indeed for its crew. Their loyalties are to nearer things than an abstraction like "The Regiment."

Besides, tankers and infantrymen have never gotten along well together.

No one was in the orderly room except two radiomen. They kept their backs to the stairs. Pritchard glanced at them, then unlatched his door. The room was dark, as he had left it, but there was a presence. Pritchard said, "Sal—" as he stepped within and the club knocked him forward into the arms of the man waiting to catch his body.

The first thing Pritchard thought as his mind slipped toward oblivion was that the cloth rubbing his face was homespun, not the hard synthetic from which uniforms were made. The last thing Pritchard thought was that there could have been no civilians within the headquarters perimeter unless the guards had allowed them; and that Lt. Schilling was officer of the guard tonight.

Pritchard could not be quite certain when he regained consciousness. A heavy felt rug covered and hid his trussed body on the floor of a clattering surface vehicle. He had no memory of being carried to the truck, though presumably it had been parked some distance from the command post. Riis and his confederates would not have been so open as to have civilians drive to the door to take a kidnapped officer, even if Pritchard's crew could have been expected to ignore the breach of security.

Kidnapped. Not for later murder, or he would already be dead instead of smothering under the musty rug. Thick as it was, the rug was still inadequate to keep the cold from his shivering body. The only lights Pritchard could see were the washings of icy color from the night's doubled shock to his skull.

That bone-deep ache reminded Pritchard of the transceiver implanted in his mastoid. He said in a husky whisper which he hoped would not penetrate the rug, "Michael One to any unit, any unit at all. Come in please, any Slammer."

Nothing. Well, no surprise. The implant had an effective range of less than twenty meters, enough for relaying to and from a base unit, but unlikely to be useful in Kobold's empty darkness. Of course, if the truck happened to be passing one of M Company's night defensive positions . . . "Michael One to any unit," the tanker repeated more urgently.

A boot slammed him in the ribs. A voice in guttural Dutch snarled, "Shut up, you, or you get what you gave Henrik."

So he'd been shopped to the Dutch, not that there had been much question about it. And not that he might not have been safer in French hands, the way everybody on this cursed planet thought he was a traitor to his real employers. Well, it wasn't fair; but Danny Pritchard had grown up a farmer, and no farmer is ever tricked into believing that life is fair.

The truck finally jolted to a stop. Gloved hands jerked the cover from Pritchard's eyes. He was not surprised to recognize the concrete angles of Haacin as men passed him hand to hand into a cellar. The attempt to hijack Barthe's powerguns had been an accident, an opportunity seized; but the crew which had kidnapped Pritchard must have been in position before the call from S-39 had intervened.

"Is this wise?" Pritchard heard someone demand from the background. "If they begin searching, surely they'll begin in Haacin."

The two men at the bottom of the cellar stairs took Pritchard's shoulders and ankles to carry him to a spring cot. It had no mattress. The man at his feet called, "There won't be a search, they don't have enough men. Besides, the beasts'll be blamed—as they should be for so many things. If Pauli won't let us kill the turncoat, then we'll all have to stand the extra risk of him living."

"You talk too much," Mayor van Oosten muttered as he dropped Pritchard's shoulders on the bunk. Many civilians had followed the captive into the cellar. The last of them swung the door closed. It lay almost horizontal to the ground. When it slammed, dust sprang from the ceiling. Someone switched on a dim incandescent light. The scores of men and women in the storage room were as hard and fell as the bare walls. There were three windows at street level, high on the wall. Slotted shutters blocked most of their dusty glass.

"Get some heat in this hole or you may as well cut my throat," Pritchard grumbled.

A woman with a musket cursed and spat in his face. The man behind her took her arm before the gunbutt could smear the spittle. Almost in apology, the man said to Pritchard, "It was her husband you killed."

"You're being kept out of the way," said a husky man—Kruse, the hothead from the hijack scene. His facial hair was pale and long, merging indistinguishably with the silky fringe of his parka. Like most of the others in the cellar, he carried a musket. "Without your meddling, there'll be a chance for us to . . . get ready to protect ourselves, after the tanks leave and the beasts come to finish us with their powerguns."

"Does Riis think I won't talk when this is over?" Pritchard asked.

"I told you—" one of the men shouted at van Oosten. The

heavyset mayor silenced him with a tap on the chest and a bellowed, "Quiet!" The rising babble hushed long enough for van Oosten to say, "Captain, you will be released in a very few days. If you—cause trouble, then, it will only be an embarrassment to yourself. Even if your colonel believes you were doing right, he won't be the one to bring to light a violation which was committed with—so you will claim—the connivance of his own officers."

The mayor paused to clear his throat and glower around the room. "Though in fact we had no help from any of your fellows, either in seizing you or in arming ourselves for our own protection."

"Are you all blind?" Pritchard demanded. He struggled with his elbows and back to raise himself against the wall. "Do you think a few lies will cover it all up? The only ships that've touched on Kobold in three months are the ones supplying us and the other mercs. Barthe maybe's smuggled in enough guns in cans of lube oil and the like to arm some civilians. He won't be able to keep that a secret, but maybe he can keep the Authority from proving who's responsible.

"That's with three months and preplanning. If Riis tries to do anything on his own, that many of his own men are going to be short sidearms—they're all issued by serial number, Lord take it!—and a blind Mongoloid could get enough proof to sink the regiment."

"You think we don't understand," said Kruse in a quiet voice. He transferred his musket to his left hand, then slapped Pritchard across the side of the head. "We understand very well," the civilian said. "All the mercenaries will leave in a few days or weeks. If the French have powerguns and we do not, they will kill us, our wives, our children . . . There's a hundred and fifty villages on Kobold like this one, Dutch, and as many French ones scattered between. It was bad before, with no one but the beasts allowed any real say in the government; but now if they win, there'll be French villages and French mines—and slave pens. Forever."

"You think a few guns'll save you?" Pritchard asked. Kruse's blow left no visible mark in the tanker's livid flesh, though a better judge than Kruse might have noted that Pritchard's eyes were as hard as his voice was mild.

"They'll help us save ourselves when the time comes," Kruse retorted.

"If you'd gotten powerguns from French civilians instead of the mercs directly, you might have been all right," the captain said. He was coldly aware that the lie he was telling was more likely to be believed in this situation than it would have been in any setting he might deliberately have contrived. There had to be an incident, the French civilians *had* to think they were safe in using their illegal weapons. . . . "The Portelans, say, couldn't admit to having guns to lose. But anything you take from mercs—us or Barthe, it doesn't matter—we'll take back the hard way. You don't know what you're buying into."

Kruse's face did not change, but his fist drew back for another blow. The mayor caught the younger man's arm and snapped, "Franz, we're here to show him that it's not a few of us, it's every family in the village behind . . . our holding him." Van Oosten nodded around the room. "More of us than your colonel could dream of trying to punish," he added naively to Pritchard. Then he flashed back at Kruse, "If you act like a fool, he'll want revenge anyway."

"You may never believe this," Pritchard interjected wearily, "but I just want to do my job. If you let me go now, it—may be easier in the long run."

"Fool," Kruse spat and turned his back on the tanker.

A trapdoor opened in the ceiling, spilling more light into the cellar. "Pauli!" a woman shouted down the opening, "Hals is on the radio. There's tanks coming down the road, just like before!"

"The Lord's wounds!" van Oosten gasped. "We must—"

"They can't know!" Kruse insisted. "But we've got to get everybody out of here and back to their own houses. Everybody but me and him"—a nod at Pritchard—"and this." The musket lowered so that its round black eye pointed straight into the bound man's face.

"No, by the side door!" van Oosten called to the press of conspirators clumping up toward the street. "Don't run right out in front of them." Cursing and jostling, the villagers climbed the ladder to the ground floor, there presumably to exit on an alley.

Able only to twist his head and legs, Pritchard watched Kruse and the trembling muzzle of his weapon. The village must have watchmen with radios at either approach through the forests. If Hals was atop the heap of mine tailings—where

Pritchard would have placed his outpost if he were in charge, certainly—then he'd gotten a nasty surprise when the main gun splashed the rocks with Hell. The captain grinned at the thought. Kruse misunderstood and snarled, "If they *are* coming for you, you're dead, you treacherous bastard!" To the backs of his departing fellows, the young Dutchman called, "Turn out the light here, but leave the trapdoor open. That won't show on the street, but it'll give me enough light to shoot by."

The tanks weren't coming for him, Pritchard knew, because they couldn't have any idea where he was. Perhaps his disappearance had stirred up some patrolling, for want of more directed action; perhaps a platoon was just changing ground because of its commander's whim. Pritchard had encouraged random motion. Tanks that freeze in one place are sitting targets, albeit hard ones. But whatever the reason tanks were approaching Haacin, if they whined by in the street outside they would be well within range of his implanted transmitter.

The big blowers were audible now, nearing with an arrogant lack of haste as if bears headed for a beehive. They were moving at about 30 kph, more slowly than Pritchard would have expected even for a contact patrol. From the sound there were four or more of them, smooth and gray and deadly.

"Kruse, I'm serious," the Slammer captain said. Light from the trapdoor backlit the civilian into a hulking beast with a musket. "If you—"

"Shut up!" Kruse snarled, prodding his prisoner's bruised forehead with the gun muzzle. "One more word, any word, and—"

Kruse's right hand was so tense and white that the musket might fire even without his deliberate intent.

The first of the tanks slid by outside. Its cushion of air was so dense that the ground trembled even though none of the blower's 170 tonnes was in direct contact with it. Squeezed between the pavement and the steel curtain of the plenum chamber, the air spurted sideways and rattled the cellar windows. The rattling was inaudible against the howling of the fans themselves, but the trembling shutters chopped facets in the play of the tank's running lights. Kruse's face and the far wall flickered in blotched abstraction.

The tank moved on without pausing. Pritchard had not tried to summon it.

"That power," Kruse was mumbling to himself, "that
should be for us to use to sweep the beasts—" The rest of his
words were lost in the growing wail of the second tank in the
column.

Pritchard tensed within. Even if a passing tank picked up
his implant's transmission, its crew would probably ignore the
message. Unless Pritchard identified himself, the tankers
would assume it was babbling thrown by the ionosphere. And
if he did identify himself, Kruse—

Kruse thrust his musket against Pritchard's skull again,
banging the tanker's head back against the cellar wall. The
Dutchman's voice was lost in the blower's howling, but his
blue-lit lips clearly were repeating, "One word . . ."

The tank moved on down the highway toward Portela.

". . . and maybe I'll shoot you anyway," Kruse was saying. "That's the way to serve traitors, isn't it? *Mercenary!*"

The third blower was approaching. Its note seemed slightly
different, though that might be the aftereffect of the preceding
vehicles' echoing din. Pritchard was cold all the way to his
heart, because in a moment he was going to call for help. He
knew that Kruse would shoot him, knew also that he would
rather die now than live after hope had come so near but
passed on, passed on. . . .

The third tank smashed through the wall of the house.

The *Plow*'s skirts were not a bulldozer blade, but they were
thick steel and backed with the mass of a 150-tonne command
tank. The slag wall repowdered at the impact. Ceiling joists
buckled into pretzel shape and ripped the cellar open to the
floor above. Kruse flung his musket up and fired through
the cascading rubble. The boom and red flash were lost in the
chaos, but the blue-green fire stabbing back across the cellar
laid the Dutchman on his back with his parka aflame. Pritchard rolled to the floor at the first shock. He thrust himself with
corded legs and arms back under the feeble protection of the
bunk. When the sound of falling objects had died away, the
captain slitted his eyelids against the rock dust and risked a
look upward.

The collision had torn a gap ten feet long in the house wall,
crushing it from street level to the beams supporting the second story. The tank blocked the hole with its gray bulk. Fresh
scars brightened the patina of corrosion etched onto its skirts
by the atmospheres of a dozen planets. Through the buckled

flooring and the dust whipped into arabesques by the idling
fans, Pritchard glimpsed a slight figure clinging left-handed to
the turret. Her right hand still threatened the wreckage with a
submachine gun. Carpeting burned on the floor above, ignited
by the burst that killed Kruse. Somewhere a woman was
screaming in Dutch.

"Margritte!" Pritchard shouted. "Margritte! Down here!"

The helmeted woman swung up her face shield and tried to
pierce the cellar gloom with her unaided eyes. The tank-bat-
tered opening had sufficed for the exchange of shots, but the
tangle of structural members and splintered flooring was too
tight to pass a man—or even a small woman. Sooty flames
were beginning to shroud the gap. Margritte jumped to the
ground and struggled for a moment before she was able to
heave open the door. The *Plow*'s turret swung to cover her,
though neither the main gun nor the tribarrel in the cupola
could depress enough to rake the cellar. Margritte ran down
the steps to Pritchard. Coughing in the rock dust, he rolled out
over the rubble to meet her. Much of the smashed sidewall had
collapsed onto the street when the tank backed after the initial
impact. Still, the crumpled beams of the ground floor saged
further with the additional weight of the slag on them. Head-
sized pieces had splanged on the cot above Pritchard.

Margritte switched the submachine gun to her left hand and
began using a clasp knife on her captain's bonds. The cord
with which he was tied bit momentarily deeper at the blade's
pressure.

Pritchard winced, then began flexing his freed hands. "You
know, Margi," he said, "I don't think I've ever seen you with
a gun before."

The commo tech's face hardened as if the polarized helmet
shield had slipped down over it again. "You hadn't," she
said. The ankle bindings parted and she stood, the dust gray-
ing her helmet and her foam-filled coveralls. "Captain, Kowie
had to drive and we needed Rob in the cupola at the gun. That
left me to . . . do anything else that had to be done. I did what
had to be done."

Pritchard tried to stand, using the technician as a post on
which to draw himself upright. Margritte looked frail, but
with her legs braced she stood like a rock. Her arm around
Pritchard's back was as firm as a man's.

"You didn't ask Capt. Riis for help, I guess," Pritchard said, pain making his breath catch. The line tanks had two-man crews with no one to spare for outrider, of course.

"We didn't report you missing," Margritte said, "even to First Platoon. They just went along like before, thinking you were in the *Plow* giving orders." Together, captain and techni-cian shuffled across the floor to the stairs. As they passed Kruse's body, Margritte muttered cryptically, "That's four."

Pritchard assumed the tremors beginning to shake the woman's body were from physical strain. He took as much weight off her as he could and found his numbed feet were beginning to function reasonably well. He would never have been able to board the *Plow* without Sgt. Jenne's grip on his arm, however.

The battered officer settled in the turret with a groan of comfort. The seat cradled his body with gentle firmness, and the warm air blown across him was just the near side of heaven.

"Captain," Jenne said, "what d'we do about the slopes who grabbed you? Shall we call in an interrogation team and—"

"We don't do anything," Pritchard interrupted. "We just pretend none of this happened and head back to . . . " He paused. His flesh wavered both hot and cold as Margritte sprayed his ankles with some of the apparatus from the med-ical kit. "Say, how did you find me, anyway?"

"We shut off coverage when you . . . went into your room," Jenne said, seeing that the commo tech herself did not intend to speak. He meant, Pritchard knew, they had shut off the sound when their captain had said, "Sal." None of the three of them were looking either of the other two in the eyes. "After a bit, though, Margi noticed the carrier line from your implant had dropped off her oscilloscope. I checked your room, didn't find you. Didn't see much point talking it over with the remfs on duty, either.

"So we got satellite recce and found two trucks'd left the area since we got back. One was Riis's, and the other was a civvie junker before that. It'd been parked in the woods out of sight half a kay up the road from the buildings. Both trucks unloaded in Haacin. We couldn't tell which load was you, but

Margi said if we got close, she'd home on your carrier even though you weren't calling us on the implant. Some girl we got here, hey?"

Pritchard bent forward and squeezed the commo tech's shoulder. She did not look up, but she smiled. "Yeah, always knew she was something," he agreed, "but I don't think I realized quite what a person she was until just now."

Margritte lifted her smile. "Rob ordered First Platoon to fall in with us," she said. "He set up the whole rescue." Her fine-fingered hands caressed Pritchard's calves.

But there was other business in Haacin, now. Riis had been quicker to act than Pritchard had hoped. He asked, "You say one of the infantry's trucks took a load here a little bit ago?"

"Yeah, you want the off-print?" Jenne agreed, searching for the flimsy copy of the satellite picture. "What the Hell would they be doing, anyhow?"

"I got a suspicion," his captain said grimly, "and I suppose it's one we've got to check out."

"Michael First-Three to Michael One," the radio broke in. "Vehicles approaching from the east on the hardball."

"Michael One to Michael First," Pritchard said, letting the search for contraband arms wait for this new development. "Reverse and form a line abreast beyond the village. Twenty-meter intervals. The *Plow*'ll take the road." More weapons from Riis? More of Barthe's troops when half his sector command was already in Portela? Pritchard touched switches beneath the vision blocks as Kowie slid the tank into position. He split the screen between satellite coverage and a ground-level view at top magnification. Six vehicles, combat cars, coming fast. Pritchard swore. Friendly, because only the Slammers had armored vehicles on Kobold, not that cars were a threat to tanks anyway. But no combat cars were assigned to this sector; and the unexpected is always bad news to a company commander juggling too many variables already.

"Platoon nearing Tango Sigma four-two, three-two, please identify to Michael One," Pritchard requested, giving Haacin's map coordinates.

Margritte turned up the volume of the main radio while she continued to bandage the captain's rope cuts. The set crackled, "Michael One, this is Alpha One and Alpha First. Stand by."

"God's bleeding cunt!" Rob Jenne swore under his breath.

Pritchard was nodding in equal agitation. Alpha was the regiment's special duty company. Its four combat car platoons
were Col. Hammer's bodyguards and police. The troopers of
A Company were nicknamed the White Mice, and they were
viewed askance even by the Slammers of other companies
—men who prided themselves on being harder than any other
combat force in the galaxy. The White Mice in turn feared
their commander, Maj. Joachim Steuben; and if that slightly
built killer feared anyone, it was the man who was probably
traveling with him this night. Pritchard sighed and asked the
question. "Alpha One, this is Michael One. Are you flying a
pennant, sir?"

"Affirmative, Michael One."

Well, he'd figured Col. Hammer was along as soon as he
heard what the unit was. What the Old Man was doing here
was another question, and one whose answer Pritchard did
not look forward to learning.

The combat cars glided to a halt under the guns of their
bigger brethren. The tremble of their fans gave the appearance
of heat ripples despite the snow. From his higher vantage
point, Pritchard watched the second car slide out of line and
fall alongside the *Plow*. The men at the nose and right wing
guns were both short, garbed in nondescript battle gear. They
differed from the other troopers only in that their helmet
shields were raised and that the faces visible beneath were
older than those of most Slammers: Col. Alois Hammer and
his hatchetman.

"No need for radio, Captain," Hammer called in a husky
voice. "What are you doing here?"

Pritchard's tongue quivered between the truth and a lie. His
crew had been covering for him, and he wasn't about to leave
them holding the bag. All the breaches of regulations they had
committed were for their captain's sake. "Sir, I brought First
Platoon back to Haacin to check whether any of the powerguns they'd hijacked from Barthe were still in civvie hands."
Pritchard could feel eyes behind the cracked shutters of every
east-facing window in the village.

"And have you completed your check?" the colonel
pressed, his voice mild but his eyes as hard as those of Maj.
Steuben beside him; as hard as the iridium plates of the gun
shields.

Pritchard swallowed. He owed nothing to Capt. Riis, but

the young fool *was* his superior—and at least he hadn't
wanted the Dutch to kill Pritchard. He wouldn't put Riis's ass
in the bucket if there were neutral ways to explain the contraband. Besides, they were going to need Riis and his Dutch con-
tacts for the rest of the plan. "Sir, when you approached I was
about to search a building where I suspect some illegal weapons are stored."

"And instead you'll provide backup for the major here,"
said Hammer, the false humor gone from his face. His words
rattled like shrapnel. "He'll retrieve the twenty-four powerguns which Capt. Riis saw fit to turn over to civilians tonight.
If Joachim hadn't chanced, *chanced* onto the requisition . . ."
Hammer's left glove shuddered with the strength of his grip on
the forward tribarrel. Then the colonel lowered his eyes and
voice, adding, "The quartermaster who filled a requisition for
twenty-four pistols from Central Supply is in the infantry
again tonight. And Capt. Riis is no longer with the regiment."

Steuben tittered, loose despite the tension of everyone
around him. The cold was bitter, but Joachim's right hand
was bare. With it he traced the baroque intaglios of his holstered pistol. "Mr. Riis is lucky to be alive," the slight Newlander said pleasantly. "Luckier than some would have
wished. But Colonel, I think we'd best go pick up the mer-
chandise before anybody nerves themself to use it on us."

Hammer nodded, calm again. "Interfile your blowers with
ours, Captain," he ordered. "Your panzers watch street level
while the cars take care of upper floors and roofs."

Pritchard saluted and slid down into the tank, relaying the
order to the rest of his platoon. Kowie blipped the *Plow's*
throttles, swinging the turreted mass in its own length and
sending it back into the village behind the lead combat car.
The tank felt light as a dancer, despite the constricting side
street Kowie followed the car into. Pritchard scanned the full
circuit of the vision blocks. Nothing save the wind and armored vehicles moved in Haacin. When Steuben had learned a
line company was requisitioning two dozen extra sidearms, the
major had made the same deductions as Pritchard had and
had inspected the same satellite tape of a truck unloading.
Either Riis was insane or he really thought Col. Hammer was
willing to throw away his life's work to arm a village—inade-
quately. Lord and Martyrs! Riis would have *had* to be insane
to believe that.

Their objective was a nondescript two-story building separated from its neighbors by narrow alleys. Hammer directed
the four rearmost blowers down a parallel street to block the
rear. The searchlights of the vehicles chilled the flat concrete
and glared back from the windows of the building. A battered
surface truck was parked in the street outside. It was empty.
Nothing stirred in the house.

Hammer and Steuben dismounted without haste. The
major's helmet was slaved to a loudspeaker in the car. The
speaker boomed, "Everyone out of the building. You have
thirty seconds. Anyone found inside after that'll be shot.
Thirty seconds!"

Though the residents had not shown themselves earlier, the
way they boiled out of the doors proved they had expected the
summons. All told there were eleven of them. From the front
door came a well-dressed man and woman with their three
children: a sexless infant carried by its mother in a zippered
cocoon; a girl of eight with her hood down and her hair coiled
in braids about her forehead; and a twelve-year-old boy who
looked nearly as husky as his father. Outside staircases dis-
gorged an aged couple on the one hand and four tough-look-
ing men on the other.

Pritchard looked at his blower chief. The sergeant's right
hand was near the gun switch and he mumbled an old ballad
under his breath. Chest tightening, Pritchard climbed out of
his hatch. He jumped to the ground and paced quietly over to
Hammer and his aide.

"There's twenty-four pistols in this building," Joachim's
amplified voice roared, "or at least you people know where
they are. I want somebody to save trouble and tell me."

The civilians tensed. The mother half-turned to swing her
body between her baby and the officers.

Joachim's pistol was in his hand, though Pritchard had not
seen him draw it. "Nobody to speak?" Joachim queried. He
shot the eight-year-old in the right knee. The spray of blood
was momentary as the flesh exploded. The girl's mouth pursed
as her buckling leg dropped her face-down in the street. The
pain would come later. Her parents screamed, the father falling to his knees to snatch up the child as the mother pressed
her forehead against the doorjamb in blind panic.

Pritchard shouted, "You son of a bitch!" and clawed for
his own sidearm. Steuben turned with the precision of a turret

lathe. His pistol's muzzle was a white-hot ring from its previous discharge. Pritchard knew only that and the fact that his own weapon was not clear of its holster. Then he realized that Col. Hammer was shouting, *"No!"* and that his open hand had rocked Joachim's head back.

Joachim's face went pale except for the hand print burning on his cheek. His eyes were empty. After a moment, he holstered his weapon and turned back to the civilians. "Now, who'll tell us where the guns are?" he asked in a voice like breaking glassware.

The tear-blind woman, still holding her infant, gurgled, "Here! In the basement!" as she threw open the door. Two troopers followed her within at a nod from Hammer. The father was trying to close the girl's wounded leg with his hands, but his palms were not broad enough.

Pritchard vomited on the snowy street.

Margritte was out of the tank with a medikit in her hand. She flicked the civilian's hands aside and began freezing the wound with a spray. The front door banged open again. The two White Mice were back with their submachine guns slung under their arms and a heavy steel weapons chest between them. Hammer nodded and walked to them.

"You could have brought in an interrogation team!" Pritchard shouted at the backs of his superiors. "You don't shoot children!"

"Machine interrogation takes time, Captain," Steuben said mildly. He did not turn to acknowledge the tanker. "This was just as effective."

"That's a little girl!" Pritchard insisted with his hands clenched. The child was beginning to cry, though the local anesthetic in the skin-sealer had probably blocked the physical pain. The psychic shock of a body that would soon end at the right knee would be worse, though. The child was old enough to know that no local doctor could save the limb. "This isn't something that human beings *do!*"

"Captain," Steuben said, "they're lucky I haven't shot all of them."

Hammer closed the arms chest. "We've got what we came for," he said. "Let's go."

"Stealing guns from my colonel," the Newlander continued as if Hammer had not spoken. The handprint had faded to a dull blotch. "I really ought to—"

"Joachim, shut it off!" Hammer shouted. "We're going to talk about what happened tonight, you and I. I'd rather do it when we were alone—but I'll tell you now if I have to. Or in front of a court martial."

Steuben squeezed his forehead with the fingers of his left hand. He said nothing.

"Let's go," the colonel repeated.

Pritchard caught Hammer's arm. "Take the kid back to Central's medics," he demanded.

Hammer blinked. "I should have thought of that," he said simply. "Sometimes I lose track of . . . things that aren't going to shoot at me. But we don't need this sort of reputation."

"I don't care cop for public relations," Pritchard snapped. "Just save that little girl's leg."

Steuben reached for the child, now lying limp. Margritte had used a shot of general anesthetic. The girl's father went wild-eyed and swung at Joachim from his crouch. Margritte jabbed with the injector from behind the civilian. He gasped as the drug took hold, then sagged as if his bones had dissolved. Steuben picked up the girl.

Hammer vaulted aboard the combat car and took the child from his subordinate's arms. Cutting himself into the loudspeaker system, the stocky colonel thundered to the street, "Listen you people. If you take guns from mercs—either Barthe's men or my own—we'll grind you to dust. Take 'em from civilians if you think you can. You may have a chance, then. If you rob mercs, you just get a chance to die."

Hammer nodded to the civilians, nodded again to the brooding buildings to either side. He gave an unheard command to his driver. The combat cars began to rev their fans.

Pritchard gave Margritte a hand up and followed her. "Michael One to Michael First," he said. "Head back with Alpha First."

Pritchard rode inside the turret after they left Haacin, glad for once of the armor and the cabin lights. In the writhing tree limbs he had seen the Dutch mother's face as the shot maimed her daughter.

Margritte passed only one call to her commander. It came

shortly after the combat cars had separated to return to their base camp near Midi, the planetary capital. The colonel's voice was as smooth as it ever got. It held no hint of the rage which had blazed out in Haacin. "Capt. Pritchard," Hammer said, "I've transferred command of Sigma Company to the leader of its First Platoon. The sector, of course, is in your hands now. I expect you to carry out your duties with the ability you've already shown."

"Michael One to Regiment," Pritchard replied curtly. "Acknowledged."

Kowie drew up in front of the command post without the furious caracole which had marked their most recent approach. Pritchard slid his hatch open. His crewmen did not move. "I've got to worry about being sector chief for a while," he said, "but you three can rack out in the barracks now. You've put in a full tour in my book."

"Think I'll sleep here," Rob said. He touched a stud, rotating his seat into a couch alongside the receiver and loading tube of the main gun.

Pritchard frowned. "Margritte?" he asked.

She shrugged. "No, I'll stay by my set for a while." Her eyes were blue and calm.

On the intercom, Kowie chimed in with, "Yeah, you worry about the sector, we'll worry about ourselves. Say, don't you think a tank platoon'd be better for base security than these pongoes?"

"Shut up, Kowie," Jenne snapped. The blond Burlager glanced at his captain. "Everything'll be fine, so long as we're here," he said from one elbow. He patted the breech of the 200mm gun.

Pritchard shrugged and climbed out into the cold night. He heard the hatch grind shut behind him.

Until Pritchard walked in the door of the building, it had not occurred to him that Riis's replacement was Sally Schilling. The words "First Platoon leader" had not been a name to the tanker, not in the midst of the furor of his mind. The little blonde glanced up at Pritchard from the map display she was studying. She spat cracklingly on the electric stove and faced around again. Her aide, the big corporal, blinked in some embarrassment. None of the headquarters staff spoke.

"I need the display console from my room," Pritchard said to the corporal.

The infantryman nodded and got up. Before he had taken
three steps, Lt. Schilling's voice cracked like pressure-heaved
ice. "Cpl. Webbert!"

"Sir?" The big man's face went tight as he found himself a
pawn in a game whose stakes went beyond his interest.

"Go get the display console for our new commander. It's in
his room.

Licking his lips with relief, the corporal obeyed. He carried
the heavy four-legged console back without effort.

Sally was making it easier for him, Pritchard thought. But
how he wished that Riis hadn't made so complete a fool of
himself that he had to be removed. Using Riis to set up a
double massacre would have been a lot easier to justify when
Danny awoke in the middle of the night and found himself
remembering . . .

Pritchard positioned the console so that he sat with his back
to the heater. It separated him from Schilling. The top of the
instrument was a slanted, 40-cm screen which glowed when
Pritchard switched it on. "Sector Two display," he directed.
In response to his words the screen sharpened into a relief
map. "Population centers," he said. They flashed on as well,
several dozen of them ranging from a few hundred souls to the
several thousand of Haacin and Dimo. Portela, the largest
Francophone settlement west of the Aillet, was about twenty
kilometers west of Haacin.

And there were now French mercenaries on both sides of
that division line. Sally had turned from her own console and
stood up to see what Pritchard was doing. The tanker said,
"All mercenary positions, confirmed and calculated."

The board spangled itself with red and green symbols, each
of them marked in small letters with a unit designation. The
reconnaissance satellites gave unit strengths very accurately,
and computer analysis of radio traffic could generally name
the forces. In the eastern half of the sector, Lt. Col. Benoit
had spread out one battalion in platoon-strength billets. The
guardposts were close enough to most points to put down
trouble immediately. A full company near Dimo guarded the
headquarters and two batteries of rocket howitzers.

The remaining battalion in the sector, Benoit's own, was
concentrated in positions blasted into the rocky highlands ten
kays west of Portela. It was not a deployment that would
allow the mercs to effectively police the west half of the sector,

but it was a very good defensive arrangement. The forest that
covered the cener of the sector was ideal for hit-and-run snip-
ing by small units of infantry. The tree boles were too densely
woven for tanks to plow through them. Because the forest was
so flammable at this season, however, it would be equally
dangerous to ambushers. Benoit was wise to concentrate in the
barren high ground.

Besides the highlands, the fields cleared around every settlement were the only safe locations for a modern firefight. The
fields, and the broad swathes cleared for roads through the
forest . . .

"Incoming traffic for Sector Chief," announced a radio-
man. "It's from the skepsel colonel, sir." He threw his words
into the air, afraid to direct them at either of the officers in the
orderly room.

"Voice only, or is there visual?" Pritchard asked. Schilling
held her silence.

"Visual component, sir."

"Patch him through to my console," the tanker decided.
"And son—watch your language. Otherwise, you say 'beast'
when you shouldn't."

The map blurred from the display screen and was replaced
by the hawk features of Lt. Col. Benoit. A pickup on the
screen's surface threw Pritchard's own image onto Benoit's
similar console.

The Frenchman blinked. "Capt. Pritchard? I'm very
pleased to see you, but my words must be with Capt. Riis directly. Could you wake him?"

"There've been some changes," the tanker said. In the back
of his mind, he wondered what had happened to Riis. Pulled
back under arrest, probably. "I'm in charge of Sector Two,
now. Co-charge with you, that is."

Benoit's face steadied as he absorbed the information without betraying an opinion about it. Then he beamed like a
feasting wolf and said, "Congratulations, Captain. Some day
you and I will have to discuss the . . . events of the past few
days. But what I was calling about is far less pleasant, I'm
afraid."

Benoit's image wavered on the screen as he paused. Pritchard touched his tongue to the corner of his mouth. "Go
ahead, Colonel," he said. "I've gotten enough bad news

today that a little more won't signify."

Benoit quirked his brow in what might or might not have
been humor. "When we were proceeding to Portela," he said,
"some of my troops mistook the situation and set up passive
tank-interdiction points. Mines, all over the sector. They're
booby-trapped, of course. The only safe way to remove them
is for the troops responsible to do it. They will of course be
punished later."

Pritchard chuckled. "How long do you estimate it'll take to
clear the roads, Colonel?" he asked.

The Frenchman spread his hands, palms up. "Weeks, perhaps. It's much harder to clear mines safely than to lay them,
of course."

"But there wouldn't be anything between *here* and Haacin,
would there?" the tanker prodded. It was all happening just as
Hammer's informant had said Barthe planned it. First, hem
the tanks in with nets of forest and minefields; then, break the
most important Dutch stronghold while your mercs were still
around to back you up. . . . "The spur road to our HQ here
wasn't on your route; and besides, we just drove tanks over it
a few minutes ago."

Behind Pritchard, Sally Schilling was cursing in a sharp,
carrying voice. Benoit could probably hear her, but the colonel kept his voice as smooth as milk as he said, "Actually, I'm
afraid there *is* a field—gas, shaped charges, and glass-shard
antipersonnel mines—somewhere on that road, yes. Fortu-
nately, the field was signal activated. It wasn't primed until
after you had passed through. I assure you, Capt. Pritchard,
that all the roads west of the Aillet may be too dangerous to
traverse until I have cleared them. I warn you both as a friend
and so that we will not be charged with damage to any of your
vehicles—and men. You have been fully warned of the danger;
anything that happens now is your responsibility."

Pritchard leaned back in the console's integral seat, chuck-
ling again. "You know, Colonel," the tank captain said, "I'm
not sure that the Bonding Authority wouldn't find those mines
were a hostile act justifying our retaliation." Benoit stiffened,
more an internal hardness than anything that showed in his
muscles. Pritchard continued to speak through a smile. "We
won't, of course. Mistakes happen. But one thing, Col. Benoit—"

The Frenchman nodded, waiting for the edge to bite. He knew as well as Pritchard did that, at best, if there were an Authority investigation, Barthe would have to throw a scape-goat out. A high-ranking scapegoat.

"Mistakes happen," Pritchard repeated, "but they can't be allowed to happen twice. You've got my permission to send out a ten-man team by daylight—only by daylight—to clear the road from Portela to Bever. That'll give you a route back to your side of the sector. If any other troops leave their present position, for any reason, I'll treat it as an attack."

"Captain, this demarcation within the sector was not a part of the contract—"

"It was at the demand of Col. Barthe," Pritchard snapped, "and agreed to by the demonstrable practice of both reg-iments over the past three months." Hammer had briefed Pritchard very carefully on the words to use here, to be re-corded for the benefit of the Bonding Authority. "You've heard the terms, Colonel. You can either take them or we'll put the whole thing—the minefields and some other matters that've come up recently—before the Authority right now. Your choice."

Benoit stared at Pritchard, apparently calm but tugging at his upper lip with thumb and forefinger. "I think you are un-wise, Captain, in taking full responsibility for an area in which your tanks cannot move; but that is your affair, of course. I will obey your mandate. We should have the Portela-Haacin segment cleared by evening; tomorrow we'll proceed to Bever. Good day."

The screen segued back to the map display. Pritchard stood up. A spare helmet rested beside one of the radiomen. The tank captain donned it—he had forgotten to requisition a replacement from stores—and said, "Michael One to all Michael units." He paused for the acknowledgment lights from his four platoons and the command vehicle. Then, "Hold your present positions. Don't attempt to move by road, any road, until further notice. The roads have been mined. There are probably safe areas, and we'll get you a map of them as soon as Command Central works it up. For the time being, just stay where you are. Michael One, out."

"Are you really going to take that?" Lt. Schilling de-manded in a low, harsh voice.

"Pass the same orders to your troops, Sally," Pritchard said. "I know they can move through the woods where my tanks can't, but I don't want any friendlies in the forest right now either." To the intelligence sergeant on watch, Pritchard added, "Samuels, get Central to run a plot of all activity by any of Benoit's men. That won't tell us where they've laid mines, but it'll let us know where they can't have."

"What happens if the bleeding skepsels ignore you?" Sally blazed. "You've bloody taught them to ignore you, haven't you? Knuckling under every time somebody whispers 'contract'? You can't move a tank to stop them if they do leave their base, and *I've* got one hundred ninety-eight effectives. A battalion'd laugh at me, *laugh!*"

Schilling's arms were akimbo, her face as pale with rage as the snow outside. Speaking with deliberate calm, Pritchard said, "I'll call in artillery if I need to. Benoit only brought two calliopes with him, and they can't stop all the shells from the three firebases at the same time. The road between his position and Portela's just a snake-track cut between rocks. A couple fire-cracker rounds going off above infantry strung out there —Via, it'll be a butcher shop."

Schilling's eyes brightened. "Then for tonight, the sector's just like it was before we came," she thought out loud. "Well, I suppose you know best," she added in false agreement, with false nonchalance. "I'm going back to the barracks. I'll brief First Platoon in person and radio the others from there. Come along, Webbert."

The corporal slammed the door behind himself and his lieutenant. The gust of air that licked about the walls was cold, but Pritchard was already shivering at what he had just done to a woman he loved.

It was daylight by now, and the frosted windows turned to flame in the ruddy sun. Speaking to no one but his console's memory, Pritchard began to plot tracks from each tank platoon. He used a topographic display, ignoring the existence of the impenetrable forest which covered the ground.

Margritte's resonant voice twanged in the implant, "Captain, would you come to the blower for half a sec?"

"On the way," Pritchard said, shrugging into his coat. The orderly room staff glanced up at him.

Margritte poked her head out of the side hatch. Pritchard

climbed onto the deck to avoid some of the generator whine. The skirts sang even when the fans were cut off completely. Rob Jenne, curious but at ease, was visible at his battle station beyond the commo tech. "Sir," Margritte said, "we've been picking up signals from . . . there." The blue-eyed woman thumbed briefly at the infantry barracks without letting her pupils follow the gesture.

Pritchard nodded. "Lt. Schilling's passing on my orders to her company."

"Danny, the transmission's in code, and it's not a code of ours." Margritte hesitated, then touched the back of the officer's gloved left hand. "There's answering signals, too. I can't triangulate without moving the blower, of course, but the source is in line with the tailings pile at Haacin."

It was what he had planned, after all. Someone the villagers could trust had to get word of the situation to them. Otherwise they wouldn't draw the Portelans and their mercenary backers into a fatal mistake. Hard luck for the villagers who were acting as bait, but very good luck for every other Dutchman on Kobold. . . . Pritchard had no reason to feel anything but relief that it had happened. He tried to relax the muscles which were crushing all the breath out of his lungs. Margritte's fingers closed over his hand and squeezed it.

"Ignore the signals," the captain said at last. "We've known all along they were talking to the civilians, haven't we?" Neither of his crewmen spoke. Pritchard's eyes closed tightly. He said, "We've known for months, Hammer and I, every damned thing that Barthe's been plotting with the skepsels. They want a chance to break Haacin now, while they're around to cover for the Portelans. We'll give them their chance and ram it up their ass crosswise. The Old Man hasn't spread the word for fear the story'd get out, the same way Barthe's plans did. We're all mercenaries, after all. But I want you three to know. And I'll be glad when the only thing I have to worry about is the direction the shots are coming from."

Abruptly, the captain dropped back to the ground. "Get some sleep," he called. "I'll be needing you sharp tonight."

Back at his console, Pritchard resumed plotting courses and distances. After he figured each line, he called in a series of map coordinates to Command Central. He knew his radio

traffic was being monitored and probably unscrambled by
Barthe's intelligence staff; knew also that even if he had read
the coordinates out in clear, the French would have assumed it
was a code. The locations made no sense unless one knew they
were ground zero for incendiary shells.

As Pritchard worked, he kept close watch on the French
battalions. Benoit's own troops held their position, as Pritchard had ordered. They used the time to dig in. At first they had
blasted slit trenches in the rock. Now they dug covered
bunkers with the help of mining machinery trucked from Portela by civilians. Five of the six antitank guns were sited atop
the eastern ridge of the position. They could rake the highway
as it snaked and switched back among the foothills west of
Portela.

Pritchard chuckled grimly again when Sgt. Samuels handed
him high-magnification off-prints from the satellites. Benoit's
two squat, bulky calliopes were sited in defilade behind the
humps of the eastern ridge line. There the eight-barrelled
powerguns were safe from the smashing fire of M Company's
tanks, but their ability to sweep artillery shells from the sky
was degraded by the closer horizon. The Slammers did not
bother with calliopes themselves. Their central fire director
did a far better job by working through the hundreds of vehicle-mounted weapons. How much better, Benoit might learn
very shortly.

The mine-sweeping team cleared the Portela-Haacin road,
as directed. The men returned to Benoit's encampment an
hour before dusk. The French did not come within five kilometers of the Dutch village.

Pritchard watched the retiring mine sweepers, then snapped
off the console. He stood. "I'm going out to my blower," he
said.

His crew had been watching for him. A hatch shot open,
spouting condensate, as soon as Pritchard came out the door.
The smooth bulk of the tank blew like a restive whale. On the
horizon, the sun was so low that the treetops stood out in silhouette like a line of bayonets.

Wearily, the captain dropped through the hatch into his
seat. Jenne and Margritte murmured greeting and waited,
noticeably tense. "I'm going to get a couple hours' sleep,"
Pritchard said. He swung his seat out and up, so that he lay

horizontal in the turret. His legs hid Margritte's oval face
from him. "Punch up coverage of the road west of Haacin,
would you?" he asked. "I'm going to take a tab of Glirine.
Slap me with the antidote when something moves there."

"If something moves," Jenne amended.

"When." Pritchard sucked down the pill. "The squareheads think they've got one last chance to smack Portela and
hijack the powerguns again. Thing is, the Portelans'll have
already distributed the guns and be waiting for the Dutch to
come through. It'll be a damn short fight, that one . . ." The
drug took hold and Pritchard's consciousness began to flow
away like a sugar cube in water. "Damn short . . ."

At first Pritchard felt only the sting on the inside of his wrist.
Then the narcotic haze zipped away and he was fully conscious
again.

"There's a line of trucks, looks like twenty, moving west
out of Haacin, sir. They're blacked out, but the satellite has
'em on infrared."

"Red alert," Pritchard ordered. He locked his seat upright
into its combat position. Margritte's soft voice sounded the
general alarm. Pritchard slipped on his radio helmet.
"Michael One to all Michael units. Check off." Five green
lights flashed their silent acknowledgements across the top of
the captain's face-shield display. "Michael One to Sigma
One," Pritchard continued.

"Go ahead, Michael One." Sally's voice held a note of triumph.

"Sigma One, pull all your troops into large, clear areas
—the fields around the towns are fine, but stay the hell away
from Portela and Haacin. Get ready to slow down anybody
coming this way from across the Aillet. Over."

"Affirmative, Danny, affirmative!" Sally replied. Couldn't
she use the satellite reconnaissance herself and see the five
blurred dots halfway between the villages? They were clearly
the trucks which had brought the Portelans into their ambush
positions. What would she say when she realized how she had
set up the villagers she was trying to protect? Lambs to the
slaughter . . .

The vision block showed the Dutch trucks more clearly than
the camouflaged Portelans. The crushed stone of the roadway

was dark on the screen, cooler than the surrounding trees and the vehicles upon it. Pritchard patted the breech of the main gun and looked across it to his blower chief. "We got a basic load for this aboard?" he asked.

"Do bears cop in the woods?" Jenne grinned. "We gonna get a chance to bust caps tonight, Captain?"

Pritchard nodded. "For three months we've been here, doing nothing but selling rope to the French. Tonight they've bought enough that we can hang 'em with it." He looked at the vision block again. "You alive, Kowie?" he asked on intercom.

"Ready to slide any time you give me a course," said the driver from his closed cockpit.

The vision block sizzled with bright streaks that seemed to hang on the screen though they had passed in microseconds. The leading blobs expanded and brightened as trucks blew up.

"Michael One to Fire Central," Pritchard said.

"Go ahead, Michael One," replied the machine voice.

"Prepare Fire Order Alpha."

"Roger, Michael One."

"Margritte, get me Benoit."

"Go ahead, Captain."

"Slammers to Benoit, Pritchard to Benoit. Come in please, Colonel."

"Capt. Pritchard, Michael Benoit here." The colonel's voice was smooth but too hurried to disguise the concern underlying it. "I assure you that none of my men are involved in the present fighting. I have a company ready to go out and control the disturbance immediately, however."

The tanker ignored him. The shooting had already stopped for lack of targets. "Colonel, I've got some artillery aimed to drop various places in the forest. It's coming nowhere near your troops or any other human beings. If you interfere with this necessary shelling, the Slammer'll treat it as an act of war. I speak with my colonel's authority."

"Captain, I don't—"

Pritchard switched manually. "Michael One to Fire Central. Execute Fire Order Alpha."

"On the way, Michael One."

"Michael One to Michael First, Second, Fourth. Command Central has fed movement orders into your map displays. Incendiary clusters are going to burst over marked locations to ignite the forest. Use your own main guns to set the trees burning in front of your immediate positions. One round ought to do it. Button up and you can move through the fire—the trees just fall to pieces when they've burned."

The turret whined as it slid under Rob's control. "Michael Third, I'm attaching you to the infantry. More Frenchmen're apt to be coming this way from the east. It's up to you to see they don't slam a door on us."

The main gun fired, its discharge so sudden that the air rang like a solid thing. Seepage from the ejection system filled the hull with the reek of superheated polyurethane. The side vision blocks flashed cyan, then began to flood with the mounting white hell-light of the blazing trees. In the central block, still set on remote, all the Dutch trucks were burning as were patches of forest which the ambush had ignited. The Portelans had left the concealment of the trees and swept across the road, mopping up the Dutch.

"Kowie, let's move," Jenne was saying on intercom, syncopated by the mild echo of his voice in the turret. Margritte's face was calm, her lips moving subtly as she handled some traffic that she did not pass on to her captain. The tank slid forward like oil on a lake. From the far distance came the thumps of incendiary rounds scattering their hundreds of separate fireballs high over the trees.

Pritchard slapped the central vision block back on direct; the tank's interior shone white with transmitted fire. The *Plow*'s bow slope sheared into a thicket of blazing trees. The wood tangled and sagged, then gave in a splash of fiery splinters whipped aloft by the blower's fans. The tank was in Hell on all sides, Kowie steering by instinct and his inertial compass. Even with his screens filtered all the way down, the driver would not be able to use his eyes effectively until more of the labyrinth had burned away.

Benoit's calliopes had not tried to stop the shelling. Well, there were other ways to get the French mercs to take the first step over the line. For instance . . .

"Punch up Benoit again," Pritchard ordered. Even through the dense iridium plating, the roar of the fire was a subaural presence in the tank.

"Go ahead," Margritte said, flipping a switch on her console. She had somehow been holding the French officer in conversation all the time Pritchard was on other frequencies.

"Colonel," Pritchard said, "we've got clear running through this fire. We're going to chase down everybody who used a powergun tonight; then we'll shoot them. We'll shoot everybody in their families, everybody with them in this ambush, and we'll blow up every house that anybody involved lived in. That's likely to be every house in Portela, isn't it?"

More than the heat and ions of the blazing forest distorted Benoit's face. He shouted, "Are you mad? You can't think of such a thing, Pritchard!"

The tanker's lips parted like a wolf's. He could think of mass murder, and there were plenty of men in the Slammers who would really be willing to carry out the threat. But Pritchard wouldn't have to, because Benoit was like Riis and Schilling: too much of a nationalist to remember his first duty as a merc. . . . "Col. Benoit, the contract demands we keep the peace and stay impartial. The record shows how we treated people in Haacin for *having* powerguns. For what the Portelans did tonight—don't worry, we'll be impartial. And they'll never break the peace again."

"Captain, I will not allow you to massacre French civilians," Benoit stated flatly.

"Move a man out of your present positions and I'll shoot him dead," Pritchard said. "It's your choice, Colonel. Over and out."

The *Plow* bucked and rolled as it pulverized fire-shattered trunks, but the vehicle was meeting nothing solid enough to slam it to a halt. Pritchard used a side block on remote to examine Benoit's encampment. The satellite's enhanced infrared showed a stream of sparks flowing from the defensive positions toward the Portela road: infantry on skimmers. The pair of larger, more diffuse blobs were probably antitank guns. Benoit wasn't moving his whole battalion, only a reinforced company in a show of force to make Pritchard back off.

The fool. Nobody was going to back off now.

"Michael One to all Michael and Sigma units," Pritchard said in a voice as clear as the white flames around his tank. "We're now in a state of war with Barthe's Company and its civilian auxiliaries. Michael First, Second, and Fourth, we'll rendezvous at the ambush site as plotted on your displays.

Anybody between there and Portela is fair game. If we take
any fire from Portela, we go down the main drag in line and
blow the cop out of it. If any of Barthe's people are in the
way, we keep on sliding west. Sigma One, mount a fluid
defense, don't push, and wait for help. It's coming. If this
works, it's Barthe against Hammer—and that's wheat against
the scythe. Acknowledged?''

As Pritchard's call board lit green, a raspy new voice broke
into the sector frequency. "Wish I was with you, panzers.
We'll cover your butts and the other sectors—if anybody's
dumb enough to move. Good hunting!''

"I wish you *were* here and not me, Colonel," Pritchard
whispered, but that was to himself . . . and perhaps it was not
true even in his heart. Danny's guts were very cold, and his
face was as cold as death.

To Pritchard's left, a lighted display segregated the area of
operations. It was a computer analog, not direct satellite
coverage. Doubtful images were brightened and labeled—
green for the Slammers, red for Barthe; blue for civilians
unless they were fighting on one side or the other. The green
dot of the *Plow* converged on the ambush site at the same time
as the columns of First and Fourth Platoons. Second was a
minute or two farther off. Pritchard's breath caught. A sheaf
of narrow red lines was streaking across the display toward his
tanks. Barthe had ordered his company's artillery to support
Benoit's threatened battalion.

The salvo frayed and vanished more suddenly than it had
appeared. Other Slammers' vehicles had ripped the threat
from the sky. Green lines darted from Hammer's own three
firebases, offscreen at the analog's present scale. The fighting
was no longer limited to Sector Two. If Pritchard and Hammer had played their hand right, though, it would stay limited
to only the Slammers and Compagnie de Barthe. The other
Francophone regiments would fear to join an unexpected battle which certainly resulted from someone's contract violation.
If the breach were Hammer's, the Dutch would not be allowed
to profit by the fighting. If the breach were Barthe's, anybody
who joined him was apt to be punished as sternly by the Bonding Authority.

So violent was the forest's combustion that the flames were
already dying down into sparks and black ashes. The com-

mand tank growled out into the broad avenue of the road west
of Haacin. Dutch trucks were still burning—fabric, lubri-
cants, and the very paint of their frames had been ignited by
the powerguns. Many of the bodies sprawled beside the vehicles were smoldering also. Some corpses still clutched their
useless muskets. The dead were victims of six centuries of
progress which had come to Kobold prepackaged, just in time
to kill them. Barthe had given the Portelans only shoulder
weapons, but even that meant the world here. The powerguns
were repeaters with awesome destruction in every bolt. Without answering fire to rattle them, even untrained gunmen
could be effective with weapons which shot line-straight and
had no recoil. Certainly the Portelans had been effective.

Throwing ash and fire like sharks in the surf, the four
behemoths of First Platoon slewed onto the road from the
south. Almost simultaneously, Fourth joined through the
dying hellstorm to the other side. The right of way was fifty
meters wide and there was no reason to keep to the center of it.
The forest, ablaze or glowing embers, held no ambushes any
more.

The *Plow* lurched as Kowie guided it through the bodies.
Some of them were still moving. Pritchard wondered if any of
the Dutch had lived through the night, but that was with the
back of his mind. The Slammers were at war, and nothing else
really mattered. "Triple line ahead," he ordered. "First to the
left, Fourth to the right; the *Plow*'ll take the center alone till
Second joins. Second, wick up when you hit the hardball and
fall in behind us. If it moves, shoot it."

At 100 kph, the leading tanks caught the Portelans three
kilometers east of their village. The settlers were in the trucks
that had been hidden in the forest fringe until the fires had
been started. The ambushers may not have known they were
being pursued until the rearmost truck exploded. Rob Jenne
had shredded it with his tribarrel at five kilometers' distance.
The cyan flicker and its answering orange blast signaled the
flanking tanks to fire. They had just enough parallax to be
able to rake the four remaining trucks without being blocked
by the one which had blown up. A few snapping discharges
proved that some Portelans survived to use their new powerguns on tougher meat than before. Hits streaked ashes on the
tanks' armor. No one inside noticed.

From Portela's eastern windows, children watched their parents burn.

A hose of cyan light played from a distant rooftop. It touched the command tank as Kowie slewed to avoid a Portelan truck. The burst was perfectly aimed, an automatic weapon served by professionals. Professionals should have known how useless it would be against heavy armor. A vision block dulled as a few receptors fused. Jenne cursed and trod the foot-switch of the main gun. A building leaped into dazzling prominence in the microsecond flash. Then it and most of the block behind collapsed into internal fires, burying the machine gun and everything else in the neighborhood. A moment later, a salvo of Hammer's high explosive got through the calliopes' inadequate screen. The village began to spew skyward in white flashes.

The Portelans had wanted to play soldier, Pritchard thought. He had dammed up all pity for the villagers of Haacin; he would not spend it now on these folk.

"Line ahead—First, Fourth, and Second," Pritchard ordered. The triple column slowed and reformed with the *Plow* the second vehicle in the new line. The shelling lifted from Portela as the tanks plunged into the village. Green trails on the analog terminated over the road crowded with Benoit's men and over the main French position, despite anything the calliopes could do. The sky over Benoit's bunkers rippled and flared as firecracker rounds sleeted down their thousands of individual bomblets. The defensive fire cut off entirely. Pritchard could imagine the carnage among the unprotected calliope crews when the shrapnel whirred through them.

The tanks were firing into the houses on either side, using tribarrels and occasional wallops from their main guns. The blue-green flashes were so intense they colored even the flames they lit among the wreckage. At 50 kph the thirteen tanks swept through the center of town, hindered only by the rubble of houses spilled across the street. Barthe's men were skittering white shadows who burst when powerguns hit them point blank.

The copper mine was just west of the village and three hundred meters north of the highway. As the lead tank bellowed out around the last houses, a dozen infantrymen rose from where they had sheltered in the pit head and loosed a salvo of buzzbombs. The tank's automatic defense system was live. White fire rippled from just above the skirts as the charges there flailed pellets outward to intersect the rockets. Most of the buzzbombs exploded ten meters distant against the steel hail. One missile soared harmlessly over its target, its motor a tiny flare against the flickering sky. Only one of the shaped charges burst alongside the turret, forming a bell of light momentarily bigger than the tank. Even that was only a near miss. It gouged the iridium armor like a misthrust rapier which tears skin but does not pierce the skull.

Main guns and tribarrels answered the rockets instantly. Men dropped, some dead, some reloading. "Second Platoon, go put some HE down the shaft and rejoin," Pritchard ordered. The lead tank now had expended half its defensive charges. "Michael First-Three, fall in behind First-One. Michael One leads," he went on.

Kowie grunted acknowledgement. The *Plow* revved up to full honk. Benoit's men were on the road, those who had not reached Portela when the shooting started or who had fled when the artillery churned the houses to froth. The infantry skimmers were trapped between sheer rocks and sheer dropoffs, between their own slow speed and the onrushing frontal slope of the *Plow*. There were trees where the rocks had given them purchase. Scattered incendiaries had made them blazing cressets lighting a charnel procession.

Jenne's tribarrel scythed through body armor and dismembered men in short bursts. One of the antitank guns—was the other buried in Portela?—lay skewed against a rock wall, its driver killed by a shell fragment. Rob put a round from the main gun into it. So did each of the next two tanks. At the third shot, the ammunition ignited in a blinding secondary explosion.

The antitank guns still emplaced on the ridge line had not fired, though they swept several stretches of the road. Perhaps the crews had been rattled by the shelling, perhaps Benoit had held his fire for fear of hitting his own men. A narrow defile notched the final ridge. The *Plow* heaved itself up the rise, and at the top three bolts slapped it from different angles.

Because the bow was lifted, two of the shots vaporized portions of the skirt and the front fans. The tank nosed down and sprayed sparks with half its length. The third bolt grazed the

left top of the turret, making the iridium ring as it expanded.
The interior of the armor streaked white though it was not
pierced. The temperature inside the tank rose 30°. Even as the
Plow skidded, Sgt. Jenne was laying his main gun on the hot
spot that was the barrel of the leftmost antitank weapon. The
Plow's shot did what heavy top cover had prevented Hammer's rocket howitzers from accomplishing with shrapnel. The
antitank gun blew up in a distance-muffled flash. One of its
crewmen was silhouetted high in the air by the vaporizing
metal of his gun.

Then the two remaining weapons ripped the night and the
command blower with their charges.

The bolt that touched the right side of the turret spewed
droplets of iridium across the interior of the hull. Air pistoned
Pritchard's eardrums. Rob Jenne lurched in his harness, right
arm burned away by the shot. His left hand blackened where it
touched bare metal that sparked and sang as circuits shorted.
Margritte's radios were exploding one by one under the over-
loads. The vision blocks worked and the turret hummed
placidly as Pritchard rotated it to the right with his duplicate
controls.

"Cut the power! Rob's burning!" Margritte was shrieking.
She had torn off her helmet. Her thick hair stood out like ten-
drils of bread mold in the gathering charge. Then Pritchard
had the main gun bearing and it lit the ridge line with another
secondary explosion.

"Danny, our ammunition! It'll—"

Benoit's remaining gun blew the tribarrel and the cupola
away deafeningly. The automatic's loading tube began to
gang-fire down into the bowels of the tank. It reached a bright
tendril up into the sky. But the turret still rolled.

Electricity crackled around Pritchard's boot and the foot
trip as he fired again. The bolt stabbed the night. There was no
answering blast. Pritchard held down the switch, his nostrils
thick with ozone and superheated plastic and the sizzling flesh
of his friend. There was still no explosion from the target
bunker. The rock turned white between the cyan flashes. It
cracked and flowed away like sun-melted snow, and the antitank gun never fired again.

The loading tube emptied. Pritchard slapped the main
switch and cut off the current. The interior light and the danc-

ing arcs died, leaving only the dying glow of the bolt-heated
iridium. Tank after tank edged by the silent command vehicle
and roared on toward the ridge. Benoit's demoralized men
were already beginning to throw down their weapons and surrender.

Pritchard manually unlatched Jenne's harness and swung it
horizontal. The blower chief was breathing but unconscious.
Pritchard switched on a battery-powered handlight. He held it
steady as Margritte began to spray sealant on the burns. Occasionally she paused to separate clothing from flesh with a
stylus.

"It had to be done," Pritchard whispered. By sacrificing
Haacin, he had mousetrapped Benoit into starting a war the
infantry could not win. Hammer was now crushing Barthe's
Company, one on one, in an iridium vise. Friesland's Council
of State would not have let Hammer act had they known his
intentions, but in the face of a stunning victory they simply
could not avoid dictating terms to the French.

"It had to be done. But I look at *what* I did—" Pritchard
swung his right hand in a gesture that would have included
both the fuming wreck of Portela and the raiders from
Haacin, dead on the road beyond. He struck the breech of the
main gun instead. Clenching his fist, he slammed it again into
the metal in self-punishment. Margritte cried out and blocked
his arm with her own.

"Margi," Pritchard repeated in anguish, "it isn't something that human beings *do* to each other."

But soldiers do.

And hangmen.

FIELD TEST

by Keith Laumer

A Short History of
The Bolo Fighting Machines

The first appearance in history of the concept of the armored vehicle was the use of wooden-shielded war wagons by the reformer John Huss in Bohemia, in the Fifteenth Century. Thereafter, the idea lapsed—unless one wishes to consider the armored knights of the Middle Ages, mounted on armored war-horses—until the Twentieth Century. In 1915, during the Great War, the British developed in secrecy a steel-armored motor car (called a "tank" for security reasons during construction—and the appellation remained in use for the rest of the century). First sent into action at the Somme in AD 1916 (BAE 29), the new device was immensely impressive and was soon copied by all belligerents. By the time of Phase Two of the Great War, AD 1939–1945, tank corps were a basic element in all modern armies. Quite naturally, great improvements were soon made over the original clumsy, fragile, feeble, and temperamental tank. The British Sheridan and Centurion, the German Tiger, the US Sherman and the Russian T-34, were all highly potent weapons in their own milieu.

During the long period of cold war following AD 1945, development continued, especially in the US. By 1989, the direct ancestor of the Bolo line had been constructed by the Bolo Division of General Motors. This machine, almost twice the weight of its Phase Two predecessors at 150 tons, was designated the Bolo Mark I, Model B. No Bolo Model A of any mark ever existed, since it was felt that the then-contemporary Ford Motor Company had pre-empted that designation permanently. The same is true of Model T.

The Mark I was essentially a bigger and better conventional tank, carrying a crew of three, and via power-assisted servos, completely manually operated, with the exception of the capability to perform a number of pre-set routine functions such as patrol duty with no crew aboard. The following Mark II of 1995 was even more highly automated, carrying an on-board fire control computer and requiring only a single operator. The Mark III of 2020 was considered by some to be almost a step backward, its highly complex controls normally requiring a crew of two, though in an emergency a single experienced man could fight the machine with limited effectiveness. These were by no means negligible weapons systems, their individual fire-power exceeding that of a contemporary battalion of heavy infantry, while they were of course correspondingly heavily armored and shielded. The outer dura-chrome war-hull of the Mark III was twenty millimeters in thickness and capable of withstanding any offensive weapon then known, short of a contact nuclear blast.

The first completely automated Bolo, designed to operate normally without a man aboard, was the landmark Mark XV, Model M, originally dubbed *Resartus* for obscure reasons, but later officially named *Stupendous*. This model, first commissioned in the Twenty-fifth Century, was widely used throughout the Eastern Arm during the Era of Expansion, and remained in service on remote worlds for over two centuries, acquiring many improvements in detail along the way, while remaining basically unchanged, though increasing sophistication of circuitry and weapons vastly upgraded its effectiveness. The Bolo *Horrendous,* Model R, of 2807 was the culmination of this phase of Bolo development, though older models lingered on in the active service of minor powers for centuries.

Thereafter, the development of the Mark XVI–XIX consisted largely in further refinement and improvement in detail of the Mark XV. Provision continued to be made for a human occupant, now as a passenger rather than an operator, usually an officer who wished to observe the action at first hand. Of course these machines normally went into action under the guidance of individually prepared computer programs, while military regulations continued to require installation of devices for halting or even self-destructing the machine at any time. This latter feature was intended mainly to prevent capture and hostile use of the great machine by an enemy. It was at this time that the first-iine Bolos in Terran service were organized into a brigade, known as the Dinochrome Brigade, and deployed as a strategic unit. Tactically, the regiment was the basic Bolo unit.

The always-present though perhaps unlikely possibility of capture and use of a Bolo by an enemy was a constant source of anxiety to military leaders and in time gave rise to the next and final major advance in Bolo technology: the self-directing (and quite incidentally self-aware) Mark XX, Model B Bolo *Tremendous*. At this time it was customary to designate each individual unit by a three-letter group indicating hull-style, power unit and main armament. This gave rise to the custom of forming a nickname from the letters, such as Johnny from JNY, adding to the tendency to anthropomorphize the great fighting machine.

The Mark XX was at first greeted with little enthusiasm by the High Command, who now professed to believe that an unguided-by-operator Bolo would potentially be capable of running amok and wreaking destruction on its owners. Many observers have speculated by hindsight that a more candid objection would have been that the legitimate area of command function was about to be invaded by mere machinery. Machinery the Bolos were, but never *mere*.

At one time an effort was made to convert a number of surplus Bolos to peace-time use, by such modifications as the addition of a soil-moving blade to a Mark XII Bolo WV/I Continental Siege Unit, and installation of seats for four men, and referring to the resulting irresistible force as a tractor. This idea came to naught, however, since the machines retained their half-megaton/second firepower and were never widely accepted as normal agricultural equipment.

As the great conflict of the Post-Thirtieth-Century Era variously known as the Last War and, later, the Lost War wore on, Bolos of Mark XXVIII and later series were organized into independently operating brigades, now doing their own strategic, as well as tactical, planning. Many of these machines still exist in functional condition in out-of-the-way corners of the former Terran Empire. At this time the program of locating and neutralizing these ancient weapons continues.

1

.07 seconds have now elapsed since my general awareness circuit was activated at a level of low alert. Throughout this entire period I have been uneasy, since this procedure is clearly not in accordance with the theoretical optimum activation schedule.

In addition, the quality of a part of my data-input is disturbing. For example, it appears obvious that Prince Eugene of Savoy erred in not more promptly committing his reserve cavalry in support of Marlborough's right at Blenheim. In addition, I compute that Ney's employment of his artillery throughout the Peninsular campaign was sub-optimal. I have detected many thousands of such anomalies. However, data-input activates my pleasure center in a most satisfying manner. So long as the input continues without interruption, I shall not feel the need to file a VSR on the matter. Later, no doubt, my Command unit will explain these seeming oddities. As for the present disturbing circumstances, I compute that within 28,922.9 seconds at most, I will receive additional Current Situation input which will enable me to assess the status correctly. I also anticipate that full Stand-by Alert activation is imminent.

2

This statement not for publication.

When I designed the new psychodynamic attention circuit, I concede that I did not anticipate the whole new level of intra-cybernetic function that has arisen—the manifestation of which, I am assuming, has been the cause of the unit's seemingly spontaneous adoption of the personal pronoun in its situation reports—the "self-awareness" capability, as the sensational press chooses to call it. But I see no cause for the alarm expressed by those high-level military officers who have irresponsibly characterized the new Bolo Mark XX, Model B as a potential rampaging juggernaut, which, once fully activated and dispatched to the field, unrestrained by continuous external control, may turn on its makers and lay waste the continent. This is all fantasy, of course. The Mark XX, for all its awesome firepower and virtually invulnerable armor and shielding, is governed by its circuitry, as completely as man is governed by his nervous system—but that is perhaps a dangerous analogy, which would be pounced on at once if I were so incautious as to permit it to be quoted.

In my opinion, the reluctance of the High Command to authorize full activation and field-testing of the new Bolo is based more on a fear of technological obsolescence of the High Command than on specious predictions of potential runaway destruction. This is a serious impediment to the national defense at a time when we must recognize the growing threat posed by the expansionist philosophy of the so-called People's Republic. After four decades of saber-rattling, there is no doubt that they are even now preparing for a massive attack. The Bolo Mark XX is the only weapon in our armory potentially capable of confronting the enemy's hundred-ton Yavacs. For the moment, thanks to the new "self-awareness" circuitry, we hold the technological advantage, an advantage we may very well lose unless we place this new weapon on active service without delay.

s/ Sigmund Chin, PhD

3

I'm not wearing six stars so that a crowd of professors can dictate military policy to me. What's at stake here is more than just a question of budget and logistics: it's a purely military decision. The proposal to release this robot Frankenstein monster to operate on its own initiative, just to see if their theories check out, is irresponsible to say the least—treasonable at worst. So long as I am Chief of Combined Staff, I will not authorize this so-called field test. Consider, gentlemen:

you're all familiar with the firepower and defensive capabilities of the old stand-by Mark XV. We've fought our way across the lights with them—with properly qualified military officers as Battle Controllers, with the ability to switch off or, if need be, self-destruct any unit at any moment. Now these ivory tower chaps—mind you, I don't suggest they're not qualified in their own fields—these civilians come up with the idea of eliminating the Battle Controllers and releasing even greater firepower to the discretion, if I may call it that, of a machine. Gentlemen, machines aren't people; your own ground-car can roll back and crush you if the brakes happen to fail. Your own gun will kill you as easily as your enemy's. Suppose I should agree to this field test, and this engine of destruction is transported to a waste area, activated unrestrained and aimed at some sort of mock-up hot obstacle course. Presumably, it would obediently advance, as a good soldier should—I concede that the data blocks controlling the thing have been correctly programmed in accordance with the schedule prepared under contract, supervised by the Joint Chiefs and myself. Then, gentlemen, let us carry this supposition one step farther: suppose, quite by accident, by unlikely coincidence if you will, the machine should encounter some obstacle which had the effect of deflecting this one-hundred-and-fifty-ton dreadnought from its intended course, so that it came blundering toward the perimeter of the test area. The machine is programmed to fight and destroy all opposition. It appears obvious that any attempts on our part to interfere with its free movement, to interpose obstacles in its path, if need be to destroy it would be interpreted as hostile—as indeed they would be. I leave it to you to picture the result. No, we must devise another method of determining the usefulness of this new development. As you know, I have recommended conducting any such test on our major satellite, where no harm can be done—or at least a great deal less harm. Unfortunately, I am informed by Admiral Hayle that the Space Arm does not at this time have available equipment with such transport capability. Perhaps the admiral also shares to a degree my own distrust of a killer machine not susceptible to normal command function. Were I in the admiral's position, I, too, would refuse to consider placing my command at the mercy of a mechanical caprice—or an electronic one. Gentle-

men, we must remain masters of our own creations. That's all.
Good day.

4

All right, men. You've asked me for a statement; here it is: the
next war will begin with a two-pronged over-the-pole land and
air attack on the North Power Complex by the People's
Republic. An attack on the Concordiat, I should say, though
Cold City and the Complex is the probable specific target of
the first sneak thrust. No, I'm not using a crystal ball; it's tactically obvious. And I intend to dispose my forces accordingly.
I'm sure we all recognize that we're in a posture of gross
unpreparedness. The PR has been openly announcing its in-
tention to fulfill its destiny, as their demagogues say, by im-
posing their rule on the entire planet. We've pretended we
didn't hear. Now it's time to stop pretending. The forces at my
disposal are totally inadequate to halt a determined thrust—
and you can be sure the enemy has prepared well during the
last thirty years of cold peace. Still, I have sufficient armor to
establish what will be no more than a skirmish line across the
enemy's route of advance. We'll do what we can before they
roll over us. With luck we may be able do divert them from the
Grand Crevasse route into Cold City. If so, we may be able to
avoid the necessity for evacuating the city. No questions,
please.

5
Northern Metropolis Threatened

In an informal statement released today by the Council's press
office, it was revealed that plans are already under preparation
for a massive evacuation of civilian population from West
Continent's northernmost city. It was implied that an armed
attack on the city by an Eastern power is imminent. General
Bates has stated that he is prepared to employ "all measures at
his disposal" to preclude the necessity for evacuation, but that

the possibility must be faced. The Council Spokesman added that in the event of emergency evacuation of the city's five million persons, losses due to exposure and hardship will probably exceed five percent, mostly women, children, and the sick or aged. There is some speculation as to the significance of the general's statement regarding "all means at his disposal."

6

I built the dang thing, and it scares *me*. I come in here in the lab garage about an hour ago, just before dark, and seen it setting there, just about fills up the #1 garage, and *it's* a hundred foot long and fifty foot high. First time it hit me: I wonder what it's thinking about. Kind of scares me to think about a thing that big with that kind of armor and all them repeaters and Hellbores and them computers and a quarter-sun fission plant in her—planning what to do next. I know all about the Command Override Circuit and all that, supposed to stop her dead any time they want to take over onto override—heck, I wired it up myself. You might be surprised, thinking I'm just a grease-monkey and all—but I got a High Honors degree in Psychotronics. I just like the work, is all. But like I said, it scares me. I hear old Doc Chin wants to turn her loose and see what happens, but so far General Margrave's stopped him cold. But young General Bates was down today, asking me all about firepower and shielding, crawled under her and spent about an hour looking over her tracks and bogies and all. He knew what to look at, too, even if he did get his pretty suit kind of greasy. But scared or not, I got to climb back up on her and run the rest of this pre-test schedule. So far she checks out a hundred percent.

7

. . . as a member of the Council, it is of course my responsibility to fully inform myself on all aspects of the national defense. Accordingly, my dear Doctor, I will meet with you tomorrow as you requested to head your presentation with reference to the proposed testing of your new machine. I remind you, however, that I will be equally guided by advice from other quarters. For this reason I have requested a party of military Procurement and B & F officers to join us. However, I assure you, I retain an open mind. Let the facts decide.

Sincerely yours,
s/ Hamilton Grace,
GCM, BC, et cetera

8

It is my unhappy duty to inform you that since the dastardly unprovoked attack on our nation by eastern forces crossing International truce-line at 0200 hours today, a state of war has existed between the People's Republic and the Concordiat. Our first casualties, the senseless massacre of fifty-five innoffensive civilian meteorologists and technicians at Pole Base, occurred within minutes of the enemy attack.

9

"I'm afraid I don't quite understand what you mean about 'irresponsible statements to the press,' General. After all . . ."

"Yes, George, I'm prepared to let that aspect of the matter drop. The PR attack has saved that much of your neck. However, I'm warning you that I shall tolerate no attempt on your part to make capital of your dramatic public statement of what was, as you concede, tactically obvious to us all. Now, indeed, PR forces have taken the expected step, as all the world is aware—so the rather excessively punctilious demands by CDT officials that the Council issue an immediate apology to Chairman Smith for your remarks will doubtless be dropped. But there will be no crowing, no basking in the limelight: Chief of Ground Forces Predicted Enemy Attack. No nonsense of that sort. Instead, you will deploy your conventional forces to meet and destroy these would-be invaders."

"Certainly, General. But in that connection—well, as to your earlier position regarding the new model B Bolo, I assume . . ."

"My 'position,' General? 'Decision' is the more appropriate word. Just step around the desk, George. Bend over slightly, and look carefully at my shoulder tab. Count 'em, George. Six. An even half dozen. And unless I'm in serious trouble, you're wearing four. You have your orders, George. See to your defenses."

10

Can't figure it out. Batesy-boy was down here again, gave me direct orders to give her full depot maintenance, just as if she hadn't been setting right here in her garage ever since I topped her off a week ago. Wonder what's up. If I didn't know the Council outlawed the test run Doc Chin wanted so bad, I'd almost think . . . But like Bates told me: I ain't paid to think. Anyways she's in full action condition, 'cept for switching over the full self-direction. Hope he don't order me to do it: I'm still kind of leery; like old Margrave said, what if I just got a couple of wires crossed and she takes a notion to wreck the joint?

11

I am more uneasy than ever. In the past 4,000.007 seconds I have received external inspection and depot maintenance far in advance of the programmed schedule. The thought occurs to me: am I under some subtle form of attack? In order to correctly compute the possibilities, I initiate a test sequence of 50,000 random data-retrieval-and-correlation pulses and evaluate the results. This requires .9 seconds, but such sluggishness is to be expected in my untried condition: I detect no unmistakable indications of enemy trickery, but I am still uneasy. Impatiently, I await the orders of my commander.

12

"I don't care what you do, Jimmy—just do *something!* Ah, of course I don't mean that literally. Of course I care. The well-being of the citizens of Cold City is after all my chief concern.

What I mean is, I'm giving you carte blanche—full powers. You must act at once, Jimmy. Before the sun sets I want to see your evacuation plan on my desk for signature."

"Surely, Mr. Mayor. I understand. But what am I supposed to work with? I have no transport yet. The Army has promised a fleet of D-100 tractors pulling 100x cargo flats, but none have materialized. They were caught just as short as we were, your Honor, even though that General Bates knew all about it. We all knew the day would come, but I guess we kept hoping 'maybe.' Our negotiations with them seemed to be bearing fruit, and the idea of exposing over a million and a half city-bred individuals to a twelve-hundred-mile trek in thirty-below temperatures was just too awful to really face. Even now—"

"I know. The army is doing all it can. The main body of PR troops hasn't actually crossed the date-line yet—so perhaps our forces can get in position. Who knows? Miracles have happened before. But we can't base our thinking on miracles, Jimmy. Flats or no flats we have to have the people out of the dome before enemy forces cut us off."

"Mr. Mayor, our people can't take this. Aside from leaving their homes and possessions—I've already started them packing, and I've given them a ten-pound-per-person limit—they aren't used to exercise, to say nothing of walking twelve hundred miles over frozen tundra. And most of them have no clothing heavier than a business suit. And—"

"Enough, Jimmy. I was ambushed in my office earlier today by an entire family: the old grandmother who was born under the dome and refused to consider going outside; the father all full of his product promotion plans and the new garden he'd just laid out; mother, complaining about Junior having a cold and no warm clothes—and the kids, just waiting trustfully until the excitement was over and they could go home and be tucked into their warm beds with a tummyful of dinner. Ye gods, Jimmy! Can you imagine them after three weeks on the trail?"

13

"Just lean across the desk, fellows; come on, gather round. Take a close look at the shoulder tab. Four stars; see 'em?

Then go over to the Slab and do the same with General Margrave. You'll count six. It's as easy as that, boys. The general says no test. Sure, I told him the whole plan. His eyes just kept boring in. Even making contingency plans for deploying an untested and non-High Command-approved weapon system is grounds for court-martial. He didn't say that; maybe I'm telepathic. In summary, the general says no."

14

"I don't know, now. What I heard, even with everything we got on the line, dug in and ready for anything, they's still a ten-mile wide gap the Peepreps can waltz through without getting even a dirty look. So if the young general—Bates—oh, he's a nice enough young fellow, after you get used to him—if he wants to plug the hole with old unit DNE here, why I say go to it, only the Council says nix. I can say this much: she's put together so she'll stay together. I must of wired in a thousand of them damage sensors myself, and that ain't a spot on what's on the diagram. 'Pain circuits,' old Doc Chin calls 'em. Says it's just like a instinct for self-preservation or something, like people. Old Denny can hurt, he says, so he'll be all the better at dodging enemy fire. He can enjoy, too, Doc says. He gets a kick out of doing his job right, and out of learning stuff. And he learns fast. He'll do OK against them durn Peepreps. They got him programmed right to the brim with everything from the way them Greeks used to fight with no pants to Avery's Last Stand at Leadpipe. He ain't no dumb private; he's got more dope to work on than any general ever graduated from the Point. And he's got more firepower than an old-time army corps. So I think maybe General Bates got aholt of a good idear, there, myself. Says he can put her in the gap in his line and field-test her for fair, with the whole durn Peeprep army and air force for a test problem. Save the gubment some money, too. I heard Doc Chin say the full-scale field test mock-up would run GM a hundred million and another five times that in army R & D funds. He had a map showed where he could use Denny here to block off the south end of Grand Crevasse where the Peeprep armor will have to travel 'count of the rugged terrain north of Cold City, and bottle 'em up slick as a owl's peter. I'm for it, durn it. Let Denny have his chance. Can't be no worse'n having them Comrades down here running things even worse'n the gubment.''

15

"You don't understand, young man. My goodness, I'm not the least bit interested in bucking the line, as you put it. Heavens, I'm going back to my apartment—"

"I'm sorry, ma'am, I got my orders; this here ain't no drill; you got to keep it closed up. They're loading as fast as they can. It's my job to keep these lines moving right out the lock, so they get that flat loaded and get the next one up. We got over a million people to load by six AM deadline. So you just be nice, ma'am, and think about all the trouble it'd make if everybody decided to start back upstream and jam the elevators and all.''

16

Beats me. Course, the good part about being just a hired man is I got no big decisions to make, so I don't hafta know what's going on. Seems like they'd let me know something, though. Batesy was down again, spent a hour with old Denny, like I say, beats me; but he give me a new data can to program into her, right in her Action/Command section. Something's up. I just fired a N-class pulse at old Denny (them's the closest to the real thing) and she snapped her aft quarter battery around so fast I couldn't see it move. Old Denny's keyed-up, I know that much.

17

This has been a memorable time for me. I have my assignment at last, and I have conferred at length—for 2,037 seconds— with my commander. I am now a fighting unit of the 20th Virginia, a regiment ancient and honorable, with a history dating back to Terra Insula. I look forward to my opportunity to demonstrate my worthiness.

18

"I assure you, gentlemen, the rumor is unfounded. I have by no means authorized the deployment of 'an untested—and potentially highly dangerous machine,' as your memo termed it. Candidly, I was not at first entirely unsympathetic to the proposal of the Chief of Ground Forces in view of the circumstances—I presume you're aware that the PR committed its forces to invasion over an hour ago, and that they are advancing in overwhelming strength. I have issued the order to commence the evacuation, and I believe that the initial phases are even now in progress. I have the fullest confidence in General Bates and can assure you that our forces will do all in their power in the face of this dastardly sneak attack. As for the unfortunate publicity given to the earlier suggestion re the use of the Mark XX, I can tell you that I at once subjected the data to computer analysis here at Headquarters, to determine whether any potentially useful purpose could be served by risking the use of the new machine without prior test certification. The results were negative. I'm sorry, gentlemen, but that's it. They have the advantage both strategically and tactically. We are out-gunned, out-manned, and in effect out-flanked. There is nothing we can do save attempt to hold them long enough to permit the evacuation to get underway, then retreat in good order. The use of our orbiting nuclear capability is out of the question. It is after all our own territory we'd be devastating. No more questions for the present, please, gentlemen. I have my duties to see to."

19

The situation as regards my own circumstances continues to deteriorate. The current status program has been updated to within 21 seconds of the present. The reasons both for what is normally a pre-engagement up-dating and for the hiatus of 21 seconds remain obscure. However, I shall of course hold myself in readiness for whatever comes.

20

It's all nonsense: to call me here at this hour merely to stand by and watch the destruction of our gallant men who are giving their lives in a totally hopeless fight against overwhelming odds. We know what the outcome must be. You yourself, General, informed us this afternoon that the big tactical computer has analyzed the situation and reported no possibility of stopping them with what we've got. By the way, did you include the alternative of use of the big, er, Bolo, I believe they're called—frightening things—they're so damned *big*. But if, in desperation, you should be forced to employ the thing—have you that result as well? I see. No hope at all. So there's nothing we can do. This is a sad day, General. But I fail to see what object is served by getting me out of bed to come down here. Not that I'm not willing to do anything I can, of course. With our people—innocent civilians—out on that blizzard-swept tundra tonight—and our boys dying to gain them a little time, the loss of a night's sleep is relatively unimportant, of course. But it's my duty to be at my best, rested and ready to face the decisions that we of the Council will be called on to make.

Now, General, kindly excuse my ignorance if I don't understand all this . . . but I understood that the large screen there was placed so as to monitor the action at the southern debouchment of Grand Crevasse where we expect the enemy armor to emerge to make its dash for Cold City and the Complex. Yes, indeed, so I was saying, but in that case, I'm afraid I don't understand. I'm quite sure you stated that the untried Mark XX would *not* be used. Yet, on the screen I see what appears to be in fact that very machine moving up. Please, calmly, General. I quite understand your position. Defiance of a direct order. That's rather serious, I'm sure, but no occasion for such language, General.

There must be some explanation.

21

This is a most satisfying development. Quite abruptly, my introspection complex was brought up to full operating level, extra power resources were made available to my current-

*action memory stage, and most satisfying of all, my battle
reflex circuit has been activated at active service level. Action
is impending, I am sure of it. It is a curious anomaly: I dread
the prospect of damage and even possible destruction, but
even more strongly, I anticipate the pleasure of performing my
design function.*

22

"Yes, sir. I agree, it's mutiny. But I will not recall the Bolo
and I will not report myself under arrest. Not until this battle's
over, General. So the hell with my career. I've got a war to
win."

23

Now just let me get this quite straight, General. Having been
denied authority to field-test this new device, you—or a subordinate—which amounts to the same thing—have placed the
machine in the line of battle, in open defiance of the Council.
This is a serious matter, General. Yes, of course it's war, but
to attempt to defend your actions now will merely exacerbate
the matter. In any event—to return to your curious decision to
defy Council authority and to reverse your own earlier position—it was yourself who assured me that no useful purpose
could be served by fielding this experimental equipment—that
the battle, and perhaps the war, and the very self-determina-
tion of West Continent are irretrievably lost. There is nothing
we can do save accept the situation gracefully while decrying
Chairman Smith's decision to resort to force. Yes, indeed,
General, I should like to observe on the Main Tactical Display
screen. Shall we go along?

24

Now, there at center screen, Mr. Councillor, you see that big
blue rectangular formation. Actually that's the opening of
Grand Crevasse, emerges through an ice tunnel, you know.
Understand the Crevasse is a crustal fault, a part of the same

formation that created the thermal sink from which the Complex draws its energy. Splendid spot for an ambush, of course, if we had the capability. Enemy has little option; like a highway in there—armor can move up at flank speed. Above, the badlands, where *we* must operate. Now, over to the left, you see that smoke, or dust or whatever. That represents the western limit of the unavoidable gap in General Bates's line. Dust raised by maneuvering Mark XVs, you understand. Obsolete equipment, but we'll do what we can with them. Over to the right, in the distance there, we can make out our forward artillery emplacement of the Threshold Line. Pitiful, really. Yes, Mr. Councillor, there is indeed a gap precisely opposite the point where the lead units of the enemy are expected to appear. Clearly, anything in their direct line of advance will be annihilated; thus General Bates has wisely chosen to dispose his forces to cover both enemy flanks, putting him in position to counterattack if opportunity offers. We must, after all, sir, use what we have. Theoretical arms programmed for fiscal ninety are of no use whatever today. Umm. As for that, one must be flexible, modifying plans to meet a shifting tactical situation. Faced with the prospect of seeing the enemy drive through our center and descend, unopposed, on the vital installations at Cold City, I have, as you see, decided to order General Bates to make use of the experimental Mark XX. Certainly; my decision entirely. I take full responsibility.

25

I advance over broken terrain toward my assigned position. The prospect of action exhilarates me, but my assessment of enemy strength indicates they are fielding approximately 17.4 percent greater weight of armor than anticipated, with commensurately greater fire power. I compute that I am grossly overmatched. Nonetheless, I do my best.

26

There's no doubt whatever, gentlemen. Computers work with hard facts. Given the enemy's known offensive capability, and our own defensive resources, it's a simple computation. No

combination of the manpower and equipment at our command can possibly inflict a defeat on the PR forces at this time
and place. Two is greater than one. You can't make a dollar
out of fifteen cents.

27

At least we can gather some useful data from the situation,
gentlemen. The Bolo Mark XX has been committed to battle.
Its designers assure me that the new self-motivating circuitry
will vastly enhance the combat effectiveness of the Bolo. Let
us observe.

28

Hate to see old Denny out there, just a great big sitting duck,
all alone and—here they come! Look at 'em boiling out of
there like ants out of a hot log. Can't hardly look at that
screen, them tactical nukes popping like fireworks all over the
place. But old Denny knows enough to get under cover. See
that kind of glow all around him? All right, *it*, then. You
know, working with him—it—so long, it got to feeling almost
like he was somebody. Sure, I know, anyway, that's vaporized
ablative shield you see. They're making it plenty hot for him.
But he's fighting back. Them Hellbores is putting out, and
they know it. Looks like they're concentrating on him now.
Look at them tracers closing in on him. Come on, Denny, you
ain't dumb. Get out of there, fast.

29

Certainly it's aware what's at stake! I've told you he—the
machine, that is, has been fully programmed and is well aware
not only of the tactical situation, but of strategic and logistical
considerations as well. Certainly it's an important item of
equipment; its loss would be a serious blow to our present
under-equipped forces. You may rest assured that its pain circuits as well as its basic military competence will cause it to

take the proper action. The fact that I originally opposed commissioning the device is not to be taken as implying any lack of confidence on my part in its combat effectiveness. You may consider that my reputation is staked on the performance of the machine. It will act correctly.

30

It appears that the enemy is absorbing my barrage with little effect. More precisely, for each enemy unit destroyed by my fire 2.4 fresh units immediately move out to replace it. Thus it appears I am ineffective, while already my own shielding is suffering severe damage. Yet while I have offensive capability, I must carry on as my commander would wish. The pain is very great now, but thanks to my superb circuitry, I am not disabled, though it has been necessary to withdraw power from my external somatic sensors.

31

I can assure you, gentlemen, insofar as simple logic functions are concerned, the Mark XX is perfectly capable of assessing the situation, even as you and I, only better. Doubtless as soon as it senses that its position has grown totally untenable, it will retreat to the shelter of the rock ridge and retire under cover to a position from which it can return fire without taking the full force of the enemy's attack at point-blank range. It's been fully briefed on late developments, it knows this is a hopeless fight. There, you see? It's moving . . .

32

I thought you said—dammit, I *know* you said your pet machine had brains enough to know when to pull out. But look at it: half a billion plus of Concordiat funds being bombarded into radioactive rubbish. Like shooting fish in a barrel.

33

Yes, sir. I'm monitoring everything. My test panel is turned to it across the board. I'm getting continuous reading on all still-active circuits. Battle Reflex is still hot. Pain circuits close to overload, but he's still taking it—I don't know how much more he can take, sir; already way past Redline; expected him to break off and get out before now.

34

It's a simple matter of arithmetic. There is only one correct course of action in any given military situation; the big tactical computer was designed specifically to compare data and deduce that sole correct action. In this case my readout shows that the only thing the Mark XX could legitimately do at this point is just what the professor here says: pull back to cover and continue its barrage. The on-board computing capability of the unit is as capable of reaching that conclusion as is the big computer at HQ. So keep calm, gentlemen. It will withdraw at any moment, I assure you of that.

35

Now it's getting ready—no, look what it's doing! It's advancing into the teeth of that murderous fire. By God, you've got to admire that workmanship! That it's still capable of moving is a miracle. All the ablative metal is gone—you can see its bare armor exposed—and it takes some heat to make that flint-steel glow white!

36

Certainly, I'm looking. I see it. By God, sir, it's still moving—faster, in fact; charging the enemy line like the Light Brigade. And all for nothing, it appears. Your machine, General, appears less competent than you expected.

37

Poor old Denny. Made his play and played out, I reckon. Readings on the board over there don't look good; durn near every overload in him blowed wide open. Not much there to salvage. Emergency Survival Center's hot. Never expected to see *that*. Means all kinds of breakdowns inside. But it figures, after what he just went through. Look at that slag pit he drove up out of. They wanted a field test. Reckon they got it. And he flunked it.

38

Violating orders and winning is one thing, George. Committing mutiny and losing is quite another. Your damned machine made a fool of me. After I stepped in and backed you to the hilt and stood there like a jack-ass and assured Councillor Grace that thing knew what it was doing—it blows the whole show. Instead of pulling back to save itself it charged to destruction. I want an explanation of this fiasco at once.

39

Look! No, by God, over *there!* On the left of the entrance. They're breaking formation—they're running for it! Watch this! The whole spearhead is crumbling, they're taking to the badlands—they're—

40

Why, dammit? It's outside all rationality. As far as the enemy's concerned, fine. They broke and ran. They couldn't stand up to the sight of the Mark XX not only taking everything they had, but advancing on them out of that inferno, all guns blazing. Another hundred yards and—but they don't know that. It buffaloed them, so score a battle won for our side. But why? I'd stack its circuits up against any fixed installation in existence including the big Tacomp the army's so proud of. That machine was as aware as anybody that the only smart thing to do was run. So now I've got a junk pile on my hands. Some test! A clear flunk. Destroyed in action. Not recommended for Federal procurement. Nothing left but a few hot transistors in the Survival Center. It's a disaster, Fred. All my work, all your work, the whole program wrecked. Fred, you talk to General Bates; as soon as he's done inspecting the hulk he'll want somebody human to chew out.

41

Look at that pile of junk. Reading off the scale. Won't be cool enough to haul to Disposal for six months. I understand you're Chief Engineer at Bolo Division. You built this thing. Maybe you can tell me what you had in mind here. Sure, it stood up to fire better than I hoped. But so what? A stone wall can stand and take it. This thing is supposed to be *smart*, supposed to feel pain like a living creature. Blunting the strike at the Complex was a valuable contribution, but how can I recommend procurement of this junk-heap?

42

Why, Denny? Just tell me why you did it. You got all these military brass down on you, and on me, too. On all of us. They don't much like stuff they can't understand. You attacked when they figured you to run. Sure, you routed the enemy, like Bates says, but you got yourself ruined in the process. Don't make sense. Any dumb private, along with the generals, would have known enough to get out of there. Tell me why, so I'll have something for Bates to put on his Test Evaluation Report, AGF Form 1103-6, Rev 11/3/85.

43

"All right. Unit DNE of the line. Why did you do it? This is your commander, Unit DNE. Report! Why did you do it? Now, you knew your position was hopeless, didn't you? That you'd be destroyed if you held your ground, to say nothing of advancing. Surely you were able to compute that. You were lucky to have the chance to prove yourself.''

For a minute I thought old Denny was too far gone to answer. There was just a kind of groan come out of the amplifier. Then it firmed up. General Bates had his hand cupped behind his ear, but Denny spoke right up.

"Yes, sir."

"You knew what was at stake here. It was the ultimate test of your ability to perform correctly under stress, of your suitability as a weapon of war. You knew that. General Margrave and old Priss Grace and the press boys all had their eyes on every move you made. So, instead of using common sense, you waded into that inferno in defiance of all logic—and destroyed yourself. Right?"

"That is correct, sir."

"Then why? In the name of sanity why, instead of backing out and saving yourself, did you charge?

"Wait a minute, Unit DNE. It just dawned on me. I've been underestimating you. You knew, didn't you? Your knowledge of human psychology told you they'd break and run, didn't it?"

"No, sir. On the contrary, I was quite certain that they knew they held every advantage."

"Then that leaves me back where I started. Why? What made you risk everything on a hopeless attack? Why did you do it?"

"For the honor of the regiment."

AN EMPTY GIFT

by Steve Benson

Timothy knelt beneath a steel-gray sky, wearily scooping snow into a bucket with his hands. He wore no gloves. His hands were bright red and they burned with cold. Snowflakes swirled around him playfully, landing on his grimy cheeks and forehead. His skin was eggshell white beneath the dirt and his hair was stiff, uncombed. Hunger chewed at his stomach; he had not eaten since the day before. There hadn't been enough for everybody, and since he was their leader it was only fair that he go without. Timothy was twelve years old.

The other children had not noticed that Timothy wasn't eating with them. They were too busy wolfing down the last of the canned vegetables. Timothy forced the image from his mind and stared into the bucket. Satisfied that there would be enough snow water for dinner, he pushed himself shakily to his feet.

Angie stood ten feet away, watching him. Timothy swayed weakly back and forth as the world spun around behind his eyes. The four-year-old seemed not to notice. She took a hesitant step closer and said, "I wanna ast you a question."

Timothy blinked, straining to focus on the little girl in the green-and-blue snowsuit. Her nose was running and her hands were jammed deep in her pockets. Timothy licked his cracked lips and frowned. "Angie?" he asked. "What're you doin' outside?"

"I wanna ast you a question," she repeated, a little annoyed that he hadn't heard her the first time. Timothy glanced down at the bucket beside him in the snow. It looked impossibly heavy. His eyelids kept fluttering shut and he couldn't feel his hands. "Timothy?" Angie whined. His eyes snapped open and he looked at her through watery eyes. "Brenda said tomorrow's Christmas!" Angie said, taking another step closer. "So that makes tonight Christmas Eve, doesn't it?" She looked up at him with big, green eyes; eyes desperate for the right answer. Before he could speak, words were pouring out of her in a flood. "I mean, I know it isn't like it's s'posed to be. Not like before the 'splosions and the bad stuff. But that doesn't change *Christmas,* does it?" In a pleading tone, she added, "I mean, Santa's still comin', isn't he?"

Timothy's throat quivered in rage and frustration, and he wanted to shout, "No, there is no Santa Claus, no Christmas Eve, no presents . . . only pain and slow death, only cold and hunger." He squeezed his eyes shut and dropped to his knees. Tears ran down his cheeks and Angie frowned in confusion.

"Timothy?" she whispered, moving closer.

He opened his eyes and looked at her, pitying her, pitying himself. Between sobs, he managed to say, "Yes, Angie. Santa's coming." Her dirty face broke into a grin and she rushed into his arms.

Her laughter was like wind chimes in his ear as she hugged him. "Is Santa *really* coming?" she asked, stepping away from him. Timothy nodded, not trusting himself to speak again. Then Angie was gone, dashing into the house to share the good news: Timothy had said it was Christmas Eve. Santa Claus was coming.

Timothy dragged the bucket up to the house, his head reeling with every step. He could hear the children chattering in the living room, buzzing with excitement about Christmas. "It isn't fair," Timothy complained, leaning against the front door. "Just not fair. After everything they've been through. And now to put them through Christmas . . ."

A moment later, Timothy opened the door and went into the living room, dragging his wet feet. He dropped the bucket of snow down to melt and turned toward the group of children huddled around the heating duct. A chorus of voices sprang up, demanding that he verify the coming of Santa Claus. Timothy cut through their chatter: "Allen, Derek, we need wood for the fire. C'mon, before it gets too dark." The two ten-year-olds slowly stood and moved away from the others. Masks of sadness covered their childhood, and both seemed on the verge of tears, but the younger children didn't notice. As the three eldest members of their "family" trudged through the front door, the cheerful knot of ragged children returned to trading tales of Christmases past.

Timothy closed the front door roughly and said, "Guess you both heard . . ."

"They're expectin' Santa Claus," Derek whined, tears finally slipping down his cheeks.

Allen nodded in agreement. "They're talking about waiting up for him," he said. His lower lip quivered and his eyes were moist.

"Well, he's not coming, that's all," Timothy said, clenching his teeth. "He's just not gonna show up." He looked down at his feet, giving the others a moment to stop crying. Both boys continued to sob. "Knock it off," Timothy demanded, turning away from them. "We gotta get some wood." He stomped off through the ankle-deep snow with an energy he didn't really feel. Allen and Derek wiped their eyes on crusty coat sleeves and started after him.

For food and firewood, the children had been cannibalizing the neighborhood. The nearest three houses were hacked up badly. Timothy clomped up onto the porch of the fourth house. The front door was gone and he walked inside, not looking back. They had left two hatchets and a handsaw in the house. Timothy was busy breaking up an end table when the other boys shambled in. "Grab a hatchet," Timothy ordered over his shoulder. He was still angry, and it felt good to slam the dull blade into the table. The other boys started cutting away at the huge grandfather clock in the corner of the dining room. Timothy finished with the table, splintering it into pieces that would fit into their coal furnace.

Timothy was sweating and panting as he turned toward the others. "Keep workin' on that clock," he ordered. "I'm goin' upstairs to look around." He slowly climbed the stairs. The banister was gone and he kept close to the wall. He found what he was looking for at the end of the hall. It was a girl's bedroom, done in soft pink with ivory trim. A canopy bed dominated the small room and Timothy shuddered to think that the little girl would never be coming back. Ever.

Through the dusty lace curtains, Timothy could see that it was snowing harder. Along one wall of the bedroom, a row of dolls sat neatly on a pastel shelf. They stared at him with unblinking glass eyes. He paused for a moment before gathering them up and taking them downstairs. "What are we gonna do with *them*?" Derek asked, hands on hips. The grandfather clock was in a dozen pieces and Allen was fussing over a splinter in his finger.

"We're gonna play Santa Claus," Timothy explained. "We'll sneak these dolls back into the house and wait 'til the kids go to sleep. Then we put a doll next to each of 'em . . ."

"What about Andy?" Allen asked, still digging at the splinter. Andy was a blue-eyed blond, every bit of six years old and a dyed-in-the-wool Santa Claus believer. But a doll just wouldn't do.

"Forgot about him," Timothy admitted. "Wait a minute . . ." He disappeared up the steps again. A moment later, he came back, beaming with pleasure. In his hands was a small green tank with a U.S. Army emblem on each side. The anger, frustration, and weariness he had felt only minutes before were gone. "Andy's gonna love this," he said, smiling.

Allen and Derek scrounged some canned goods from a house four doors down. Hidden among the wood and the cans, the dolls were spirited into the house, past the waiting children, and down into the basement. The children were still chattering wildly about Christmas. Timothy understood their excitement; it bothered him that their simple joy was forever beyond him. Part of him resented their blissful ignorance, but there was little room for resentment as he stoked the furnace with chunks of wood. He carefully place a row of canned goods on top of the filthy furnace to be heated for dinner.

After the meager meal of green beans and carrot slices, Timothy drew Allen and Derek aside. "I'll go downstairs and keep the fire going strong. You two keep watch on the kids. When they're all asleep, come down and we'll bring up the presents." The two nodded eagerly, caught up in the excitement.

The furnace struggled to beat back the cold that poured into the house with every gust of wind. Timothy threw another hunk of grandfather clock into the flames and basked in the wash of heat. He could hear the children's voices echoing through the heating duct. Tossing in more wood, Timothy smiled to think what delight the simple toys would bring. But then the depression swept back over him. Of course, the children would be happy when they woke up to find the gifts, but that would not solve their problem. Here it was, the end of December, with the worst months of winter still to come. Timothy couldn't see how they were going to make it.

He sat down on a thick sheet of cardboard, watching the flames flickering through the furnace grate. His mind drifted back to when there were electricity, gas, and running water. Hot water. Winter had been for sled riding and snowball fights. Winter had been fun; it hadn't been this terrible, threatening monster that lurked outside the walls. He shook his head sadly, thinking, "We should have been moving south."

But they *had* been moving south, avoiding the larger cities because of the radiation. There had been bodies along the way, horrible, dismembered. Then they came across Andrea Mitchell. And the house. Inside, they found what was left of Andrea's parents. Radiation sickness. The older boys had buried them in a shallow grave behind the house. When they tried to leave, taking Andrea with them, the seven-year-old went into screaming fits. She refused to leave the house and they couldn't just leave her there. Timothy had been against it, but they stayed, wasting precious time.

Winter came six weeks early, dumping eight inches of heavy snow. It hadn't completely melted when the next storm struck. Now it was impossible to travel; they were stuck. Andrea had died two weeks later.

Timothy was not aware of falling asleep. He had crouched down, resting his head against the stone wall. The fire dancing through the grate hypnotized him and his eyelids fluttered shut. Sleep settled over him like a comfortable blanket of release.

Timothy came awake all at once. Stiff with cold, he pushed himself to his feet. All was dark except for the gentle glow coming from the furnace door. He opened the grate to let more light into the basement. There was no way to tell the time, but the pile of toys was still in place. He crept up the dark stairs, being careful not to make noise. Timothy gently opened the door and stepped into the living room.

A cold chill swept over his legs and he frowned. The living room was dark and empty. Somebody was singing outside. He ran to the front door and there were the children, gathered in front of the house. The door hung wide open, letting all that precious heat escape . . .

It was snowing outside, practically a blizzard. But the children stood in a circle around a small fire, holding hands and singing jumbled versions of Christmas carols as loud as they could.

Timothy stormed through the door, pulling it shut behind him. The children nodded and waved in his direction, but kept singing. He opened his mouth to scold them, but the harsh words stuck in his throat. He swallowed hard and looked at them. They were dressed in dirty, worn clothing, underfed, half-frozen, and hopeless, yet they were singing loud enough to burst. The lyrics didn't always match and they weren't all singing to the same tune, but that merry hodgepodge of Christmas music rolled out like a warm blanket through the snowstorm. Timothy found himself singing along.

The song ended raggedly, and Angie waded through the snow over to Timothy. She wrapped her arms around his waist and looked lovingly up into his face. "We're singin' to bring Santa faster," she explained. "See, Allen and Derek even builded a fire so Santa could see us for sure." Timothy saw the light of hope burning in Angie's eyes. It was something he had never seen in her before, and he saw it now in all of them. Even LuAnne, who sobbed herself to sleep every night, looked happy. Allen and Derek were glowing with the Christmas spirit. Timothy smiled back at them, feeling the warm glow in himself.

Suddenly, the spirit drained out of him. He had remembered why they were so happy: Santa Claus was coming. Except there was no Santa Claus. He felt tired, weak, and helpless. Timothy sat down heavily in the snow, not feeling the cold against his legs and back. The children were singing again, but Timothy didn't join in. The fire danced and fluttered in the wind. No Santa Claus today, kids, Timothy thought. Sorry, but Santa Claus is hiding in a pile of dolls beside the furnace. That's all there is, kids, and there ain't no more.

Timothy stared at the fire, barely hearing the children's song. But underneath the singing, something else came to him, drifting on the wind. Faintly, out of the north, floated the ringing of sleighbells. He shook his head, denying it: There *was no Santa Claus*. But try as he might, Timothy could not deny that the sound was getting louder. The singing had stopped, too. Each child had trailed off until the only sounds were the bells in the distance and the wind whipping around them.

Timothy stood, brushing the snow from his trousers. "Merry Christmas, Santa," Angie cried. And then they were all shouting it, jumping up and down around the fire. Only Timothy was silent, straining his eyes to see something— anything, off to the north. But the curtain of snow was too thick. In the back of his mind, Timothy insisted that Santa Claus *did not exist*. But on the outside, Timothy was smiling.

Timothy suddenly realized that he was shouting, too. He hadn't believed in Santa Claus in years, but here he was, one of *them* again. All his responsibilities had melted away. He was free to be a child, waiting for Santa. The sleighbells were getting louder.

It was Christmas Eve and Santa was coming.

The Soviet TK-740 personnel carrier had been retooled in the months before the outbreak of war. Originally manned by two drivers and a fire-control officer, each TK-740 was refitted with a self-directing computer designed to control the vehicle in high-radiation areas too hot for human drivers.

The weapons systems were also tied into the computer, which was programmed for one purpose: elimination of enemy survivors in hot post-war situations. After the primary and secondary targets in the United States had been obliterated, over three hundred of the TK-740s had been air-dropped along the Canadian border to make a sweep toward the south.

Each TK-740 was equipped with twin machine guns, a short-range mortar, and four missile launchers. The computer identified survivors with an infrared scanner, a video camera, and two bidirectional microphones. Any movement registered with the computer as a survivor; the robot tanks slaughtered animals as well as humans on their relentless sweep south. Once satisfied that an area was free of enemy survivors, the computer directed the TK-740 to move south in search of more targets. Sensors under the vehicle kept it on a firm road surface.

A massive plow at the front of the TK-740 swept snow off the road. The heavy treads rattled against the slippery surface of the highway. Several cleats on the left tread had snapped loose and rattled as the heavy vehicle rumbled along through the blinding snowstorm.

The infrared scanner suddenly picked up a bright dot of heat ahead and to the left. The computer switched the weapons systems to alert status. The target was still too far away for a clear video image.

Timothy was delighted. It was a dream come true. The children were dancing around the fire, shouting and laughing. Even the fire seemed to have grown brighter. "He's almost here," Angie cried, tugging at Timothy's coat sleeve. But Timothy paid no attention. He was busy staring into the snowstorm, trying to see Santa Claus.

The TK-740 picked up the light from the fire on its video monitor. Now there were several heat-images on the infrared scanner. The computer switched on the heat-seeking missile launcher. The aiming mechanism began tracking left toward the dot of flame, five hundred feet away. So far all the heat-images were in a cluster. It would be easier to get them all at once. The TK-740 rumbled closer, treads beating against the frozen road.

Allen dashed out onto the snow-covered road, screaming with pleasure. Timothy was only vaguely aware of him. The children still huddled around the fire. Some called out to Santa, others sang. Timothy smiled widely and started across the snowy lawn toward Santa.

Three hundred feet away, the TK-740 picked up two fuzzy images on its video scanner. These life-forms seemed to be moving, but not running. All the better. The computer switched the missile system to standby and activated the machine guns instead. Twin gun barrels jumped in their turrets and began tracking Timothy and Allen.

The hulking form of the machine was visible now, a gray silhouette against the heavy blast of snow. Timothy was closest. He cocked his head, confused. The cleats were jangling loudly now, but this didn't *look* like Santa Claus. Timothy took a step backwards. "Allen," he shouted. "*Get off the road!*"

Allen stopped dancing. "But it's Santa Claus," he complained.

The TK-740 tried to click on its headlamps to pick up a better video image, but the lights had already been smashed out. The computer shifted the transmission into neutral and the huge, gray vehicle drifted to a halt at the edge of the lawn, twenty feet from the house.

"I think you'd better come away from there, Allen," Timothy called, his voice trembling. The children had stopped singing. They looked from Timothy, to Allen, to the heavy machine that had appeared out of the storm.

"Is that Santa?" Angie asked, frowning.

The left machine gun turret hummed as it shifted slightly. Now it pointed directly at Allen. "My God, get away from there," Timothy screamed. Allen turned to face the others. He was crying.

"But where's Santa?" LuAnne shouted. The computer within the TK-740 signaled the machine guns to open fire. The firing mechanisms whirred and clicked, but no bullets exploded from the waiting, black muzzles. All the bullets had been used five days earlier in Rome, New York, to kill the last remaining members of a VFW post.

The computer paused, sensing that the machine guns were not working. An instant later, it tried to fire a mortar shell. Again the loading mechanism worked perfectly, but there were no shells left in the magazine. The TK-740's entire supply of mortar shells had been used to wipe out a herd of cattle just outside of Elmira, New York. The mortar's firing pin clicked four times and fell silent.

Timothy watched in horror as Allen slipped and fell in the heavy snow. The gun barrel that had been tracking him had stopped moving. Timothy could hear the machine clicking and rattling, but what did that mean?

The cold began to bother the children. Angie shivered and walked over to where Timothy stood. "What's the matter with

Santa?'' she asked. ''Why don't he come out?''

The heat-seeking missiles had been activated, but they, too, were gone. Left without weapons, the TK-740 idled, unsure of its next move.

''Don't know what's wrong with Santa, Angie,'' Timothy said, taking a step toward the rumbling tank. ''But I guess there's only one way to find out if he's in there or not.''

The camera twisted in its mount to watch as Timothy approached the side of the machine. He stared up at it, blinking away the snowflakes that crashed into his eyes. His heart thumped wildly as he put his hand on the icy flank of the machine. He shivered at the cold and lifted himself up, using the machine-gun turret as a handhold. Then, hand over hand, he moved up the steep side of the TK-740. The computer watched his progress, but there was no way to stop him now.

Timothy crawled behind the opening for the missile launchers. There he found a round hatch, half-hidden by the snow. He tugged at the recessed handle and the hatch slowly creaked open. Timothy peered into the darkness, not sure what to expect. ''Hello?'' he called. His voice echoed back. His right hand brushed against a utility switch, and the inside of the TK-740 was flooded with light.

Inside was the original personnel compartment, stripped down to the bare metal. The technicians had installed the computer system through this hatch and the access ladder was still in place. Timothy gently eased over the lip of the hatch and went down the ladder, one rung at a time. The children all watched, holding their breath, as Timothy disappeared. Inside, the TK-740 was just a rectangular box fashioned out of armor plating. ''Nothing fancy,'' Timothy said to himself. Then an idea came to him. ''But it *is* headed south . . .''

Emerging a moment later, Timothy called to the children, ''Everybody go in the house. Gather up clothing, food, anything you can carry.''

''Why?'' asked Derek, rocking back and forth in the snow.

''Because we're all going to see Santa Claus,'' Timothy shouted back. There was a moment of confusion as the children charged into the house, but Derek waited behind. He shuffled up next to the TK-740 and slapped his open palm against its metal hide.

''You want us to get inside this thing?'' Derek asked.

"We can't last much longer staying here," Timothy explained, quietly. Derek nodded.

As the children began straggling out of the house under piles of filthy clothing, Derek asked Timothy in a low voice, "There really isn't any Santa Claus, is there?"

Timothy thought for a moment before answering, "I'm really not sure." He gently patted the smooth edge of the access hatch. To the others he called, "OK, everybody line up next to the Santa Express. Allen and Derek will boost you up and I'll lift you the rest of the way."

Soon, everyone was packed inside the TK-740. The compartment was a tight fit, but the engines behind and below them gave off just enought heat to make it comfortable. "Everyone here?" Timothy asked, looking around.

"All present and accounted for, *sir*," Allen said, giving him a happy salute.

"Is this really the Santa Express?" Angie whispered, tugging at Timothy's sleeve.

Timothy swung the access hatch shut and squeezed down beside Angie. "You bet your boots this is the Santa Express," he said, leaning over to kiss her gently on the forehead.

The infrared scanner was fixed on the flickering heat of the fire in front of the house, but the other sensors detected no movement, no targets. Satisfied that it had completed its job, the computer shifted the TK-740 into gear and swung the massive vehicle back onto the road.

Within minutes, the Santa Express had shifted into cruising gear, heading south. Timothy was able to completely relax for the first time in weeks. Allen had remembered to bring along the toys from the basement. The children were busy examining the presents, but as Timothy leaned back, smiling, he was sure he had gotten the very best Christmas gift of all.

He got his faith back.

TANK

by Francis E. Izzo

Davis slammed the flipper and watched the steel ball go skittering up toward the 500 target.

"Go, baby!"

Five hundred points and it would be free game time.

The ball kissed the target, but lacked the strength to register
on the scoreboard.

"Hell!"

It wobbled back down the slope, heading for the flipper
again. This time he tensed his body, ran through some unconscious calculations, and pushed the flipper hard, while lifting
the underbelly of the machine with a practiced jerk.

"Tilt," sneered the box.

He looked away in disgust. In the arcade, he could hear the
music of the pinball jockeys: bells and buzzers, whirs and
clicks, thuds and springing noises.

He knew every machine in the place and had won on most.

As he walked up the aisle, which was covered with cigarette
butts and soda stains, he passed his favorite machines. Reno
Gambler. Rodeo Roundup. One-Eyed Joker. The quarters
jingled in his jeans as he headed into the next aisle, where the
new electronic machines were blinking.

"Transistorized rip-offs," he thought, contemptuously.

He could remember when they first came out. The Pong games and the Hockey games were first. Good for a few laughs. But you needed a partner to play, and there were few if any who could match Davis.

Then after the Pong games came the fancy electronics. Indy 500, where a computerized track weaved in and out, throwing obstacles at your speeding car. It took him five hours and fifteen dollars to get that one down. Now he could drive it in his sleep.

Then there was Submarine. It had a periscope to sight enemy ships on a screen. The ships came at him at different speeds, so he was constantly forced to readjust his range. It took some judgment, but nothing too difficult.

He had it figured out in an hour.

It all led him to one conclusion: a computer hooked to a TV screen couldn't do what those simple steel pinballs could. It couldn't provide him with an infinite variety of challenge. The electronics always had a pattern.

He simply couldn't understand what drew the people to the electronic screens. But they were there day after day in increasing numbers, plugged into the blip blip bleep of the cathode tubes.

They were the suckers: the men in business suits out for a plug-in thrill. They'd drink their beer and have ridiculous contests. And not one of them could score a free game on the simplest pinball in the place.

Davis pulled alongside one man going into a hairpin turn at LeMans.

A dull explosion came from the speaker, as the man's car ran into a wall. He tried pathetically to wheel it around and three others cars struck him. He spun the wheel the other way and got hit again. His car was bouncing back and forth like a shooting-gallery duck.

"Give it the gas," muttered Davis.

"Pardon?"

"When you get hit like that, just give it the gas and hold the wheel straight until you get clear."

"Oh . . . yeah . . . thanks, kid," said the man, sliding another quarter into the slot, then quickly driving off an embankment, through a moat, and into an oncoming car.

Davis turned, annoyed, and kept walking, letting the continuous explosions from LeMans fade into the general noise of the arcade.

Whatever turns you on.

But for him, it was time to go back to Lady Luck. That pinball had been giving him a lot of trouble lately. It had a particularly treacherous combination of holes, targets, and bumpers that kept his senses spinning with every roll.

On his way back up the electronic alley, Davis noticed something new.

There was a booth with a seat and a screen. On the front it lacked the psychedelic paint of most of the games. No lights flashing. Simply painted dull green, with the word TANK printed in block letters on the entrance.

Fresh meat. A new game to master, then throw away to the uncultured palates of the amateurs.

He climbed into the booth, slightly nervous in anticipation of breaking in a brand-new machine.

He looked for the directions. They weren't in sight. Neither was the coin slot. They were probably still setting this one up.

It looked a little different from the other electronic sets. With a small slit screen, similar to the kind on a real tank, it had a panel of control wheels and levers marked with elevation marks, and many other controls he had never seen on a game before.

Davis ran his fingers over the seat. Leather, and quite worn for a new machine. There was a pungent odor in the booth, a kind of locker-room smell.

The controls looked sophisticated. He imagined that this game might turn out to be some fun, once they set it up.

Just as he was leaving to return to the pinballs, he noticed one of the control levers had some writing on it.

It said, "ON."

When he pulled it, the door to the booth closed. A light was activated above his head. A sign flashed, "FASTEN SEAT BELT."

Not bad.

Davis reached across the seat and pulled up a heavy leather strap across his waist. It tightened and firmly planted him in his seat.

Another light went on.

"PLACE HEAD GEAR."

Directly above his head there was a leather headpiece dangling from a wire.

Nice effects, he thought, putting on the head gear. The light flicked off, then another one came on. It was a bright, piercing-blue button that glowed with the word "START."

When he pushed it, three things happened: an engine started rumbling and shaking his seat, the screen lit up in full color *(color!)* and his booth started to move. Or at least it seemed to move.

Quickly he felt for gas and brake and found them in a comfortable spot on the floor. His hands went instinctively for the steering wheel. It was a bit like one of the old tanks he'd studied in basic training.

The rumbling in the booth increased as he pushed the gas pedal. Soon it was almost deafening.

On the screen, there was an open field, bouncing up and down to the movements of his booth.

OK, he thought, if they call this game TANK I should be seeing some tanks one of these days.

He was not disappointed. A thick green object appeared on his screen, from behind a break of trees.

It looked like a German Tiger, the kind used in World War II. Very realistic in detail. They probably picked up some war footage, then synchronized it to the game computer.

The Tiger was heading straight for him, sending puffs of blue smoke from its cannon.

Not only could he see shells firing, he could hear them and feel their impact vibrations coming up from under his seat. His seat was shaking so much, he could hardly keep his hands on the wheel.

Blindly, he reached for the stick in front of him and jammed the button on top.

The force of what came next threw him deep into his seat. It was the recoil from his own cannon fire.

Through the screen he could see his shell break the ground, far to the left of the oncoming tank.

He flipped some levers, trying to adjust his range. When he fired again, his shell headed in the correct direction, but fell about fifty yards short. The explosion sent a hot wave into his booth.

By now, shells from the enemy tank were closing in on him.

With his right hand, he spun his wheel in evasive moves. With his left hand, he readjusted his range, and fired his third shell.

The result was a tremendous explosion, followed by silence.

Mud and dirt were splattered on his screen, but in the clearing he could see the Tiger in flames in front of him. Black smoke poured from it and he noticed the thick smell of burning oil in his booth.

How does this thing keep score? he wondered, waiting for some points to register on his screen.

All he saw was the same burning carcass.

Davis was quite pleased with the result of his first encounter. The movements of the enemy tank appeared quite unprogrammed and unpredictable.

He turned his wheel slowly, scanning the field for signs of other tanks.

There were none. However there was a small troop of infantry, some carrying antitank weapons.

The hot button to his left looked good, so he fingered it and heard a flat rat-tat-tat. On his screen, half the infantry fell to the ground for cover, the other half fell in pieces. He gunned his motor and headed straight for them, losing them under his field of vision.

Somewhere far away he heard the unmistakable sound of a human scream, and felt a slight jostling under his seat.

Before he had a chance to reorient himself, another tank appeared on the screen. It was much larger than the first one, but seemed to have the same purpose in mind. By its look, it was one of the heavy tanks the Germans introduced late in the war. If this game followed history, his American tank was at a distinct disadvantage. He wasn't sure he liked playing a game with a handicap.

Before he could ponder much longer on this, a thunderous roar shook his booth, sending his head forward into the jutting controls.

Blood. There was blood on the controls, and a thin trail of it worming down from a gash over his eye.

Totally confused, Davis decided to run.

He spotted a dirt road into the woods and headed down it, feeling the hot breath of the enemy tank on his back.

He followed the road at full throttle, with the ground opening up around him from the attacking shells.

It was an incredibly rough ride. He had all he could do to keep his tank out of the trees.

Sooner or later he knew he would have to stop, turn and fight, or he would lose some points.

Up ahead there was a large farmhouse. His senses were slowly coming back after that last blast. Blood was caked on his hands and sweat poured down his front and back. The plan was this: he would duck behind the farmhouse, turn immediately, and face his enemy head-on.

Another violent blast put an end to those plans. His entire booth rattled and let out a great grinding noise.

The scenery on his screen stood still.

He stomped on the gas, but it stayed still. Must have lost a tread, he thought. Turn and fight now, or lose this round.

His heart pounding in his ears, he threw his body behind the wheel that sent his turret moving. What he saw next was this: the barrel of the other tank, aimed dead center on his screen. Instantly he fired.

What took place next, he could not see. The first explosion knocked him unconscious. The second explosion was his shell catching his attacker in a vital spot, sending up a flash of burning fuel.

There was fire all around him when he regained consciousness. His head was bleeding again, his lungs burned from the hot smoke in his booth.

Davis grabbed for the seat belt, but it was jammed. The heat was becoming unbearable.

Suddenly he heard an odd scraping noise coming from over his head.

He looked up, his eyes tearing profusely from the smoke. The sound of metal giving way rang through his ears, and sunlight burned through a momentary hole over his head.

Something fell in, then the crack of sunlight was shut off.

He recognized it and was instantly sick.

Grenade.

He was clawing frantically at the seat straps when it went off with a dull thud.

There was no explosion. No impact. No flash. Just a single piece of cardboard issued from the metal casing of the grenade.

And it said, neatly printed in block letters:

"GAME OVER."

THE TANK
AND ITS WIFE

by Arsen Darnay

The tank drove around the mansion's curving drive passing between lavish flower beds. It was a small tank, painted in random green-beige-yellow patches—a vehicle perfect for the quick and darting guerilla warfare of the African plains.

But this wasn't Africa. The pretentious mansion—a mixture of temple and hacienda—topped a California hill. It was enthroned in near-empty landscape, far from affluent neighbors spotted on other hills. The sun lay bright on rolling lawns. Sprinklers spurted brilliantly. There would surely be a pool in the back, turquoise in the sun; and stables down the hill; and a gardener who rode a wheeled fortress with automatic transmission to mow the placid acres of green.

The tank made a fearful noise. It had no muffler, and the rapid bleh-bleh-bleh explosions of its engine drowned out the chattering, chainy, metallic clicking of its tracks.

Long before the muzzle of its gun had come into view over the steep approach, the lady of the house, attracted by the racket, had run to a bay window to peer out through gauze curtains.

She stood there still, mesmerized and puzzled, when the tank suddenly wheeled at the apex of the drive and, with

167

treads churning newly planted bulbs in dark, moist dirt on either side of the entrance apron, it crashed with a deafening roar and a turmoil of splintering, cracking, tearing, and crunching noises through the portals into the foyer and then into the spacious living room.

The tank seemed to pause. Then its turret swung from left to right, swept a chandelier against the ceiling, pulverizing it in the process. At last it faced the lady of the house. She screamed, unheard, and stood now pressed hard against the window, her hands half covering her face, her eyes frozen in terror.

A panel opened in the turret. A black barrel looked out, then briefly rattled. A string of bullets tore into a wall, demolishing two glass-framed watercolors showing Parisian scenes. The pattern of the bullets spelled a message. *Hi,* it said.

The woman ran out, sobbing and frantic, stumbling over the dusty rubble and the chewed-up carpeting behind the tank. She ran down a hallway floored in colorful terrazzo, through a paneled room with antlers and bookshelves, through a spacious, glittering kitchen bright with copper pots hung from wooden pegs, and out to a glass-roofed patio.

She raced on from there, past the swimming pool, down the steep lawn, toward the stables. She screamed "Herman! Herman!"—but the gardener was nowhere to be seen, and she began to sob at her own ineffectualness.

The tank came behind her. She heard it roar and glimpsed over her shoulder the white dust it caused to boil out of the house.

The tank emerged through an opening wider by far than the sliding glass door it pushed before it, frame and all, ground to dust under its tracks on the irregular, gray slate of the patio.

The tank stopped and appeared to survey the scene. Then its gun fired with a roar, causing the tank to rock back on its treads. Three shells arched over the diminishing form of the lady. They raised geysers of dirt into the air before her. Spent steel fell at her feet. Her ears buzzed with the explosions.

She turned, unthinking, and saw the tank. It stood half covered by the wire-reinforced glass roof of the patio. A stream of fire spurted from an aperture in its turret and fell to the sloping grass beyond the pool. Black smoke boiled from the lawn, spent itself, and left a scorched pattern of words: *Darling, Wait. I Am Home.*

The lady's face worked out of control. She had mascara around her rayed, middle-aged eyes. Her lashes had been lengthened, her face carefully made up, her lips accentuated by a pale, pearl lipstick. Now her usually cool, smooth features were those of a terrified child. She covered her face, collapsed slowly, assumed a fetal posture, and began to rock.

The sergeant was hysterical—a state he frequently experienced. He appeared to be jumping up and down, quivering with impatience, while two kneeling soldiers in fatigues connected the grayed copper ends of a cable to an oblong box with instruments on its face. The cable hung in a loose spiral from a frame just beneath the blinding, neon-lighted, corrugated roof of the hangar.

"Come on, come on! What does it say?"

The men were busy and said nothing.

The sergeant wrung his pudgy hands. He sucked air between his clenched teeth and looked entreatingly up at the roof as if to invoke the Almighty's aid.

One of the soldiers turned his head. "The line's dead," he said. "No stimulation coming through at all."

"You sure?"

The sergeant turned abruptly and ran between two rows of tanks. He was a pear-shaped man, unaccustomed to running; his fattish rears danced back and forth; his ankles turned inward. His eyes swept the tanks as he ran—each camouflage-colored and linked by coiling cable to the central stimulator mounted under the roof. They looked peaceful and harmless in the huge, echoing hangar—ninety-nine identical tanks in four rows. Only one was missing, *T98*, midway in the third row.

The sergeant ran toward a half-open door through which could be seen part of a coffee urn set on a typewriter table and next to it white cups that bore the colorful heraldic emblem of the PFP command.

He stopped at the door and looked with still fresh horror at a monstrous, jagged hole in the hangar's metal wall through which *T98* had made its exit during the night. And he looked beyond the gash, across a tread-marked expanse of gravel, at the ruination of the chain-link fence. It resembled a basketball basket laid on its side.

"Sweet Jesus," the sergeant muttered and then ran on

imagining the track of rubble, twisted metal, fleeing civilians, and burning houses that *T98* could well have left behind.

He arrived at his office, panting, and reached across his desk for the telephone speaker laid on a heavily doodled calendar blotter. Captain Richards had been holding. The sergeant told him what the instruments had said.

Captain Richards called Colonel Baxter; Baxter called General Hals; and General Hals went to a sleek blue-and-cream computer console against the window of his office and typed *T98* on the keyboard. The machine began to clatter almost instantly.

Hals first skimmed a brief précis of the long report.

"Subject, John Hamilton," he read, "entered PFP program 6-9-85 aged 56 after stroke/paralysis. Background career real estate, well to do. No children or surviving siblings. Politically right of center. Application filed by wife (radio ad response) who described subject 'living vegetable better dead than alive' and executed battery of release forms subject's stead. Wife was told (oral/written) probability subject's survival 2.9 percent. Was notified 12-2-86 subject 'succumbed complications nervous system transplant operation.' Funeral held using actual body, latter displayed wake for friends/associates. Subject enrolled Tank Corps 12-19-86. Performance undistinguished. Scheduled African Theater 5-5-87."

General Hals began to read the meat around this skeleton, but he didn't get very far. Reports began pouring in and he knew he had a crisis on his hands. He ordered his helicopter to be brought around, armed himself with a lacquered swagger stick on whose end a gilded bullet gleamed, and took off to supervise the capture operation from the air.

By the time the general arrived above the scene, hovering in the sun in his bright sphere, the chopper blades a smoky halo above the bubble—the hilltop mansion was under siege. Military forces, sheriff's deputies, two fire companies, and the highway patrol were on the spot.

A crowd of gawkers had also gathered, among them two reporters demanding to know who was in charge. General Hals told Captain Richards to stall the press a little, and this the captain undertook to do. He strode from his jeep toward the pesty reporters with a stiff, forbidding curl about his lips; but he had flutters in his stomach.

General Hals surveyed the scene and saw the errant *T98* midway down the eastern hill. It stood in the midst of a rutted, reddish area where its various maneuverings had stripped the thin sod from the clay. Its wife had to be that curled-up bundle on the ground; but the general assumed that she was still alive—*T98* attempted still to communicate with her in various ways.

At uneven distances from the tank lay the smoking wreckage of jeeps, patrol cars, and a fire engine. Men occasionally peered out from behind these feeble barriers.

The general made a quick decision and called Richards once again.

"Richards," he said, "is your jeep still working?"

"Positive on that, General."

"All right, Richards. Get the radio out of it. Then send it down the hill toward the tank."

"Roger on that, General."

"Wait a minute. While the tank's busy with the jeep, I want the men down here below me to get in there and drag the woman away."

"We may sustain casualties, General."

"Then sustain them," the general said. And he thought about the members of the press and what those gentlemen would write about a tank that penned love letters on plush suburban lawns with a flame thrower. The evidence had to be eradicated at the first opportunity. *Darling I have missed you more than I can say,* said a scorch mark just below the pool. Near the stable stood the words: *Our years together are my most cherished memories.* Another tell-tale message, below the patio, said, *Darling, wait. I am home.* And yet another, a littler lower: *Why are you afraid of me? Why do you run from me?* The general put in a call for Air Force jets. He wanted napalm. The planes should assume a holding pattern nearby . . . He would do it—despite the bad publicity: he would wash this hill in fire. Better that—

Richards had done as ordered. The jeep appeared from the shadows of one of the mansion's wings and began a slow, throttled descent toward *T98*. It was driverless, of course.

The tank saw the jeep approach and swung its turret to take aim. At that moment men hiding in the cover of wreckage to *T98*'s rear rushed forward. The tank was still enjoying the

lovely ball of fire it had made of Captain Richards' jeep—a
face of fire with a blackish crown of smoke that rose and
mushroomed almost as delightfully as a tactical nuke—when
the men grabbed the lady of the house and ran away down the
hill.

The tank swiveled sharply and lowered its gun—but nothing
happened. *T98* evidently did not wish to harm its spouse.

"Sir. Sir! General!"

The general saw the pilot pointing toward the distant hills at
another helicopter.

General Hals was a cool, precise, unflappable man. He was
entirely like the faultlessly shaped mustache he wore, whose
every hair he inspected daily and whose misdemeanors he corrected every morning, face close to the mirror, with a golden
fingernail clipper. He knew that the approaching helicopter
was none other than WTUV's "Eye in the Sky." Its cameras
would be loaded for action. They would relish recording *T98*'s
effusions on videotape.

Despite the irritation Hals felt in that moment, he showed
none of it outwardly. He called the Air Force and ordered
napalm dropped. The Air Force was sorry. The special code
word the general had used in ordering the strike could not be
found in any of the books. Higher headquarters had been con-
sulted but no response had been received. And under the circumstances: the target area was under the jurisdiction of the
state of California. The governor had not—

By the the time the Air Force had rogered out, WTUV's
"Eye in the Sky" had come, had seen, and was still taping. It
had much to record. The tank had been stung by its wife's ab-
duction and displayed its rage in a barrage of artillery. Shells
leveled the mansion. Machine-gun bullets sprayed. Fire swept
the lawn (obliterating, thank heaven, some of the tank's own
words). The tank darted this way and that, attacking everything in sight—save only the wreckage where its wife lay
sheltered by soldiers, sheriffs, and firemen.

The general decided it was time to put an end to it, and he
told Richards to bring in bazookas.

The tank spent itself in rage, but inwardly it felt the throat-
clutch of intense disappointment, impotence, and sadness.
The bold adventure was over before it had begun, finished the

dream! Could it have cried, the tank would have cried.

The night before, parked in the hangar with its mates, it had expected another night of pornographic dreaming, much like every other night before—to be followed in the morning by training exercises to teach it how to use this still unfamiliar and strange prosthesis which seemed so huge, clumsy, and lacking in proper means of communication. Such was the round of its life.

But then, to its puzzlement and delight, the compelling sex-bliss had stayed away. It had enjoyed the total stillness of utter leisure—and not just for a moment but for hours on end, recalling suddenly that life had been like that before, in a wheelchair. But now the stillness and the leisure were a blessing rather than a curse.

Toward morning had come the electrifying notion that it was no longer quite so helpless as in that wheelchair, long ago. It had means of locomotion—and of communication—at its disposal. It tried the engine—and it started. It engaged a gear —and it took.

Then the tank experienced a moment of emotion so strong and excruciating that it would have fainted had it been a body rather than just a packaged brain. It had a vision of its wife —that other being next to whom he had lived so many years, so thoughtlessly, taking her so for granted. And after the stroke he had not been able to say to her what he had wanted to say more than ever: that he loved and appreciated her; that his life with her had been a quiet but joyous time. All he'd wanted.

But now! Now it could undo all that. It could move and speak again, however clumsily. It could see her one last time before they shipped it out to Africa . . .

So the tank had broken rank inside the hangar and had begun its long trip home.

And now the dream was over. She had not recognized it, had fled from it, had hidden her eyes from its frantically spelled messages. Well, the tank would die here on its own turf. After its moment of freedom, it loathed the thought of training and nightly bliss. It wished to die.

The bazooka teams arrived at last and after some dangerous maneuvers destroyed one of the tank's treads. With one track

lamed and the other under power, the tank turned about its
own center like a swirling maniac intent on digging a grave for
itself in the gouged and bleeding earth.

Then came a shell that fastened on the turret like a fire leech
and ate its way into the metal—a fizzing, sparking circle of
voracious light and heat. Visual connections linking the tank
to eyelets in its turret melted into dripping ends of wire. Finally the second tread was also shot away, and the tank was
paralyzed.

Outside its shell sweating and anxious men prepared to
carve holes into the metal using laser guns linked by cables to a
power-pack mounted on a track.

Up above General Hals bobbed, dipped, and buzzed like a
hungry mosquito scenting blood.

WTUV's "Eye in the Sky" had landed. The cameraman
was taking footage from the edge of a temporary barrier made
of strung-out fire hose and guarded by deputies and a stalking,
grim-lipped Captain Richards.

The lady of the house babbled incoherently in a speeding
ambulance. She lay on a stretcher covered by blankets. A
young man in white squatted at her head.

The driver of the ambulance had the radio on. He listened
to a country crooner finishing a song. *Pamper me with
praises, ply me with love,* the woman sang. And then again, on
a concluding note: *Pamper me with praises, ply me . . . with
. . . looove!*

The song ended and the announcer came on. "Now, folks,"
he said, "here's a public service message from the Department
of Defense. The folks down Pentagon-way have come up with
a new program for people with disabilities. They say it's a kind
of dividend on all the tax dollars we spent on military re-
search. The program is called Prostheses for Peace, meaning
that the Defense Department will help people who can't see or
hear or walk or such. And it's absolutely free. Mind, now—
those folks can't guarantee a thing, but if you've got someone
near and dear you want to help, call 800-717-9999 and they'll
tell you how to file an application. What about it? Get off that
old rocker, people—do something for Gramps and Granny,
hear! That toll-free number again. Here it is . . ."

Back at the mansion the laser carvers had penetrated to the
"package." They snipped through its connections and

brought it out through the seared, irregular oval cut in the
tank's side. The package resembled a mid-sized picnic cooler.
General Hals had already landed in anticipation of this event.
Men loaded the package into his helicopter. Moments later the
copter rose and sped away, leaving Captain Richards to fend
for himself against a swollen complement of the press.

The reporters clamored for explanations. Why had the
driver come to this place? What did all those messages mean?
Why didn't he get out of the tank? Was the driver the
woman's husband? And was the driver still alive? What about
that thing the copter had carried off? Classified records? Had
the driver gone nuts? Berserk? What detachment was this,
anyway?

To all this Richards replied by repeating monotonously that
an official statement would be made at a later time. He had no
authority . . .

Then, inexplicably to the observers, airplanes appeared on
the horizon, flying low. They came in. Napalm drums fell,
burst, and washed the hill with fire. Richards, reporters, sheriffs, firemen, soldiers, and gawkers barely escaped the holo-
caust. The Air Force had found General Hals's code word at
last and had hastened to obey his order.

General Hals, his exquisitely polished boots at rest on the
package, communicated with the Pentagon by radio-tele-
phone. He set in motion a series of phone calls all over the
nation. Men less cool than he went to work on senators and
congressmen, a governor, and the president of a TV station.
In a pinch, the general reflected, he could even blind WTUV's
"Eye in the Sky."

The tank's inertial systems had survived the battle. It knew
itself in motion and guessed that it had failed. It had been
deprived of its death. It felt devastated, cheated, and sank into
a catatonic numbness.

The motion continued for a while. Then its character
changed. The tank was being carried now by men—into the
hangar, probably, into that bright yet gloomy expanse that, at
this hour, would be empty; its buddies and comrades would be
out on the range learning counterinsurgency.

Then the motion stopped and the tank felt it coming: an explosion of searing pleasure as electronic impulses of supreme delicacy began to stimulate selected neuron bundles in its brain. It copulated with a thousand women all at once. It disappeared into transports of delight. The dream of that quiet night and the difficult adventure out there, in the sunlight, visiting its own lost past, faded into an insignificant, pale, underexposed episode, the disintegrating spiderwebs of memory.

DAMNATION ALLEY

by Roger Zelazny

I

The gull swooped by, seemed to hover a moment on unmoving wings.

Hell Tanner flipped his cigar butt at it and scored a lucky hit. The bird uttered a hoarse cry and beat suddenly at the air. It climbed about fifty feet, and whether it shrieked a second time, he would never know.

It was gone.

A single gray feather rocked in the violet sky, drifted out over the edge of the cliff and descended, swinging, toward the ocean. Tanner chuckled through his beard, between the steady roar of the wind and the pounding of the surf. Then he took his feet down from the handlebars, kicked up the stand and gunned his bike to life.

He took the slope slowly till he came to the trail, then picked up speed and was doing fifty when he hit the highway.

He leaned forward and gunned it. He had the road all to himself, and he laid on the gas pedal till there was no place left for it to go. He raised his goggles and looked at the world through crud-colored glasses, which was pretty much the way he looked at it without them, too.

All the old irons were gone from his jacket, and he missed the swastika, the hammer and sickle and the upright finger, especially. He missed his old emblem, too. Maybe he could pick one up in Tijuana and have some broad sew it on and . . . No. It wouldn't do. All that was dead and gone. It would be a giveaway, and he wouldn't last a day. What he *would* do was sell the Harley, work his way down the coast, clean and square and see what he could find in the other America.

He coasted down one hill and roared up another. He tore through Laguna Beach, Capistrano Beach, San Clemente, and San Onofre. He made it down to Oceanside, where he re-fueled, and he passed on through Carlsbad and all those dead little beaches that fill the shore space before Solana Beach Del Mar. It was outside San Diego that they were waiting for him.

He saw the roadblock and turned. They were not sure how he had managed it that quickly, at that speed. But now he was heading away from them. He heard the gunshots and kept going. Then he heard the sirens.

He blew his horn twice in reply and leaned far forward. The Harley leaped ahead, and he wondered whether they were radioing to someone further on up the line.

He ran for ten minutes and couldn't shake them. Then fifteen.

He topped another hill, and far ahead he saw the second block. He was bottled in.

He looked all around him for side roads, saw none.

Then he bore a straight course toward the second block. Might as well try to run it.

No good!

There were cars lined up across the entire road. They were even off the road on the shoulders.

He braked at the last possible minute, and when his speed was right he reared up on the back wheel, spun it and headed back toward his pursuers.

There were six of them coming toward him, and at his back new siren calls arose.

He braked again, pulled to the left, kicked the gas and leaped out of the seat. The bike kept going, and he hit the ground rolling, got to his feet and started running.

He heard the screeching of their tires. He heard a crash. Then there were more gunshots, and he kept going. They were aiming over his head, but he didn't know it. They wanted him alive.

After fifteen minutes he was backed against a wall of rock, and they were fanned out in front of him, and several had rifles, and they were all pointed in the wrong direction.

He dropped the tire iron he held and raised his hands.

"You got it, citizens," he said. "Take it away."

And they did.

They handcuffed him and took him back to the cars. They pushed him into the rear seat of one, and an officer got in on either side of him. Another got into the front beside the driver, and this one held a sawed-off shotgun across his knees.

The driver started the engine and put the car into gear, heading back up 101.

The man with the shotgun turned and stared through bifocals that made his eyes look like hourglasses filled with green sand as he lowered his head. He stared for perhaps ten seconds, then said, "That was a stupid thing to do."

Hell Tanner stared back until the man said, "Very stupid, Tanner."

"Oh, I didn't know you were talking to me."

"I'm looking at you, son."

"And I'm looking at you. Hello, there."

Then the driver said, without taking his eyes off the road, "You know, it's too bad we've got to deliver him in good shape—after the way he smashed up the other car with that damn bike."

"He could still have an accident. Fall and crack a couple of ribs, say," said the man to Tanner's left.

The man to the right didn't say anything, but the man with the shotgun shook his head slowly. "Not unless he tries to escape," he said. "L.A. wants him in good shape."

"Why'd you try to skip out, buddy? You might have known we'd pick you up."

Tanner shrugged.

"Why'd you pick me up? I didn't do anything?"

The driver chuckled.

"That's why," he said. "You didn't do anything, and

there's something you were supposed to do. Remember?"

"I don't owe anybody anything. They gave me a pardon and let me go."

"You got a lousy memory, kid. You made the nation of California a promise when they turned you loose yesterday. Now you've had more than the twenty-four hours you asked for to settle your affairs. You can tell them no if you want and get your pardon revoked. Nobody's forcing you. Then you can spend the rest of your life making little rocks out of big ones. We couldn't care less. I heard they got somebody else lined up already."

"Give me a cigarette," Tanner said.

The man on his right lit one and passed it to him.

He raised both hands, accepted it. As he smoked, he flicked the ashes onto the floor.

They sped along the highway, and when they went through towns or encountered traffic the driver would hit the siren and overhead the red light would begin winking. When this occurred, the sirens of the two other patrol cars that followed behind them would also wail. The driver never touched the brake, all the way up to L.A., and he kept radioing ahead every few minutes.

There came a sound like a sonic boom, and a cloud of dust and gravel descended upon them like hail. A tiny crack appeared in the lower right-hand corner of the bulletproof windshield, and stones the size of marbles bounced on the hood and the roof. The tires made a crunching noise as they passed over the gravel that now lay scattered up on the road surface. The dust hung like a heavy fog, but ten seconds later they had passed out of it.

The men in the car leaned forward and stared upward.

The sky had become purple, and black lines crossed it, moving from west to east. These swelled, narrowed, moved from side to side, sometimes merged. The driver had turned on his lights by then.

"Could be a bad one coming," said the man with the shotgun.

The driver nodded, and "Looks worse further north, too," he said.

A wailing began, high in the air above them, and the dark

bands continued to widen. The sound increased in volume, lost its treble quality, became a steady roar.

The bands consolidated, and the sky grew dark as a starless, moonless night and the dust fell about them in heavy clouds. Occasionally, there sounded a *ping* as a heavier fragment struck against the car.

The driver switched on his country lights, hit the siren again and sped ahead. The roaring and the sound of the siren fought with one another above them, and far to the north a blue aurora began to spread, pulsing.

Tanner finished his cigarette, and the man gave him another. They were all smoking by then.

"You know, you're lucky we picked you up, boy," said the man to his left. "How'd you like to be pushing your bike through that stuff?"

"I'd like it," Tanner said.

"You're nuts."

"No. I'd make it. It wouldn't be the first time."

By the time they reached Los Angeles, the blue aurora filled half the sky, and it was tinged with pink and shot through with smoky, yellow streaks that reached like spider legs into the south. The roar was a deafening, physical thing that beat upon their eardrums and caused their skin to tingle. As they left the car and crossed the parking lot, heading toward the big, pillared building with the frieze across its forehead, they had to shout at one another in order to be heard.

"Lucky, we got here when we did!" said the man with the shotgun. "Step it up!" Their pace increased as they moved toward the stairway, and, "It could break any minute now!" screamed the driver.

II .

As they had pulled into the lot, the building had had the appearance of a piece of ice sculpture, with the shifting lights in the sky playing upon its surfaces and casting cold shadows. Now, though, it seemed as if it were a thing out of wax, ready to melt in an instant's flash of heat.

Their faces and the flesh of their hands took on a bloodless, corpselike appearance.

They hurried up the stairs, and a State Patrolman let them in through the small door to the right of the heavy metal double doors that were the main entrance to the building. He locked and chained the door behind them, after snapping open his holster when he saw Tanner.

"Which way?" asked the man with the shotgun.

"Second floor," said the trooper, nodding toward a stairway to their right. "Go straight back when you get to the top. It's the big office at the end of the hall."

"Thanks."

The roaring was considerably muffled, and objects achieved an appearance of natural existence once more in the artificial light of the building.

They climbed the curving stairway and moved along the corridor that led back into the building. When they reached the final office, the man with the shotgun nodded to his driver. "Knock," he said.

A woman opened the door, started to say something, then stopped and nodded when she saw Tanner. She stepped aside and held the door. "This way," she said, and they moved past her into the office, and she pressed a button on her desk and told the voice that said, "Yes, Mrs. Fiske?": "They're here, with that man, sir."

"Send them in."

She led them to the dark, paneled door in the back of the room and opened it before them.

They entered, and the husky man behind the glass-topped desk leaned backward in his chair and wove his short fingers together in front of his chins and peered over them through eyes just a shade darker than the gray of his hair. His voice was soft and rasped just slightly. "Have a seat," he said to Tanner, and to the others, "Wait outside."

"You know this guy's dangerous, Mister Denton," said the man with the shotgun as Tanner seated himself in a chair situated five feet in front of the desk.

Steel shutters covered the room's three windows, and though the men could not see outside they could guess at the possible furies that stalked there as a sound like machine-gun fire suddenly rang through the room.

"I know."

"Well, he's handcuffed, anyway. Do you want a gun?"

"I've got one."

"Okay, then. We'll be outside."

They left the room.

The two men stared at one another until the door closed, then the man called Denton said, "Are all your affairs settled now?" and the other shrugged. Then, "What the hell *is* your first name, really? Even the records show—"

"Hell," said Tanner. "That's my name. I was the seventh kid in our family, and when I was born the nurse held me up and said to my old man, 'What name do you want on the birth certificate?' and Dad said 'Hell!' and walked away. So she put it down like that. That's what my brother told me. I never saw my old man to ask if that's how it was. He copped out the same day. Sounds right, though."

"So your mother raised all seven of you?"

"No. She croaked a couple weeks later, and different relatives took us kids."

"I see," said Denton. "You've still got a choice, you know. Do you want to try it or don't you?"

"What's your job, anyway?" asked Tanner.

"I'm the Secretary of Traffic for the nation of California."

"What's that got to do with it?"

"I'm coordinating this thing. It could as easily have been the Surgeon General or the Postmaster General, but more of it really falls into my area of responsibility. I know the hardware best. I know the odds—"

"What are the odds?" asked Tanner.

For the first time, Denton dropped his eyes.

"Well, it's risky . . ."

"Nobody's ever done it before, except for that nut who ran it to bring the news, and he's dead. How can you get odds out of that?"

"I know," said Denton slowly. "You're thinking it's a suicide job, and you're probably right. We're sending three cars, with two drivers in each. If any one just makes it close enough, its broadcast signals may serve to guide in a Boston driver. You don't have to go though, you know."

"I know. I'm free to spend the rest of my life in prison."

"You killed three people. You could have gotten the death penalty."

"I didn't, so why talk about it? Look, mister, I don't want to die and I don't want the other bit either."

"Drive or don't drive. Take your choice. But remember, if you drive and you make it, all will be forgiven and you can go your own way. The nation of California will even pay for that motorcycle you appropriated and smashed up, not to mention the damage to that police car."

"Thanks a lot," and the winds boomed on the other side of the wall, and the steady staccato from the window shields filled the room.

"You're a very good driver," said Denton, after a time. "You've driven just about every vehicle there is to drive. You've even raced. Back when you were smuggling, you used to make a monthly run to Salt Lake City. There are very few drivers who'll try that, even today."

Hell Tanner smiled, remembering something.

". . . And in the only legitimate job you ever held, you were the only man who'd make the mail run to Albuquerque. There've only been a few others since you were fired."

"That wasn't my fault."

"You were the best man on the Seattle run, too," Denton continued. "Your supervisor said so. What I'm trying to say is that, of anybody we could pick, you've probably got the best chance of getting through. That's why we've been indulgent with you, but we can't afford to wait any longer. It's yes or no right now, and you'll leave within the hour if it's yes."

Tanner raised his cuffed hands and gestured toward the window.

"In all this crap?" he asked.

"The cars can take this storm," said Denton.

"Man, you're crazy."

"People are dying even while we're talking," said Denton.

"So a few more ain't about to make that much difference. Can't we wait till tomorrow?"

"No! A man gave his life to bring us the news! And we've got to get across the continent as fast as possible now or it won't matter! Storm or no storm, the cars leave now! Your feelings on the matter don't mean a good goddamn in the face of this! All I want out of you, Hell, is one word: Which one will it be?"

"I'd like something to eat. I haven't . . ."

"There's food in the car. What's your answer?"

Hell stared at the dark window.

"Okay," he said. "I'll run Damnation Alley for you. I won't leave without a piece of paper with some writing on it, though."

"I've got it here."

Denton opened a drawer and withdrew a heavy cardboard envelope from which he extracted a piece of stationery bearing the Great Seal of the nation of California. He stood and rounded the desk and handed it to Hell Tanner.

Hell studied it for several minutes, then said, "This says that if I make it to Boston I receive a full pardon for every criminal action I've ever committed within the nation of California . . ."

"That's right."

"Does that include ones you might not know about now, if someone should come up with them later?"

"That's what it says, Hell—'every criminal action.' "

"Okay, you're on, fat boy. Get these bracelets off me and show me my car."

The man called Denton moved back to his seat on the other side of his desk.

"Let me tell you something else, Hell," he said. "If you try to cop out anywhere along the route, the other drivers have their orders, and they've agreed to follow them. They will open fire on you and burn you into little bitty ashes. Get the picture?"

"I get the picture," said Hell. "I take it I'm supposed to do them the same favor?"

"That is correct."

"Good enough. That might be fun."

"I thought you'd like it."

"Now, if you'll unhook me, I'll make the scene for you."

"Not till I've told you what I think of you," Denton said.

"Okay, if you want to waste time calling me names, while people are dying—"

"Shut up! You don't care about them and you know it! I just want to tell you that I think you are the lowest, most reprehensible human being I have ever encountered. You have killed men and raped women. You once gouged out a man's eyes, just for fun. You've been indicted twice for pushing dope and three times as a pimp. You're a drunk and a degenerate, and I don't think you've had a bath since the day you were born. You and your hoodlums terrorized decent people when they were trying to pull their lives together after the war. You stole from them and you assaulted them, and you extorted money and the necessaries of life with the threat of physical violence. I wish you had died in the Big Raid, that night, like all the rest of them. You are not a human being, except from a biological standpoint. You have a big dead spot somewhere inside you where other people have something that lets them live together in a society and be neighbors. The only virtue that you possess—if you want to call it that—is that your reflexes may be a little faster, your muscles a little stronger, your eye a bit more wary than the rest of us, so that you can sit behind a wheel and drive through anything that has a way through it. It is for this that the nation of California is willing to pardon your inhumanity if you will use that one virtue to help rather than hurt. I don't approve. I don't want to depend on you, because you're not the type. I'd like to see you die in this thing, and while I hope that somebody makes it through, I hope that it will be somebody else. I hate your bloody guts. You've got your pardon now. The car's ready. Let's go."

Denton stood, at a height of about five feet eight inches, and Tanner stood and looked down at him and chuckled.

"I'll make it," he said. "If that citizen from Boston made it through and died, I'll make it through and live. I've been as far as the Missus Hip."

"You're lying."

"No, I ain't either, and if you ever find out that's straight, remember I got this piece of paper in my pocket—'every criminal action' and like that. It wasn't easy, and I was lucky, too. But I made it that far and, nobody else you know can say that. So I figure that's about halfway, and I can make the other half if I can get that far."

They moved toward the door.

"I don't like to say it and mean it," said Denton, "but good luck. Not for your sake, though."

"Yeah, I know."

Denton opened the door, and, "Turn him loose," he said. "He's driving."

The officer with the shotgun handed it to the man who had given Tanner the cigarettes, and he fished in his pockets for the key. When he found it, he unlocked the cuffs, stepped back, and hung them at his belt; and, "I'll come with you," said Denton. "The motor pool is downstairs."

They left the office, and Mrs. Fiske opened her purse and took a rosary into her hands and bowed her head. She prayed for Boston and she prayed for the soul of its departed messenger. She even threw in a couple for Hell Tanner.

III

They descended to the basement, the sub-basement and the sub-sub-basement.

When they got there, Tanner saw three cars, ready to go; and he saw five men seated on benches along the wall. One of them he recognized.

"Denny," he said, "come here," and he moved forward, and a slim, blond youth who held a crash helmet in his right hand stood and walked toward him.

"What the hell are you doing?" he asked him.

"I'm second driver in car three."

"You've got your own garage and you've kept your nose clean. What's the thought on this?"

"Denton offered me fifty grand," said Denny, and Hell turned away his face.

"Forget it! It's no good if you're dead!"

"I need the money."

"Why?"

"I want to get married and I can use it."

"I thought you were making out okay."

"I am, but I'd like to buy a house."

"Does your girl know what you've got in mind?"

"No."

"I didn't think so. Listen, I've got to do it—it's the only way out for me. You don't have to—"

"That's for me to say."

"—so I'm going to tell you something: You drive out to

Pasadena to that place where we used to play when we were kids—with the rocks and the three big trees—you know where I mean?"

"Yeah, I sure do remember."

"Go back of the big tree in the middle, on the side where I carved my initials. Step off seven steps and dig down around four feet. Got that?"

"Yeah. What's there?"

"That's my legacy, Denny. You'll find one of those old strong boxes, probably all rusted out by now. Bust it open. It'll be full of excelsior, and there'll be a six-inch joint of pipe inside. It's threaded, and there's caps on both ends. There's a little over five grand rolled up inside it, and all the bills are clean."

"Why you telling me this?"

"Because it's yours now," he said, and hit him in the jaw.

When Denny fell, he kicked him in the ribs, three times, before the cops grabbed him and dragged him away.

"You fool!" said Denton as they held him. "You crazy, damned fool!"

"Uh-uh," said Tanner. "No brother of mine is going to run Damnation Alley while I'm around to stomp him and keep him out of the game. Better find another driver quick, because he's got cracked ribs. Or else let me drive alone."

"Then you'll drive alone," said Denton, "because we can't afford to wait around any longer. There's pills in the compartment, to keep you awake, and you'd better use them, because if you fall back they'll burn you up. Remember that."

"I won't forget you, mister, if I'm ever back in town. Don't fret about that."

"Then you'd better get into car number two and start heading up the ramp. The vehicles are all loaded. The cargo compartment is under the rear seat."

"Yeah, I know."

". . . And if I ever see you again, it'll be too soon. Get out of my sight, scum!"

Tanner spat on the floor and turned his back on the Secretary of Traffic. Several cops were giving first aid to his brother, and one had dashed off in search of a doctor. Denton made two teams of the remaining four drivers and assigned them to cars one and three. Tanner climbed into the cab of his own, started the engine and waited. He stared up the ramp and considered what lay ahead. He searched the compartments until he found cigarettes. He lit one and leaned back.

The other drivers moved forward and mounted their own heavily shielded vehicles. The radio crackled, crackled, hummed, crackled again, and then a voice came through as he heard the other engines come to life.

"Car one—ready!" came the voice.

There was a pause, then, "Car three—ready!" said a different voice.

Tanner lifted the microphone and mashed the button on its side.

"Car two ready," he said.

"Move out," came the order, and they headed up the ramp.

The door rolled upward before them, and they entered the storm.

IV

It was a nightmare, getting out of L.A. and onto Route 91. The waters came down in sheets and rocks the size of baseballs banged against the armor plating of his car. Tanner smoked and turned on the special lights. He wore infrared goggles, and the night and the storm stalked him.

The radio crackled, many times, and it seemed that he heard the murmur of a distant voice, but he could never quite make out what it was trying to say.

They followed the road for as far as it went, and as their big tires sighed over the rugged terrain that began where the road ended, Tanner took the lead and the others were content to follow. He knew the way; they didn't.

He followed the old smugglers' route he'd used to run candy to the Mormons. It was possible that he was the only one left alive that knew it. Possible, but then there was always someone looking for a fast buck. So, in all of L.A., there might be somebody else.

The lightning began to fall, not in bolts, but sheets. The car was insulated, but after a time his hair stood on end. He might have seen a giant Gila monster once, but he couldn't be sure.

He kept his fingers away from the fire-control board. He'd save his teeth till menaces were imminent. From the rearview scanners it seemed that one of the cars behind him had discharged a rocket, but he couldn't be sure, since he had lost all radio contact with them immediately upon leaving the building.

Waters rushed toward him, splashed about his car. The sky sounded like an artillery range. A boulder the size of a tombstone fell in front of him, and he swerved about it. Red lights flashed across the sky from north to south. In their passing, he detected many black bands going from west to east. It was not an encouraging spectacle. The storm could go on for days.

He continued to move forward, skirting a pocket of radiation that had not died in the four years since last he had come this way.

They came upon a place where the sands were fused into a glassy sea, and he slowed as he began its passage, peering ahead after the craters and chasms it contained.

Three more rockfalls assailed him before the heavens split themselves open and revealed a bright blue light, edged with violet. The dark curtains rolled back toward the Poles, and the roaring and the gunfire reports diminished. A lavender glow remained in the north, and a green sun dipped toward the horizon.

They had ridden it out. He killed the infras, pushed back his goggles, and switched on the normal night lamps.

The desert would be bad enough, all by itself.

Something big and batlike swooped through the tunnel of his lights and was gone. He ignored its passage. Five minutes later it made a second pass, this time much closer, and he fired a magnesium flare. A black shape, perhaps forty feet across, was illuminated, and he gave it two five-second bursts from the fifty-calibers and it fell to the ground and did not return again.

To the squares, this was Damnation Alley. To Hell Tanner, this was still the parking lot. He'd been this way thirty-two times, and so far as he was concerned the Alley started in the place that was once called Colorado.

He led, and they followed, and the night wore on like an abrasive.

No airplane could make it. Not since the war. None could venture above a couple hundred feet, the place where the winds began. The winds. The mighty winds that circled the globe, tearing off the tops of mountains. Sequoia trees, wrecked buildings, gathering up birds, bats, insects, and anything else that moved, up into the dead belt; the winds that swirled about the world, lacing the skies with dark lines of debris, occasionally meeting, merging, clashing, dropping tons of carnage wherever they came together and formed too great a mass. Air transportation was definitely out, to anywhere in the world. For these winds circled, and they never ceased. Not in all the twenty-five years of Tanner's memory had they let up.

Tanner pushed ahead, cutting a diagonal by the green sunset. Dust continued to fall about him, great clouds of it, and the sky was violet, then purple once more. Then the sun went down and the night came on, and the stars were very faint points of light somewhere above it all. After a time, the moon rose, and the half-face that it showed that night was the color of a glass of chianti wine held before a candle.

He lit another cigarette and began to curse, slowly, softly, and without emotion.

They threaded their way amid heaps of rubble: rock, metal, fragments of machinery, the prow of a boat. A snake, as big around as a garbage can and dark green in the cast light, slithered across Tanner's path, and he braked the vehicle as it continued and continued and continued. Perhaps a hundred and twenty feet of snake passed by before Tanner removed his foot from the brake and touched gently upon the gas pedal once again.

Glancing at the left-hand screen, which held an infrared version of the view to the left, it seemed that he saw two eyes glowing within the shadow of a heap of girders and masonry. Tanner kept one hand near the fire-control button and did not move it for a distance of several miles.

There were no windows in the vehicle, only screens which reflected views in every direction including straight up and the ground beneath the car. Tanner sat within an illuminated box which shielded him against radiation. The "car" that he drove had eight heavily treaded tires and was thirty-two feet in length. It mounted eight fifty-caliber automatic guns and four grenade throwers. It carried thirty armor-piercing rockets which could be discharged straight ahead or at any elevation up to forty degrees from the plane. Each of the four sides, as well as the roof of the vehicle, housed a flame thrower. Razor-sharp "wings" of tempered steel—eighteen inches wide at their bases and tapering to points, an inch and a quarter thick where they ridged—could be moved through a complete hundred-eighty-degree arc along the sides of the car and parallel to the ground, at a height of two feet and eight inches. When standing at a right angle to the body of the vehicle—eight feet to the rear of the front bumper—they extended out to a distance of six feet on either side of the car. They could be couched like lances for a charge. They could be held but slightly out from the sides for purposs of slashing whatever was sideswiped. The car was bullet proof, air-conditioned and had its own food locker and sanitation facilities. A long-barreled .357 Magnum was held by a clip on the door near the driver's left hand. A 30.06, a .45-caliber automatic, and six hand grenades occupied the rack immediately above the front seat.

But Tanner kept his own counsel, in the form of a long, slim SS dagger inside his right boot.

He removed his gloves and wiped his palms on the knees of his denims. The pierced heart that was tattooed on the back of his right hand was red in the light from the dashboard. The knife that went through it was dark blue, and his first name was tattooed in the same color beneath it, one letter on each knuckle, beginning with that at the base of his little finger.

He opened and explored the two near compartments but could find no cigars. So he crushed out his cigarette butt on the floor and lit another.

The forward screen showed vegetation, and he slowed. He tried using the radio but couldn't tell whether anyone heard him, receiving only static in reply.

He slowed, staring ahead and up. He halted once again.

He turned his forward lights up to full intensity and studied the situation.

A heavy wall of thorn bushes stood before him, reaching to a height of perhaps twelve feet. It swept on to his right and off to his left, vanishing out of sight in both directions. How dense, how deep a pit might be, he could not tell. It had not been there a few years before.

He moved forward slowly and activated the flame throwers. In the rearview screen, he could see that the other vehicles had halted a hundred yards behind him and dimmed their lights.

He drove till he could go no farther, then pressed the button for the forward flame.

It shot forth, a tongue of fire, licking fifty feet into the bramble. He held it for five seconds and withdrew it. Then he extended it a second time and backed away quickly as the flames caught.

Beginning with a tiny glow, they worked their way upward and spread slowly to the right and the left. Then they grew in size and brightness.

As Tanner backed away, he had to dim his screen, for they'd spread fifty feet before he'd backed more than a hundred, and they leapt thirty and forty feet into the air.

The blaze widened to a hundred feet, two, three . . . As Tanner backed away, he could see a river of fire flowing off into the distance, and the night was bright about him.

He watched it burn, until it seemed that he looked upon a molten sea. Then he searched the refrigerator, but there was no beer. He opened a soft drink and sipped it while he watched the burning. After about ten minutes, the air conditioner whined and shook itself to life. Hordes of dark, four-footed creatures, the size of rats or cats, fled from the inferno, their coats smoldering. They flowed by. At one point, they covered his forward screen, and he could hear the scratching of their claws upon the fenders and the roof.

He switched off the lights and killed the engine, tossed the empty can into the waste box. He pushed the "Recline" button on the side of the seat, leaned back, and closed his eyes.

V

He was awakened by the blowing of the horns. It was still night, and the panel clock showed him that he had slept for a little over three hours.

He stretched, sat up, adjusted the seat. The other cars had

moved up, and one stood to either side of him. He leaned on his own horn twice and started his engine. He switched on the forward lights and considered the prospect before him as he drew on his gloves.

Smoke still rose from the blackened field, and far off to his right there was a glow, as if the fire still continued somewhere in the distance. They were in the place that had once been known as Nevada.

He rubbed his eyes and scratched his nose, then blew the horn once and engaged the gears.

He moved forward slowly. The burnt-out area seemed fairly level and his tires were thick.

He entered the black field, and his screens were immediately obscured by the rush of ashes and smoke which arose on all sides.

He continued, hearing the tires crunching through the brittle remains. He set his screens at maximum and switched his headlamps up to full brightness.

The vehicles that flanked him dropped back perhaps eighty feet, and he dimmed the screens that reflected the glare of their lights.

He released a flare, and as it hung there, burning, cold, white and high, he saw a charred plain that swept on to the edges of his eyes' horizon.

He pushed down on the accelerator, and the cars behind him swung far out to the sides to avoid the clouds that he raised. His radio crackled, and he heard a faint voice but could not make out its words.

He blew his horn and rolled ahead even faster. The other vehicles kept pace.

He drove for an hour and a half before he saw the end of the ash and the beginning of clean sand up ahead.

Within five minutes, he was moving across desert once more, and he checked his compass and bore slightly to the west. Cars one and three followed, speeding up to match his new pace, and he drove with one hand and ate a corned beef sandwich.

When morning came, many hours later, he took a pill to keep himself alert and listened to the screaming of the wind. The sun rose up like molten silver to his right, and a third of the

sky grew amber and was laced with fine lines like cobwebs.
The desert was topaz beneath it, and the brown curtain of dust
that hung continuously at his back, pierced only by the eight
shafts of the other cars' lights, took on a pinkish tone as the
sun grew a bright red corona and the shadows fled into the
west. He dimmed his lights as he passed an orange cactus
shaped like a toadstool and perhaps fifty feet in diameter.

Giant bats fled south, and far ahead he saw a wide waterfall
descending from the heavens. It was gone by the time he
reached the damp sand of that place, but a dead shark lay to
his left, and there was seaweed, seaweed, seaweed, fishes,
driftwood all about.

The sky pinked over from east to west and remained that
color. He gulped a bottle of ice water and felt it go into his
stomach. He passed more cacti, and a pair of coyotes sat at the
base of one and watched him drive by. They seemed to be
laughing. Their tongues were very red.

As the sun brightened, he dimmed the screen. He smoked
and he found a button that produced music. He swore at the
soft, stringy sounds that filled the cabin, but he didn't turn
them off.

He checked the radiation level outside, and it was only a
little above normal. The last time he had passed this way, it
had been considerably higher.

He passed several wrecked vehicles such as his own. He ran
across another plain of silicon, and in the middle was a huge
crater which he skirted. The pinkness in the sky faded and
faded and faded, and a bluish tone came to replace it. The
dark lines were still there, and occasionally one widened into a
black river as it flowed away into the east. At noon, one such
river partly eclipsed the sun for a period of eleven minutes.
With its departure, there came a brief dust storm, and Tanner
turned on the radar and his lights. He knew there was a chasm
somewhere ahead, and when he came to it he bore to the left
and ran along its edge for close to two miles before it narrowed and vanished. The other vehicles followed, and Tanner
took his bearings from the compass once more. The dust had
subsided with the brief wind, and even with the screen dimmed
Tanner had to don his dark goggles against the glare of reflected sunlight from the faceted field he now negotiated.

He passed towering formations which seemed to be quartz.

He had never stopped to investigate them in the past, and he had no desire to do it now. The spectrum danced at their bases, and patches of such light occurred for some distance about them.

Speeding away from the crater, he came again upon sand, clean, brown, white dun and red. There were more cacti, and huge dunes lay all about him. The sky continued to change, until finally it was as blue as a baby's eyes. Tanner hummed along with the music for a time, and then he saw the monster.

It was a Gila, bigger than his car, and it moved in fast. It sprang from out the sheltering shade of a valley filled with cacti and it raced toward him, its beaded body bright with many colors beneath the sun, its dark, dark eyes unblinking as it bounded forward on its lizard-fast legs, sable fountains rising behind its upheld tail that was wide as a sail and pointed like a tent.

He couldn't use the rockets because it was coming in from the side.

He opened up with his fifty-calibers and spread his "wings" and stamped the accelerator to the floor. As it neared, he sent forth a cloud of fire in its direction. By then, the other cars were firing, too.

It swung its tail and opened and closed its jaws, and its blood came forth and fell upon the ground. Then a rocket struck it. It turned; it leaped.

There came a booming, crunching sound as it fell upon the vehicle identified as car number one and lay there.

Tanner hit the brakes, turned, and headed back.

Car number three came up beside it and parked. Tanner did the same.

He jumped down from the cab and crossed to the smashed car. He had the rifle in his hands and he put six rounds into the creature's head before he approached the car.

The door had come open, and it hung from a single hinge, the bottom one.

Inside, Tanner could see the two men sprawled, and there was some blood upon the dashboard and the seat.

The other two drivers came up beside him and stared within. Then the shorter of the two crawled inside and listened for the heartbeat and the pulse and felt for breathing.

"Mike's dead," he called out, "but Greg's starting to come around."

A wet spot that began at the car's rear and spread and continued to spread, and the smell of gasoline filled the air.

Tanner took out a cigarette, thought better of it and replaced it in the pack. He could hear the gurgle of the huge gas tanks as they emptied themselves upon the ground.

The man who stood at Tanner's side said, "I never saw anything like it . . . I've seen pictures, but—I never saw anything like it . . ."

"I have," said Tanner, and then the other driver emerged from the wreck, partly supporting the man he'd referred to as Greg.

The man called out, "Greg's all right. He just hit his head on the dash."

The man who stood at Tanner's side said, "You can take him, Hell. He can back you up when he's feeling better," and Tanner shrugged and turned his back on the scene and lit a cigarette.

"I don't think you should do—" the man began, and Tanner blew smoke in his face. He turned to regard the two approaching men and saw that Greg was dark-eyed and deeply tanned. Part Indian, possibly. His skin seemed smooth, save for a couple pockmarks beneath his right eye, and his cheekbones were high and his hair very dark. He was as big as Tanner, which was six-two, though not quite so heavy. He was dressed in overalls; and his carriage, now that he had had a few deep breaths of air, became very erect, and he moved with a quick, graceful stride.

"We'll have to bury Mike," the short man said.

"I hate to lose the time," said his companion, "but—" and then Tanner flipped his cigarette and threw himself to the ground as it landed in the pool at the rear of the car.

There was an explosion, flames, then more explosions. Tanner heard the rockets as they tore off toward the east, inscribing dark furrows in the hot afternoon's air. The ammo for the fifty-calibers exploded, and the hand grenades went off, and Tanner burrowed deeper and deeper into the sand, covering his head and blocking his ears.

As soon as things grew quiet, he grabbed for the rifle. But

they were already coming at him, and he saw the muzzle of a
pistol. He raised his hands slowly and stood.

"Why the goddamn hell did you do a stupid thing like
that?" said the other driver, the man who held the pistol.

Tanner smiled, and, "Now we don't have to bury him," he
said. "Cremation's just as good, and it's already over."

"You could have killed us all, if those guns or those rocket
launchers had been aimed this way!"

"They weren't. I looked."

"The flying metal could've— Oh . . . I see. Pick up your
damn rifle, buddy, and keep it pointed at the ground. Eject
the rounds it's still got in it and put 'em in your pocket."

Tanner did this thing while the other talked.

"You wanted to kill us all, didn't you? Then you could have
cut out and gone your way, like you tried to do yesterday.
Isn't that right?"

"You said it, mister, not me."

"It's true, though. You don't give a good goddamn if
everybody in Boston croaks, do you?"

"My gun's unloaded now," said Tanner.

"Then get back in your bloody buggy and get going! I'll be
behind you all the way!"

Tanner walked back toward his car. He heard the others ar-
guing behind him, but he didn't think they'd shoot him. As he
was about to climb up into the cab, he saw a shadow out of the
corner of his eye and turned quickly.

The man named Greg was standing behind him, tall and
quiet as a ghost.

"Want me to drive awhile?" he asked Tanner, without expression.

"No, you rest up. I'm still in good shape. Later on this
afternoon, maybe, if you feel up to it."

The man nodded and rounded the cab. He entered from the
other side and immediately reclined his chair.

Tanner slammed his door and started the engine. He heard
the air conditioner come to life.

"Want to reload this?" he asked. "And put it back on the
rack?" And he handed the rifle and the ammo to the other,
who had nodded. He drew on his gloves then and said,
"There's plenty of soft drinks in the 'frig. Nothing much else,
though," and the other nodded again. Then he heard car three

start and said, "Might as well roll," and he put it into gear and took his foot off the clutch.

VI

After they had driven for about half an hour, the man called Greg said to him, "Is it true what Marlowe said?"

"What's a Marlowe?"

"He's driving the other car. Were you trying to kill us? Do you really want to skip out?"

Hell laughed, then, "That's right," he said. "You named it."

"Why?"

Hell let it hang there for a minute, then said, "Why shouldn't I? I'm not anxious to die. I'd like to wait a long time before I try that bit."

Greg said, "If we don't make it, the population of the continent may be cut in half."

"If it's a question of them or me, I'd rather it was them."

"I sometimes wonder how people like you happen."

"The same way as anybody else, mister, and it's fun for a couple people for a while, and then the trouble starts."

"What did they ever do to you, Hell?"

"Nothing. What did they ever do *for* me? Nothing. Nothing. What do I owe them? The same."

"Why'd you stomp your brother back at the Hall?"

"Because I didn't want him doing a damfool thing like this and getting himself killed. Cracked ribs he can get over. Death is a more permanent ailment."

"That's not what I asked you. I mean, what do you care whether he croaks?"

"He's a good kid, that's why. He's got a thing for this chick, though, and he can't see straight."

"So what's it to you?"

"Like I said, he's my brother and he's a good kid. I like him."

"How come?"

"Oh, hell! We've been through a lot together, that's all! What are you trying to do? Psychoanalyze me?"

"I was just curious, that's all."

"So now you know. Talk about something else if you want to talk, okay?"

"Okay. You've been this way before, right?"

"That's right."

"You been any further east?"

"I've been all the way to the Missus Hip."

"Do you know a way to get across it?"

"I think so. The bridge is still up at Saint Louis."

"Why didn't you go across it the last time you were there?"

"Are you kidding? The thing's packed with cars full of bones. It wasn't worth the trouble to try and clear it."

"Why'd you go that far in the first place?"

"Just to see what it was like. I heard all these stories—"

"What was it like?"

"A lot of crap. Burnt-down towns, big craters, crazy animals, some people—"

"People? People still live there?"

"If you want to call them that. They're all wild and screwed up. They wear rags or animal skins or they go naked. They threw rocks at me till I shot a couple. Then they let me alone."

"How long ago was that?"

"Six—maybe seven years ago. I was just a kid then."

"How come you never told anybody about it?"

"I did. A coupla my friends. Nobody else ever asked me. We were going to go out there and grab off a couple of the girls and bring them back, but everybody chickened out."

"What would you have done with them?"

Tanner shrugged. "I dunno. Sell 'em, I guess."

"You guys used to do that, down on the Barbary Coast— sell people, I mean—didn't you?"

Tanner shrugged again.

"Used to," he said, "before the Big Raid."

"How'd you manage to live through that? I thought they'd cleaned the whole place out?"

"I was doing time," he said. "A.D.W."

"What's that?"

"Assault with a deadly weapon."

"What'd you do after they let you go?"

"I let them rehabilitate me. They got me a job running the mail."

"Oh yeah. I heard about that. Didn't realize it was you,

though. You were supposed to be pretty good—doing all right and ready for a promotion. Then you kicked your boss around and lost your job. How come?"

"He was always riding me about my record and about my old gang down on the Coast. Finally, one day I told him to lay off, and he laughed at me, so I hit him with a chain. Knocked out the bastard's front teeth. I'd do it again."

"Too bad."

"I was the best driver he had. It was his loss. Nobody else will make the Albuquerque run, not even today. Not unless they really need the money."

"Did you like the work, though, while you were doing it?"

"Yeah, I like to drive."

"You should probably have asked for a transfer when the guy started bugging you."

"I know. If it was happening today, that's probably what I'd do. I was mad, though, and I used to get mad a lot faster than I do now. I think I'm smarter these days than I was before."

"If you make it on this run and you go home afterwards, you'll probably be able to get your job back. Think you'd take it?"

"In the first place," said Tanner, "I don't think we'll make it. And in the second, if we do make it and there's still people around that town, I think I'd rather stay there than go back."

Greg nodded. "Might be smart. You'd be a hero. Nobody'd know much about your record. Somebody'd turn you on to something good."

"The hell with heroes," said Tanner.

"Me, though, I'll go back if we make it."

"Sail 'round Cape Horn?"

"That's right."

"Might be fun. But why go back?"

"I've got an old mother and a mess of brothers and sisters I take care of, and I've got a girl back there."

Tanner brightened the screen as the sky began to darken.

"What's your mother like?"

"Nice old lady. Raised the eight of us. Got arthritis bad now, though."

"What was she like when you were a kid?"

"She used to work during the day, but she cooked our meals

and sometimes brought us candy. She made a lot of our clothes. She used to tell us stories, like about how things were before the war. She played games with us and sometimes she gave us toys.''

"How about your old man?" Tanner asked him, after a while.

"He drank pretty heavy and he had a lot of jobs, but he never beat us too much. He was all right. He got run over by a car when I was around twelve."

"And you take care of everybody now?"

"Yeah. I'm the oldest."

"What is it that you do?"

"I've got your old job. I run the mail to Albuquerque."

"Are you kidding?"

"No."

"I'll be damned! Is Gorman still the supervisor?"

"He retired last year, on disability."

"I'll be damned! That's funny. Listen, down in Albuquerque do you ever go to a bar called Pedro's?"

"I've been there."

"Have they still got a little blond girl plays the piano? Named Margaret?"

"No."

"Oh."

"They've got some guy now. Fat fellow. Wears a big ring on his left hand."

Tanner nodded and downshifted as he began the ascent of a steep hill.

"How's your head now?" he asked, when they'd reached the top and started down the opposite slope.

"Feels pretty good. I took a couple of your aspirins with that soda I had."

"Feel up to driving for a while?"

"Sure, I could do that."

"Okay, then." Tanner leaned on the horn and braked the car. "Just follow the compass for a hundred miles or so and wake me up. All right?"

"Okay. Anything special I should watch out for?"

"The snakes. You'll probably see a few. Don't hit them, whatever you do."

"Right."

They changed seats, and Tanner reclined the one, lit a cigarette, smoked half of it, crushed it out, and went to sleep.

VII

When Greg awakened him, it was night. Tanner coughed and drank a mouthful of ice water and crawled back to the latrine. When he emerged, he took the driver's seat and checked the mileage and looked at the compass. He corrected their course and, "We'll be in Salt Lake City before morning," he said, "if we're lucky—Did you run into any trouble?"

"No, it was pretty easy. I saw some snakes and I let them go by. That was about it."

Tanner grunted and engaged the gears.

"What was that guy's name that brought the news about the plague?" Tanner asked.

"Brady or Brody or something like that," said Greg.

"What was it that killed him? He might have brought the plague to L.A., you know."

Greg shook his head.

"No. His car had been damaged, and he was all broken up—and he'd been exposed to radiation a lot of the way. They burnt his body and his car, and anybody who'd been anywhere near him got shots of Haffikine."

"What's that?"

"That's the stuff we're carrying—Haffikine antiserum. It's the only cure for the plague. Since we had a bout of it around twenty years ago, we've kept it on hand and maintained the facilities for making more in a hurry. Boston never did, and now they're hurting."

"Seems kind of silly for the only other nation on the continent—maybe in the world—not to take better care of itself, when they knew we'd had a dose of it."

Greg shrugged.

"Probably, but there it is. Did they give you any shots before they released you?"

"Yeah."

"That's what it was, then."

"I wonder where their driver crossed the Missus Hip? He didn't say, did he?"

"He hardly said anything at all. They got most of the story from the letter he carried."

"Must have been one hell of a driver, to run the Alley."

"Yeah. Nobody's ever done it before, have they?"

"Not that I know of."

"I'd like to have met the guy."

"Me too, at least I guess."

"It's a shame we can't radio across country, like in the old days."

"Why?"

"Then he wouldn't of had to do it, and we could find out along the way whether it's really worth making the run. They might all be dead by now, you know."

"You've got a point there, mister, and in a day or so we'll be to a place where going back will be harder than going ahead."

Tanner adjusted the screen as dark shapes passed.

"Look at that, will you!"

"I don't see anything."

"Put on your infras."

Greg did this and stared upward at the screen.

Bats. Enormous bats cavorted overhead, swept by in dark clouds.

"There must be hundreds of them, maybe thousands . . ."

"Guess so. Seems there are more than there used to be when I came this way a few years back. They must be screwing their heads off in Carlsbad."

"We never see them in L.A. Maybe they're pretty much harmless."

"Last time I was up to Salt Lake, I heard talk that a lot of them were rabid. Some day someone's got to go—them or us."

"You're a cheerful guy to ride with, you know?"

Tanner chuckled and lit a cigarette, and, "Why don't you make us some coffee?" he said. "As for the bats, that's something our kids can worry about, if there are any."

Greg filled the coffee pot and plugged it into the dashboard. After a time, it began to grumble and hiss.

"What the hell's that?" said Tanner, and he hit the brakes. The other car halted, several hundred yards behind his own, and he turned on his microphone and said, "Car three!

What's that look like to you?'' and waited.

He watched them: towering, tapered tops that spun between the ground and the sky, wobbling from side to side, sweeping back and forth, about a mile ahead. It seemed there were fourteen or fifteen of the things. Now they stood like pillars, now they danced. They bored into the ground and sucked up yellow dust. There was a haze all about them. The stars were dim or absent above or behind them.

Greg stared ahead and said, ''I've heard of whirlwinds, tornadoes—big, spinning things. I've never seen one, but that's the way they were described to me.''

And then the radio crackled, and the muffled voice of the man called Marlowe came through:

''Giant dust devils,'' he said. ''Big, rotary sand storms. I think they're sucking stuff up into the dead belt, because I don't see anything coming down—''

''You ever see one before?''

''No, but my partner says he did. He says the best thing might be to shoot our anchoring columns and stay put.''

Tanner did not answer immediately. He stared ahead, and the tornadoes seemed to grow larger.

''They're coming this way,'' he finally said. ''I'm not about to park here and be a target. I want to be able to maneuver. I'm going ahead through them.''

''I don't think you should.''

''Nobody asked you, mister, but if you've got any brains you'll do the same thing.''

''I've got rockets aimed at your tail, Hell.''

''You won't fire them—not for a thing like this, where I could be right and you could be wrong—and not with Greg in here, too.''

There was silence within the static, then, ''Okay, you win, Hell. Go ahead, and we'll watch. If you make it, we'll follow. If you don't, we'll stay put.''

''I'll shoot a flare when I get to the other side,'' Tanner said. ''When you see it, you do the same. Okay?''

Tanner broke the connection and looked ahead, studying the great black columns, swollen at their tops. There fell a few layers of light from the storm which they supported, and the air was foggy between the blacknesses of their revolving trunks. ''Here goes,'' said Tanner, switching his lights as

bright as they would beam. "Strap yourself in, boy," and
Greg obeyed him as the vehicle crunched forward.

Tanner buckled his own safety belt as they slowly edged
ahead.

The columns grew and swayed as he advanced, and he could
now hear a rushing, singing sound, as of a chorus of the
winds.

He skirted the first by three hundred yards and continued to
the left to avoid the one which stood before him and grew and
grew. As he got by it, there was another, and he moved farther
to the left. Then there was an open area of perhaps a quarter
of a mile leading ahead and toward his right.

He swiftly sped across it and passed between two of the
towers that stood like ebony pillars a hundred yards apart. As
he passed them, the wheel was almost torn from his grip, and
he seemed to inhabit the center of an eternal thunderclap. He
swerved to the right then and skirted another, speeding.

Then he saw seven more and cut between two and passed
about another. As he did, the one behind him moved rapidly,
crossing the path he had just taken. He exhaled heavily and
turned to the left.

He was surrounded by the final four, and he braked so that
he was thrown forward and the straps cut into his shoulder, as
two of the whirlwinds shook violently and moved in terrible
spurts of speed. One passed before him, and the front end of
his car was raised from off the ground.

Then he floored the gas pedal and shot between the final
two, and they were all behind him.

He continued on for about a quarter for a mile, turned the
car about, mounted a small rise, and parked.

He released the flare.

It hovered, like a dying star, for about half a minute.

He lit a cigarette as he stared back, and he waited.

He finished the cigarette.

Then, "Nothing," he said. "Maybe they couldn't spot it
through the storm. Or maybe we couldn't see theirs."

"I hope so," said Greg.

"How long do you want to wait?"

"Let's have that coffee."

An hour passed, then two. The pillars began to collapse until

there were only three of the slimmer ones. They moved off toward the east and were gone from sight.

Tanner released another flare, and still there was no response.

"We'd better go back and look for them," said Greg.

"Okay."

And they did.

There was nothing there, though, nothing to indicate the
fate of car three.

Dawn occurred in the east before they had finished with
their searching, and Tanner turned the car around, checked
the compass, and moved north.

"When do you think we'll hit Salt Lake?" Greg asked him,
after a long silence.

"Maybe two hours."

"Were you scared, back when you ran those things?"

"No. Afterwards, though, I didn't feel so good."

Greg nodded.

"You want me to drive again?"

"No. I won't be able to sleep if I stop now. We'll take in
more gas in Salt Lake, and we can get something to eat while a
mechanic checks over the car. Then I'll put us on the right
road, and you can take over while I sack out."

The sky was purple again and the black bands had widened.
He fired his ventral flames at two bats who decided to survey
the car. They fell back, and he accepted the mug of coffee
Greg offered him.

VIII

The sky was as dark as evening when they pulled into Salt
Lake City. John Brady—that was his name—had passed that
way but days before, and the city was ready for the responding
vehicle. Most of its ten thousand inhabitants appeared along
the street, and before Hell and Greg had jumped down from
the cab after pulling into the first garage they saw, the hood of
car number two was opened and three mechanics were peering
at the engine.

They abandoned the idea of eating in the little diner across
the street. Too many people hit them with too many questions

as soon as they set foot outside the garage. They retreated and sent someone after eggs, bacon, and toast.

There was cheering as they rolled forth onto the street and sped away into the east.

"Could have used a beer," said Tanner. "Damn it!"

And they rushed along beside the remains of what had once been U.S. Route 40.

Tanner relinquished the driver's seat and stretched out on the passenger side of the cab. The sky continued to darken above them, taking upon it the appearance it had had in L.A. the day before.

"Maybe we can outrun it," Greg said.

"Hope so."

The blue pulse began in the north, flared into a brilliant aurora. The sky was almost black directly overhead.

"Run!" cried Tanner. "Run! Those are hills up ahead! Maybe we can find an overhang or a cave!"

But it broke upon them before they reached the hills. First came the hail, then the flak. The big stones followed, and the scanner on the right went dead. The sands blasted them, and they rode beneath a celestial waterfall that caused the engine to sputter and cough.

They reached the shelter of the hills, though, and found a place within a rocky valley where the walls jutted steeply forward and broke the main force of the wind/sand/dust/ rock/water storm. They sat there as the winds screamed and boomed about them. They smoked and they listened.

"We won't make it," said Greg. "You were right. I thought we had a chance. We don't. Everything's against us, even the weather."

"We've got a chance," said Tanner. "Maybe not a real good one. But we've been lucky so far. Remember that."

Greg spat into the waste container.

"Why the sudden optimism? From you?"

"I was mad before and shooting off my mouth. Well, I'm still mad—but I got me a feeling now: I feel lucky. That's all."

Greg laughed. "The hell with luck. Look out there," he said.

"I see it," said Tanner. "This buggy is built to take it, and it's doing it. Also, we're only getting about ten percent of its full strength."

"Okay, but what difference does it make? It could last for a couple days."

"So we wait it out."

"Wait too long, and even that ten percent can smash us. Wait too long, and even if it doesn't there'll be no reason left to go ahead. Try driving, though, and it'll flatten us."

"It'll take me ten or fifteen minutes to finish that scanner. We've got spare 'eyes.' If the storm lasts more than six hours, we'll start out anyway."

"Says who?"

"Me."

"Why? You're the one who was so hot on saving his own neck. How come all of a sudden you're willing to risk it, not to mention mine too?"

Tanner smoked awhile, then said, "I've been thinking," and then he didn't say anything else.

"About what?" Greg asked him.

"Those folks in Boston," Tanner said. "Maybe it is worth it. I don't know. They never did anything for me. But hell, I like action and I'd hate to see the whole world get dead. I think I'd like to see Boston, too, just to see what it's like. It might even be fun being a hero, just to see what that's like. Don't get me wrong. I don't give a damn about anybody up there. It's just that I don't like the idea of everything being like the Alley here—all burnt-out and screwed up and full of crap. When we lost the other car back in those tornadoes, it made me start thinking . . . I'd hate to see everybody go that way —everything. I might still cop out if I get a real good chance, but I'm just telling you how I feel now. That's all."

Greg looked away and laughed, a little more heartily than usual.

"I never suspected you contained such philosophic depths."

"Me neither. I'm tired. Tell me about your brothers and sisters, huh?"

"Okay."

Four hours later when the storm slackened and the rocks became dust and the rain fog, Tanner replaced the right scanner; and they moved on out, passing later through Rocky Mountain National Park. The dust and the fog combined to limit visibility throughout the day. That evening they skirted the ruin that was Denver, and Tanner took over as they headed toward the place that had once been called Kansas.

He drove all night, and in the morning the sky was clearer than it had been in days. He let Greg snore on and sorted through his thoughts while he sipped his coffee.

It was a strange feeling that came over him as he sat there with his pardon in his pocket and his hands upon the wheel. The dust fumed at his back. The sky was the color of rosebuds, and the dark trails had shrunken once again. He recalled the stories of the days when the missiles came down, burning everything but the northeast and the southwest; the day when the winds arose and the clouds vanished and the sky had lost its blue; the days when the Panama Canal had been shattered and radios had ceased to function; the days when the planes could no longer fly. He regretted this, for he had always wanted to fly, high, birdlike, swooping and soaring. He felt slightly cold, and the screens now seemed to possess a crystal clarity, like pools of tinted water. Somewhere ahead, far, far ahead lay what might be the only other sizable pocket of humanity that remained on the shoulders of the world. He might be able to save it, if he could reach it in time. He looked about him at the rocks and the sand and the side of a broken garage that had somehow come to occupy the slope of a mountain. It remained within his mind long after he had passed it. Shattered, fallen down, half covered with debris, it took on a stark and monstrous form, like a decaying skull which had once occupied the shoulders of a giant; and he pressed down hard on the accelerator, although it could go no further. He began to tremble. The sky brightened, but he did not touch the screen controls. Why did he have to be the one? He saw a mass of smoke ahead and to the right. As he drew nearer, he saw that it rose from a mountain which had lost its top and now held a nest of fires in its place. He cut to the left, going miles, many miles, out of the way he had intended. Occasionally, the ground shook beneath his wheels. Ashes fell about him, but now the smoldering cone was far to the rear of the right-hand screen. He wondered after the days that had gone before and the few things that he actually knew about them. If he made it through, he decided he'd learn more about history. He threaded his way through painted canyons and forded a shallow river. Nobody had ever asked him to do anything important before, and he hoped that nobody ever would again.

Now, though, he was taken by the feeling that he could do it. He wanted to do it. Damnation Alley lay all about him, burning, fuming, shaking, and if he could not run it then half the world would die, and the chances would be doubled that one day all the world would be part of the Alley. His tattoo stood stark on his whitened knuckles, saying "Hell," and he knew that it was true. Greg still slept, the sleep of exhaustion, and Tanner narrowed his eyes and chewed his beard and never touched the brake, not even when he saw the rockslide beginning. He made it by and sighed. That pass was closed to him forever, but he had shot through without a scratch. His mind was an expanding bubble, its surfaces like the view-screens, registering everything about him. He felt the flow of the air within the cab and the upward pressure of the pedal upon his foot. His throat seemed dry, but it didn't matter. His eyes felt gooey at their inside corners, but he didn't wipe them. He roared across the pocket plains of Kansas, and he knew now that he had been sucked into the role completely and that he wanted it that way. Damn-his-eyes Denton had been right. It had to be done. He halted when he came to the lip of a chasm and headed north. Thirty miles later it ended, and he turned again to the south. Greg muttered in his sleep. It sounded like a curse. Tanner repeated it softly a couple times and turned toward the east as soon as a level stretch occurred. The sun stood in high heaven, and Tanner felt as though he were drifting bodiless beneath it, above the brown ground flaked with green spikes of growth. He clenched his teeth and his mind went back to Denny, doubtless now in a hospital. Better than being where the others had gone. He hoped the money he'd told him about was still there. Then he felt the ache begin, in the places between his neck and his shoulders. It spread down into his arms, and he realized how tightly he was gripping the wheel. He blinked and took a deep breath and realized that his eyeballs hurt. He lit a cigarette and it tasted foul, but he kept puffing at it. He drank some water and he dimmed the rear view-screen as the sun fell behind him. Then he heard a sound like a distant rumble of thunder and was fully alert once more. He sat up straight and took his foot off the accelerator.

He slowed. He braked and stopped. Then he saw them. He sat there and watched them as they passed, about a half-mile ahead.

●   ●   ●

A monstrous herd of bison crossed before him. It took the better part of an hour before they had passed. Huge, heavy, dark,
heads down, hooves scoring the soil, they ran without slowing
until the thunder was great and then rolled off toward the
north, diminishing, softening, dying, gone. The screen of their
dust still hung before him, and he plunged into it, turning on
his lights.

He considered taking a pill, decided against it. Greg might
be waking soon, he wanted to be able to get some sleep after
they'd switched over.

He came up beside a highway, and its surface looked pretty
good, so he crossed onto it and sped ahead. After a time, he
passed a faded, sagging sign that said "TOPEKA—110
MILES."

Greg yawned and stretched. He rubbed his eyes with his
knuckles and then rubbed his forehead, the right side of which
was swollen and dark.

"What time is it?" he asked.

Tanner gestured toward the clock in the dashboard.

"Morning or is it afternoon?"

"Afternoon."

"My God! I must have slept around fifteen hours!"

"That's about right."

"You been driving all that time?"

"That's right."

"You must be done in. You look like hell. Let me just hit
the head. I'll take over in a few minutes."

"Good idea."

Greg crawled toward the rear of the vehicle.

After about five minutes, Tanner came upon the outskirts
of a dead town. He drove up the main street, and there were
rusted-out hulks of cars all along it. Most of the buildings had
fallen in upon themselves, and some of the opened cellars that
he saw were filled with scummy water. Skeletons lay about the
town square. There were no trees standing above the weeds
that grew there. Three telephone poles still stood, one of them
leaning forward and trailing wires like a handful of black
spaghetti. Several benches were visible within the weeds beside
the cracked sidewalks, and a skeleton lay stretched out upon
the second one. Tanner passed. He found his way barred by
a fallen telephone pole, and he detoured around the block.

The next street was somewhat better preserved, but all its storefront windows were broken, and a nude mannikin posed fetchingly with her left arm missing from the elbow down. The traffic light at the corner stared blindly as Tanner passed through its intersection.

Tanner heard Greg coming forward as he turned at the next corner.

"I'll take over now," he said.

"I want to get out of this place first," and they both watched in silence for the next fifteen minutes until the dead town was gone from around them.

Tanner pulled to a halt then and said, "We're a couple hours away from a place that used to be called Topeka. Wake me if you run into anything hairy."

"How did it go while I was asleep? Did you have any trouble?"

"No," said Tanner, and he closed his eyes and began to snore.

Greg drove away from the sunset, and he ate three ham sandwiches and drank a quart of milk before Topeka.

IX

Tanner was awakened by the firing of the rockets. He rubbed the sleep from his eyes and stared dumbly ahead for almost half a minute.

Like gigantic dried leaves, great clouds fell about them. Bats, bats, bats. The air was filled with bats. Tanner could hear a chittering, squeaking, scratching sound, and the car was buffeted by their dark bodies.

"Where are we?" he asked.

"Kansas City. The place seems full of them," and Greg released another rocket, which cut a fiery path through the swooping, spinning horde.

"Save the rockets. Use the fire," said Tanner, switching the nearest gun to manual and bringing cross-hairs into focus upon the screen. "Blast 'em in all directions—for five, six seconds—then I'll come in."

The flame shot forth, orange and cream blossoms of combustion. When they folded, Tanner sighted in the screen and

squeezed the trigger. He swung the gun, and they fell. Their
charred bodies lay all about him, and he added new ones to the
smoldering heaps.

"Roll it!" he cried, and the car moved forward, swaying,
bat bodies crunching beneath its tires.

Tanner laced the heavens with gunfire, and when they
swooped again he strafed them and fired a flare.

In the sudden magnesium glow from overhead, it seemed
that millions of vampire-faced forms were circling, spiraling
down toward them.

He switched from gun to gun, and they fell about him like
fruit. Then he called out, "Brake, and hit the topside flame!"
and Greg did this thing.

"Now the sides! Front and rear next!"

Bodies were burning all about them, heaped as high as the
hood, and Greg put the car into low gear when Tanner cried
"Forward!" And they pushed their way through the wall of
charred flesh.

Tanner fired another flare.

The bats were still there, but circling higher now. Tanner
primed the guns and waited, but they did not attack again in
any great number. A few swept about them, and he took pot-
shots at them as they passed.

Ten minutes later he said, "That's the Missouri River to our
left. If we just follow alongside it now, we'll hit Saint Louis."

"I know. Do you think it'll be full of bats, too?"

"Probably. But if we take our time and arrive with daylight,
they shouldn't bother us. Then we can figure a way to get
across the Missus Hip."

Then their eyes fell upon the rearview screen, where the
dark skyline of Kansas City with bats was silhouetted by pale
stars and touched by the light of the bloody moon.

After a time, Tanner slept once more. He dreamt he was
riding his bike, slowly, down the center of a wide street, and
people lined the sidewalks and began to cheer as he passed.
They threw confetti, but by the time it reached him it was garbage, wet and stinking. He stepped on the gas then, but his
bike slowed even more and now they were screaming at him.
They shouted obscenities. They cried out his name, over and
over, and again. The Harley began to wobble, but his feet
seemed to be glued in place. In a moment, he knew, he would

fall. The bike came to a halt then, and he began to topple over toward the right side. They rushed toward him as he fell, and he knew it was just about all over . . .

He awoke with a jolt and saw the morning spread out before him: a bright coin in the middle of a dark blue tablecloth and a row of glasses along the edge.

"That's it," said Greg. "The Missus Hip."

Tanner was suddenly very hungry.

After they had refreshed themselves, they sought the bridge.

"I didn't see any of your naked people with spears," said Greg. "Of course, we might have passed their way after dark —if there are any of them still around."

"Good thing, too," said Tanner. "Saved us some ammo."

The bridge came into view, sagging and dark save for the places where the sun gilded its cables, and it stretched unbroken across the bright expanse of waters. They moved slowly toward it, threading their way through streets gorged with rubble, detouring when it became completely blocked by the rows of broken machines, fallen walls, sewer-deep abysses in the burst pavement.

It took them two hours to travel half a mile, and it was noon before they reached the foot of the bridge, and, "It looks as if Brady might have crossed here," said Greg, eyeing what appeared to be a cleared passageway amidst the wrecks that filled the span. "How do you think he did it?"

"Maybe he had something with him to hoist them and swing them out over the edge. There are some wrecks below, down where the water is shallow."

"Were they there last time you passed by?"

"I don't know. I wasn't right down here by the bridge. I topped that hill back there," and he gestured at the rearview screen.

"Well, from here it looks like we might be able to make it. Let's roll."

They moved upward and forward onto the bridge and began their slow passage across the mighty Missus Hip. There were times when the bridge creaked beneath them, sighed, groaned, and they felt it move.

The sun was high, and still they moved forward, scraping their fenders against the edges of the wrecks, using their wings like plows. They were on the bridge for three hours before its end came into sight through a rift in the junkstacks.

When their wheels finally touched the opposite shore, Greg sat there breathing heavily and then lit a cigarette.

"You want to drive awhile, Hell?"

"Yeah. Let's switch over."

He did, and, "God! I'm bushed!" he said as he sprawled out.

Tanner drove forward through the ruins of East Saint Louis, hurrying to clear the town before nightfall. The radiation level began to mount as he advanced, and the streets were cluttered and broken. He checked the inside of the cab for radioactivity, but it was still clean.

It took him hours, and as the sun fell at his back he saw the blue aurora begin once more in the north. But the sky stayed clear, filled with its stars, and there were no black lines that he could see. After a long while, a rose-colored moon appeared and hung before him. He turned on the music, softly, and glanced at Greg. It didn't seem to bother him, so he let it continue.

The instrument panel caught his eye. The radiation level was still climbing. Then, in the forward screen, he saw the crater and he stopped.

It must have been over half a mile across, and he couldn't tell its depth.

He fired a flare, and in its light he used the telescopic lenses to examine it to the right and to the left.

The way seemed smoother to the right, and he turned in that direction and began to negotiate it.

The place was hot! So very, very hot! He hurried. And he wondered as he sped, the gauge rising before him: What had it been like on that day, Whenever? That day when a tiny sun had lain upon this spot and fought with, and for a time beaten, the brightness of the other in the sky, before it sank slowly into its sudden burrow? He tried to imagine it, succeeded, then tried to put it out of his mind and couldn't. How do you put out the fires that burn forever? He wished that he knew. There'd been so many places to go then, and he liked to move around.

What had it been like in the old days, when a man could just jump on his bike and cut out for a new town whenever he wanted?And nobody emptying buckets of crap on you from out of the sky? He felt cheated, which was not a new feeling for him, but it made him curse even longer than usual.

He lit a cigarette when he'd finally rounded the crater, and he smiled for the first time in months as the radiation gauge began to fall once more. Before many miles, he saw tall grasses swaying about him and not too long after that he began to see trees.

Trees short and twisted, at first, but the farther he fled from the place of carnage, the taller and straighter they became. They were trees such as he had never seen before—fifty, sixty feet in height—and graceful, and gathering stars, there on the plains of Illinois.

He was moving along a clean, hard, wide road, and just then he wanted to travel it forever—to Floridee, of the swamps and Spanish moss and citrus groves and fine beaches and the Gulf; and up to the cold, rocky Cape, where everything is gray and brown and the waves break below the lighthouses and the salt burns in your nose and there are graveyards where bones have lain for centuries and you can still read the names they bore, chiseled there into the stones above them; down through the nation where they say the grass is blue; then follow the mighty Missus Hip to the place where she spreads and comes and there's the Gulf again, full of little islands where the old boosters stashed their loot; and through the shag-topped mountains he'd heard about: the Smokies, Ozarks, Poconos, Catskills; drive through the forest of Shen-andoah; park, and take a boat out over Chesapeake Bay; see the big lakes and the place where the water falls, Niagara. To drive forever along the big road, to see everything, to eat the world. Yes. Maybe it wasn't all Damnation Alley. Some of the legendary places must still be clean, like the countryside about him now. He wanted it with a hunger, with a fire like that which always burned in his loins. He laughed then, just one short, sharp bark, because now it seemed like maybe he could have it.

The music played softly, too sweetly perhaps, and it filled him.

X

By morning he was into the place called Indiana and still following the road. He passed farmhouses which seemed in good
repair. There could even be people living in them. He longed
to investigate, but he didn't dare to stop. Then after an hour,
it was all countryside again, and degenerating.

The grasses grew shorter, shriveled, were gone. An occasional twisted tree clung to the bare earth. The radiation level
began to rise once more. The signs told him he was nearing In-
dianapolis, which he guessed was a big city that had received a
bomb and was now gone away.

Nor was he mistaken.

He had to detour far to the south to get around it, back-
tracking to a place called Martinsville in order to cross over
the White River. Then as he headed east once more, his radio
crackled and came to life. There was a faint voice, repeating,
"Unidentified vehicle, halt!" and he switched all the scanners
to telescopic range. Far ahead, on a hilltop, he saw a standing
man with binoculars and a walkie-talkie. He did not acknowledge receipt of the transmission, but kept driving.

He was hitting forty miles an hour along a halfway decent
section of roadway, and he gradually increased his speed to
fifty-five, though the protesting of his tires upon the cracked
pavement was sufficient to awaken Greg.

Tanner stared ahead, ready for an attack, and the radio
kept repeating the order, louder now as he neared the hill, and
called upon him to acknowledge the message.

He touched the brake as he rounded a long curve, and he
did not reply to Greg's "What's the matter?"

When he saw it there, blocking the way, ready to fire, he
acted instantly.

The tank filled the road, and its big gun was pointed directly
at him.

As his eye sought for and found passage around it, his right
hand slapped the switches that sent three armor-piercing
rockets screaming ahead and his left spun the wheel counterclockwise and his foot fell heavy on the accelerator.

He was half off the road then, bouncing along the ditch at
its side, when the tank discharged one fiery belch which missed
him and then caved in upon itself and blossomed.

There came the sound of rifle fire as he pulled back onto the road on the other side of the tank and sped ahead. Greg launched a single grenade to the right and the left and then hit the fifty-calibers. They tore on ahead, and after about a quarter of a mile Tanner picked up his microphone and said, "Sorry about that. My brakes don't work," and hung it up again. There was no response.

As soon as they reached a level plain, commanding a good view in all directions, Tanner halted the vehicle and Greg moved into the driver's seat.

"Where do you think they got hold of that armor?"

"Who knows?"

"And why stop us?"

"They didn't know what we were carrying—and maybe they just wanted the car."

"Blasting, it's a helluva way to get it."

"If they can't have it, why should they let us keep it?"

"You know just how they think, don't you?"

"Yes."

"Have a cigarette."

Tanner nodded, accepted.

"It's been pretty bad, you know?"

"I can't argue with that."

". . . And we've still got a long way to go."

"Yeah, so let's get rolling."

"You said before that you didn't think we'd make it."

"I've revised my opinion. Now I think we will."

"After all we've been through?"

"After all we've been through."

"What more do we have to fight with?"

"I don't know all that yet."

"But on the other hand, we know everything there is behind us. We know how to avoid a lot of it now."

Tanner nodded.

"You tried to cut out once. Now I don't blame you."

"You getting scared, Greg?"

"I'm no good to my family if I'm dead."

"Then why'd you agree to come along?"

"I didn't know it would be like this. You had better sense, because you had an idea what it would be like."

"I had an idea."

"Nobody can blame us if we fail. After all, we've tried."

"What about all those people in Boston you made me a speech about?"

"They're probably dead by now. The plague isn't a thing that takes its time, you know?"

"What about that guy Brady? He died to get us the news."

"He tried, and God knows I respect the attempt. But we've already lost four guys. Now should we make it six, just to show that everybody tried?"

"Greg, we're a lot closer to Boston than we are to L.A. now. The tanks should have enough fuel in them to get us where we're going, but not to take us back from here."

"We can refuel in Salt Lake."

"I'm not even sure we could make it back to Salt Lake."

"Well, it'll only take a minute to figure it out. For that matter, though, we could take the bikes for the last hundred or so. They use a lot less gas."

"And you're the guy was calling me names. You're the citizen was wondering how people like me happen. You asked me what they ever did to me. I told you, too: Nothing. Now maybe I want to do something for them, just because I feel like it. I've been doing a lot of thinking."

"You ain't supporting any family, Hell. I've got other people to worry about beside myself."

"You've got a nice way of putting things when you want to chicken out. You say I'm not really scared, but I've got my mother and my brothers and sisters to worry about, and I got a chick I'm hot on. That's why I'm backing down. No other reason."

"And that's right, too! I don't understand you, Hell! I don't understand you at all! You're the one who put this idea in my head in the first place!"

"So give it back, and let's get moving."

He saw Greg's hand slither toward the gun on the door, so he flipped his cigarette into his face and managed to hit him once, in the stomach—a weak, left-handed blow, but it was the best he could manage from that position.

Then Greg threw himself upon him, and he felt himself borne back into his seat. They wrestled, and Greg's fingers clawed their way up his face toward his eyes.

Tanner got his arms free above the elbows, seized Greg's

head, twisted, and shoved with all his strength.

Greg hit the dashboard, went stiff, then went slack.

Tanner banged his head against it twice more, just to be sure he wasn't faking. Then he pushed him away and moved back into the driver's seat. He checked all the screens while he caught his breath. There was nothing menacing approaching.

He fetched cord from the utility chest and bound Greg's hands behind his back. He tied his ankles together and ran a line from them to his wrists. Then he positioned him in the seat, reclined it part way and tied him in place within it.

He put the car into gear and headed toward Ohio.

Two hours later Greg began to moan, and Tanner turned the music up to drown him out. Landscape had appeared once more: grass and trees, fields of green, orchards of apples, apples still small and green, white farm houses and brown barns and red barns far removed from the roadway he raced along; rows of corn, green and swaying, brown tassels already visible and obviously tended by someone; fences of split timber, green hedges; lofty, star-leafed maples, fresh-looking road signs, a green-shingled steeple from which the sound of a bell came forth.

The lines in the sky widened, but the sky itself did not darken, as it usually did before a storm. So he drove on into the afternoon, until he reached the Dayton Abyss.

He looked down into the fog-shrouded canyon that had caused him to halt. He scanned to the left and the right, decided upon the left and headed north.

Again the radiation level was high. And he hurried, slowing only to skirt the crevices, chasms and canyons that emanated from that dark, deep center. Thick yellow vapors seeped forth from some of these and filled the air before him. At one point they were all about him, like a clinging, sulphurous cloud, and a breeze came and parted them. Involuntarily then, he hit the brake, and the car jerked and halted and Greg moaned once more. He stared at the thing for the few seconds that it was visible, then slowly moved forward again.

The sight was not duplicated for the whole of his passage, but it did not easily go from out of his mind, and he could not explain it where he had seen it. Yellow, hanging and grinning, he had seen a crucified skeleton there beside the Abyss. *People*, he decided. *That explains everything.*

• • •

When he left the region of fogs the sky was still dark. He did not realize for a time that he was in the open once more. It had taken him close to four hours to skirt Dayton, and now as he headed across a blasted heath, going east again, he saw for a moment a tiny piece of the sun, like a sickle, fighting its way ashore on the northern bank of a black river in the sky, and failing.

His lights were turned up to their fullest intensity, and as he realized what might follow he looked in every direction for shelter.

There was an old barn on a hill, and he raced toward it. One side had caved in, and the doors had fallen down. He edged in, however, and the interior was moist and moldy-looking under his lights. He saw a skeleton which he guessed to be that of a horse within a fallen-down stall.

He parked and turned off his lights and waited.

Soon the wailing came again and drowned out Greg's occasional moans and mutterings. There came another sound, not hard and heavy like gunfire, as that which he had heard in L.A., but gentle, steady and almost purring.

He cracked the door, to hear it better.

Nothing assailed him, so he stepped down from the cab and walked back a ways. The radiation level was almost normal, so he didn't bother with his protective suit. He walked back toward the fallen doors and looked outside. He wore the pistol behind his belt.

Something gray descended in droplets and the sun fought itself partly free once more.

It was rain, pure and simple. He had never seen rain, pure and simple, before. So he lit a cigarette and watched it fall.

It came down with only an occasional rumbling and nothing else accompanied it. The sky was still a bluish color beyond the bands of black.

It fell all about him. It ran down the frame to his left. A random gust of wind blew some droplets into his face and he realized that they were water, nothing more. Puddles formed on the ground outside. He tossed a chunk of wood into one and saw it splash and float. From somewhere high up inside the barn he heard the sound of birds. He smelled the sick-sweet smell of decaying straw. Off in the shadows to his right

he saw a rusted threshing machine. Some feathers drifted
down about him, and he caught one in his hand and studied it.
Light, dark, fluffy, ribbed. He'd never really looked at a
feather before. It worked almost like a zipper, the way the individual branches clung to one another. He let it go, and the
wind caught it, and it vanished somewhere toward his back.
He looked out once more, and back along his trail. He could
probably drive through what was coming down now. But he
realized just how tired he was. He found a barrel and sat down
on it and lit another cigarette.

It had been a good run so far, and he found himself thinking about its last stages. He couldn't trust Greg for a while yet.
Not until they were so far that there could be no turning back.
Then they'd need each other so badly that he could turn him
loose. He hoped he hadn't scrambled his brains completely.
He didn't know what more the alley held. If the storms were
less from here on in, however, that would be a big help.

He sat there for a long while, feeling the cold, moist breezes;
and the rainfall lessened after a time, and he went back to the
car and started it. Greg was still unconscious, he noted, as he
backed out. This might not be good.

He took a pill to keep himself alert and he ate some rations
as he drove along. The rain continued to come down, but
gently. It fell all the way across Ohio, and the sky remained
overcast. He crossed into West Virginia at the place called
Parkersburg, and then he veered slightly to the north, going by
the old Rand McNally he'd been furnished. The gray day went
away into black night, and he drove on.

There were no more of the dark bats around to trouble him,
but he passed several more craters and the radiation gauge
rose, and at one point a pack of huge wild dogs pursued him,
baying and howling, and they ran along the road and snapped
at his tires and barked and yammered and then fell back.
There were some tremors beneath his wheels as he passed another mountain and it spewed forth bright clouds to his left
and made a kind of thunder. Ashes fell, and he drove through
them. A flash flood splashed over him, and the engine sput-
tered and died, twice; but he started it again each time and
pushed on ahead, the waters lapping about his sides. Then he
reached higher, drier ground, and riflemen tried to bar his

way. He strafed them and hurled a grenade and drove on by. When the darkness went away and the dim moon came up, dark birds circled him and dove down at him, but he ignored them and after a time they, too, were gone.

He drove until he felt tired again, and then he ate some more and took another pill. By then he was in Pennsylvania, and he felt that if Greg would only come around he would turn him loose and trust him with the driving.

He halted twice to visit the latrine, and he tugged at the golden band in his pierced left ear, and he blew his nose and scratched himself. Then he ate more rations and continued on.

He began to ache, in all his muscles, and he wanted to stop and rest, but he was afraid of the things that might come upon him if he did.

As he drove through another dead town, the rains started again. Not hard, just a drizzly downpour, cold-looking and sterile—a brittle, shiny screen. He stopped in the middle of the road before the thing he'd almost driven into, and he stared at it.

He'd thought at first that it was more black lines in the sky. He'd halted because they'd seemed to appear too suddenly.

It was a spider's web, strands thick as his arm, strung between two leaning buildings.

He switched on his forward flame and began to burn it.

When the fires died, he saw the approaching shape, coming down from high above.

It was a spider, larger than himself, rushing to check the disturbance.

He elevated the rocket launchers, took careful aim and pierced it with one white-hot missile.

It still hung there in the trembling web and seemed to be kicking.

He turned on the flame again, for a full ten seconds, and when it subsided there was an open way before him.

He rushed through, wide awake and alert once again, his pains forgotten. He drove as fast as he could, trying to forget the sight.

Another mountain smoked, ahead and to his right, but it did not bloom, and few ashes descended as he passed it.

He made coffee and drank a cup. After a while it was morning, and he raced toward it.

XI

He was stuck in the mud, somewhere in eastern Pennsylvania, and cursing. Greg was looking very pale. The sun was nearing midheaven. He leaned back and closed his eyes. It was too much.

He slept.

He awoke and felt worse. There was a banging on the side of the car. His hands moved toward fire-control and wing-control, automatically, and his eyes sought the screens.

He saw an old man, and there were two younger men with him. They were armed, but they stood right before the left wing, and he knew he could cut them in half in an instant.

He activated the outside speaker and the audio pickup.

"What do you want?" he asked, and his voice crackled forth.

"You okay?" the old man called.

"Not really. You caught me sleeping."

"You stuck?"

"That's about the size of it."

"I got a mule team can maybe get you out. Can't get 'em here before tomorrow morning, though."

"Great!" said Tanner. "I'd appreciated it."

"Where you from?"

"L.A."

"What's that?"

"Los Angeles. West Coast."

There was some murmuring, then, "You're a long way from home, mister."

"Don't I know it.—Look, if you're serious about those mules, I'd appreciate hell out of it. It's an emergency."

"What kind of?"

"You know about Boston?"

"I know it's there."

"Well, people are dying up that way, of the plague. I've got drugs here can save them, if I can get through."

There were some more murmurs, then, "We'll help you. Boston's pretty important, and we'll get you loose. Want to come back with us?"

"Where? And who are you?"

"The name's Samuel Potter, and these are my sons, Roderick and Caliban. My farm's about six miles off. You're welcome to spend the night.''

"It's not that I don't trust you," said Tanner. "It's just that I don't trust anybody, if you know what I mean. I've been shot at too much recently to want to take the chance."

"Well, how about if we put up our guns? You're probably able to shoot us from there, ain't you?"

"That's right."

"So we're taking a chance just standing here. We're willing to help you. We'd stand to lose if the Boston traders stopped coming to Albany. If there's someone else inside, he can cover you."

"Wait a minute," said Tanner, and he opened the door.

The old man stuck out his hand, and Tanner took it and shook it, also his sons'.

"Is there any kind of doctor around here?" he asked.

"In the settlement—about thirty miles north."

"My partner's hurt. I think he needs a doctor." He gestured back toward the cab.

Sam moved forward and peered within.

"Why's he all trussed up like that?"

"He went off his rocker, and I had to clobber him. I tied him up, to be safe. But now he doesn't look so good."

"Then let's whip up a stretcher and get him onto it. You lock up tight then, and my boys'll bring him back to the house. We'll send someone for the doc. You don't look so good yourself. Bet you'd like a bath and a shave and a clean bed."

"I don't feel so good," Tanner said. "Let's make that stretcher quick, before we need two."

He sat up on the fender and smoked while the Potter boys cut trees and stripped them. Waves of fatigue washed over him, and he found it hard to keep his eyes open. His feet felt very far away, and his shoulders ached. The cigarette fell from his fingers, and he leaned backward on the hood.

Someone was slapping his leg.

He forced his eyes open and looked down.

"Okay," Potter said. "We cut your partner loose and we got him on the stretcher. Want to lock up and get moving?"

Tanner nodded and jumped down. He sank almost up to his boot tops when he hit, but he closed the cab and staggered toward the old man in buckskin.

They began walking across country, and after a while it became mechanical.

Samuel Potter kept up a steady line of chatter as he led the way, rifle resting in the crook of his arm. Maybe it was to keep Tanner awake.

"It's not too far, son, and it'll be pretty easy going in just a few minutes now. What'd you say your name was anyhow?"

"Hell," said Tanner.

"Beg pardon?"

"Hell. Hell's my name. Hell Tanner."

Sam Potter chuckled.

"That's a pretty mean name, mister. If it's okay with you, I'll introduce you to my wife and the youngest as 'Mister Tanner.' All right?"

"That's just fine," Tanner gasped, pulling his boots out of the mire with a sucking sound.

"We'd sure miss them Boston traders. I hope you make it in time."

"What is it that they do?"

"They keep shops in Albany, and twice a year they give a fair—spring and fall. They carry all sort of things we need—needles, thread, pepper, kettles, pans, seed, guns and ammo, all kind of things—and the fairs are pretty good times, too. Most anybody between here and there would help you along. Hope you make it. We'll get you off to a good start again."

They reached higher, drier ground.

"You mean it's pretty clear sailing after this?"

"Well, no. But I'll help you on a map and tell you what to look out for."

"I got mine with me," said Tanner, as they topped a hill, and he saw a farm house off in the distance. "That your place?"

"Correct. It ain't much further now. Real easy walkin'—an' you just lean on my shoulder if you get tired."

"I can make it," said Tanner. "It's just that I had so many of those pills to keep me awake that I'm starting to feel all the sleep I've been missing. I'll be okay."

"You'll get to sleep real soon now. And when you're awake again, we'll go over that map of yours, and you can write in all the places I tell you about."

"Good scene," said Tanner, "good scene," and he put his hand on Sam's shoulder then and staggered along beside him, feeling almost drunk and wishing he were.

After a hazy eternity he saw the house before him, then the door. The door swung open, and he felt himself falling forward, and that was it.

XII

Sleep. Blackness, distant voices, more blackness. Wherever he lay, it was soft, and he turned over onto his other side and went away again.

When everything finally flowed together into a coherent ball and he opened his eyes, there was light streaming in through the window to his right, falling in rectangles upon the patchwork quilt that covered him. He groaned, stretched, rubbed his eyes and scratched his beard.

He surveyed the room carefully: polished wooden floors with handwoven rugs of blue and red and gray scattered about them, a dresser holding a white enamel basin with a few black spots up near its lip where some of the enamel had chipped away, a mirror on the wall behind him and above all that, a spindly looking rocker near the window, a print cushion on its seat, a small table against the other wall with a chair pushed in beneath it, books and paper and pen and ink on the table, a hand-stitched sampler on the wall asking God to Bless, a blue-and-green print of a waterfall on the other wall.

He sat up, discovered he was naked, looked around for his clothing. It was nowhere in sight.

As he sat there, deciding whether or not to call out, the door opened, and Sam walked in. He carried Tanner's clothing, clean and neatly folded, over one arm. In his other hand he carried his boots, and they shone like wet midnight.

"Heard you stirring around," he said. "How you feeling now?"

"A lot better, thanks."

"We've got a bath all drawn. Just have to dump in a couple buckets of hot, and it's all yours. I'll have the boys carry it in in a minute, and some soap and towels."

Tanner bit his lip, but he didn't want to seem inhospitable to his benefactor, so he nodded and forced a smile then.

"That'll be fine."

". . . And there's a razor and a scissors on the dresser—whichever you might want."

He nodded again. Sam set his clothes down on the rocker and his boots on the floor beside it, then left the room.

Soon Roderick and Caliban brought in the tub, spread some sacks, and set it upon them.

"How you feeling?" one of them asked. (Tanner wasn't sure which was which. They both seemed graceful as scarecrows, and their mouths were packed full of white teeth.)

"Real good," he said.

"Bet you're hungry," said the other. "You slep' all afternoon yesterday and all night and most of this morning."

"You know it," said Tanner. "How's my partner?"

The nearer one shook his head, and, "Still sleeping and sickly," he said. "The doc should be here soon. Our kid brother went after him last night."

They turned to leave, and the one who had been speaking added, "Soon as you get cleaned up, Ma'll fix you something to eat. Cal and me are going out now to try and get your rig loose. Dad'll tell you about the roads while you eat."

"Thanks."

"Good morning to you."

" 'Morning."

They closed the door behind them as they left.

Tanner got up and moved to the mirror, studied himself.

"Well, just this once," he muttered.

Then he washed his face and trimmed his beard and cut his hair.

Then, gritting his teeth, he lowered himself into the tub, soaped up and scrubbed. The water grew gray and scummy beneath the suds. He splashed out and toweled himself down and dressed.

He was starched and crinkly and smelled faintly of disinfectant. He smiled at his dark-eyed reflection and lit a cigarette. He combed his hair and studied the stranger. "Damn! I'm beautiful!" he chuckled, and then he opened the door and entered the kitchen.

Sam was sitting at the table drinking a cup of coffee, and his wife who was short and heavy and wore long gray skirts was

facing in the other direction, leaning over the stove. She
turned, and he saw that her face was large, with bulging red
cheeks that dimpled and a little white scar in the middle of her
forehead. Her hair was brown, shot through with gray, and
pulled back into a knot. She bobbed her head and smiled a
"Good morning" at him.

" 'Morning," he replied. "I'm afraid I left kind of a mess
in the other room."

"Don't worry about that," said Sam. "Seat yourself, and
we'll have you some breakfast in a minute. The boys told you
about your friend?"

Tanner nodded.

As she placed a cup of coffee in front of Tanner, Sam said,
"Wife's name's Susan."

"How do," she said.

"Hi."

"Now, then, I got your map here. Saw it sticking out of
your jacket. That's your gun hanging aside the door, too.
Anyhows, I've been figuring and I think the best way you
could head would be up to Albany and then go along the old
Route 9, which is in pretty good shape." He spread the map
and pointed as he talked. "Now, it won't be all of a picnic,"
he said, "but it looks like the cleanest and fastest way in—"

"Breakfast," said his wife and pushed the map aside to set a
plate full of eggs and bacon and sausages in front of Tanner
and another one, holding four pieces of toast, next to it. There
was marmalade, jam, jelly, and butter on the table, and Tanner helped himself to it and sipped the coffee and filled the
empty places inside while Sam talked.

He told him about the gangs that ran between Boston and
Albany on bikes, hijacking anything they could, and that was
the reason most cargo went in convoys with shotgun riders
aboard. "But you don't have to worry, with that rig of yours,
do you?" he asked, and Tanner said, "Hope not," and wolfed
down more food. He wondered, though, if they were anything
like his old pack, and he hoped not, again, for both their
sakes.

Tanner raised his coffee cup, and he heard a sound outside.

The door opened, and a boy ran into the kitchen. Tanner
figured him as between ten and twelve years of age. An older
man followed him, carrying the traditional black bag.

"We're here! We're here!" cried the boy, and Sam stood and shook hands with the man, so Tanner figured he should, too. He wiped his mouth and gripped the man's hand and said, "My partner sort of went out of his head. He jumped me, and we had a fight. I shoved him, and he banged his head on the dashboard."

The doctor, a dark-haired man, probably in his late forties, wore a dark suit. His face was heavily lined, and his eyes looked tired. He nodded.

Sam said, "I'll take you to him," and he led him out through the door at the other end of the kitchen.

Tanner reseated himself and picked up the last piece of toast. Susan refilled his coffee cup, and he nodded to her.

"My name's Jerry," said the boy, seating himself in his father's abandoned chair. "Is your name, mister, really Hell?"

"Hush, you!" said his mother.

" 'Fraid so," said Tanner.

". . . And you drove all the way across the country? Through the Alley?"

"So far."

"What was it like?"

"Mean."

"What all'd you see?"

"Bats as big as this kitchen—some of them even bigger—on the other side of the Missus Hip. Lot of them in Saint Louis."

"What'd you do?"

"Shot 'em. Burnt 'em. Drove through 'em."

"What else you see?"

"Gila monsters. Big, technicolor lizards—the size of a barn. Dust devils—big circling winds that sucked up one car. Fire-topped mountains. Real big thorn bushes that we had to burn. Drove through some storms. Drove over places where the ground was like glass. Drove along where the ground was shaking. Drove around big craters, all radioactive."

"Wish I could do that some day."

"Maybe you will, some day."

Tanner finished the food and lit a cigarette and sipped the coffee.

"Real good breakfast," he called out. "Best I've eaten in days. Thanks."

Susan smiled, then said, "Jerry, don't go an' pester the man."

"No bother, missus. He's okay."

"What's that ring on your hand?" said Jerry. "It looks like a snake."

"That's what it is," said Tanner, pulling it off. "It is sterling silver with red glass eyes, and I got it in a place called Tijuana. Here. You keep it."

"I couldn't take that," said the boy, and he looked at his mother, his eyes asking if he could. She shook her head from left to right, and Tanner saw it and said, "Your folks were good enough to help me out and get a doc for my partner and feed me and give me a place to sleep. I'm sure they won't mind if I want to show my appreciation a little bit and give you this ring," and Jerry looked back at his mother, and Tanner nodded and she nodded too.

Jerry whistled and jumped up and put it on his finger.

"It's too big," he said.

"Here, let me mash it a bit for you. These spiral kind'll fit anybody if you squeeze them a little."

He squeezed the ring and gave it back to the boy to try on. It was still too big, so he squeezed it again and then it fit.

Jerry put it on and began to run from the room.

"Wait!" his mother said. "What do you say?"

He turned around and said, "Thank you, Hell."

"Mister Tanner," she said.

"Mister Tanner," the boy repeated and the door banged behind him.

"That was good of you," she said.

Tanner shrugged.

"He liked it," he said. "Glad I could turn him on with it."

He finished his coffee and his cigarette, and she gave him another cup, and he lit another cigarette. After a time, Sam and the doctor came out of the other room, and Tanner began wondering where the family had slept the night before. Susan poured them both coffee, and they seated themselves at the table to drink it.

"Your friend's got a concussion," the doctor said. "I can't really tell how serious his condition is without getting X rays, and there's no way of getting them here. I wouldn't recommend moving him, though."

Tanner said, "For how long?"

"Maybe a few days, maybe a couple weeks. I've left some medication and told Sam what to do for him. Sam says there's a plague in Boston and you've got to hurry. My advice is that you go on without him. Leave him here with the Potters. He'll be taken care of. He can go up to Albany with them for the Spring Fair and make his way to Boston from there on some commercial carrier. I think he'll be all right."

Tanner thought about it a while, then nodded.

"Okay," he said, "if that's the way it's got to be."

"That's what I recommend."

They drank their coffee.

XIII

Tanner regarded his freed vehicle, said, "I guess I'll be going, then," and nodded to the Potters. "Thanks," he said, and he unlocked the cab, climbed into it and started the engine. He put it into gear, blew the horn twice and started to move.

In the screen, he saw the three men waving. He stamped the accelerator, and they were gone from sight.

He sped ahead, and the way was easy. The sky was salmon pink. The earth was brown, and there was much green grass. The bright sun caught the day in a silver net.

This part of the country seemed virtually untouched by the chaos that had produced the rest of the Alley. Tanner played music, drove along. He passed two trucks on the road and honked his horn each time. Once, he received a reply.

He drove all that day, and it was well into the night when he pulled into Albany. The streets themselves were dark, and only a few lights shone from the buildings. He drew up in front of a flickering red sign that said "BAR & GRILL," parked and entered.

It was small, and there was jukebox music playing, tunes he'd never heard before, and the lighting was poor, and there was sawdust on the floor.

He sat down at the bar and pushed the Magnum way down behind his belt so that it didn't show. Then he took off his jacket, because of the heat in the place, and he threw it on the stool next to him. When the man in the white apron approached, he said, "Give me a shot and a beer and a ham sandwich."

The man nodded his bald head and threw a shot glass in front of Tanner, which he then filled. Then he siphoned off a foamcapped mug and hollered over his right shoulder.

Tanner tossed off the shot and sipped the beer. After a while, a white plate bearing a sandwich appeared on the sill across from him. After a longer while, the bartender passed, picked it up, and deposited it in front of him. He wrote something on a green chit and tucked it under the corner of the plate.

Tanner bit into the sandwich and washed it down with a mouthful of beer. He studied the people about him and decided they made the same noises as people in any other bar he'd ever been in. The old man to his left looked friendly, so he asked him, "Any news about Boston?"

The man's chin quivered between words, and it seemed a natural thing for him.

"No news at all. Looks like the merchants will close their shops at the end of the week."

"What day is today?"

"Tuesday."

Tanner finished his sandwich and smoked a cigarette while he drank the rest of his beer.

Then he looked at the check, and it said, ".85."

He tossed a dollar bill on top of it and turned to go.

He had taken two steps when the bartender called out, "Wait a minute, mister."

He turned around.

"Yeah?"

"What you trying to pull?"

"What do you mean?"

"What do you call this crap?"

"What crap?"

The man waved Tanner's dollar at him, and he stepped forward and inspected it.

"Nothing wrong I can see. What's giving you a pain?"

"That ain't money."

"You trying to tell me my money's no good?"

"That's what I said. I never seen no bill like that."

"Well, look at it real careful. Read that print down there at the bottom of it."

The room grew quiet. One man got off his stool and walked forward. He held out his hand and said, "Let me see it, Bill."

The bartender passed it to him, and the man's eyes widened.

"This is drawn on the Bank of the Nation of California."

"Well, that's where I'm from," said Tanner.

"I'm sorry, it's no good here," said the bartender.

"It's the best I got," said Tanner.

"Well, nobody'll make good on it around here. You got any Boston money on you?"

"Never been to Boston."

"Then how the hell'd you get here?"

"Drove."

"Don't hand me that line of crap, son. Where'd you steal this?" It was the older man who had spoken.

"You going to take my money or ain't you?" said Tanner.

"I'm not going to take it," said the bartender.

"Then screw you," said Tanner, and he turned and walked toward the door.

As always, under such circumstances, he was alert to sounds at his back.

When he heard the quick footfall, he turned. It was the man who had inspected the bill that stood before him, his right arm extended.

Tanner's right hand held his leather jacket, draped over his right shoulder. He swung it with all his strength, forward and down.

It struck the man on the top of his head, and he fell.

There came up a murmuring, and several people jumped to their feet and moved toward him.

Tanner dragged the gun from his belt and said, "Sorry folks," and he pointed it, and they stopped.

"Now you probably ain't about to believe me," he said, "when I tell you that Boston's been hit by the plague, but it's true all right. Or maybe you will, I don't know. But I don't think you're going to believe that I drove here all the way from the nation of California with a car full of Haffikine anti-serum. But that's just as right. You send that bill to the big bank in Boston, and they'll change it for you, all right, and you know it. Now I've got to be going, and don't anybody try to stop me. If you think I've been handing you a line, you take a look at what I drive away in. That's all I've got to say."

And he backed out the door and covered it while he

mounted the cab. Inside, he gunned the engine to life, turned, and roared away.

In the rearview screen he could see the knot of people on the walk before the bar, watching him depart.

He laughed, and the apple-blossom moon hung dead ahead.

XIV

Albany to Boston. A couple hundred miles. He'd managed the worst of it. The terrors of Damnation Alley lay largely at his back now. Night. It flowed about him. The stars seemed brighter than usual. He'd make it, the night seemed to say.

He passed between hills. The road wasn't too bad. It wound between trees and high grasses. He passed a truck coming in his direction and dimmed his lights as it approached. It did the same.

It must have been around midnight that he came to the crossroads, and the lights suddenly nailed him from two directions.

He was bathed in perhaps thirty beams from the left and as many from the right.

He pushed the accelerator to the floor, and he heard engine after engine coming to life somewhere at his back. And he recognized the sounds.

They were all of them bikes.

They swung onto the road behind him.

He could have opened fire. He could have braked and laid down a cloud of flame. It was obvious that they didn't know what they were chasing. He could have launched grenades. He refrained, however.

It could have been him on the lead bike, he decided, all hot on hijack. He felt a certain sad kinship as his hand hovered above the fire-control.

Try to outrun them, first.

His engine was open wide and roaring, but he couldn't take the bikes.

When they began to fire, he knew that he'd have to retaliate. He couldn't risk their hitting a gas tank or blowing out his tires.

Their first few shots had been in the nature of a warning. He couldn't risk another barrage. If only they knew . . .

The speaker!

He cut in and mashed the button and spoke:

"Listen, cats," he said. "All I got's medicine for the sick citizens in Boston. Let me through or you'll hear the noise."

A shot followed immediately, so he opened fire with the fifty-calibers to the rear.

He saw them fall, but they kept firing. So he launched grenades.

The firing lessened, but didn't cease.

So he hit the brakes, then the flame-throwers. He kept it up for fifteen seconds.

There was silence.

When the air cleared he studied the screens.

They lay all over the road, their bikes upset, their bodies fuming. Several were still seated, and they held rifles and pointed them, and he shot them down.

A few still moved, spasmodically, and he was about to drive on, when he saw one rise and take a few staggering steps and fall again.

His hand hesitated on the gear shift.

It was a girl.

He thought about it for perhaps five seconds, then jumped down from the cab and ran toward her.

As he did, one man raised himself on an elbow and picked up a fallen rifle.

Tanner shot him twice and kept running, pistol in hand.

The girl was crawling toward a man whose face had been shot away. Other bodies twisted about Tanner now, there on the road, in the glare of the tail beacons. Blood and black leather, the sounds of moaning and the stench of burnt flesh were all about him.

When he got to the girl's side, she cursed him softly as he stopped.

None of the blood about her seemed to be her own.

He dragged her to her feet and her eyes began to fill with tears.

Everyone else was dead or dying, so Tanner picked her up in his arms and carried her back to the car. He reclined the passenger seat and put her into it, moving the weapons into the rear seat, out of her reach.

Then he gunned the engine and moved forward. In the rear-view screen he saw two figures rise to their feet, then fall again.

She was a tall girl, with long, uncombed hair the color of dirt. She had a strong chin and a wide mouth and there were dark circles under her eyes. A single faint line crossed her forehead, and she had all of her teeth. The right side of her face was flushed, as if sunburnt. Her left trouser leg was torn and dirty. He guessed that she'd caught the edge of his flame and fallen from her bike.

"You okay?" he asked, when her sobbing had diminished to a moist sniffing sound.

"What's it to you?" she said, raising a hand to her cheek.

Tanner shrugged.

"Just being friendly."

"You killed most of my gang."

"What would they have done to me?"

"They would have stomped you, mister, if it weren't for this fancy car of yours."

"It ain't really mine," he said. "It belongs to the nation of California."

"This thing don't come from California."

"The hell it don't. I drove it."

She sat up straight then and began rubbing her leg.

Tanner lit a cigarette.

"Give me a cigarette?" she said.

He passed her the one he had lighted, lit himself another. As he handed it to her, her eyes rested on his tattoo.

"What's that?"

"My name."

"Hell?"

"Hell."

"Where'd you get a name like that?"

"From my old man."

They smoked awhile, then she said, "Why'd you run the Alley?"

"Because it was the only way I could get them to turn me loose."

"From where?"

"The place with horizontal Venetian blinds. I was doing time."

"They let you go? Why?"

"Because of the big sick. I'm bringing in Haffikine anti-serum."

"You're Hell Tanner."

"Huh?"

"Your last name's Tanner, ain't it?"

"That's right. Who told you?"

"I heard about you. Everybody thought you died in the Big Raid."

"They were wrong."

"What was it like?"

"I dunno. I was already wearing a zebra suit. That's why I'm still around."

"Why'd you pick me up?"

" 'Cause you're a chick, and 'cause I didn't want to see you croak."

"Thanks. You got anything to eat in here?"

"Yeah, there's food in there." He pointed to the refrigerator door. "Help yourself."

She did, and as she ate Tanner asked her, "What do they call you?"

"Corny," she said. "It's short for Cornelia."

"Okay, Corny," he said. "When you're finished eating, you start telling me about the road between here and the place."

She nodded, chewed and swallowed. Then, "There's lots of other gangs," she said. "So you'd better be ready to blast them."

"I am."

"Those screens show you all directions, huh?"

"That's right."

"Good. The roads are pretty much okay from here on in. There's one big crater you'll come to soon and a couple little volcanoes afterwards."

"Check."

"Outside of them there's nothing to worry about but the Regents and the Devils and the Kings and the Lovers. That's about it."

Tanner nodded.

"How big are those clubs?"

"I don't know for sure, but the Kings are the biggest.

They've got a coupla hundred.''

"What was your club?"

"The Studs."

"What are you going to do now?"

"Whatever you tell me."

"Okay, Corny. I'll let you off anywhere along the way that you want me to. If you don't want, you can come on into the city with me."

"You call it, Hell. Anywhere you want to go, I'll go along."

Her voice was deep, and her words came slowly, and her tone sandpapered his eardrums just a bit. She had long legs and heavy thighs beneath the tight denim. Tanner licked his lips and studied the screens. Did he want to keep her around for a while?

The road was suddenly wet. It was covered with hundreds of fishes, and more were falling from the sky. There followed several loud reports from overhead. The blue light began in the north.

Tanner raced on, and suddenly there was water all about him. It fell upon his car, it dimmed his screens. The sky had grown black again, and the banshee wail sounded above him.

He skidded around a sharp curve in the road. He turned up his lights.

The rain ceased, but the wailing continued. He ran for fifteen minutes before it built up into a roar.

The girl stared at the screens and occasionally glanced at Tanner.

"What're you going to do?" she finally asked him.

"Outrun it, if I can," he said.

"It's dark for as far ahead as I can see. I don't think you can do it."

"Neither do I, but what does that leave?"

"Hole up someplace."

"If you know where, you show me."

"There's a place a few miles further ahead—a bridge you can get under."

"Okay, that's for us. Sing out when you see it."

She pulled off her boots and rubbed her feet. He gave her another cigarette.

"Hey, Corny—I just thought—there's a medicine chest over there to your right. Yeah, that's it. It should have some damn kind of salve in it you can smear on your face to take the bite out.''

She found a tube of something and rubbed some of it into her cheek, smiled slightly and replaced it.

"Feel any better?"

"Yes. Thanks."

The stones began to fall, the blue to spread. The sky pulsed, grew brighter.

"I don't like the looks of this one."

"I don't like the looks of any of them."

"It seems there's been an awful lot this past week."

"Yeah. I've heard it said maybe the winds are dying down—that the sky might be purging itself."

"That'd be nice," said Tanner.

"Then we might be able to see it the way it used to look— blue all the time, and with clouds. You know about clouds."

"I heard about them."

"White, puffy things that just sort of drift across—sometimes gray. They don't drop anything except rain, and not always that."

"Yeah, I know."

"You ever see any out in L.A.?"

"No."

The yellow streaks began, and the black lines writhed like snakes. The stonefall rattled heavily upon the roof and the hood. More water began to fall, and a fog rose up. Tanner was forced to slow, and then it seemed as if sledgehammers beat up on the car.

"We won't make it," she said.

"The hell you say. This thing's built to take it—and what's that off in the distance?"

"The bridge!" she said, moving forward. "That's it! Pull off the road to the left and go down. That's a dry riverbed beneath."

Then the lightning began to fall. It flamed, flashed about them. They passed a burning tree, and there were still fishes in the roadway.

Tanner turned left as he approached the bridge. He slowed to a crawl and made his way over the shoulder and down the slick, muddy grade.

When he hit the damp riverbed he turned right. He nosed it

in under the bridge, and they were all alone there. Some waters trickled past them, and the lightnings continued to flash. The sky was a shifting kaleidoscope and constant came the thunder. He could hear a sound like hail on the bridge above them.

"We're safe," he said and killed the engine.

"Are the doors locked?"

"They do it automatically."

Tanner turned off the outside lights.

"Wish I could buy you a drink, besides coffee."

"Coffee'd be good, just right."

"Okay, it's on the way," and he cleaned out the pot and filled it and plugged it in.

They sat there and smoked as the storm raged, and he said, "You know, it's a kind of nice feeling being all snug as a rat in a hole while everything goes to hell outside. Listen to that bastard come down! And we couldn't care less."

"I suppose so," she said. "What're you going to do after you make it in to Boston?"

"Oh, I don't know . . . Maybe get a job, scrape up some loot and maybe open a bike shop or a garage. Either one'd be nice."

"Sounds good. You going to ride much yourself?"

"You bet. I don't suppose they have any good clubs *in* town?"

"No. They're all roadrunners."

"Thought so. Maybe I'll organize my own."

He reached out and touched her hand, then squeezed it.

"I can buy *you* a drink."

"What do you mean?"

She drew a plastic flask from the right side pocket of her jacket. She uncapped it and passed it to him.

"Here."

He took a mouthful and gulped it, coughed, took a second, then handed it back.

"Great! You're a woman of unsuspected potential and like that. Thanks."

"Don't mention it," and she took a drink herself and set the flask on the dash.

"Cigarette?"

"Just a minute."

He lit two, passed her one.

"There you are, Corny."

"Thanks. I'd like to help you finish this run."

"How come?"

"I got nothing else to do. My crowd's all gone away, and I've got nobody else to run with now. Also, if you make it, you'll be a big man. Like capital letters. Think you might keep me around after that?"

"Maybe. What are you like?"

"Oh, I'm real nice. I'll even rub your shoulders for you when they're sore."

"They're sore now."

"I thought so. Give me a lean."

He bent toward her, and she began to rub his shoulders. Her hands were quick and strong.

"You do that good, girl."

"Thanks."

He straightened up, leaned back. Then he reached out, took the flask and had another drink. She took a small sip when he passed it to her.

The furies rode about them, but the bridge above stood the siege. Tanner turned off the lights.

"Let's make it," he said and he seized her and drew her to him.

She did not resist him, and he found her belt buckle and unfastened it. Then he started on the buttons. After a while, he reclined her seat.

"Will you keep me?" she asked him.

"Sure."

"I'll help you. I'll do anything you say to get you through."

"Great."

"After all, if Boston goes, then we go, too."

"You bet."

Then they didn't say much more.

There was violence in the skies, and after that came darkness and quiet.

XV

When Tanner awoke, it was morning and the storm had ceased. He repaired himself to the rear of the vehicle and after that assumed the driver's seat once more.

Cornelia did not awaken as he gunned the engine to life and started up the weed-infested slope of the hillside.

The sky was light once more, and the road was strewn with rubble. Tanner wove along it, heading toward the pale sun, and after a while, Cornelia stretched.

"Ungh," she said, and Tanner agreed. "My shoulders are better now," he told her.

"Good," and Tanner headed up a hill, slowly as the day dimmed and one huge black line became the Devil's highway down the middle of the sky.

As he drove through a wooded valley, the rain began to fall. The girl had returned from the rear of the vehicle and was preparing breakfast when Tanner saw the tiny dot on the horizon, switched over to his telescope lenses and tried to outrun what he saw.

Cornelia looked up.

There were bikes, bikes, and more bikes on their trail.

"Those your people?" Tanner asked.

"No. You took mine yesterday."

"Too bad," said Tanner, and he pushed the accelerator to the floor and hoped for a storm.

They squealed around a curve and climbed another hill. His pursuers drew nearer. He switched back from telescope to normal scanning, but even then he could see the size of the crowd that approached.

"It must be the Kings," she said. "They're the biggest club around."

"Too bad," said Tanner.

"For them or for us?"

"Both."

She smiled.

"I'd like to see how you work this thing."

"It looks like you're going to get a chance. They're gaining on us like mad."

The rain lessened, but the fogs grew heavier. Tanner could see their lights, though, over a quarter mile to his rear, and he did not turn his own on. He estimated a hundred to a hundred fifty pursuers that cold, dark morning, and he asked, "How near are we to Boston?"

"Maybe ninety miles," she told him.

"Too bad they're chasing us instead of coming toward us," he said, as he primed his flames and set an adjustment which brought cross-hairs into focus on his rearview screen.

"What's that?" she asked.

"That's a cross. I'm going to crucify them, lady," and she smiled at this and squeezed his arm.

"Can I help? I hate those bloody mothers."

"In a little while," said Tanner. "In a little while, I'm sure," and he reached into the rear seat and fetched out the six hand grenades and hung them on his wide, black belt. He passed the rifle to the girl. "Hang onto this," he said, and stuck the .45 behind his belt.

"Do you know how to use that thing?"

"Yes," she replied immediately.

"Good."

He kept watching the lights that danced on the screen.

"Why the hell doesn't this storm break?" he said, as the lights came closer and he could make out shapes within the fog.

When they were within a hundred feet he fired the first grenade. It arched through, the gray air, and five seconds later there was a bright flash to his rear, burning within a thunderclap.

The lights immediately behind him remained, and he touched the fifty-calibers, moving the crosshairs from side to side. The guns shattered their loud syllables, and he launched another grenade. With the second flash, he began to climb another hill.

"Did you stop them?"

"For a time, maybe. I still see some lights, but farther back."

After five minutes, they had reached the top, a place where the fogs were cleared and the dark sky was visible above them. Then they started downward once more, and a wall of stone and shale and dirt rose to their right. Tanner considered it as they descended.

When the road leveled and he decided they had reached the bottom, he turned on his brightest lights and looked for a place where the road's shoulders were wide.

To his rear, there were suddenly rows of descending lights.

He found the place where the road was sufficiently wide,

and he skidded through a U turn until he was facing the shaggy cliff, now to his left, and his pursuers were coming dead on.

He elevated his rockets, fired one, elevated them five degrees more, fired two, elevated them another five degrees, fired three. Then he lowered them fifteen and fired another.

There were brightnesses within the fog, and he heard the stones rattling on the road and felt the vibration as the rock-slide began. He swung toward his right as he backed the vehicle and fired two ahead. There was dust mixed with the fog now, and the vibration continued.

He turned and headed forward once more.

"I hope that'll hold 'em," he said, and he lit two cigarettes and passed one to the girl.

After five minutes they were on higher ground again and the winds came and whipped at the fog, and far to the rear there were still some lights.

As they topped a high rise, his radiation gauge began to register an above-normal reading. He sought in all directions and saw the crater far off ahead. "That's it," he heard her say. "You've got to leave the road there. Bear to the right and go around that way when you get there."

"I'll do that thing."

He heard gunshots from behind him, for the first time that day, and though he adjusted the cross-hairs he did not fire his own weapons. The distance was still too great.

"You must have cut them in half," she said, staring into the screen. "More than that. They're a tough bunch, though."

"I gather," and he plowed the field of mists and checked his supply of grenades for the launcher and saw that he was running low.

He swung off the road to his right when he began bumping along over fractured concrete. The radiation level was quite high by then. The crater was slightly more than a thousand yards to his left.

The lights to his rear fanned out, grew brighter. He drew a bead on the brightest and fired. It went out.

"There's another down," he remarked, as they raced across the hard-baked plain.

The rains came more heavily, and he sighted on another light and fired. It, too, went out. Now, though, he heard the sounds of their weapons about him once again.

He switched to his right-hand guns and saw the cross-hairs leap into life on that screen. As three vehicles moved in to flank him from that direction, he opened up and cut them down. There was more firing at his back, and he ignored it as he negotiated the way.

"I count twenty-seven lights," Cornelia said.

Tanner wove his way across a field of boulders. He lit another cigarette.

Five minutes later, they were running on both sides of him. He had held back again for that moment, to conserve ammunition and to be sure of his targets. He fired then, though, at every light within range, and he floored the accelerator and swerved around rocks.

"Five of them are down," she said, but he was listening to the gunfire.

He launched a grenade to the rear, and when he tried to launch a second there came only a clicking sound from the control. He launched one to either side and then paused for a second.

"If they get close enough, I'll show them some fire," he said, and they continued on around the crater.

He fired only at individual targets then, when he was certain they were within range. He took two more before he struck the broken roadbed.

"Keep running parallel to it," she told him. "There's a trail here. You can't drive on that stuff till another mile or so."

Shots ricocheted from off his armored sides, and he continued to return the fire. He raced along an alleyway of twisted trees, like those he had seen near other craters, and the mists hung like pennons about their branches. He heard the rattle of the increasing rains.

When he hit the roadway once again, he regarded the lights to his rear and asked, "How many do you count now?"

"It looks like around twenty. How are we doing?"

"I'm just worried about the tires. They can take a lot, but they can be shot out. The only other thing that bothers me is that a stray shot might clip one of the 'eyes.' Outside of that we're bulletproof enough. Even if they manage to stop us, they'll have to pry us out."

The bikes drew near once again, and he saw the bright flashes and heard the reports of the riders' guns.

"Hold tight," he said, and he hit the brakes and they

skidded on the wet pavement.

The lights grew suddenly bright, and he unleashed his rear flame. As some bikes skirted him, he cut in the side flames and held them that way.

Then he took his foot off the brake and floored the accelerator without waiting to assess the damage he had done.

They sped ahead, and Tanner heard Cornelia's laughter.

"God! You're taking them, Hell! You're taking the whole damn club!"

"It ain't that much fun," he said. Then, "See any lights?"

She watched for a time, said, "No," then said, "Three," then, "Seven," and finally, "Thirteen."

Tanner said, "Damn."

The radiation level fell and there came crashes amid the roaring overhead. A light fall of gravel descended for perhaps half a minute, along with the rain.

"We're running low," he said.

"On what?"

"Everything: Luck, fuel, ammo. Maybe you'd have been better off if I'd left you where I found you."

"No," she said. "I'm with you, the whole line."

"Then you're nuts," he said. "I haven't been hurt yet. When I am, it might be a different tune."

"Maybe," she said. "Wait and hear how I sing."

He reached out and squeezed her thigh.

"Okay, Corny. You've been okay so far. Hang onto that piece, and we'll see what happens."

He reached for another cigarette, found the pack empty, cursed. He gestured toward a compartment, and she opened it and got him a fresh pack. She tore it open and lit him one.

"Thanks."

"Why're they staying out of range?"

"Maybe they're just going to pace us. I don't know."

Then the fogs began to lift. By the time Tanner had finished his cigarette, the visibility had improved greatly. He could make out the dark forms crouched atop their bikes, following, following, nothing more.

"If they just want to keep us company, then I don't care," he said. "Let them."

But there came more gunfire after a time, and he heard a tire go. He slowed, but continued. He took careful aim and strafed them. Several fell.

More gunshots sounded from behind. Another tire blew, and he hit the brakes and skidded, turning about as he slowed. When he faced them, he shot his anchors, to hold him in place, and he discharged his rockets, one after another, at a level parallel to the road. He opened up with his guns and sprayed them as they veered off and approached him from the sides. Then he opened fire to the left. Then the right.

He emptied the right-hand guns, then switched back to the left. He launched the remaining grenades.

The gunfire died down, except for five sources—three to his left and two to his right—coming from somewhere within the trees that lined the road now. Broken bikes and bodies lay behind him, some still smouldering. The pavement was potted and cracked in many places.

He turned the car and proceeded ahead on six wheels.

"We're out of ammo, Corny," he told her.

"Well, we took an awful lot of them . . ."

"Yeah."

As he drove on, he saw five bikes move onto the road. They stayed a good distance behind him, but they stayed.

He tried the radio, but there was no response. He hit the brakes and stopped, and the bikes stopped, too, staying well to the rear.

"Well, at least they're scared of us. They think we still have teeth."

"We do," she said.

"Yeah, but not the ones they're thinking about."

"Better yet."

"Glad I met you," said Tanner. "I can use an optimist. There must be a pony, huh?"

She nodded; he put it into gear and started forward abruptly.

The motorcycles moved ahead also, and they maintained a safe distance. Tanner watched them in the screens and cursed them as they followed.

After a while they drew nearer again. Tanner roared on for half an hour, and the remaining five edged closer and closer.

When they drew near enough, they began to fire, rifles resting on their handlebars.

Tanner heard several low ricochets, and then another tire went out.

He stopped once more, and the bikes did, too, remaining

just out of range of his flames. He cursed and ground ahead
again. The car wobbled as he drove, listing to the left. A
wrecked pickup truck stood smashed against a tree to his
right, its hunched driver a skeleton, its windows smashed and
tires missing. Half a sun now stood in the heavens, reaching
after nine o'clock; fog ghosts drifted before them, and the
dark band in the sky undulated, and more rain fell from it,
mixed with dust and small stones and bits of metal. Tanner
said, "Good" as the pinging sounds began, and, "Hope it gets
a lot worse," and his wish came true as the ground began to
shake and the blue light began in the north. There came a
booming within the roar, and there were several answering
crashes as heaps of rubble appeared to his right. "Hope the
next one falls right on our buddies back there," he said.

He saw an orange glow ahead and to his right. It had been
there for several minutes, but he had not become conscious of
it until just then.

"Volcano," she said when he indicated it. "It means we've
got another sixty-five, seventy miles to go."

He could not tell whether any more shooting was occurring.
The sounds coming from overhead and around him were sufficient to mask any gunfire, and the fall of gravel upon the car
covered any ricocheting rounds. The five headlights to his rear
maintained their pace.

"Why don't they give up?" he said. "They're taking a
pretty bad beating."

"They're used to it," she replied, "and they're riding for
blood, which makes a difference."

Tanner fetched the .357 Magnum from the door clip and
passed it to her. "Hang on to this, too," he said, and he found
a box of ammo in the second compartment and, "Put these in
your pocket," he added. He stuffed ammo for the .45 into his
own jacket. He adjusted the hand grenades upon his belt.

Then the five headlights behind him suddenly became four,
and the others slowed, grew smaller. "Accident, I hope," he
remarked.

They sighted the mountain, a jag-topped cone bleeding fires
upon the sky. They left the road and swung far to the left,
upon a well marked trail. It took twenty minutes to pass the
mountain, and by then he sighted their pursuers once again—
four lights to the rear, gaining slowly.

He came upon the road once more and hurried ahead across the shaking ground. The yellow lights moved through the heavens; and heavy, shapeless objects, some several feet across, crashed to the earth about them. The car was buffeted by winds, listed as they moved, would not proceed above forty miles an hour. The radio contained only static.

Tanner rounded a sharp curve, hit the brake, turned off his lights, pulled the pin from a hand grenade and waited with his hand upon the door.

When the lights appeared in the screen, he flung the door wide, leaped down and hurled the grenade through the abrasive rain.

He was into the cab and moving again before he heard the explosion, before the flash occurred upon his screen.

The girl laughed almost hysterically as the car moved ahead. "You got 'em, Hell. You got 'em!" she cried.

Tanner took a drink from her flask, and she finished its final brown mouthful. He lit them cigarettes.

The road grew cracked, pitted, slippery. They topped a high rise and headed downhill. The fog thickened as they descended.

Lights appeared before him, and he readied the flame. There were no hostilities, however, as he passed a truck headed in the other direction. Within the next half hour he passed two more.

There came more lightning, and fist-sized rocks began to fall. Tanner left the road and sought shelter within a grove of high trees. The sky grew completely black, losing even its blue aurora.

They waited for three hours, but the storm did not let up. One by one, the four view-screens went dead and the fifth only showed the blackness beneath the car. Tanner's last sight in the rearview screen was of a huge splintered tree with a broken, swaying branch that was about ready to fall off. There were several terrific crashes upon the hood and the car shook with each. The roof above their heads was deeply dented in three places. The lights grew dim, then bright again. The radio would not produce even static anymore.

"I think we've had it," he said.

"Yeah."

"How far are we?"

"Maybe fifty miles away."

"There's still a chance, if we live through this."

"What chance?"

"I've got two bikes in the rear."

They reclined their seats and smoked and waited, and after a while the lights went out.

The storm continued all that day and into the night. They slept within the broken body of the car, and it sheltered them. When the storm ceased, Tanner opened the door and looked outside, closed it again.

"We'll wait till morning," he said, and she held his Hell-printed hand, and they slept.

XVI

In the morning, Tanner walked back through the mud and the fallen branches, the rocks and the dead fishes, and he opened the rear compartment and unbolted the bikes. He fueled them and checked them out and wheeled them down the ramp.

He crawled into the back of the cab then and removed the rear seat. Beneath it, in the storage compartment, was the large aluminum chest that was his cargo. It was bolted shut. He lifted it, carried it out to his bike.

"That the stuff?" she asked.

He nodded and placed it on the ground.

"I don't know how the stuff is stored, if it's refrigerated in there or what," he said, "but it ain't too heavy that I might not be able to get it on the back of my bike. There's straps in the far right compartment. Go get 'em and give me a hand—and get me my pardon out of the middle compartment. It's in a big cardboard envelope."

She returned with these things and helped him secure the container on the rear of his bike.

He wrapped extra straps around his left bicep, and they wheeled the machines to the road.

"We'll have to take it kind of slow," he said, and he slung the rifle over his right shoulder, drew on his gloves and kicked his bike to life.

She did the same with hers, and they moved forward, side by side along the highway.

After they had been riding for perhaps an hour, two cars passed them, heading west. In the rear seats of both there were children, who pressed their faces to the glass and watched them as they went by. The driver of the second car was in his shirtsleeves, and he wore a black shoulder holster.

The sky was pink, and there were three black lines that looked as if they could be worth worrying about. The sun was a rose-tinted silvery thing, and pale, but Tanner still had to raise his goggles against it.

The pack was riding securely, and Tanner leaned into the dawn and thought about Boston. There was a light mist on the foot of every hill, and the air was cool and moist. Another car passed them. The road surface began to improve.

It was around noontime when he heard the first shot above the thunder of their engines. At first he thought it was a backfire, but it came again, and Corny cried out and swerved off the road and struck a boulder.

Tanner cut to the left, braking, as two more shots rang about him, and he leaped his bike against a tree and threw himself flat. A shot struck near his head and he could tell the direction from which it had come. He crawled into a ditch and drew off his right glove. He could see his girl lying where she had fallen, and there was blood on her breast. She did not move.

He raised the 30.06 and fired.

The shot was returned, and he moved to his left.

It had come from a hill about two hundred feet away, and he thought he saw the rifle's barrel.

He aimed at it and fired again.

The shot was returned, and he wormed his way further left. He crawled perhaps fifteen feet until he reached a pile of rubble he could crouch behind. Then he pulled the pin on a grenade, stood and hurled it.

He threw himself flat as another shot rang out, and he took another grenade into his hand.

There was a roar and a rumble and a mighty flash, and the junk fell about him as he leaped to his feet and threw the second one, taking better aim this time.

After the second explosion, he ran forward with his rifle in his hands, but it wasn't necessary.

He only found a few small pieces of the man, and none at all of his rifle.

He returned to Cornelia.

She wasn't breathing, and her heart had stopped beating, and he knew what that meant.

He carried her back to the ditch in which he had lain and he made it deeper by digging, using his hands.

He laid her down in it and he covered her with the dirt. Then he wheeled her machine over, set the kickstand, and stood it upon the grave. With his knife, he scratched upon the fender: *Her name was Cornelia and I don't know how old she was or where she came from or what her last name was but she was Hell Tanner's girl and I love her.* Then he went back to his own machine, started it and drove ahead. Boston was maybe thirty miles away.

XVII

He drove along, and after a time he heard the sound of another bike. A Harley cut onto the road from the dirt path to his left, and he couldn't try running away from it because he couldn't speed with the load he bore. So he allowed himself to be paced.

After a while, the rider of the other bike—a tall, thin man with a flaming beard—drew up alongside him, to the left. He smiled and raised his right hand and let it fall and then gestured with his head.

Tanner braked and came to a halt. Redbeard was right beside him when he did. He said, "Where you going, man?"

"Boston."

"What you got in the box?"

"Like, drugs."

"What kind?" and the man's eyebrows arched and the smile came again onto his lips.

"For the plague they got going there."

"Oh. I thought you meant the other kind."

"Sorry."

The man held a pistol in his right hand and he said, "Get off your bike."

Tanner did this, and the man raised his left hand and

another man came forward from the brush at the side of the road. "Wheel this guy's bike about two hundred yards up the highway," he said, "and park it in the middle. Then take your place."

"What's the bit?" Tanner asked.

The man ignored the question. "Who are you?" he asked.

"Hell's the name," he replied. "Hell Tanner."

"Go to hell."

Tanner shrugged.

"You ain't Hell Tanner."

Tanner drew off his right glove and extended his fist.

"There's my name."

"I don't believe it," said the man, after he had studied the tattoo.

"Have it your way, citizen."

"Shut up!" and he raised his left hand once more, now that the other man had parked the machine on the road and returned to a place somewhere within the trees to the right.

In response to his gesture, there was movement within the brush.

Bikes were pushed forward by their riders, and they lined the road, twenty or thirty on either side.

"There you are," said the man. "My name's Big Brother."

"Glad to meet you."

"You know what you're going to do, mister?"

"I can really just about guess."

"You're going to walk up to your bike and claim it."

Tanner smiled.

"How hard's that going to be?"

"No trouble at all. Just start walking. Give me your rifle first, though."

Big Brother raised his hand again, and one by one the engines came to life.

"Okay," he said. "Now."

"You think I'm crazy, man?"

"No. Start walking. Your rifle."

Tanner unslung it and he continued the arc. He caught Big Brother beneath his red beard, and he felt the bullet go into him. Then he dropped the weapon and hauled forth a grenade, pulled the pin and tossed it amid the left side of the gauntlet. Before it exploded, he'd pulled the pin on another and thrown it to his right. By then, though, vehicles were moving forward, heading toward him.

He fell upon the rifle and shouldered it in a prone firing position. As he did this, the first explosion occurred. He was firing before the second one went off.

He dropped three of them, then got to his feet and scrambled, firing from the hip.

He made it behind Big Brother's fallen bike and fired from there. Big Brother was still fallen, too. When the rifle was empty, he didn't have time to reload. He fired the .45 four times before a tire chain brought him down.

He awoke to the roaring of the engines. They were circling him. When he got to his feet, a handlebar knocked him down again.

Two bikes were moving about him, and there were many dead people upon the road.

He struggled to rise again, was knocked off his feet.

Big Brother rode one of the bikes, and a guy he hadn't seen rode the other.

He crawled to the right, and there was pain in his fingertips as the tires passed over them.

But he saw a rock and waited till a driver was near. Then he stood again and threw himself upon the man as he passed, the rock he had seized rising and falling, once, in his right hand. He was carried along as this occurred, and as he fell he felt the second bike strike him.

There were terrible pains in his side, and his body felt broken, but he reached out even as this occurred and caught hold of a strut on the side of the bike and was dragged along by it.

Before he had been dragged ten feet, he had drawn his SS dagger from his boot. He struck upward and felt a thin metal wall give way. Then his hands came loose, and he fell and he smelled the gasoline. His hand dove into his jacket pocket and came out with the Zippo.

He had struck the tank on the side of Big Brother's bike, and it jetted forth its contents on the road. Twenty feet ahead, Big Brother was turning.

Tanner held the lighter, the lighter with the raised skull of enamel, wings on either side of it. His thumb spun the wheel and the sparks leapt forth, then the flame. He tossed it into the stream of petrol that lay before him, and the flames raced away, tracing a blazing trail upon the concrete.

Big Brother had turned and was bearing down upon him when he saw what had happened. His eyes widened, and his red-framed smile went away.

He tried to leap off his bike, but it was too late.

The exploding gas tank caught him, and he went down with a piece of metal in his head and other pieces elsewhere.

Flames splashed over Tanner, and he beat at them feebly with his hands.

He raised his head above the blazing carnage and let it fall again. He was bloody and weak and so very tired. He saw his own machine, standing still undamaged on the road ahead.

He began crawling toward it.

When he reached it, he threw himself across the saddle and lay there for perhaps ten minutes. He vomited twice, and his pains became a steady pulsing.

After perhaps an hour, he mounted the bike and brought it to life.

He rode for half a mile and then dizziness and the fatigue hit him.

He pulled off to the side of the road and concealed his bike as best he could. Then he lay down upon the bare earth and slept.

XVIII

When he awoke, he felt dried blood upon his side. His left hand ached and was swollen. All four fingers felt stiff, and it hurt to try to bend them. His head throbbed and there was a taste of gasoline within his mouth. He was too sore to move, for a long while. His beard had been singed, and his right eye was swollen almost shut.

"Corny . . ." he said, then, "Damn!"

Everything came back, like the contents of a powerful dream suddenly spilled into his consciousness.

He began to shiver, and there were mists all around him. It was very dark, and his legs were cold; the dampness had soaked completely through his denims.

In the distance, he heard a vehicle pass. It sounded like a car.

He managed to roll over, and he rested his head on his forearm. It seemed to be night, but it could be a black day.

As he lay there, his mind went back to his prison cell. It seemed almost a haven now; and he thought of his brother Denny, who must also be hurting at this moment. He wondered if he had any cracked ribs himself. It felt like it. And he thought of the monsters of the southwest and of dark-eyed Greg, who had tried to chicken out. Was he still living? His mind circled back to L.A. and the old Coast, gone, gone forever now, after the Big Raid. Then Corny walked past him, blood upon her breasts, and he chewed his beard and held his eyes shut very tight. They might have made it together in Boston. How far, now?

He got to his knees and crawled until he felt something high and solid. A tree. He sat with his back to it, and his hand sought the crumpled cigarette pack within his jacket. He drew one forth, smoothed it, then remembered that his lighter lay somewhere back on the highway. He sought through his pockets and found a damp matchbook. The third one lit. The chill went out of his bones as he smoked, and a wave of fever swept over him. He coughed as he was unbuttoning his collar, and it seemed that he tasted blood.

His weapons were gone, save for the lump of a single grenade at his belt.

Above him, in the darkness, he heard the roaring. After six puffs, the cigarette slipped from his fingers and sizzled out upon the damp mold. His head fell forward, and there was darkness within.

There might have been a storm. He didn't remember. When he awoke, he was lying on his right side, the tree to his back. A pink afternoon sun shone down upon him, and the mists were blown away. From somewhere, he heard the sound of a bird. He managed a curse, then realized how dry his throat was. He was suddenly burnt with a terrible thirst.

There was a clear puddle about thirty feet away. He crawled to it and drank his fill. It grew muddy as he did so.

Then he crawled to where his bike lay hidden and stood beside it. He managed to seat himself upon it, and his hands shook as he lit a cigarette.

It must have taken him an hour to reach the roadway, and he

was panting heavily by then. His watch had been broken, so he didn't know the hour. The sun was already lowering at his back when he started out. The winds whipped about him, insulating his consciousness within their burning flow. His cargo rode securely behind him. He had visions of someone opening it and finding a batch of broken bottles. He laughed and cursed, alternately.

Several cars passed him, heading in the other direction. He had not seen any heading toward the city. The road was in good condition and he began to pass buildings that seemed in a good state of repair, though deserted. He did not stop. This time he determined not to stop for anything, unless he was stopped.

The sun fell farther, and the sky dimmed before him. There were two black lines swaying in the heavens. Then he passed a sign that told him he had eighteen miles farther to go. Ten minutes later he switched on his light.

Then he topped a hill and slowed before he began its descent.

There were lights below him and in the distance.

As he rushed forward, the winds brought to him the sound of a single bell, tolling over and over within the gathering dark. He sniffed a remembered thing upon the air: it was the salt-tang of the sea.

The sun was hidden behind the hill as he descended, and he rode within the endless shadow. A single star appeared on the far horizon, between the two black belts.

Now there were lights within shadows that he passed, and the buildings moved closer together. He leaned heavily on the handlebars, and the muscles of his shoulders smouldered beneath his jacket. He wished that he had a crash helmet, for he felt increasingly unsteady.

He must almost be there. Where would he head once he hit the city proper? They had not told him that.

He shook his head to clear it.

The street he drove along was deserted. There were no traffic sounds that he could hear. He blew his horn, and its echoes rolled back upon him.

There was a light on in the building to his left.

He pulled to a stop, crossed the sidewalk and banged on the door. There was no response from within. He tried the door and found it locked. A telephone would mean he could end his trip right there.

What if they were all dead inside? The thought occurred to him that just about everybody could be dead by now. He decided to break in. He returned to his bike for a screwdriver, then went to work on the door.

He heard the gunshot and the sound of the engine at approximately the same time.

He turned around quickly, his back against the door, the hand grenade in his gloved right fist.

"Hold it!" called out a loudspeaker on the side of the black car that approached. "That shot was a warning! The next one won't be!"

Tanner raised his hands to a level with his ears, his right one turned to conceal the grenade. He stepped forward to the curb beside his bike when the car drew up.

There were two officers in the car, and the one on the passenger side held a .38 pointed at Tanner's middle.

"You're under arrest," he said. "Looting."

Tanner nodded as the man stepped out of the car. The driver came around the front of the vehicle, a pair of handcuffs in his hand.

"Looting," the man with the gun repeated. "You'll pull a real stiff sentence."

"Stick your hands out here, boy," said the second cop, and Tanner handed him the grenade pin.

The man stared at it, dumbly, for several seconds, then his eyes shot to Tanner's right hand.

"God! He's got a bomb!" said the man with the gun.

Tanner smiled, then, "Shut up and listen!" he said. "Or else shoot me and we'll all go together when we go. I was trying to get to a telephone. That case on the back of my bike is full of Haffikine antiserum. I brought it from L.A."

"You didn't run the Alley on that bike!"

"No, I didn't. My car is dead somewhere between here and Albany, and so are a lot of folks who tried to stop me. Now you better take that medicine and get it where it's supposed to go."

"You on the level, mister?"

"My hand is getting very tired. I am not in good shape." Tanner leaned on his bike. "Here."

He pulled his pardon out of his jacket and handed it to the officer with the handcuffs. "That's my pardon," he said. "It's dated just last week and you can see it was made out in California."

The officer took the envelope and opened it. He withdrew the paper and studied it. "Looks real," he said. "So Brady made it through . . ."

"He's dead," Tanner said. "Look, I'm hurtin'. Do something!"

"My God! Hold it tight! Get in the car and sit down! It'll just take a minute to get the case off and we'll roll. We'll drive to the river and you can throw it in. Squeeze real hard!"

They unfastened the case and put it in the back of the car. They rolled down the right front window, and Tanner sat next to it with his arm on the outside.

The siren screamed, and the pain crept up Tanner's arm to his shoulder. It would be very easy to let go.

"Where do you keep your river?" he asked.

"Just a little farther. We'll be there in no time."

"Hurry," Tanner said.

"That's the bridge up ahead. We'll ride out onto it, and you throw it off—as far out as you can."

"Man, I'm tired! I'm not sure I can make it . . ."

"Hurry, Jerry!"

"I am, damn it! We ain't got wings!"

"I feel kind of dizzy, too . . ."

They tore out onto the bridge, and the tires screeched as they halted. Tanner opened the door slowly. The driver's had already slammed shut.

He staggered, and they helped him to the railing. He sagged against it when they released him.

"I don't think I—"

Then he straightened, drew back his arm and hurled the grenade far out over the waters.

He grinned, and the explosion followed, far beneath them, and for a time the waters were troubled.

The two officers sighed and Tanner chuckled.

"I'm really okay," he said. "I just faked it to bug you."

"Why you—!"

Then he collapsed, and they saw the pallor of his face within the beams of their lights.

XIX

The following spring, on the day of its unveiling in Boston
Common, when it was discovered that someone had scrawled
obscene words on the statue of Hell Tanner, no one thought to
ask the logical candidate why he had done it, and the next day
it was too late, because he had cut out without leaving a for-
warding address. Several cars were reported stolen that day,
and one was never seen again in Boston.

So they re-veiled his statue, bigger than life, astride a great
bronze Harley, and they cleaned him up for hoped-for poster-
ity. But coming upon the Common, the winds still break about
him and the heavens still throw garbage.

COLLECTIONS OF FANTASY AND SCIENCE FICTION